# GODS & GHOSTS

GODS & GHOSTS BOOK 1

CYNTHIA D. WITHERSPOON

T.H. MORRIS

Published 2020 by Shadow City – A Next Chapter Imprint

Cover art by CoverMint

*Previously Published as*
*Grave Endowments: Volume 1*

# PROLOGUE

## EVA MCRAYNE

*June 24th*

*Elliot Lancaster is trying to kill me.*

*You know Elliott. I've written about him before - first, when we were friends, then as he became my enemy. But for the sake of documentation, I will write of him again. We became friends in college - the University of Georgia, English Literature 101 to be exact. He started showing up wherever I was on campus. I was flattered at the time - I'd pretty much kept myself hidden away except cheerleading, which I was forced to do for my scholarship.*

*Flattered and naive. I didn't see the warning signs of his madness. How his sudden appearances were more attuned to stalking than friendship. One thing led to another and after graduation, I took the job as his co-host on the television show, Grave Messages.*

*Things spiraled out of control real quick. Elliott became jealous then downright hateful. He began sending me to locations where I had to fight for my life against beings I had no business dealing with. All for the sake of the show. Things came to a head last year when he betrayed me.*

*Yes. Betrayed. Like in an old novel or television show. See, I became the Sibyl four years ago. To put matters simply, I can talk to the dead through mirrors. I was granted immortality thanks to Apollo.*

*The Apollo. The Olympian Apollo. As fate would have it, he is also my biological father. A fact I learned two months ago and am still grappling with.*

*Why am I rehashing all this in my own journal? Why, since I wrote about the events as they happened? Maybe it's to keep things straight in my own mind. Or maybe, it's to better understand Elliott's motives.*

*He has done horrible things to me over the years. We have a history that I don't understand. A history riddled with hateful words and violence.*

*I'm on a plane at the moment. Elliott and by extension, Theia Productions, has sent me to Rome, North Carolina to film Grave Messages in an old house that has been abandoned for over a decade. There are even bodies buried in the basement - disturbing, I know, but it adds to the creepiness factor. It's the perfect location for a paranormal reality show.*

*A little too perfect.*

*I shouldn't be so anxious about all this. I know what I am doing. I know what I have survived. The last time Elliott attacked me directly, I'd physically died. Hermes - the god, not the handbag - gave me a choice. Pass over into the ether or return to the living.*

*I'm on a plane flying to North Carolina so you know the choice I made. If I can survive getting shoved out of a four-story window, then I can survive anything.*

*I hope so, though Cyrus - my mentor for this whole Sibyl thing - is not happy with this trip. Apollo is insistent that I stay at a place called Grannison-Morris estate. It's a huge compound of sorts, filled with ethereal beings. That is one of the main reasons why Cyrus isn't happy. He swore he is friends with the proprietor of the estate, but he doesn't care for the students who live there.*

*My Keeper won't explain why. As far as I know, he's never met them. Then again, there's a lot about Cyrus that I don't know. He is literally ancient - an immortal who has served Apollo since the days Socrates and Plato roamed the earth.*

*I'm writing so much because I'm nervous. I tend to ramble when I'm anxious. If there are people at this estate, then I'm putting them in danger by being there. I don't know if I'm strong enough now to protect them. Maybe Cyrus was right. Maybe we should have just taken a room at the local hotel.*

*It's too late now. The proprietor of Grannison-Morris is expecting us. It would be rude to turn down his invitation while we were flying to our destination.*

*One week. That's my filming schedule. I can survive one week.*

*I hope.*

# ONE

## JONAH ROWE

AT THIS MOMENT, Jonah couldn't help but feel like he'd gotten the shaft.

It was summer, which was always when the Grannison-Morris estate was at its emptiest, and the only residents left were the eight to nine people who everyone else had affectionately dubbed the "skeleton crew."

Only this time, that wasn't the case.

Any and everybody had somewhere to go for either half the summer or the whole season. This one saw Liz and her family trek to Las Vegas. Her parents rewarded her for achieving the Dean's List for the second consecutive time, as well as a consecutive 4.0 grade point average. Liz happily accepted the gift, and it also didn't hurt that Bobby and Vera went along with her family as well. Spader was off doing...something. No one really wanted to know. Douglas had been forced to spend summer with family he didn't even like. Even Malcolm, the most reserved of them all, was occupied for the summer. He'd given some carpentry insights that had been so invaluable that he'd been invited to teach a couple wood shop summer courses.

So, everyone had something to do.

Everyone, that was, except for Jonah, Terrence, and Reena.

After the ordeal that they'd experienced, everyone felt the three of them should have the luxury of being bored. Liz, for one, thought that it was a courtesy to allow the three of them to rest and not have to "expend mental energy."

Malcolm threw in his two cents right before his departure. "You can't possibly recharge your batteries while out having fun and running yourself ragged," he'd said. "Sometimes, sitting back and taking perspective is the most advantageous thing."

So, here the three of them were, in the family room of the estate, bored out of their minds. This wasn't relaxing. This wasn't battery recharging. This was—

"Bullshit." said Terrence aloud. "This is total bullshit. Why do we have to be stuck here like this? This feels like kid's table crap."

Reena rolled her eyes. "You know that's not the case, Terrence. We weren't left out. Everyone felt like they did us a kindness and an honor to leave us to rest."

"Not helping anything, Reena." murmured Jonah. "Don't even pretend like you want to be here with us. We all know that you'd rather be locked up in some hotel room with Kendall right now."

Reena took a breath and closed her eyes. "Not possible at the moment," She grumbled. "Thanks to Jonathan. He felt like I needed to get my emotions in order. Let's just leave it at that."

"It wouldn't be so bad if we weren't the *only* ones at the entire estate," complained Terrence. "I hope that that was luck of the draw. Surely that wasn't done by design—"

"Would it be that huge of a matter if that was the case?"

Jonathan was there. Their mentor and trainer always looked the same, button down, tan duster, and infinity medallion around his neck. This image was so commonplace to Jonah nowadays that he barely noticed it. He certainly didn't notice it right now, as he'd fastened on to what Jonathan just said.

"What did you say, Jonathan?" He queried. "You isolated us on purpose?"

"It wasn't isolation." said Jonathan, "I sincerely believe that the three of you need to have your spirits replenished. But I never intended for you to sit here slothfully doing nothing at all. I have a simple task for you all. Should be easy as can be."

Jonah glanced at Terrence and Reena. What the hell would *this* be?

"What's that, Jonathan?"

Jonathan pocketed his hands. "Have you ever heard of Eva McRayne?"

"No," said Jonah and Reena at once.

"Hell yeah!" exclaimed Terrence, who hopped up from his seat. "She's awesome! The centerpiece of *Grave Messages!*"

"*Grave* what?" asked Jonah.

Terrence looked at Jonah in disbelief. "Seriously, Jonah?" he breathed. "You've never heard of the Sibyl?"

Now Jonah was really befuddled. "Wait. Sibyl? What's she got to do with *Eva?*"

"They are one and the same, Jonah," clarified Terrence. "Eva McRayne is the Sibyl. *Grave Messages* is her show. She is the best. Smart, intense, and smokin' hot—"

"Whoa," interrupted Jonah, "*Grave Messages* is a TV show? You guys know me well enough to know that the only thing I watch on TV is *Supernatural.* Everything else is Netflix. What, pray tell, is this show about?"

Now Terrence looked a bit sheepish. Jonathan spoke up once more.

"It's best if I take over now, Terrence," he said. "Eva McRayne is a superbly talented spiritual conduit who communicates with—"

Now Jonah was the one that rose out of his seat. His meter went from zero to octane in a nanosecond.

"Forgive me, Jonathan, but *are you out of your damn mind?* After everything that happened with Landry over the past few months?"

Jonathan's eyes narrowed. "Mind your tone, Jonah," He said with quiet authority. "This is an entirely different situation. Miss McRayne is no charlatan. She has a spiritual gift."

"So you say," said Reena, equally as riled as Jonah. "If she is authentic, then where exactly did she get this gift?"

"That's the best part!" said Terrence. "It's the show I told you that I started watching once I checked out on *ScarYous Tales*. It's nothing ethereal—I mean, nothing that deals with us! Like Jonathan said, she ain't a charlatan! She said that it comes from Apollo."

Terrence's words left dumbfounded silence in their wake. Jonah ran his tongue over his teeth, like he always did when he heard bona fide bullshit.

"Please, Terrence," He supplicated, "Do not tell me that you mean *Apollo* Apollo."

"The very same, Jonah," said Jonathan. "Apollo, the god. Patron of Delphi, symbolized by the lyre, healer, prophetic deity—"

"I know the stories, Jonathan," interrupted Jonah. "I've done book reports on mythology. Mythology. As in lie. If she fancies herself to be aligned with Apollo, then I suppose she's calling herself Sibyl after the Sibyl no one ever believed—"

"That was Cassandra, actually," corrected Reena.

"And that woman was a prophetess. Eva is a medium." Terrence added. "Dude, you gotta watch-"

"Whoever," spat Jonah. "Point is she's lying. And if she's on TV— "

"Jonah, stop," said Terrence. "And while you're at it, calm down a bit, alright? We're supposed to be de-stressing, recall that?"

With difficulty, Jonah desisted. Yeah, Terrence was right, but that was before Jonathan mentioned this fresh hell.

Reena, who seemed to have successfully put a lid on her own thoughts, directed her attention to Jonathan.

"Sir, clearly, we've gotten way off the point," She said as in level a voice as she could muster. "Your initial question was whether or not we've ever heard of this woman. Why does that matter?"

Jonathan smoothly moved his weight from one foot to the other.

"She is coming to Rome," He replied. "Today."

"So what?" Jonah raised an eyebrow. "What's that got to do with us?"

"Miss McRayne's patron god is a friend of mine." Jonathan explained. "In light of recent events, he contacted me to offer her haven as they film a new episode of *Grave Messages* here in Rome. When I had another protector guide support the suggestion, I agreed."

Jonah shook his head. "You cannot possibly have said yes, Jonathan."

"I did indeed say yes," Jonathan responded.

Jonah threw his hands in the air. What was Jonathan's deal? After everything that had happened with Landry and *ScarYous Tales of the Paranormal,* why was he subjecting them to this *Grave Messages* crap? And this McRayne woman would be crashing at the estate? For the love of God, she could probably buy out a hotel floor! Why the hell did Jonathan have to lodge her?

"Back up." said Reena. "You said someone else suggested this? Who?"

"Akraia," answered Jonathan. "She is another Protector Guide. Apparently, she got wind that *Grave Messages'* production company was interested as Rome for a potential filming site, so she contacted me after I had spoken to Apollo. This is part of my sphere of protection; therefore, I have the right to know any and everything that goes on around here."

"Huh," said Terrence, who looked intrigued. "That Akraia guide must have been around Elliot Lancaster if she got wind of that—"

"Who?" said Reena and Jonah simultaneously.

"Elliot Lancaster," repeated Terrence like it should have been obvious. "His dad runs the company that does *Grave Messages*. He was a presenter on the show, but now he's the day-to-day producing consultant, something like that. I think he scaled back his responsibilities for that Helakos woman."

"What are you talking about, Terrence?" questioned Jonah.

Terrence sighed. "I read that Elliott's supposedly messing around with this billionaire heiress who's recently moved to Beverly Hills named Juno Helakos." he said. "They spend a *lot* of time together—she's been labeled a cougar. Eva's got a new partner on the show. It's a blind guy named Leyton. Well, he *was* her new partner. But his dumb ass left for *ScarYous*."

Jonah eyed Terrence intently. He noticed that Reena, and surprisingly, Jonathan, did too. Reena was the one who broke the silence.

"You read all this, you say," she said slowly, "do you mean…as in…tabloid gossip?"

"Dear Lord," said Jonah, who now questioned his best friend's sanity. "This just keeps getting better and better."

"I read celebrity gossip!" said Terrence, unabashed. "So *what?!* It's not like I'm living these crazy lives, I just read about them!"

"It's not so much that, Terrence," said Jonah, "it's just that one would think that—"

"Look," interrupted Terrence with a trace of heat in his voice, "I'm well aware of what happened. You think it's possible that I'd forget? Turk Landry can go to hell for what he did and is *still* doing. But *Grave Messages* is good TV. I love it, and I ain't ashamed of it. It's a part of all the TV that I watch. I'm a janitor, remember? So, any release that I got from nasty teenagers, clogged sinks, and shitty toilets is a blessed one. TV and celebrity gossip provide such releases. Sorry for the swearing, Jonathan," He added hastily.

Jonathan waved a hand, but regarded Reena, who looked pensive. "What's on your mind, Reena?" he asked.

"It's just…weird," She murmured. "Juno Helakos? Her surname is Greek, and Eva McRayne claims to be blessed by a Greek god. The name Juno is from Ancient Rome, and we live in *Rome,* North Carolina. It's just a bunch of coincidences, and they just—stirred in my brain is all."

Jonah looked at her. Reena made some crazy connections there. He hadn't even noticed those things, and he probably should have. Emotions clouded his rationale at the moment.

"Might be an alias." suggested Terrence. "Lots of rich folks have those."

"True indeed," said Jonathan, "but Ms. Helakos is not the issue here. Miss McRayne's flight will land at a private airport in Raleigh in two hours, and I want the three of you to meet her and her people there. You have my authorization to use the *Astralimes*, and Akraia has seen to it that a car will be there to collect you all and bring you back to Rome. I personally would have preferred if you all could simply use the *Astralimes* to come back, but with the Phasmastis Curaie's strictures on Tenth Percenters using ethereal travel, it's just better that you ride back in the car. Road trips clear the mind. You guys go ahead and get dressed."

"Wait. Hold on for just a damn minute." Jonah held up his hands when he faced Jonathan. "You said in light of recent events earlier. What the hell does that mean?"

"You haven't heard?" Terrence looked shocked. "Jonah, it's been all over the news."

"Netflix, remember?"

"Eva tried to commit suicide after her parents were murdered." Terrence shifted on his feet. "Or at least, that's what the news has been reporting. She survived and was still healing up. In fact, I didn't think she would be back on the show for a while."

Terrence grinned when he whirled around to face Jonathan. "This is her first show back, ain't it? She must be back one hundred precent, then!"

Terrence bounded the stairs so exuberantly one would have thought that he needed the toilet. He must have a crush on this Eva McRayne. Dear Lord. Reena ascended the stairs more slowly; she was probably deep in thought about more random coincidences, as well as these new people about to be introduced to the estate. Jonah let them head upstairs, and then turned back around to Jonathan.

"A suicidal spiritual conduit?" Jonah narrowed his eyes. "Really?"

"The girl is not suicidal." Jonathan folded his hands

together in front of him. "She was in the middle of a fight with the one called Lancaster. It was he who harmed her."

"Don't tell me you watch this crap, too."

"No." Jonathan gave him a tight-lipped smile. "I have much more reliable resources than television."

"I still have strong feelings about this, Jonathan," he said in a sharp whisper.

"I would be surprised if you didn't, Jonah," said Jonathan calmly. "I do, too."

Jonathan's response stunned Jonah. "Then why did you green light this?" he asked. "Surely you don't believe in this Greek gods and monsters sh—stuff, right?"

Jonathan contemplated Jonah's question for a minute or so before he answered. "The realms of life are infinite, Jonah," he said at last. "We know that life never ends; what other secrets does life hold? With the vastness of life, who am I to refute the possibilities? Is Eva McRayne the genuine article? I do not know, never having met her. But it's far from impossible. But the thing that I *do* know is that I am a Protector Guide over everything in this region that I survey. Miss McRayne is a new element. I don't know if her presence is blessing or threat. Events will unfold right here —where I can do something about either eventuality."

---

Jonah, Terrence, and Reena awaited Eva McRayne and her crew at the private airstrip in Raleigh. Reena simply changed out of her relax clothes, which meant her new outfit didn't have paint splattered all over it and rearranged her hair into a tighter ponytail. Terrence was clad in Dockers, loafers, and a snug black polo shirt. Jonah didn't change a damn thing. He didn't view this as important enough for changing. Plus, he didn't care if McRayne or her buddies judged him based on appearance. It wasn't like they would be friends. Though he had given the *Grave Messages* website a glance so that he wouldn't be completely in the dark.

He got the website and more. Terrence wasn't kidding when he mentioned McRayne had been all over the news. Article after article detailed the gruesome murders of one Janet and Martin McRayne, followed by more propaganda regarding the woman's suicide attempt. It was deemed a miraculous recovery based off her so-called immortality.

Yeah. Right.

"Why would she come here?" He wanted to know. "RDU is just a hop, skip, and a jump away."

"Jonathan said that they wanted to be incognito," Reena reminded him. "Celebrities, influential people—they all want the smaller airports so that they can avoid paparazzi and psychos and all that. A commercial airliner doesn't allow privacy for anyone, but in remote places like this? Famous folks can call ahead, and the airport powers-that-be can arrange transport." She gestured to the stretch limousine that had been there before they showed up. "The people land, get in, and put road behind them with almost no one being the wiser."

Jonah thought on it. Made sense. Enough.

Terrence paid no attention to any of their words. He bounced on his heels like a kid and watched the sky as though he could will the arrival to be sooner. Jonah looked over Terrence's outfit once more and had to admit that he was pretty sharp. Despite that, he just didn't think that it would impress a celebrity. But he wasn't about to tear down his friend. Jonah had a feeling that it would happen soon enough.

"Showtime." announced Reena and Jonah threw his eyes skyward.

A private jet descended, made a smooth landing, and taxied to a point not very far from the limo. Jonah had expected to see some fancy words emblazoned across the jet, but McRayne—or whoever handled transportation—did the thing properly. It still didn't sit well with him. It wasn't like everyone had jets to fly them everywhere, and limos to whisk them away the minute they landed. Why did McRayne need all the secrecy? Wasn't shouting from the highest mountain all a part of the celeb protocol?

"Take off the dampener, Reena," said Jonah as the jet doors lowered. "Do us a favor and peg these people right now."

"That isn't the way I do things, Jonah," said Reena in a blunt tone. "You know that. No advantages. We all need to be on even ground. That's always the best way to make a first impression."

Jonah shook his head. "Reena, do you realize that you're saying this about a suicidal woman getting off of a *private jet?*"

The occupants of the jet quickly descended the steps. The first guy seemed a bit happy-go-lucky, but at the same time, it looked forced.

"That's the camera dude," revealed Terrence. "Don't really see much of him, obviously, but the Theia Productions website sings his praises. I think his name's Joey."

After Joey, a positively hardcore-looking man made a quick scan of the airstrip like an attack was imminent. That could only be Eva's bodyguard. Damn, was the guy retired Special Forces or something? It would probably be best to stay on his good side.

Lastly, Jonah got his first official look at Eva McRayne. It was weird. She appeared to be a contradiction. On the one hand, she fit the profile of a vapid, spoiled celebrity to a

T: Honey-blond hair with every strand in place, athletic figure, and that indefinable air of someone who had no money problems whatsoever. But on the other hand, there was something different.

There was a preternatural air about her. It wasn't anything he could see. It was something that he *sensed.* Her features seemed a bit haunted, but if she'd just lost her parents, that was no surprise. And her eyes—wait, were they *gold?* Terrence hadn't mentioned that one. The eyes had an interesting effect, and Jonah caught himself wondering that maybe there *was* something to this lady.

What the hell was he thinking? They were fake, duh. Granted, he had never seen golden eye contacts, but she probably had them specially made to accentuate her whole "Sybil" image. The fact that she lost her parents was terrible. But the woman could probably buy her way out of her grief. She had the jet and limo, after all.

The woman stopped halfway down the stairs and stared at him. In that moment, the strangest thought hit Jonah like a brick. No, not a thought.

A memory.

Three weeks before, he'd joined Reena and Terrence on a road trip to the coast. On the way home, they had stopped at a small county festival outside of Raleigh. It was a chance to stretch their legs after the day on the road and somehow, they ended up in a small booth where a woman claimed to be able to tell you your future for twenty bucks

Yeah, right. Jonah had been skeptical, but he went along when Terrence damn near dragged him over to it. The woman told Terrence that he would continue to explore his love of cooking and eventually, make it his career.

No surprise there. Jonah's informal brother was a master with food. He had even wearing his favorite t-shirt to barbeque in, so he smelled a little like smoke and sweet sauce. For Reena, the woman divined that she would focus more on her art and her family. Again, no surprise. Even after days on the road, Reena still had paint from her latest project buried under her nails.

But Jonah wouldn't be so easy to read. There were no clues for the woman to use as he sat across from her. He passed over his twenty bucks and she took his hand to study his palm.

"Oh," She breathed. "Your life is about to change."

"Yeah? How is that?"

"I see...I see a woman. You've met before, though you don't realize it yet. She is your soulmate. The one you've been waiting to return to you."

Jonah snorted. Clearly, she was talking about Vera Halliday. He had been in love with that woman since he met her, but nothing substantial had happened between them.

So again, no surprising breakthroughs. He had half a mind to make Terrence pay him back the twenty he just wasted.

"Um, ma'am? I already know. I'm working on it."

"No." She shook her head. "No, you don't. I see..."

The woman pauses then frowned. "There is something about gold. Gold hair? Gold eyes? I can't tell. But you will be transferred into a whole other world. A financially wealthy one. You will have much strife, but the rewards will greatly outweigh the hardships."

Jonah had to bite his tongue to keep from laughing out loud.

"I think you just described a reality show, ma'am. Or the plot to the Beverly Hillbillies. I'm a lapsed accountant who works part-time at a library. The only reason why I ain't panhandling is because I have free room and board. So unless you're counting the denominations on the fake poker chips I use with my goth friend, you might have some wires crossed."

"You laugh because you don't see what I see."

"I laugh because I know the truth of my situation."

"Your current situation, yes. I am talking about the future. The near future."

"Alright, fine. Tell me what to look for so I can identify this savior of mine."

"Gold. I know that for certain. She is...entertainment? In entertainment? Yes. I see that. An actress, maybe."

Jonah nodded. "Okay. A vapid, vacuous movie star is my soulmate. Okay."

"I'm serious-"

"So am I. Terrence, give me my twenty dollars back."

"Listen," The woman tightened her grip on his hand. "Look for gold. Look for fame. This is a once in a lifetime opportunity and if you miss it, you will both suffer."

"Noted, ma'am," Jonah muttered. "Thanks for the entertainment."

He rose from the table. "Terrence, you will pay me my twenty back, and I want two large cheesesteaks. Understand?"

"Fine. Mock me. But you will see. You will remember my words when the time comes."

Jonah led the way out of the booth without another word. Terrence muttered under his breath as he took out a twenty and passed it to Jonah.

"You gonna give me that back if her words end up being true."

"They won't."

"How do you know?"

"I don't like blondes."

"Come on, J!" Reena looped her arm through his. "You never know what's going to happen."

"Reena, every single blonde I've met, not counting Liz, has been a bitch. Every. Single. One." Jonah sniffed. "Priscilla was a bitch *and* the last straw. So if there is a blonde in my future, she had better dye it and take the secret to her grave."

"You're no fun." Reena laughed. "You didn't even mention how we're in the middle of nowhere. What celebrity is going to come to Rome?"

"No one," Jonah said. "The last celebrity was Turk Landry, and he was an ass. And oh yeah, *blonde*."

"Dude, that was the worst blonde dye job ever," Terrence said.

"Still," Jonah murmured, "He was blonde."

And yet, here he was on the side of a landing strip watching a blonde celebrity pull down her sunglasses from her head to hide her golden eyes.

No. No way in hell was that psychic right. Jonah shook the memory away. In no time at all, McRayne, her muscle, and Joey were face-to-face with them. Joey and Terrence high-fived like they were already bosom buddies, but it was clear that Terrence's attention was on Eva. The bodyguard shook Reena's hand, and unless Jonah was much mistaken, they were sizing each other up. What was the deal with that? Did this man assume that Reena was the muscle of this trio, and gravitated to a kindred spirit?

For some reason, the thought kind of offended Jonah. He wasn't the one who needed the bodyguard, after all. That was the woman who was in front of him at the moment, shaking his hand with neither zeal nor thrill.

"It's a pleasure to meet you, Eva," welcomed Jonah in a practiced voice. "The name's—"

"I know your name, Country," said Eva in a terse voice. "Jonah Rowe. Former accountant. Current—what do you do again? And that's Terrence Aldercy, standing by Reena

Katoa. Despite what you may believe, I'm not stupid. Do you really think I would stay with people and not know who they are?"

Jonah pulled away his hand, narrowing his eyes. That was yet another check on the list of criteria for a spoiled celebrity brat.

"If you know who I am, then you know not to call me *Country,"* He replied. "And I wouldn't talk if I were you. I looked you up. You're from Charleston, Superstar. You're just as Southern as the rest of us."

Eva turned pale at the mention of Charleston, but she rolled her eyes when she spoke.

"So, you've seen the show. Read a couple of websites. You think you know everything there is to know about me. Country and a fan boy? Cyrus, great job setting up our living arrangements. Really."

"Wait, what?" said Jonah, caught off-guard, "you got it wrong, *Terrence* is the one who—"

But Eva wasn't interested. With a scoff, she turned her back on Jonah and got in the limo. Joey, Special Forces dude—whom Jonah overheard say his name was Cyrus or something—and Terrence were already heading that way.

Terrence hadn't noticed anything past Eva already knowing his name, so conversation with him was out. Jonah still had Reena, though. He noticed that she hadn't entered the limo just yet. She stared at it, shaking her head.

"I'm in full agreement," He grumbled to her. "She is quite a little—"

"No, Jonah," said Reena, "McRayne is scared. Terrified. Something isn't right."

Jonah blinked. "I thought you had your dampener on," he said.

"Oh, I do," confirmed Reena. "I know it because I'm not stupid. I didn't need my essence reading to know that."

Jonah wasn't convinced. "How can she be afraid of anything with Cyrus the Action Figure following her around like a shadow?"

"Damn if I know," said Reena with a shrug. "I just met these people."

She lowered herself into the limo. Jonah approached the door and sighed.

"Goddamn, Jonathan," he said under his breath. "De-stress, my ass."

# TWO

## EVA MCRAYNE

I WAS SHAKING.

I couldn't stop it. I wasn't used to this feeling of pure fear. And I didn't like it. I felt weak. Helpless. The utter desire of fight or flight was so prevalent, I almost jumped out of the limo as the last two joined me. But I was better than that. I was stronger than that.

I won't lie. I had spent the entire flight from California to North Carolina in a daze. Sure, I could have dozed off. But the feeling of Elliot's hands on my throat remained. The sound of wind as it rushed past my ears remained no matter what song I listened to while I tried to drown it all out.

Tried. Tried and failed. I knew that he was after me. I knew that the traitor wouldn't stop until one of us was in our grave. And though Cyrus swore that I had nothing to worry about, I still worried.

"Are you sure that we aren't going to put these people in danger?"

I had ripped my headphones out of my ears as I posed the question to Cyrus for the fiftieth time. That was my main concern. If a crazed serial killer was after my head -

after murdering my mother and the man who had posed as my father - what was going to stop him from slashing his way through a house full of strangers?

"Eva," Cyrus sighed and patted my hand like I was five. A move he knew I absolutely hated. "They are going to be just fine. Jonathan's students are all ethereal. They were born with abilities and have been training to fight."

"Besides, Cy said that the place was going to be deserted."

I raised an eyebrow at my best friend and cameraman, Joey Lawson, who grinned back at me.

"Yeah. I was listening. And if you are so worried, why not spring for a hotel?"

"A hotel cannot provide the same level of security that the estate can, according to Lord Apollo," Cyrus answered for me as he refilled my wine. "Just be cautious, dear girl. Do not get close to anyone. Elliot won't have any recourse when he sees that there is no one to threaten."

Yeah. Like that was going to stop him. I downed the glass like water. It was just after noon eastern time. We would be there in no time. And I needed all the alcohol I could get before we landed.

Don't get me wrong. I hadn't been trying to get smashed before I met Apollo's old friend who had been kind enough to put us up while we filmed in Rome, North Carolina. But my nerves were shot. I was scared out of my mind.

And there was absolutely nothing I could do about it.

"You might want to go easy on that wine, baby girl." Joey fiddled with his phone as Cyrus hooked me up again. "We land in less than ten minutes."

"Leave her be, Joey. She has been through too much lately. And this recent threat isn't helping matters one bit."

I had glowered at Cyrus. Normally, I could look past

him coddling me. I don't know why it was pissing me off so much today. Before I could respond though, a voice came over the loudspeaker.

"Miss. McRayne, we are approaching the air strip now. Be prepared to land in five."

So much for that bottle of red. I buckled myself in and brushed the curls away from my face with annoyance. Maybe Cyrus was right. Maybe I did need to unwind a little.

I watched out the window as we descended. I had requested a private airfield this go round. I wasn't up to the crowds or the paps today. And given my mood since I woke up to fly across the country at four a.m., the bitch persona I was perfecting was in full swing.

I waited when the attendant came up and told us we could get off the jet. I watched as Joey bounded down the aisle and Cyrus followed him. Finally, I stood and stretched.

I took my time. Straightening out my shirt. Brushing away the nonexistent wrinkles in my $500 pair of Calvin's. I wanted to look every bit the part of the television star Jonathan knew me to be

It would make things easier. People tended to be intimidated by money. By fame. I could keep them away from me like I did my clients.

I swung my messenger bag over my shoulder and stepped off the plane. Making sure to lower my sunglasses to keep the sun from blinding me. There were three people already talking with Cyrus and Joey at the base of the stairs. A woman who looked like a damn force to be reckoned with. A stocky black man dressed to the nines. And a tall dark-haired guy who looked like he wanted to be anywhere else but here.

I couldn't blame him. I didn't want him here, either.

I had been heading down when the man pulled his

sunglasses off and I froze at the sight of his face. He looked like someone I had met before. A man I'd met for one night on a beach in South Carolina then spent the next six months trying to get out of my head.

No. There was no way in hell he would be here. Not after all these years.

I had to move. They were going to take off with me still dumbstruck on the stairs if I didn't.

I couldn't stop staring as I worked my way down. I couldn't take my eyes off of his face as I closed the distance between us. I caught a whiff of his cologne and went weak in the knees when I stopped in front of him.

Gods, help me. I had Cyrus and my mind was most certainly betraying him now as I envisioned what this man could do to me.

I forced myself to snap at him when he tried to introduce himself. And when he snapped back, I had to walk away. Because the force in his tone was the hottest thing I had ever experienced.

Maybe it was the wine. Maybe I needed more of it.

I folded myself up in the limo and thanked the gods for my few moments alone. I had to do this. I had to push them away. All of them. I was going insane. That was the only explanation for me wanting a stranger sent to pick me up at the damn airport.

But by Apollo, I did. There was nothing in this world I wanted more than the man who had tried to introduce himself as Jonah Rowe.

I had to shake out of this. I turned my thoughts back to my duties. My job as the Sibyl and as the Representative of the Olympian Council.

Zeus, Hecate, Medusa—they all believed in me. I made a promise to myself that Elliot would not scare me away from the show I'd helped create. I felt more confident after kicking his ass but having Hera in his corner definitely helped him. Despite that, Elliott wouldn't make me go away.

No matter what he could do now. Or what he had done.

So, I clenched my phone in my hand and kept staring out the window. Even though Elliot was supposed to be across the country from me, I knew better. Hera had empowered him. She granted him abilities that not even Cyrus could explain to me. I kept waiting for him to show up. Slip out of the darkness to finish what he had started.

I swallowed down my tears before they could get started. I was in North Carolina, which was far too close to Charleston and the memories I was trying so hard to forget.

The *Greetings from Charleston* postcard. My parents calling out to me through the mirror. The inevitable fight with Elliot that had left me in the hospital for weeks. The fact that Apollo was my father, not the man I'd known throughout my childhood—

No. I couldn't think about that here. Not now. Although, those thoughts had worked well to get my mind off the man sitting diagonally from me.

I leaned forward until my head touched the glass. We were pulling out of the airfield and on our way to the manor Cyrus swore would keep us safe while we filmed the episode.

One week and I would be back across the country. Back in California where I could keep an eye on Elliot to make sure he didn't hurt anyone else.

Not that I had done any good. I bit my lip as the driver pulled out onto a highway. I hadn't been able to protect anyone. Not really. Ash, the Native American who became Elliot's first victim. The others he sacrificed in Hera's name to grant himself power. Even my own mother and father—no, *not* my father, just the man who raised me.

I had to get used to that, but damn, it was hard. When you called a man your father for twenty-four years, the label stuck.

No. I had to stop. I had a job to do. Get it done then start on the next one.

I felt my phone buzz in my hand. I glanced down at the screen to see Cyrus had sent me a message despite sitting right next to me.

I sighed, pulled the phone down, and opened the screen with a single swipe of my thumb.

*Breathe. I'm right here.*

I shook my head as he reached out to squeeze my hand. Cyrus was known as a Keeper. My guide, mentor, and guard against all things which threatened me.

*I'm fine.* I typed back as quickly as I could. *Promise.*

He gave me a look that told me he didn't believe me. He was right to do so. I wasn't fine. I wasn't sure if I ever would be again.

But I had to act fine. Smile for the camera. Keep the show going. Maybe I was a better actress than I thought.

I kept my eyes on the passing road, but I turned my attention to what was going on around me. The three people who came to greet us at the airfield were representatives of the Grannison-Morris Estate. I wasn't kidding when I said I'd done my research on them. I had to make sure they weren't agents under Hera's control. I didn't find anything suspicious about them. Just listings on white pages and the standard social media sites. There was nothing that would alarm me. No real interest in the paranormal or the Greek pantheon. They seemed stable. Boring.

That was all I wanted to know. I didn't dare get close enough to any of them with the threat Elliot would pose if he found out I'd befriended them.

"Eva? Earth to Eva." Joey leaned in to snap his fingers in front of my nose. "You still with us?"

"Somewhat." I gave him a small smile. Joey had been with me from the beginning. He was also on Elliot's hit list since he was under my protection. "What's up?"

"Reena was asking about our location. Since you snatched up the files and refused to give me a copy, I haven't read about it yet. Care to enlighten us?"

"Oh." I dropped my phone back into my lap. "It's nothing spectacular. The Covington mansion not far from the Grannison-Morris Estate."

"The what?" Jonah sounded bored. But that didn't stop my heart from flipping again at the sound of his accent. "Never heard of it."

"Covington mansion. I'm not surprised you've never heard of it. It's not something you'd learn about binge watching Netflix."

"She got you there, Jonah." The man named Terrence laughed. "You should see him. He won't move for days unless you make him."

Jonah gave me a dark look and mumbled, "So someone read my page on Facebook."

I smiled as sweetly as possible.

"To put it simple, it's a big house on a big hill cursed by the original owner. For those who are actually interested, the mansion was built entirely out of granite back in 1823 by the founder of Covington Textile Mills, George S. Covington. His entire family died when a fever swept through the area, save him. So, he built the house as a memorial to them. He even went so far as installing a tomb beneath the parlor and had them buried there. But in doing so, he also put things in it to invite the spirits in. He studied Spiritualism. Held séances. At the time of his death, he cursed anyone who would dare to change anything about his beloved memorial. Families moved in, and then back out within a week. It was eventually boarded up."

"Until now." Joey piped up, rubbing his hands together. "So, we're going to check out an abandoned, cursed mansion with bodies buried beneath it? Awesome find, Evie."

I didn't have the heart to tell him that it was *Elliot's* find, not my own, but I winked at him and started to reply before Cyrus joined in.

"If this man invited spirits in, then it could be a portal." He narrowed his eyes at me. "I don't know how comfortable I am with this, Eva. Perhaps there is another haunted pile of rubble for you to play in."

I shrugged. "Everywhere I go is a portal, Cyrus, as long as it has a mirror in it. No one will die. It's an in-and-out. I'm not that concerned."

"Oh, no you don't." Jonah snapped. "First thing, we don't say *die.* That is fiction. And don't you dare think.... don't you even consider it. What if a spirit attaches itself to you? Do you have any idea—"

Cyrus turned his own dark gaze towards the man while Reena gave him an identical look. She spoke before Cyrus could.

"Jonah, stop. They are here by Jonathan's invitation. As such, we must respect them." The woman shook her ponytail. "Look, Ms. McRayne, I don't know what forces brought you to our home, nor do I wish to know what you are facing. But do not expect us to become involved. We will respect your privacy as long as you respect ours."

"Agreed."

I nodded, feeling a strange kinship with this woman. There was an aura of strength about her that I could relate to. It was how I had been before the Charleston fiasco. I also tried hard to ignore the twinge of disquiet I felt when

Jonah said death was fiction. Cyrus called it something similar. A change? A transformation? Yeah. That sounded right.

"It is my hope that we are out of your hair within a few days."

"Thank God." Jonah muttered as the limo turned down a driveway. "The sooner you are gone, the better."

"Wait, Reena. Don't go saying I won't help if I can." Terrence held up his hand as the car came to a stop. "We're not doing anything. And it might do us some good to get out of the house before we pass into Spirit from boredom."

Pass into Spirit? That was such a waste of breath. Why couldn't he just say die?

"Such a poor choice of words, dear man." I tucked my phone down into my messenger bag before reaching for the door handle. "But I would prefer it if you left this one to the professionals."

I stepped out of the car to see that Jonah had gotten out as well and beaten me to the other side. For a fleeting moment, I thought he was going to grab me, push me against the car, and kiss me until I went weak in the knees. Instead, he jabbed a finger into my shoulder as he hissed at me.

"I don't know who you think you are, Superstar, and I don't give a damn. But here? On this estate? *We* are the professionals. We're the ones saving your ass from—something. So, you can drop the attitude."

I grabbed his hand and twisted it back at the wrist before Cyrus decided to step in. I ignored the shock of electricity that seemed to go through me. "You have no idea what I am dealing with. And if you and your people are smart? You'll leave me alone to do that."

"Oh, I'm sorry." Jonah chided as he jerked himself free from me. "Let me guess. Your biggest problem is what color your fingernail polish is going to be, right? That is, if you don't decide to take a leap off a four-story building..."

"Stop."

Jonah whirled around and I huffed as an older man stepped forward. He looked as distinguished as the massive building behind him. This must be the Jonathan that Cyrus had told me about.

"Jonah, go inside and wait for us." Jonathan offered me his hand. "Ms. McRayne, forgive Jonah's rudeness. Please, call me Jonathan."

"Then you must call me Eva." I shook his hand, amazed as the anxiety which had filled me earlier disappeared in his presence. "Sir, I must speak with you as soon as possible."

"Come inside. The driver will take care of your things." The man fell in step beside me as we walked across a stone walkway to enter inside. "Welcome to Grannison-Morris Estate. While you are here, you may have free reign of the grounds and the house. I hope you find this place to be a sanctuary of sorts."

"I already do." I glanced over to see Cyrus bowing his head towards the stranger. I would have to remember to ask him about it later. "I hear that you are already familiar with Cyrus. And the lollygagger with his mouth open? That's Joey."

"Yes, I am quite familiar with the great Cyrus of Crete." The man nodded with a smile that Cyrus mimicked. "I have heard a great deal about your service to Apollo. I look forward to speaking with you after dinner. I am certain it will be quite an enlightening experience."

"Dinner? Great! I'm starving!" Joey lifted his camera bag so that it hung over his shoulder. "It was a long flight and Sentinel Sibyl over here refused to stop for fast food so that I could eat on the plane."

I scowled at Joey as he disappeared with Terrence

down the hallway. I was sure they were heading towards the kitchen. Reena stayed behind Jonathan as Jonah dismissed us with a wave of his hand and went through a pair of impressive double doors.

"Jonah, your presence is still required."

Jonathan spoke with a quiet tone, but apparently, the man heard him. He popped his head back through the doors, rolled his eyes, and stepped back into the foyer.

"Would you like to rest before we speak?" Jonathan dusted off a piece of imaginary lint from his sleeve. "Or can we get you anything?"

"Wine, if you have it. It's too late for coffee." I sat my bag down on a table which lined the wall. "We may as well get everything out into the open. The sooner the better."

---

Jonathan was a master at hospitality. He got us settled in a large family room with drinks and a plate of cut vegetables to stave off Joey's hunger. He and Terrence attacked the plate with a fervor that was embarrassing. I took a minute to glance around the room as everyone else took their seats.

"I swear, I've seen this place before."

I took a sip of my wine and sat it down on the wooden coffee table. Jonah scoffed as he took the overstuffed chair farthest away from me.

"Where? In a dream? A premonition?"

"A comic book." I raised my eyebrow in his direction. "With a small sign at the gate announcing it as a school for gifted students."

Terrence chuckled. Joey smirked. Cyrus simply sighed as he stood behind me.

"It is an accurate description of the Grannison-Morris Estate, Eva." Jonathan entered the room and took a seat across from us. "But I am most interested in your own story. Tell me about yourself."

I hated this part. I hated having to tell the story repeatedly. But I did it each time I asked. It was all part and parcel of my role. So, I started from the only place I could. The beginning. I explained to those in the room how I had been tricked - or so I thought - by my predecessor into speaking Apollo's oath. I told them about the mirror, and the history behind it. How the first Sibyl became immortal as punishment for breaking a deal with Apollo. How Persephone took pity on the girl and granted her the ability to speak with the dead. Apollo awarded that same girl with the mirror to break her immortality if she wished it. But only if she passed it onto another woman who would take her place.

But that was all they'd get. It wasn't their business that Apollo was my actual father. Only the gods and Cyrus knew the truth. I planned on keeping it that way.

I told them the basics. But what I needed to tell them, what I had to tell them, was much more important. I took a deep breath, ignored the skeptical looks from our new roommates, and continued.

"Look, I pose a very serious threat to you and yours while being here, Jonathan. I know Apollo has told you that Elliot Lancaster, a producer for *Grave Messages,* has become something...horrible. The official name for what he has become is..."

"Skinwalker." Terrence piped up as he leaned forward. "So that Montana episode wasn't theatrics for the show? He really is a psychotic monster?"

"Everything you see on the show is real, I'm afraid." I took a gulp of my drink as Cyrus squeezed my shoulder to let me know he was still there. Jonah leaned his head against his hand and had such a look of disbelief, it was painful. "And yes. He has become a Skinwalker. A monster transformed by Hera. He is a killer. The problem is, I haven't figured out how to stop him yet. Not without Hera bailing him out every chance she gets."

Terrence shook his head. "I wonder if the Helakos woman knows about that,"

I didn't know what to say to that, so I let it pass. I knew nothing about Elliot's dealings with the billionaire woman from the tabloids. It paled in comparison to everything else.

Now that Terrence mentioned it, though, it was a bit of a surprise that Elliott hadn't offered *her* up to Hera for slaughter, too. Maybe he relished her company too much to kill her. Maybe she was a physical means to an end. Who knew?

Jonah broke out into laughter, which ended the brief silence in the room. He started to applaud before standing.

"You tell a good tale, Superstar, but surely you don't think we'll fall for it. Me thinks you've been out in the California glitz too long."

I stood up to face him with my arms crossed over my chest. "You may think so, Rowe. I wish it was fake. My life would be far less tragic if it were. I've had to fight for, then fight against, a man I cared for once. A man who is hell bound to see me suffer at his hands."

"Fight? Right." Jonah chuckled. "I don't see that happening. You might mess up your hair in the process."

"Jonathan, may I demonstrate something to your charge?" I turned to face my host. "It involves a weapon, but I won't use it. Yet."

Jonathan gestured his approval as the others tensed up around me. Reena leaned forward on her seat. Even happy-go-lucky Terrence looked as if he were ready to strike. I took a deep breath and willed for my weapon to appear. Cyrus had taught me how to call it forth when Zeus had given it to me, but he never explained the mechanics of it. Truth was, I didn't think to ask. Chalk it up as another thing I needed to talk to my Keeper about.

My right hand shimmered just before my short sword appeared out of thin air. The blade was white gold. The handle? Gold as well. I balanced it between my hands before sitting it on the table next to my wine. In the late afternoon sunlight, the Phoenix symbol rising out of the Sun gleamed, as did the swirls of yellow gold that crossed the white of the blade.

"The official name for my weapon is the Ceremonial Sword of the Sibyl. According to Zeus, it was crafted by Hephaestus himself. The weapon was a gift, but it has come in handy more often than I would like to admit."

The four strangers leaned over the sword, each studying it with veiled expressions. Finally, Terrence spoke up.

"It's beautiful, but, um—" He scratched the bridge of his nose. "Who is Hephaestus?"

"The weapon maker of the Gods." Cyrus finally spoke. "Who is also a son of Hera."

"Still trying to convince us this whole Greek mythology thing is real, aren't you?" Jonah slumped back down in his chair. "I don't think some fancy trick of the light is going to make your case for you."

I took up the sword, ignoring the sudden hurt in my chest as it disappeared. Some people were believers. Some were not. It didn't matter to me one way or the other what this Jonah thought.

That was a lie. For some reason, despite my fears, I felt the need to impress him.

“Look, I’m sure you’ve all heard about my supposed suicide attempt. It wasn’t suicide. Elliot enlisted Kampe’s help through Hera. He nearly killed me. He won’t hesitate to do the same to any of you.”

"Dinner." Terrence rubbed his hands together, a little eager to change the subject. "Let's talk about that. What can I make you, Eva? I can throw together anything you'd want."

I shook my head to cut him off, but his look of disappointment was so strong, I felt horrible. "Let me take a rain check, Terrence. I would love to try your cooking. Tomorrow. For now, I really just want to see my room and crash before we head to the site tomorrow."

Cyrus offered me his arm, but I waved it away. "No. I'll be fine. I'm sure you have much to discuss with Jonathan. I'm going to unpack and get some sleep."

"I'll join you as soon as I can." Cyrus dropped his arm. "There are some matters I wish to cover with the Elevenths."

I frowned, knowing that Cyrus had called the Grannison-Morris Estate the home of the Eleventh Percenters, but I didn't ask him to elaborate. When Cyrus started talking about different planes of existence and "ethereal" powers, my eyes glazed over. Just as I knew they would now if I stuck around for this conversation.

"Tell me later?" I waited until he nodded before Terrence hopped up from his seat on the couch.

"Let me show you to your room, Eva."

"Alright." I turned to follow him, trying to hide the smile this man elicited from me. He was as excited as a puppy as he explained how to get around the massive house. Finally, he stopped before a wooden door.

"This is it. Yours for a week." He grinned as he stuffed his hands in his pockets. "And don't pay Jonah any never mind. We have all had a—a trying few months. He's spun about concerning this, but he'll get over it."

"Yeah? Me, too." I started to open the door but stopped before I could. "Terrence, I didn't see any mirrors in the rooms we went into earlier. Are there any in my room?"

"No." He swelled up, quite proud of himself. "I took them all down the minute Jonathan told us you were arriving. I know how dangerous they are to you."

I leaned forward and squeezed his hand. "Thank you, Terrence. That means a lot to me."

I slipped through the door before he could fall over. I knew how excited fans got and he was obviously a fan.

I gave the room a once over as I closed the door. The pile of luggage stacked up neat in the far-right corner by the closet. I had a lot of work to do before tomorrow. We were going to view the Covington property. Joey had even scheduled an interview with the owner. But I couldn't handle it right now. I collapsed on my bed with a sigh.

I rubbed my hands over my face as I considered how important this was. I had been gone from *Grave Messages* for a long while. First, with the deaths of my parents. Then, while I healed up from Elliot's attack. And lastly, the magic goddess boot-camp at an Olympian training ground called the Academy.

If I could survive Charleston, Hecate, and Medusa, then I could survive anything. I could get through a week without falling all over Jonah.

At least, I hoped I could.

# THREE

## JONAH ROWE

JONAH HAD HAD ENOUGH. Superstar McRayne was allowed to go to bed, so he excused himself.

Jonathan and Cyrus looked as though they'd speak for hours, so his departure was seamless. Reena was in pragmatist mode. She could be the voice of reason here. There was no point in a conversation with Terrence because he was too enamored to be of much use at the moment. Looked like Jonah was on his own for this one.

How dare McRayne condescend? How dare she say "Leave it to the professionals?"

The estate was their zone. This wasn't a damn Hollywood studio where fantasy became reality courtesy of lights, makeup, and clockwork. What the hell did she know about fighting?

As a writer, he had to give her credit. Her story was superb. Her producer was now a Skinwalker slave to Hera and wanted to kill her.

It was definitely original. But Terrence had already said that that Lancaster dude was in Beverly Hills, mooching off of a billionaire heiress. What man in his right mind would be thinking about murder when he had it like that?

Eva had storytelling down. Her little sleight of hand with the sword? Cute. The hallmark of a bona fide Hollywood illusionist. But when you got down to the root of it? Eva McRayne was indeed a superstar.

A superstar bitch.

Jonah had taken a spiritual endowment before they'd used the Astralimes to get to Raleigh. He didn't know how vigilant he'd have to be with the celebrities around, but Joey was cool, and Cyrus seemed too reserved to be an asshole. But Eva?

Whatever.

*One week, Jonah,* He thought to himself. *You tolerated Essa, Langton, and Bane for months. You can deal with the diva medium for a week.*

He could do it. He'd been through worse. Seven days. Seven little sunsets, and Superstar would be gone, and life would be uneventful once again. With that satisfied thought, he fell asleep.

He was standing on the lushest lawn he'd ever seen. It was like Superbowl grass, and even better than the grounds at the estate, and that was saying something.

But the lawn was nothing compared to the house.

It was huge, and done in the style of Frank Lloyd Wright. That was the only style he knew and enjoyed, so he knew it when he saw it. A sudden weight in his pocket caught his attention, and he reached there.

They were keys.

Jonah stared at them. They hadn't been there before. Had they? So this house was—

"Yours, darling," said a smoky voice.

Jonah actually jumped. There was a woman on the porch

whose smile was disarming as hell. She had a perfect figure. On a scale of one to ten, she was a two hundred fifty. Her attire was simple, but daunting. A snow-white top that left little to the imagination, and a skirt that was so short it should have been criminal. How could Jonah have not noticed her before?

"Um…" murmured Jonah, "who are you?"

"I'm whoever you want me to be." The woman descended the steps, chuckling as she did so. "I'm yours, just like this house."

Then it all came back to Jonah. Had he forgotten things that quickly? He'd written a five-book steampunk series that had struck gold. The books were a resounding success. It was like he could do no wrong. No one could explain how his books had been such runaway hits. He'd negotiated a book deal for an amount of money so high that it could cause vertigo. He'd just closed on this beautiful new house last week, which he'd dubbed Beech in honor of his grandmother's maiden name. That was all familiar. But he didn't know the woman. She was a blank.

"I—I remember everything now," said Jonah slowly. "I just don't know you."

Even though the woman descended the steps, she hadn't come any further. "Think of me as your housewarming present," she purred. "And I'm not alone. My sisters are here for you, too."

She gestured to the front porch, and two women sauntered out of the front door. Their figures were as perfect and outfits as scandalous as hers. Jonah didn't know what to make of it. It was quite a sight.

"What are you waiting for, Jonah?" said Smoky Voice quietly. "It isn't like you don't deserve what you're about to receive."

Something about that statement didn't sit well with

Jonah, but he let it pass. Seduction could be an uncomfortable thing, after all.

Jonah was tempted. No sane man wouldn't be. His books were successful now. He could remember every award, every signing, every convention—all of it. He was the real deal. Finally ! Why shouldn't he enjoy his success?

This success felt great. Perfect.

Maybe a little too perfect.

But wasn't that the way it was sometimes? Huge successes that felt too good to be true? Too perfect?

"Why do you doubt this, my dear?" said Smoky Voice. "Your mystery novels are simply the best! Now come on in here and let's enjoy ourselves!"

"Mystery?" Jonah frowned. "I do steampunk."

"That's what I meant to say," said Smoky Voice hastily. "But it doesn't matter, does it? A book's a book, no matter the genre!"

"Let's not worry about books right now," said one of the women on the porch. "Let's just think about all of the fun that the four of us are about to have."

But now Jonah was just a bit rattled. They were adamant about getting him into that strange house. It seemed to go a little beyond seduction.

Wait. Strange house? Where had that come from? It was his house! Right?

"How exactly did you all get in my house?" he asked them.

Smoky Voice rolled her eyes. "The keys of course! You left them for us!"

The first red flag went up in Jonah's head. "How could I have left them for you if you were a housewarming surprise?" he quizzed. "And the keys are right here! I've always had them—no—they appeared in my pocket!"

Smoky Voice threw a look at her sisters on the porch. The second red flag went up in Jonah's head.

"Why do you ask all these questions?" she asked, but her voice seemed a little different. A little colder. "Can't you just come into this place and bed us?"

"Bed you?" repeated Jonah. "Is this the eighteen-forties?"

"It's a figure of speech, Rowe," said Smoky Voice, whose seductive tone was now nonexistent. "Now, if you please—"

"No." These women were the textbook definition of gorgeous. There was no question about that. But this entire thing just didn't mesh with Jonah. It was a gut feeling. He even doubted his successes as a writer. It was just too perfect. "I don't know what this is, but I don't want any part of it. Thanks, but no thanks."

Smoky Voice looked stunned. Her sisters looked as if they'd gotten punched in the gut. Jonah didn't care if he'd hurt their feelings. He turned his back on them but before he could take a step, a strong hand gripped his shoulder.

"You dare to resist us, mortal?"

In the time it took for Jonah to get spun around, the entire landscape changed. The lush grounds were replaced by rocks, stones, and briar patches. The Frank Lloyd Wright was gone, replaced by a bone ridden cave that stuck out of the ground like a gaping mouth. Only Smoky Voice and her sisters remained, but they, to Jonah's surprise, were not fazed by these stark changes. They were almost iridescent with rage.

"What the—?"

Then the sisters changed. The lustrous hair became patchy clumps. The eyes became blood red, with black dots for pupils. Their skin became deep-sunk and sallow, and their shapely figures devolved into emaciated, gaunt, and bent postures.

"HOLY SH—!"

Jonah didn't get the chance to finish. One of the hideous apparitions lunged forward and throttled the expletive right out of him.

"You belong to us!" she screeched, her voice now an archaic rasp. "You will never leave our lair!"

"Says you, bitch!" snarled Jonah. Due to his struggling against her, the creature's clutch on his throat wasn't as tight as she probably desired. He had to think. Fight or flight had kicked in, but Jonah knew that if he simply attempted to flee, he wouldn't make it far. He had to fight for a chance to flee.

For some reason, the keys were still in his grasp, even though the house never existed. He didn't question it. He simply swiped the metal across the apparition's face, rupturing an eye in the process. With a howl, she released him and clutched at the injury. A second one snarled in rage and gave Jonah a hard shove, which knocked him into a briar patch.

Jonah felt every sting and laceration that the briars made on his legs, but did his best to file them away. He knew that if he didn't put space between himself and these demon bitches, he'd feel something worse than briar cuts.

The one who shoved him grabbed his throat and lifted him as though he weighed nothing. When he was eye-level, the red-eyed, sagging face morphed back into the gorgeous façade of Smoky Voice. The face contrasted massively with the emaciated and gaunt body.

"It would have been more enjoyable for you if you'd just said yes," she told him in a voice that was restored once again to sultry.

"But it makes no difference. Now, you die."

The words caused a memory to flash across Jonah's mind. It felt like an electric shock in his brain.

"Death isn't real," he grumbled.

He conjured all the concentration he could, and willed his batons to appear in his hands. It was a hunch, but if this place made no sense, then actions could be far-fetched as well.

Miraculously, they appeared right in his hands, and even cackled with blue current from his spiritual endowment. The wraith-woman's false visage slipped as she witnessed the phenomena. Jonah took advantage of the opportunity to crack her ragged jaw. She cried out and released him.

Jonah had no idea what was going on. But he knew that every memory he had before was a lie. He wasn't an author with a fancy house and women fawning at his feet. He was the Blue Aura.

The confused as hell Blue Aura, but at least he knew who he was.

"Stay back!" he roared. "I'll break your bones! They look brittle enough as it is!"

Strangely, they didn't even register his threat. Even the one who now only had one eye regarded him with alarm.

"What is this?" said the one on the left. "What manner of mortal are you, Jonah Rowe?"

"It doesn't matter!" said the one who had had the Smoky Voice disguise. "Kill him!"

Jonah knew that fight time was over. It was flight time now. He didn't know where to go, but it had to be anyplace else but where he stood. Spinning on his heel, he fled—

—And sat bolt upright in his bed, struggling this way and that. He nearly rolled off of the thing as realization hit him.

*It had been a dream. A dream. A dream.*

As he repeated it in his mind, his heart rate returned to normal. His breathing slowed. He settled back into his own skin and was himself again.

That had been one of the most vivid dreams he'd ever experienced. What brought about that dream? He hadn't watched anything freaky on Netflix, he hadn't had spicy food before bed—he hadn't done anything that warranted such insanity.

It had to be random. It was a random, sick dream that was now over.

"Yeah," he said aloud. "It's over. Get a grip, Jonah."

The sound of his own voice calmed him a great deal. Everything was cool. Hell, that dream may have the makings of a novel.

With a snicker at that, he moved to straighten out the sheet that had been twisted all to hell when he'd thrashed.

"Ow, damn." There was discomfort below his knees. He threw off the sheet to inspect, and froze.

On the lower half of his legs were multiple cuts and lacerations. He didn't feel them until his legs brushed the cover, which must have aggravated them. The cuts were in the same places where he'd felt pain when he'd been shoved into that briar patch in the dream.

A thrill of horror overtook him, and he grabbed both of his batons from the nightstand. Blue current danced up and down the things, but he took no notice of it as he stormed out of his room with one destination in the forefront of his mind.

He reached Eva's door and burst in without preamble. She made an exclamation before she swung her sword at him. He instinctively blocked her weapon by throwing his batons up in an X formation. So she hadn't been asleep, after all.

The two of them stood there breathing heavily, sword on batons.

"What the hell have you brought on us, McRayne?" Jonah whispered.

"What the hell are you doing in my room, Rowe?" Eva shook hair from her face, clearly confused. "And what's the deal with these blue glow sticks?"

Jonah had neither the time nor the patience for circular conversation. "Answer the damn question!"

"What are you talking about?" Eva shot back.

"Bitch, you'd better start talking!"

"Bitch—?!"

"Whoa there!"

Jonathan and Cyrus stormed the scene. They must have overheard things unfold.

"What is going on here?" Cyrus demanded. "Jonah, lower your batons!"

"Hell no!" snapped Jonah. "Superstar here would have cleaved my head in two!"

"You were the one who came in here, blue blazing!" shouted Eva.

"Lower. The. Weapons."

Jonathan spoke with such absolute authority Jonah and Eva complied in spite of themselves. Even Cyrus gave him a double take.

"Now then," said Jonathan in his usual tone. "Get to the family room, right this minute. I'll summon Bast to rouse Joey, Terrence, and Reena. Explanations for these behaviors are in order."

# FOUR

## EVA MCRAYNE

"WHY THE HELL am I in trouble?" I hissed at Cyrus as we followed Jonathan and damned Rowe down the hall. "I didn't do anything."

"You're not in trouble." Cyrus placed his hand on my lower back. "By god, Eva. You're not going to be reprimanded. But we do need to know what is going on here."

"Yeah? Well, it sure does feel like it." I huffed. "What was he thinking, barging in like that? I really would have cut him to pieces if he hadn't been armed."

I didn't want to tell Cyrus what Rowe had said about me bringing trouble to their doorstep. I knew that already. Hell, I'd warned them all about the darkness that seemed to follow me. But did Mr. Smart Ass want to listen? No.

I watched the object of my irritation fall into the chair across from the couch. No matter how handsome he was, Jonah had scared me to death. I had been unpacking, but the second I heard my door bang open, all I could think of was Elliot choking me.

Jonah Rowe really was lucky.

A cat sat so still by the stairs, I thought it was a statue. When everyone had reconvened into the family room, Terrence looked between us with a stunned expression.

"Jonah, did you really go into Eva's room armed?" He seemed to stare at me a little longer than necessary before he turned back to his friend. "What were you thinking about?"

"Before any more words are spoken," Jonathan reached out and beckoned to Jonah, "Your batons."

Jonah handed them over, never taking his eyes off of me when Cyrus spoke up as well.

"Eva, your sword."

Two could play this game. I glared at Rowe as I lowered my weapon to the coffee table. I'd be damned if he saw me relinquish it.

"Well, now. That's done." Jonathan took a spot between the furniture where Jonah and I sat. "Now, Jonah. Explain yourself."

"Gladly."

Jonah launched into a story of the dream he had about three women who wanted him. I rolled my eyes until he concluded by lifting up his sweats. His legs were covered in nicks and cuts from the knee down. I watched as he studied his friends as if waiting for them to speak, but he spoke to the wrong audience. Joey clasped his hand around my arm as we both recognized the horror that had happened to Jonah.

A person was most vulnerable to attacks when they were asleep. Elliot had attacked me through my dreams before I had been sent to the Academy. If it hadn't been for Hecate's tutelage, I'd be a demented fool right now.

I tried to wipe the fear off of my face and mirror the confusion on the other faces around me, but it was hard. I knew Elliot had enlisted the help of Pasithea, the wife of the god of sleep, to gain access to the dreamscape. But it was surprising how quick he had been to attack Jonah. I didn't want to admit to myself that he had been right.

This was all my fault.

Truth be told, the only occupants in the room who showed no emotion were Jonathan and Cyrus. I jumped when I heard the admiration in my keeper's voice instead of the anger I expected.

"Congratulations, Jonah Rowe." Cyrus broke the tension that filled the room. "You encountered the Sirens, and are still here to tell the tale."

"Look Cyrus," Jonah leaned forward on his elbows as he began. "I don't believe this shit, but despite myself, I'll humor you. I know about the Sirens because I read about them when I was a kid. They lured men to their ruin at sea. In case you hadn't noticed, this isn't the sea. And on top of that, the Sirens tempted men by singing. I assure you, there were no tunes."

"True," agreed Cyrus. "But times do progress. It's a 'brave new world,' as people say. Do you think the gods and the monsters don't adapt as well? You don't think that the Sirens' temptations can't be just as effective on land? And who said they always had to sing to a man to get him to compromise his morals?"

Jonah turned away from Cyrus as if he was ignoring him, but I wasn't. I stared at Rowe as I realized the one thing I would have known if I'd paid attention to Cyrus' lecture about the Eleventh Percenters on the flight to Raleigh. These people were strong. Far stronger than I had given them credit for.

I felt my expression soften, so I closed my eyes and willed the bitch in me forward. I couldn't get close to him. I couldn't even play with the spike of thrill that sprung up every time I saw him. I wouldn't start admiring him. It would be deadly for all of them if I did.

I had to remember that more than anything else.

"A more interesting thing, though," continued Cyrus, "Is Jonah's ability to resist them. Older, wiser men have fallen victim to the seductions of the Sirens. They fill your mind with false experiences, sometimes leaving no trace of the true memories. How did you manage it?"

"That would have to be attributed to Jonah's ethereality." Jonathan beamed at his pupil with pride.

"'Ethereality?'" I opened my eyes with a snort. "Sounds like something off a cheap perfume commercial."

Yeah. The bitch was back. I knew my words had hit home when Jonah straightened up in his seat.

"Well, see, Superstar," He had regained his bastard form as well, "For those of us who have an I.Q. higher than Kanye and the Kardashians, ethereality is something that keeps us physically alive."

Ok. That one hurt. I narrowed my eyes at him when Jonathan broke in.

"Now, Jonah."

Jonathan stepped forward as if we were about to go at each other's throats. It might have happened if Jonah put my intelligence on par with a damned Kardashian again. The leader of this little ragtag group cleared his throat as he continued.

"I think that this would be an opportune time to implement some of the anger control techniques Felix taught you these past few months. Eva was kind enough to explain the inner workings of her abilities as the Sibyl. Would you please share the Eleventh Percent with her and Joey?"

Jonah's mouth twisted. He shifted in his seat as if

explaining his abilities was the last thing on earth he wanted to do.

"If you aren't up to the task," Jonathan spoke with an obvious annoyance, "I'll gladly ask Reena or Terrence to do it— "

"No, I got it," interrupted Jonah. "I'm good. Now, Joey, Superstar, we are what you call ethereal humans..."

He went on from there. He told us about them having access to the extra portion of their brains. Told us about interactions with and influencing the spiritual world. Told us about how "death" was just a label we "Tenth Percenters" used, and that that transition was actually someone passing into Spirit, going from a physical life to a spiritual one. I felt Joey tighten his grip around my arm as Jonah explained how they believed that some spirits and spiritesses stayed on Earthplane and the Astral Plane while some decided to cross on to The Other Side. It was at that point that Joey interrupted.

"Other Side?" He repeated. "You mean like the Underworld? I'm just trying to keep up here."

"No, son," said Jonathan. "The Other Side isn't a place that any of us can access. People don't return from there once they go. The Underworld is an entirely separate matter. Jonah, please continue."

Jonah cleared his throat, and kept going. I was with Joey. I tried to wrap my mind around how Eleventh Percenters couldn't see spirits of other Eleventh Percenters, nor could they see the spirits of people that they were emotionally close to. He concluded with how some spirits enjoyed bouncing between the Earthplane and the Astral Plane.

When he was done, I couldn't help myself. His explanations were too damned close to what I had experienced as my time as the Sibyl. But I wouldn't let him know that. Instead, I began to cast looks on the strangers that were about as skeptical as the ones they'd given to me when I explained my own abilities.

"So let me get this straight." I leaned back against the couch so that Joey would be forced to loosen his grip. He was trying hard to show he wasn't rattled, but in the process, he was leaving bruises on my arm. "You people are like some glorified superheroes, or something?"

Jonah gritted his teeth, but Terrence chimed in before he could respond.

"That was awesome, Jonah," He said. "But I'll help you out now, man. Jonathan, is that okay?"

Jonathan opened his hands in a welcoming gesture. He looked like a proud parent who had just successfully launched a child into the world. Reena, on the other hand, looked skeptical.

"You're sure, Terrence?" Reena asked. "I'll wrap it up, no problem."

"Nah, I'm good."

Clearly, he did not want to be deprived of his chance to impress me. I hid my smile behind my hand. Some fans were annoying. Others were adorable in their hero worship. Terrence fit into the latter category.

"Eva, Joey, our access to the ethereal world lets us use powers when we have spiritual endowments," He began. "We've been endowed all day, and when we touch things made of ethereal steel, they gleam with the color of our aura. Here."

For a reason known only to himself, Terrence already had weapons ready. He passed Reena a dagger, and pulled his own steel knuckles out of his pocket. The weapons turned yellow for Reena, and burnt orange for Terrence. I sat up again when I saw the weapons begin to glow. It was beautiful, dangerous, and thrilling all at the same time.

"As you can see, our colors," announced Terrence. "Tenths' aura colors change at the drop of a hat, but for Elevenths, the color is always the root of our personality. I'm burnt orange, Reena is yellow, and Jonah is the Blue Aura."

I raised an eyebrow at Jonah despite the fact that I was talking to Terrence. "The Blue Aura? Is that like a big deal, or something?"

"Supposedly, it's a very big deal, Superstar." Jonah interrupted Terrence before he could open his mouth "I've been told that I'm only the eighth Blue Aura in history. I've been at this a few years, and I still don't have it all figured out. I've got gifts on top of gifts that I didn't even ask for."

I stared at him as a strange feeling of kinship and respect washed over me. I clasped my hands together then rubbed my thumbs over each other as I whispered my response. "I can relate."

No. I won't. I couldn't. I gritted my teeth, unlatched my fingers, and began tapping them against my knee.

"Look, it doesn't matter. Tell me about these powers you all seem to possess."

"Eleventh Percenters all have powers that are brought about by the ethereal world," explained Jonathan. "But all have areas of expertise. Signatures, if you will. The aura colors that you see here are three of many, though Jonah is the only one that's blue. Terrence has strength-based skills. Reena can alter her speed, create cold spots, and read essence. Jonah has...many gifts. The most prominent gift is balance, which is one of the things that the Blue Aura is all about. It's that balancing power that saved him from the Sirens. It regulated his mind, gave him glimpses of his true self, and kept him from weakness."

"That may be true, but it's only a partial piece of it, Jonathan." Cyrus still stood behind me. Still held onto my shoulder as if to keep me upright during this mess of a conversation. "To overcome the temptations of the Sirens, one must have a tether to their true nature. A powerful tether. Something to reel them in, if you will. So Jonah has abilities that include balance? Excellent. But there was definitely something that pulled him back from succumbing. What was it?"

Jonah swallowed. He visibly swallowed. It was as if Cyrus had asked him the secrets of the universe and expected a response.

"It—It was something my Nana used to say," he answered. "The women in the dream—or whatever it was—were a little too eager and willing to let me have my way with them. It seemed to be their only thought. Nana used to say 'Watch out for women who are hot in the pants and empty in the head.' She used to say that all the time. That was in my head when they tried so hard to get me to join them."

Liar.

I bit my lip to keep my mouth shut. It was true that I depended on Cyrus to tell me what I needed to know about the monsters I dealt with, but I was damn good at reading people. Jonah was hiding something. I could feel it.

Maybe he had a girlfriend. The realization made my stomach sink. I couldn't explain why it bothered me. I had to remind myself that I had Cyrus. I was happy.

No, I wasn't. I was lying to myself.

"Wise woman, your Nana," Cyrus told Jonah. "Family influence, particularly positive ones, are definitely powerful tethers. Even across planes of existence, your Nana still saved your life."

I rubbed my hands over my eyes as a sharp pain filled my heart. Family influence and tethers hadn't been enough to keep me tied to my parents. I took a deep breath and began to count until the guilt lessened. It had been months since the murders, and I'll admit, I'd made progress. But damned if it didn't kill me when I was reminded of them.

Joey piped up from his spot beside me. He leaned forward to clasp Terrence on the shoulder.

"This is intense, man!"

"How do you think I feel?" responded Terrence. "I've been exposed to ethereal things my entire life!"

The new bosom buddies broke into a conversation all their own, so I ignored them. I clasped Cyrus' hand when he squeezed my shoulder. But instead of the secured feeling I was used to when I was around him, I felt nothing.

I just wanted to be left alone. I wanted to get away from Jonah and the feelings he seemed to illicit from me.

Too bad Jonathan picked that very moment to make his announcement.

"Jonah, Eva," he said, "you cannot be forced to believe. But belief is not necessary at this point, because the both of you have seen proof of the existence of each other's' respective realities. Jonah, the Greek myths are not myths. Eva, there is much more in this world than gods and monsters. All the nuances of divination—magic, 'magick,' or whatever semantics you choose to employ—they are all ethereality. No matter the realm or sphere of influence. The people that you see in the mirrors are still very much alive. They are simply no longer physical beings. Like it or not, our paths have been joined, and we have to adapt."

I studied Jonah as he looked down at the cuts on his legs. When he met my gaze, I saw his expression shift from contemplation to fear.

"Superstar," He breathed, "Your eyes are green. How in the hell did you do that?"

I felt the blood drain out of my face at his words. The only way my eyes could turn back to their natural shade was if I had lost my abilities as the Sibyl. It had happened twice since I'd taken Apollo's oath. Both times were due to my injuries thanks to Athena's Blade. So to say that Jonah's words scared the hell out of me?

Understatement of the year.

"No, they aren't." I snapped. "There is no way. Give me a mirror!"

I stopped myself as I realized what I was about to expose myself to. "Wait, no! Don't—don't do that."

"It's fine," said Jonathan hastily. "I can protect you. In my presence, the spirits and spiritesses will be held at bay. Please do not try any mirror stunts on your own, though."

Joey pressed a button on his cell phone and passed it over to me. I snatched it and frowned.

"Why do you have a mirror app on your phone?" I knew I was deflecting, but I couldn't help myself. I didn't want to see what the others saw. I didn't want to face the questions reeling through my mind. "I mean, I knew you were vain, Joey, but—"

"Just look." Jonah shoved the phone upright until I was forced to look at myself. There were no whispers from the dead. No faces flickering across Joey's phone. It was just me as I had been. Green eyes and all.

I did the only thing I could think of. I blinked. Hard. Then again until my eyes shifted back to the gold I'd grown used to. I couldn't stop staring at my damned reflection as I realized what this could mean.

The wound from Athena's Blade hadn't been healed by the concoction Hecate's apprentices had administered in Washington. No matter how fast my other injuries had healed, the one that had caused the most damage was still seeping poison into my blood despite the mark of the gods now tattooed on the skin of my left side.

After a few minutes, my eyes remained resolutely

golden. But I couldn't breathe. And I couldn't reveal my concern to Cyrus. He would have me encased in bubble wrap and shipped back to California before daybreak.

I had to get out of here.

I pushed up from the couch to head towards the door as my concerns about the stab wound I had suffered brought forth my memories of Elliot's threats. How he swore to destroy anyone who tried to help me. No matter who or what they were.

He had already proven himself capable. After all, Jonah had been hurt thanks to his brief interaction with me. I shouldn't have cared given that he nearly broke down my bedroom door to voice his displeasure of my presence. But I did. A little too much.

The monsters under Hera's control were closing in, and there was nothing I could do to stop it.

"Eva, stop."

Cyrus caught up with me before I could leave the room. He snagged my arm and forced me to face him.

"Let's go upstairs. You need to calm down in light of these recent developments."

"No." I closed my eyes, afraid that when I opened them, they would have changed back to green. "Cyrus, I need some air."

"You need— "

"Please," I whispered as my heart began to break. I had fooled myself into believing that I could get past my fears. I had convinced myself that I was stronger than ever. But I was wrong. Dead wrong.

I felt my eyes burning from the tears that wanted to fall, but I kept them in check. "I won't go far, I promise. I'll even stay on the porch."

"Eva, you need more time to heal. The power of Athena's Blade is still affecting you, despite the ministrations of Hecate's Ambassadors." Cyrus narrowed his eyes at me. "Surely it would be best if you stay close enough where I can reach you if needed."

I nodded. "I'll be fine. I just—I need time to think. And I can call you if I need to. I'm sure you'll hear me if I holler for you."

Cyrus still looked skeptical, but he didn't argue as I turned on my heel to walk out of the room. I tried to remember what Terrence had said about maneuvering around this massive place. Soon enough, I found the front door.

The humid air hit me the moment I stepped out on the porch. I breathed in with blessed relief as my muddled thoughts began to clear. It was obvious that Jonah deemed me as an idiot. A dangerous one. Reena seemed much more guarded, which was good. Most likely, it was the only thing that had saved her when the Sirens attacked. Terrence? He reminded me of Joey. Happy. Thrilled to be considered special.

And possibly vulnerable. I shuddered. Could he hold a candle to Elliott?

Before I had been transformed into the Sibyl, I would have laughed at these people who called themselves Eleventh Percenters. I mean, come on. Mysterious mentor. Big house in the middle of nowhere. Everyone has special powers. A modern day comic book come to life.

But that was before. I propped my elbows up onto the porch rail and buried my face into my hands. Now, my life was nothing but monsters. Monsters and ghosts and revenge. It was horrible. My losses were great.

Yet, despite everything I'd been through, I couldn't imagine my life being anything less than what it is now.

This was the main reason why I was so freaked out when I saw my eyes had changed. I was in serious trouble with only Cyrus and my abilities as the Sibyl to protect me. But there was another factor that weighed heavy on my mind.

"Evangelina."

I jerked my head up to stare at a woman I hadn't seen in over a year. Longer, since seeing your mother's urn didn't count as actually seeing her.

"Look at you. You've always been a fucking mess." She sneered in that trademark Charleston accent of hers. "Always running away. Always trying to find a man to hide behind. Didn't I teach you better than that? There is no help for you, Evangelina. There never was."

I stared at her with a mixture of fear and hatred. I had my reasons. Reasons that tried to bubble up to the surface the more I looked at her.

"You're not supposed to be here." I managed. "I'm not supposed to see you. Apollo forbade-"

Janet broke out into a cruel laughter. "Apollo has no power over the likes of me, little girl."

"Yes, he-"

Janet waved her hand and within moments, I wasn't on the porch anymore. I reappeared in a forest. Woods. There were trees all around me. I stood up to brush myself off when someone grabbed me from behind and slung me against the nearest tree. I cried out as my head cracked against the wood. I landed in a crouch then prayed to Apollo for the pain shooting across my abdomen to subside and my vision to return to normal. When I stood to face my attacker, I remembered something Cyrus had taught me on day one of my training. Not too long ago, Medusa reiterated it.

Always be aware of your surroundings.

There were eleven total. Each one stepping out of the trees to encircle me.

"Who are you?" I spoke, surprised to hear the steel underlying my words. "What role do you have in Hera's fight with me?"

"Oh, darling Sibyl." The shadow man laughed as he closed in the distance between us. "You elate me so! Perhaps I am a simple spirit, wishing for attention from the Daughter of Apollo herself. Perhaps I have a message for you."

"Don't be ridiculous." I felt discomfort at these words. The phrase Daughter of Apollo engendered such uneasiness now. But my anger resurfaced as I watched the image of my mother disappear. "Wait. Where did she go?"

The man's eyes glowed a familiar green before he struck out again. He punched me so hard, I landed flat on my back. Within moments, he grabbed me and the others parted as he slammed me against another tree.

"So pretty. So strong." He hissed as he pressed himself against me. He freed one hand long enough to twirl a strand of my hair around one shadowed finger. "Some things are worth going to Hell for, Sibyl."

"Yeah? Then by all means, let me help you get there."

I couldn't move my arms thanks to the hold this man had on me, but if I had learned anything during my time as the Sibyl, it was that there was more than one method of escape. I slammed my knee upwards, connecting with his center. The creature howled as my sword shimmered into view. He stumbled backwards and it was my turn.

I brought the sword up to slam the hilt against his throat. When he fell to his knees, I brought the blade down in a single motion. He disappeared within an instant.

I lifted the sword up and held it just in front of my face as I turned my attention to the ones who still circled me.

"Who sent you?" I called out, ignoring the blood that

ran down my cheek from the blow I'd taken. "Who do you serve if not Hera?"

The dark beings around me lunged forward as a single unit. I would have cursed out loud if there had been time. I should have called out to Cyrus, but I didn't want to. I wanted to lose myself in battle. I wanted to forget about the image of my mother. The hatefulness in her eyes.

So I fought.

I blocked their hands as they grabbed at me. Those who got in a hit met my blade the fastest. I thought I was doing pretty well until I felt a sharp pain slice across my side. It was so intense that I dropped my sword as I fell. I rolled onto my back as the creature scrambled past my legs to crawl on top of me.

"Dammit!"

I grunted as the thing scratched at my eyes. I turned my head to see the other beings following suit to circle me in a realm of shadow.

I stopped trying to get the creatures off of me as I raised my arms to block my face. Ideas flew through my mind as I took blow after blow. I thought about my Keeper's suggestion to stay inside. I knew I would be land blasted for not listening to him the moment I got back.

But the worst part?

I couldn't figure out how I was going to get out of this one.

I really was in trouble.

# FIVE

## JONAH ROWE

JONAH WAS PISSED.

But it was a multilayered thing.

So, he had encountered the Sirens. The *Sirens*. He'd always found them creepy when he read about them as a kid, but he always wrote it off as mythology.

Well, that same mythology had just entered his consciousness and screwed with his emotions. He even had cuts and scrapes on his lower legs from the experience.

Why did those psycho bitches have to go into his mind and do that? Anyone who knew him knew all about his writing troubles. So for them to go inside his mind and fabricate an illusion of his success infuriated him hugely. After what he'd gone through with the 49er and the Haunts, he had pretty much had it with people messing around in his head.

He'd managed to fight them off and win. He remained safe because something "tethered him to the truth," as Cyrus put it. It had been quick thinking on his part to throw out that quote that his Nana used to say. That part was true.

But it wasn't thoughts of Nana that saved him. The truth would remain in his head, though. He'd be damned if he discussed that with Cyrus and Eva around.

Eva...

Jonah sighed. He had been certain that his disdain for her would remain absolute. He hadn't viewed her much better than he viewed Turk Landry. It also didn't help matters that the first thing she asked for when they got to the estate was a drink. But his disdain had been shaken by Jonathan's and Cyrus's explanations.

He was now convinced that the whole "bitch" thing was a front. He didn't know at first, but when she said that she could relate to how he felt as the Blue Aura, a glimmer of her true self shone through. It happened again when she looked on Joey's phone and saw that her eyes were green again. That scared the shit out of her. So much so that her mask slipped again. Eva had that bitch mask on to hide fear.

This Elliott guy, the murderer, had Eva so frightened that she had to piss people off to hide it.

What had she gotten them into?

Terrence stood up and extended his hand.

"You owe me twenty bucks."

"What? What for?"

"You know what for. That psychic was right on the money. My money. Pass it over."

"Hell no," Jonah scoffed. "She said I'd fall in love with her. That I'd be rich and get a golden parachute. Superstar doesn't look like she's about to give us handouts."

"Come on, J! You just met her!" Terrence began to tick off his points with each finger. "Blonde? Check. Golden eyes? Check. Gold? Olympus counts, so check. Insanely wealthy? Also check. And did I mention famous? Triple check."

"I'll see you, and I will raise you." Jonah ticked off his own fingers. "Blonde? Coincidence. Golden eyes are kinda green now. Olympus. Eh. Wealthy and famous, but on T.V., not movies."

"Fine. I'll raise you." Terrence seemed to be getting way too much amusement out of this. "Blonde? Natural. Golden eyes? Green came and went so that don't count. Olympus? It's real, dude. T.V. famous is still famous. The woman never said movie star, just entertainment. You were the one who threw in movies. And how are you gonna explain why you keep stealing glances at her? You already falling, and you know it."

"Falling? I'm on watch." Jonah shrugged. "This lady is a magnet for trouble. Plus, she is afraid and doesn't want us knowing. I'm not stealing glances. I'm observing."

"Uh huh. Ok," Terrence nodded. "Then you won't care if I try to take my shot. You know how many magazines I got saved up just because she does pin-up shoots? That girl is sexy as hell."

"Shoot your shot, brother," Jonah said. "Hopefully, she'll be enthralled. Cyrus won't approve, just so you know."

Terrence raised an eyebrow. "That wasn't the response I was expecting."

"I know what you're trying to do here. It ain't happenin'. Besides, I got Vera-"

"Who runs off every chance she gets and barely gives you the time of day." Terrence snorted. "Reena! Tell J. to give me my money back."

Reena abandoned her conversation with Joey and approached them.

"What money?"

"The twenty bucks from the psychic. J. doesn't believe

that Eva is the one she was talking about and he won't listen to reason."

Reena laughed. "Yeah, J. You lost this one. Pretty decisively."

"Ok. Look, there's absolutely nothing there. Nothing."

"Yeah? I'll believe that when pigs fly." Reena smirked. "You two keep playing the 'I hate you' game to hide the fact that you just want to rip each other's clothes off."

"Reena!"

"It's true." She shrugged. "I know that look on a woman's face. She got hit by lightning when she saw you. Now, she don't know what to do about it."

"Hit by lightning?" Jonah frowned. "She's been a Mean Girl...a *Karen* ever since we've met! For the smart one, you kinda overshot that one."

"It's a front, J.," Reena rolled her eyes. "I told you that she's scared. On that same note, you've been an asshole to her. Why? Are you trying to deny how you feel or something?"

"Hell no," Jonah muttered. "I saw her asshole, and matched her. It was that simple."

"Ok." Reena nodded. "So if she came over and kissed you right now, you'd push her away? Or would you get into it?"

"That's never going to happen."

"That's not an answer."

"But it's the answer you got," Jonah said. "She's got the old guy, anyway."

"I think that's just for appearances sake." Reena tapped her fingers against her chin. "Notice how they barely interact with each other? That doesn't scream red hot romance to me."

"Why are we even having this discussion?"

"Because its fun to torture you?"

"Funny."

"I'm gonna go talk to her. See if I can shoot that shot we talked about." Terrence clapped Jonah on the shoulder. "Since you don't mind and all."

"I don't," Jonah said heartily. "It's just...she has Old Dusty. Brace yourself."

"Where'd she go?"

"She went out to get some air." Jonah responded. "The front porch. Probably."

"Good. That means she's alone." Terrence grinned. "Wish me luck."

Terrence started to walk away, but got ten steps before he threw up his hands and stormed back over to them.

"What? I thought you were going to shoot that shot."

"And I thought you were going to try and stop me! What the hell, J.?"

"Why would I stop you?" Jonah said in an innocent tone. "I'm interested to see if she shoots you down, or lovingly *lets* you down. Because it ain't gonna work."

"And why is that, exactly?" Terrence crossed his arms over his chest. "Because of the old dude? If she's the vapid celebrity type, then the old dude don't matter."

"She just...seems like she needs a Hollywood type," Jonah said. "Not you know, us bumpkins. For God's sakes, you invite her to a barbecue, she'll probably shoot it down and say she only eats grass-fed, free-range cardboard."

"Stop torturing me, J.! Alright. Fine. I'll go talk to her for you."

"For me?"

"Yeah. I already told her that you weren't really an asshole and that we've been through a lot lately. When I walked her to her room." Terrence grinned. "She thanked me for my insight of removing all the mirrors so she wouldn't have to worry about a spirit trying to come through. Cause I - unlike you - recognize a good thing when I see it."

Jonah shrugged, feeling a relief he didn't understand. "This has been fun, y'all. I'll be in the weight room. If you shoot your shot or what have you, you can come by and tell me how good it went."

"Will do-"

Terrence stepped back in a moment later with a frown on his face. He crossed over to them.

"That was fast."

"Eva's not outside." Terrence shook his head. "At least, not on the porch. You didn't see her come through, did you?"

"Haven't seen her, brother," Jonah said. "I'm sure she wouldn't be in the gym."

"She would have walked right by us." Reena tugged her ponytail down then put it right back up. "Maybe she went for a walk on the grounds."

"Dammit," Terrence sighed. "I just got my courage up. I'll try again tonight. Maybe I can walk her to her room."

"Maybe she'll invite you in." Reena grinned.

"Have fun, man," Jonah told him, oddly relieved again. "And when you're disappointed, come find me. We can game, okay?"

"I'm not getting under your skin at all, am I?"

"Would it make you feel better if you were?" Jonah asked.

"Yes because then I would know I'm right and you would give me my twenty bucks back!"

"Terrence!" Reena laughed. "So your whole schiek has been to get twenty bucks? What would you have done if she said yes?"

"You know what I would do, Re." Terrence pulled out his phone and showed them a screenshot of Eva. It was an obvious photoshoot, but she was dressed in nothing but a tiny skirt as she walked down a beach. "I'd take care of things."

Jonah took a breath, but shook his head. "That's stalker-y, man."

"It's only stalkerish if I actually tried to contact her. Who knew she'd show up here?" Terrence tucked his phone away. "I mean, other than that psychic."

"You better lock your phone," Jonah said. "If she sees that, she'll put you away in the prison everyone wanted to put Kevin Spacey in."

"She'll never see it." Terrence shrugged. "Just like Charlize Theron will never see her pictures on my phone. Or-"

"You have more than one?"

"I'm a man, Re. Of course I do. And we're getting off topic. How are we gonna actually set Jonah up with Eva so I can get my money back?"

"Dude, if the twenty means that much to you, I'll PayPal you," Jonah said. "You will *not* be my gilded pimp."

"I'm not gilded, I'm golden." Terrence grinned widened. "I think you're afraid."

"Afraid of what?"

"Afraid that something might happen to make you happy. You get nervous when shit gets too good, J."

""I'm good, brother," Jonah insisted. "No nerves. Though I'd like to know why she's so scared."

"I think it has to do with Elliott."

"What's his story anyway?" Jonah shook his head. "I don't get how someone who is immortal could be afraid of anything."

"Elliott is just an ass, dude. He's pretty much known for it." Terrence shook his head. "He's the creative director and co-host of the show, so he determines their locations. But he is forever sticking Eva in situations where she ends up either hurt or traumatized."

"Traumatized?"

"Yeah. Like, in their first season. One of the clients died of a heart attack right in front of her. The season finale? He had her be bait for a rapey spirit who turned out to be a flesh and blood employee of the hotel they were at. You know that shit had to leave its mark."

Jonah frowned. "And the boss of the show...agrees to this shit? What kind of people does she work for? Good ol' boys?"

"Yeah. Elliot is the son of the CEO and founder of Theia. Their staff have all been there forever, so they go along with all kinds of things. As long as *Grave* keeps bringing in the big bucks, nobody dares to step in."

"So the more successful Eva is, the more danger she gets put in," Jonah said. "Great."

"Exactly." Terrence glanced back at the front door. "*Forbes* reported that she takes home nearly three hundred thousand per episode now. That's before her percentage of the ad revenue. And each season is twenty-two episodes long, so you can do the math on that."

"No wonder she's rich as fuck," Jonah said.."I hope she invests most of it."

"What she doesn't invest, she gives to charity. It's that Hollywood liberal influence."

"Are you seriously talking like that's a bad thing?"

"Not at all. I'm just saying that there's more to her than her looks, is all."

"Uh huh," Jonah said. "They believed the same thing about Miley Cyrus. Then she released *Bangers*, and everything went to shit."

"You can't put those two in the same category." Terrence shook his head. "Eva lays low, which is why the paparazzi love to ambush her. Her only scandal has been this supposed suicide attempt which we all know was false."

"What happened exactly?"

"Nobody except Eva and Cyrus really know. She was in Charleston for her parents' funeral back in the fall. The papers reported that she jumped out of a four-story building, but there's holes in that story."

"Holes?" Reena decided to rejoin their conversation. "Like what?"

"She had a wicked stab wound in her side right where her mark of the Sibyl is." Terrence leaned in like he was giving them good gossip. "And there was evidence that she had been in a physical fight prior to that. Busted face, fist bruises, shit like that."

"Well she's immortal, supposedly?" Jonah said. "In Greek mythology, the only thing that could injure an immortal was Athena's Blade. Assuming, of course, that's real. So unless Elliott shanked her with that, she'd be hard pressed to prove her story. "

"What do you know of Athena's Blade?"

The three of them turned to see Cyrus standing close by. He studied Jonah with a cold expression.

"I've read mythology." Jonah shrugged. "That was one thing that stuck with me."

"What happened in that hotel room, Cyrus?" Reena frowned. "Seriously?"

"Eva is a very...fragile...individual." He responded. "It would be best for everyone involved if our worlds did not mix together."

"Dude, we ain't the one that mixed us together," Jonah reminded Cyrus. "That was your boy Apollo. So if you're butthurt about that, kindly don't take it out on us."

"Besides all that," Terrence said with a frown, "What's the deal with that, man? If I didn't know any better, I'd say that you're telling us Eva can only have friends you give her permission to have. Please tell me I'm assuming wrong."

"It is my duty to make sure Eva is protected." Cyrus gave them a tight smile. "Anyone who attempts to become friends with the Sibyl must be vetted and they must be able to hold their own."

"You are the one who does the vetting?" Reena asked. "Sounds like that's a job for Apollo, don't you think? It just seems like a weird thing that you would be the final say on that."

"Then allow me to clarify." Cyrus sounded annoyed. "Eva doesn't have friends. It is far too dangerous for her and for them. I ask that each of you keep your distance from her while we are here. Jonah's dream of the Sirens is proof enough of how dangerous it is to be under the same roof with her."

"Ain't happening, bro," Jonah said. "Jonathan brought you guys into our zone. There will be no reticence on our end. If Apollo declared it, whatever, but...and no disrespect to you, bro, but...your word isn't enough. Eva has no friends because *you* call it? Uh uh. Sorry."

"We shall see."

"What the hell does that mean?"

"Exactly what I said." Cyrus stuffed his hands in his suit pants pockets. "If Apollo deems it so, then we will follow his directive. Yet, that directive will be over soon. If you must aid Eva in filming her show, then so be it. But don't expect anything further than that."

Jonah's eyes narrowed. Something about that way Cyrus said that didn't sit well with him. "No expectations either way, man. I'm just saying that Eva is a grown woman, with her own mind, and own opinions and viewpoints. I say this with full respect, no one here needs to talk to you first. If you were her publicist, yeah. But you're the muscle. Nothing personal. Just a different set of rules."

"Muscle, yes. I suppose so."

"Speaking of," Terrence spoke up. "Where were you when Elliot pushed Eva out of that window?"

"You are assuming Lancaster was involved."

"Eva said-"

"Eva says a lot of things in an attempt to keep her public persona intact, Terrence."

"Oh," Reena said in a knowing tone. "It's like that."

"Like what, dear Reena?"

"Don't call me, 'dear,'" Reena said, "And it's like the situation where you prefer the narrative controlled as much as possible. Why is that, Cyrus? Why do you feel that Eva needs to be micromanaged?"

"As I said, my charge is an extremely fragile individual," His eyes darkened as he turned to Reena. "And given the dangers she faces on a daily basis, it is imperative that as much control as possible is utilized to ensure her safety. Eleventh Percenters face dangers, yes, but not to this extreme. I would prefer that you not put ideas to the contrary in the Sibyl's mind. My job is hard enough as is."

"There you go again, dude," Jonah said. "What *you* prefer. What *you* want. What *you* desire. We can't actually put thoughts in Eva's head. But it seems like *you* want to be the only one who puts thoughts there. If I'm wrong, tell me. Sounds like you are acting like a mixture of her dad and husband."

"You have no right to speak like that to me," Cyrus glared at Jonah. "You do not know our world-"

"Shut up." Reena held her hand up. "Eva's essence just changed."

"What?"

They all saw Eva's sword vanish from the coffee table.

When Jonah started to go around him, Cyrus held out an arm.

"Do not, Blue Aura, believe you can interfere."

"And do not, Cretan, believe you can control me," Jonah fired back. "Now I may not know your world, but I do know these grounds. Now if you'll excuse me. Jonathan, give me back my batons, We'll find out what's up."

"Jonah," Cyrus attempted to empty the tension out of his voice, "Eva is not your responsibility—"

"Save it, man." Jonah was so thankful to have his batons back that he twisted them in his hands a few times. "You don't want my help? Tough shit."

He spun on his heel and hurried out before anyone could say anything about thinking or planning. He was on the porch in about a minute, with Cyrus right behind him.

At that moment, clear as a bell, they heard Eva scream. Their heads both shot in that direction.

"Woods!"

Jonah nearly knocked Cyrus over as the two of them tore off towards the woods. He didn't know what to expect when they reached Eva.

And once they did, he still didn't know.

"What the hell?"

Eva was surrounded by shadow people. But the composition of their bodies was a bit denser, like soot. They put Jonah in mind of other shadowy, soot-like beings.

"Shades!" Cyrus yelled. "Stop this at once!"

"I don't think that worked, dude!"

Jonah called over to him. He thought of the Sirens messing with his head again, and the combination lit Jonah with such anger that all thought of worry got stamped out.

He threw down his batons and began to concentrate.

"Jonah, what are you doing? Eva needs us!"

"Get Eva out of the way," commanded Jonah.

"I need to cut a line through the beasts—"

"Don't touch a single one!" snapped Jonah as the ground began to tremble. "You might want to get Eva now!"

Cyrus disappeared into the shadows. The shadow beings realized that the ground was trembling beneath their feet, and alarmed, ceased attacking Eva. Cyrus phased into view right next to Eva and pulled her aside. The shadow people didn't even notice.

Jonah's concentration came to fruition as the mental cage door closed in his mind. The second it did, that familiar spectral blue cage erupted out of the ground and trapped every shadow beast within. One touched a bar and howled in agony.

"What is this?" cried one of them. "No Greek mortal is capable of such things!"

"I'm not Greek, I'm Southern," growled Jonah. "And you ain't welcome on this land."

He closed his fists, and then cage closed in on the things. The blue cage wiped them out in minutes.

Jonah lowered his hands. Cyrus and Eva looked at him in shock.

"What was that?" asked Eva.

Jonah took slow breaths to calm himself. "It's got some fancy name, but I call it a Mind Cage."

"Why were you riled so?" asked Cyrus.

Jonah felt himself return to center. "They reminded me of something else."

Cyrus's eyes narrowed, but he let the matter drop as he returned his attention to Eva.

"Dammit," He snapped. "What are you doing out here?"

Jonah rolled his eyes and extended a hand to Eva. "Apparently, superstars do whatever they please. I hear they refuse to listen to anything. Especially when it's for their own damn good."

Eva took Jonah's hand, and then jerked him down and to the side. Jonah was ready to call her everything except her given name, but then he realized a shadowy form on her sword. The thing gave a final twitch as it faded into the night.

"You missed one, Country," she muttered. "You can thank me later."

Eva shoved Jonah hard enough to cause him to roll over on his back. Jonah rolled his eyes again as Cyrus reached down to pull Eva up on her feet. He filed his snarky response away. Now was not the time for it since Eva had taken one hell of a beating. Cyrus's eyes narrowed as he turned his full attention to Eva.

"Your injuries are your own fault, Eva," He snapped. "I told you to stay on the porch."

Before Eva could respond, Cyrus continued.

"You of all people know what dangers you face right now and yet, you rush off without thinking? If it hadn't been for the fact we were still in the family room, we never would have realized you needed help."

Eva crossed her arms in front of herself and nodded. "You're right. I'm sorry, Cyrus."

"When we get back to the house, I want you to go straight to your room and stay there." Cyrus grabbed her arm right above the elbow and Jonah could have sworn he saw a wince flicker across her features. "Let's go."

"Hey, dude!" Jonah exclaimed. "If you grab Eva like that, you'll bruise her worse than the Shades! Want to cool it a bit?"

"What did I tell you about interfering, Rowe?" Cyrus glared at Jonah as they began to walk. "Since you are so concerned-"

"It's fine," Eva interrupted as she stared straight ahead. "I'm fine. I swear it. Thank you for your help. Both of you."

"If you hadn't left the porch, there wouldn't have been a need for help."

"You're right, Cyrus. I should have listened to you. I'm sorry."

"Eva, you don't have to apologize for walking twenty goddamn feet," Jonah spat. "Cyrus, it's not interference, it's a question. The website says Eva's dad's name was Martin, not Cyrus. Jonathan wouldn't have a woman manhandled like that. Neither will the rest of us. Now loosen your grip. The blood is draining from Eva's arm."

Eva said nothing as Cyrus released a sound that was a cross between a sigh and a growl. He loosened his grip, but Jonah could see he was pissed.

What the hell was going on between the two of them? Really?

Once they reached the front porch, Cyrus steered Eva towards the stairs only to stop when Reena called out to them.

"You. Get in the kitchen. We'll check you over."

"I can't," Eva cleared her throat as she tried again. "I'm fine. It was just a scuffle."

"I won't ask again," Reena said, stern. "Sit and be inspected."

Eva moved into the kitchen with her head down, arms still crossed over herself. The second she was out of earshot, Cyrus turned to Jonah.

"You have no idea what our world is like, Rowe," He glared at him. "Kindness is a weakness that is exploited. You question my methods through the eyes of ignorance."

"Kindness...don't give me that shit," Jonah said, "Eva being in danger from violence, so you respond *with* violence? If you think that is a valid approach, the only ignorant one is your ass. Your world ain't no different from the rest of them. That shit was  borderline abuse. There is no other explanation."

Cyrus inhaled then responded.

"Eva is my charge. She is my responsibility. She is not a student at the estate. Jonathan nor you have any influence on what happens between us. I want to make that point perfectly clear."

Jonah didn't back down. "Eva is Apollo's charge, with you as his chosen hand. Nah, she isn't a student here, but she isn't your student, either. If you are in Jonathan's domain, under his roof, then he *does* have influence, whether your ego accepts it or not. If you keep acting like as big a threat as those shadow things, or as an even bigger one, I want to make it perfectly clear to *you* that you will be treated accordingly. Got me, dude?"

"Perfectly. Now, if you will excuse me, I need to check on Apollo's charge."

Cyrus went towards the kitchen and Jonah watched him until Terrence bounded over to him.

"What the hell could attack Eva here?" He demanded. "We're protected by every resource imaginable."

"Shady-looking things, man." Jonah shrugged soreness out of his shoulders. "Something or someone is mixing our Greek and ethereal stuff. Got through some defenses out there."

"So what happened?"

"What do you mean?"

"You looked pissed, bro. I'm willing to bet it wasn't those shady things unless they destroyed one of your batons or something."

Jonah gritted his teeth. "It seems Cyrus the Muscle is a bit old school."

"Old-school? As in mentality?"

"Yeah," Jonah answered, "As well as in how he treats women. Eva got attacked out there, and then he chewed her out for leaving the porch. See that red on her arm? That didn't come from those Shade things. That came from him grabbing her in frustration."

"Wait. Cyrus did that?" Terrence looked confused. "I'm sure it was just a mistake."

"A mistake? I saw him do it!"

"Come on, J. If Eva was being abused, somebody would have noticed and spoke up. More so, she would have left him. The woman has houses all over the world. It ain't like she's dependent on him or anything."

Jonah took a deep breath so as to let Terrence's words in. "Alright, fine. I ain't entirely convinced, but I hear you."

"You're awfully protective of a woman you don't like." Terrence's face was shrewd.

"It could be Jessica Hale, as much as I hate her, I'd still step on if I thought she was being battered," Jonah said.

"Yeah, I hear ya."

Terrence and Jonah headed into the kitchen, but stopped just inside the door. Eva sighed when Reena slathered suave on her arm above the elbow.

"I maintain this is completely unnecessary."

"And I maintain that you should get taken care of," Reena grumbled. "What about between now and when you're healed?"

"Then I've learned my lesson about taking on a mob of eleven assholes by myself?"

Jonah almost laughed. If she thought she could spurn Reena's attempts to aid her, she had another thing coming. Apparently, Cyrus couldn't withhold his admonitions even with this big of an audience.

"I told you so," He said to her. "How could you be so careless?"

Cyrus paced in front of the chair while Eva took, at least in Jonah's eyes, more time than necessary to answer him. After the earful she had gotten in the woods, he almost told Cyrus to drop it. How many times was that old bastard going to keep bringing up that this was her fault?

"Cyrus, I'm fine." She winced as Reena put some sort of cream on the wound across her side. "In fact, I'm not even sure why y'all are going through all the trouble to bandage me up. My wounds will be gone before morning."

"This conversation is going to drive me crazy," announced Jonah. "What were those things? They looked like Haunts in the shapes of people. You said there were eleven of those things? I only saw five ."

"Eleven." Eva confirmed as she shook out the arm Reena had been working on. "I took out five of them before I got ambushed from behind. Six, if you count the one I saved your ass from. And what exactly is a Haunt?"

Jonah stared at her. She took out five by herself, huh? He kind of wished he'd seen that.

"Fine," said Eva. Apparently, she didn't want Jonah to tell her what a Haunt was. "Where is Jonathan? If I'm going to tell this, I may as well do it with everyone here."

Jonah watched Reena pack up the healing satchel that she used with almost as much aptitude as Liz. They all filed through the kitchen so as to reach the family room. Eva grabbed an entire bottle of wine. Christ alive, where did she put all that liquor? But Joey cleared his throat, took it, and poured her a glass. Jonah shook his head. Beyond remedying the effects of a Haunting, he had no use for liquor. He hoped she didn't expect that crap to clear her mind.

"I am here, Eva." Jonathan appeared though the door. He nodded to Jonah and Cyrus as he perched himself on the arm of the couch where Eva seated herself. "You did well, Jonah."

Jonah shrugged. He was more concerned with those Haunt-looking things than praise.

"Look, this is going to be painful to talk about." Eva started with a ragged breath. "I saw my mom."

"Your mom?" Terrence leaned forward with his elbows pressed against his knees. "You saw your mom in spiritess form?"

"Yes," murmured Eva as Cyrus stood over her. "I shouldn't have seen her. Apollo forbade it. The two of us have a...a horrible history."

"Exactly right." Cyrus stood stiff in front of her. "Apollo forbade it. Try again, Eva."

Eva rubbed her hand over her face. "If it wasn't Janet-"

"It wasn't. You decided to ignore a perfectly rational suggestion to stay where I could help you."

Eva's face became completely blank. She was shutting down. Jonah knew that sort of look anywhere.

"Why don't you let Eva tell us what happened instead of interrupting her every five seconds?"

"Because Eva has been known to lie on occasion. Especially when she knows she has gone against orders set out for her own protection."

"Eva," Jonathan raised an eyebrow at Cyrus before he focused on her. "Please tell us what happened."

"I walked right into a trap." She responded in a flat voice. "The incident in the woods was my fault. I apologize for putting Jonah and Cyrus in harm's way. May I be excused?"

"Not yet. There is more, I think." Jonathan glanced around the inhabitants of the room, and then at Eva. "Tell us about this trap."

"What is there to say?" Eva stared at a spot on the wall

behind Cyrus' head. "I got slammed against a tree. Their leader told me there were some things worth going to hell for. Said I was a threat to harmony or something. Then I started a good old-fashioned brawl."

"That's when we showed up." Jonah had to describe those beasts. "Jonathan, those things looked like human-shaped Haunts."

"Those weren't Haunts, Jonah." Cyrus spoke, but he didn't take his eyes off of Eva. "They are called Shades. Powerful creatures blessed by Hera herself. They were believed to be soldiers who had fallen on the battlefield. Only the best were brought forth from the Underworld to serve the Queen of the Heavens."

"So she has an army of her own now?" sighed Eva. "Great."

But Jonah ignored her. He wasn't about to give up that easily. "Why did they look like Haunts?"

"They are products of the same Astral material," Jonathan explained. "Hera is mixing our worlds to create new monsters."

Jonah hung his head. So this woman—goddess—whatever, was borrowing from both their worlds to make shadow soldiers. Swell.

And then Jonathan had to go and make things even more swell.

"Jonah," He said with his eyes on Eva, "I want you to remain with Ms. McRayne throughout the duration of her stay here at the Grannison-Morris estate."

"What?" Jonah blinked. "But Eva already has a bodyguard. Besides, why me? Why not Terrence? He's the big fan."

"Emotions will do no good when you encounter a threat." Jonathan held up a hand as everyone started to protest. "Cyrus, I understand your position. Yet, I believe the threat your Sibyl is facing is far more dangerous than anything we've ever encountered before."

"I accept your offer." Cyrus nodded, but Jonah saw him grit his teeth before he continued.. "Any assistance will be greatly appreciated."

Jonah raised an eyebrow. Really? He was fine with it?

"But now," Cyrus took Eva's arm above the bandage Reena had covered her elbow with and helped her to her feet, "I believe it is time for Eva to retire. It has been quite the eventful evening."

She said her goodnights to all of them as Cyrus steered her towards the door. She stopped at the threshold and turned to face Jonah.

"Thanks, Jonah. I really appreciate your help back there. I'm sorry I got you pulled into a mess."

The appreciation took Jonah by surprise, but he recovered nicely. "Don't mention it, Superstar. Thank you for getting that one that was behind me."

Cyrus guided her out. Jonah plopped down as Terrence whacked Joey on the shoulder with no force behind the hit.

"Let me show you your room, Joey," He said. "It's a couple doors down from mine."

"Sure, man," said Joey, "How many rooms do you guys have?"

"Oh Lord." Reena rose and untied her hair. "The number of people in here is in single digits, and still there is bromance. I'm going to paint."

She headed for her art studio, which left Jonah alone with Jonathan.

"Who thought so much bull—sorry—B.S. could fit into one day?" Jonah asked. "But I'm more than happy to put it behind me. 'Night, Jonathan."

"Not so quick, Jonah." Jonathan never took his eyes off of the door that Eva and Cyrus used to leave. "Remember how I told you that I wished you to remain with Ms. McRayne?"

"Duh, Jonathan, you just said it five minutes ago."

"I want that to begin now."

Jonah stared at his mentor. "Um, what?"

Jonathan's expression didn't change. "You heard, son."

"At one a.m.?"

"Time makes no difference, Jonah. You know that."

"But Jonathan!" Why the hell was Jonathan doing this? "She is in a room with Cyrus!"

"Exactly," said Jonathan. "His judgment is not what it should be at a juncture like this. And she doesn't need the distraction that the keeper is undoubtedly causing her at this time. You two have a mutual experience with each other's worlds. We should strike while the iron is hot. Besides, Cyrus can assist me in assessing the new defenses. "

"Oh come on, man!" Jonah kind of understood what Jonathan meant, but the timing was garbage. "Just give her the night, Jonathan. I'll link up with Eva in the morning. If I go in there now, there is no telling what I might be interrupting—"

"Your presence may very well interrupt something," said Jonathan. "An innocent woman from experiencing a horrific beating."

That one stopped Jonah in his tracks. Jonathan had to go there, did he?

"You know something, Jonathan?"

"Not for certain, but I recognize the signs. And I won't have our guest harmed under this roof."

"Alright, Jonathan," He said. "Fine."

---

Jonah hated ruining moments. Then again, after what he had witnessed in the woods, he wasn't sure what kind of moment he would be interrupting.

He returned to Eva's door, no violent intent this time around, and knocked.

He heard stirring, steps, and then the door opened. It was Cyrus.

"What?"

Jonah stiffened at the tone in Cyrus' voice. He wanted to play the asshole? Fine. Jonah could give it right back to him.

"Jonathan wants me staying with Superstar."

Cyrus looked at him. "Now?"

"Yeah," said Jonah. " Right now."

Cyrus shook his head. "She is already asleep. Perhaps it would be best if you waited until—"

Then he heard Eva's voice. "Can't it wait until daybreak? I'm all for the extra babysitter. But at one o'clock in the morning?"

Jonah shrugged. These were the same questions that he had asked Jonathan himself. Why couldn't they understand that?

"Jonathan doesn't really care about time," He told them. "When I asked him those same questions, he said Eva and I have a mutual experience now and it's best to expound on that sooner rather than later. Plus, he'd like your assistance with shoring up defenses, Cyrus. He didn't want those Shades anywhere near here again."

Cyrus' aggravation was still evident on his face, but he relented. "Very well," He said. "I'll depart. But if Eva needs me—"

"Cyrus, I swear to you," Jonah said, "If Eva needs you, I'll personally see to it that you know about it. Deal?"

Cyrus took a breath through his nostrils. "Alright. See you in the morning—well, later in the morning, Eva."

Finally, he departed. Jonah stepped into the room to take it in. He saw Eva sitting up with the comforter over her legs. She rubbed sleep out of her eyes; a movement that caused the strap of her shirt to fall from her shoulder. Jonah took a breath as his mind flew in the exact opposite direction he wanted it to go in. The picture Terrence had shown him earlier flashed before his eyes and he shook his head to clear it.

*Calm down. Jesus,* He admonished himself. *It's just a little skin.*

Jonah threw an awkward glance at Eva as he pushed those unnecessary thoughts to the back of his mind. Eva stared back at him.

"So what's the sleeping arrangement?" She asked with a raised eyebrow. "Because I don't share my bed with anyone."

"I doubt that," Jonah snorted. "I bet Cyrus would be pissed to hear you say that."

"We don't have that kind of relationship," Eva glared at him. "And I'm not a whore. So no, I don't share my bed."

"Calm down, Superstar," Jonah dropped the sleep bag at the foot of the bed. He couldn't help but notice there was far less venom in his voice now. "I've got sleeping equipment here. All is well."

Eva shook her head and turned on her side. "I maintain that we don't have to share a bedroom. We could have just met back up at seven-thirty."

"My feelings exactly," murmured Jonah. It was the truth. There was no point in sugar-coating it. "But when Jonathan says something, it gets done."

Eva scoffed. "Do you always do what you're told?"

"Hell no," said Jonah, "but I'm cool with doing this one."

He placed his batons within reach and their blue gleam faded. He stretched out on the mat he'd brought then placed his hands behind his head. Jonathan owed him for this one.

*Big time.*

Initially, he didn't want to be anywhere around this woman. But then she showed a trace of backbone. Okay, it was more than a trace. She had some badass in her. But then Jonathan had to ruin the ride and stick them together like this. Didn't he know that the last thing they needed right now was to be shoved down each other's throats?

This was going to be a long week. How many times was that going to run across his mind?

"This is wonderful. Just wonderful." said Eva. "I'm not going to be able to sleep now."

Jonah shook his head. Badass, but still bratty.

"You're a grown woman, Eva," he muttered. "I promise you that you can sleep without your boyfriend for a few nights."

"I told you. It's not like that."

"Then what is it like?"

"We don't have sex, if that's what you mean," She snorted. "Cyrus usually hangs out long enough to make sure I'm asleep then he goes and does his own thing."

"His own thing," Jonah let that just linger there for a moment. "I saw you in the woods. He didn't seem all that indifferent then, and you were just walking on the grounds."

"That's because I disobeyed an order. Cyrus used to be a general in the Creten army, so he doesn't take kindly to people who defy him."

"Even you?"

"Especially me," Eva brushed a strand of hair from her eyes. "It is what it is."

"That's bullshit, Eva." Jonah's tongue might've been too loose at the moment, but he didn't really care. "You are this Sybil, yes? You are the golden girl of Apollo. If this were *Richie Rich,* Cyrus would be on the same level as Cadbury. And you wouldn't see Cadbury behaving like Cyrus did. He is there to protect you, not scold you and demand directives of you. He needs to learn his place because he seems to have forgotten it. I bet he wouldn't be that liberal with his authority if Apollo was around."

"What did you say?"

"You heard-"

"Did you just pull a *Richie Rich* reference?" She sat up with a laugh. "Seriously?"

"Damn right," Jonah said, snorting. "The cartoon was before my time, but Nana got them on VHS tapes. I read the comic book and loved the movie. No shame, Superstar. Zero."

Eva giggled; an act Jonah was sure she didn't do often.

"I have a confession to make," She smoothed out her expression as he sat up to look at her. "I have never seen that movie."

"Never?"

"Nope. I never watched movies or T.V. when I was a kid, and if I slow down enough now to watch anything, it's usually AMC."

"Well, the critics hated it, but they seemed to have it in for Macaulay Culkin post-*Home Alone,*" Jonah said. "Besides, what do they know, anyway? If you ever get free time, watch it. Good fun from the nineties."

"What else do you like?"

"Why do you ask?"

"Just curious," Eva shook her head. "You don't have to

answer if you don't want to and that's ok. I'm not good with this whole socializing thing and I'm pretty sure you don't want to socialize with me after how I acted today. I really am sorry about it. I can be a real bitch sometimes."

"Well, you were, no denying that," Jonah said, "but I haven't exactly been a paragon of virtue, either. I love mindless action movies. Arnold Schwarzenegger. Stallone. Van Damme. Even Steven Segal. Terrible actor, amazing fighter. I like *WWE*. Mysteries. All things Marvel, some DC. And the old westerns and old-ass game shows I watched with Nana."

"I can see that."

"See what?"

"Why you like mindless movies," She gave him a small smile. "Sometimes, it's nice to shut your brain down for awhile. Not think about anything."

"Absolutely," Jonah said. "I do like adventure stuff as well. Like one of my favorite movies, bar none, is *Raiders*."

"Never seen it."

Jonah felt his eyes bulge. Did she just say that? "You've never seen *Raiders of The Lost Ark*? This is scandalous!"

Eva laughed. "I'm serious! If a movie came out after 1955, I haven't seen it."

"What? Why?"

"I don't know. I just like the classic ones. Everything is so beautifully vintage and everyone was so classy. That element is lacking in modern movies."

"They also lack diversity."

"I beg your pardon?"

Jonah sighed. "Eva, I promise I'm not about to climb on a soapbox or anything, but there are tons of movies in the classic era that I don't much care for."

"Why not?"

"I'm not the hugest fan of classic movies and period

pieces because it's the perfect excuse for those stuffy execs to make everyone white. There are exceptions, like *The Godfather*, or basically anything with Brando or Sinatra, Serpico, The Sound of Music, and of course those Westerns with Nana. But I *hate* whitewashing. And Hollywood was good for it."

"They are still good for it." Eva pointed out. "And typecasting is a very real thing. It sucks, but they do that because beauty brings in money. And since the beauty standard hasn't really changed in over a hundred years, Hollywood keeps pushing the same narrative. White, attractive, thin. Anyone who is different is either - again - typecast or put in administrative roles."

"Right," Jonah muttered. "I had a friend - black guy - who had a dream to make movies. He pitched some ideas, with actors of color, but they all got shot down. He was told that they didn't have 'universal appeal.' Anyone with a fully functional brain knew what that meant. He abandoned movies and went into the tech world. Very sad."

"What's his name?"

"Does it matter?"

"Of course it matters. Give me his information and I'll pull some strings. If movies really are his dream, then I can help with that."

Jonah was slightly surprised. "Asa Russ James. He's done an indie film or two, but that's about it. But you can find his name."

"It won't be that hard. Hollywood circles are small, but we have great investigators."

The word investigators sparked something in Jonah's memory. The last celebrity who had come to Rome had used investigators to exploit people. He asked his next question before he even thought about it.

"Have you ever met Turk Landry?"

"Yeah," Eva snorted. "How could I not? He's the competition. Not much of one, mind you, but we run in the same circles."

"You don't sound too happy."

"I can't stand him. My last interaction with him was at a premiere for *Shadowed Histories* - that one season spin-off of his show that literally lasted five episodes? He wanted to do a Halloween special together. When I said no, he gave me the choice to either do the special or sleep with him. Otherwise, he'd find dirt on me and spread it to the media."

"What happened?"

"I threw him in the fountain headfirst."

Damn, Jonah wished he had seen that. He started to say those very words when Eva frowned. She was looking at the spot behind him.

"What? Jonah looked behind him then did a double take when he noticed a thick white mist hovering in the air. He rolled and got to his feet seconds before a man appeared. "What the actual hell?"

"Elliot." Eva whispered.

Jonah gave the man a double take. Elliott looked like a bluish-white hologram. He looked like a spirit. But he wasn't in Spirit. So what was the deal?

He looked down at his form and flashed one of the coldest leers Jonah had ever seen.

"Oh man," Elliot commented, "I gotta admit this is cool."

"How the hell are you in here?" Jonah had to know. "There are defenses!"

"Relax," said Elliot in a bored voice. "Your respective masters have pooled their resources, and unfortunately, they've been effective. I can't breach the grounds of the Grannison-Morris estate at this time. But it doesn't matter. The Shades were able to breach, and I will be able to soon enough. How am I here, you ask? Truth is, I'm not. I'm miles away, on your Astral Plane."

Jonah shook his head. It couldn't be true. There was no possible way.

"Are you talking about Astral Projection?!" He croaked. "But you're a Tenth Percenter!"

"Those little details tend not to matter when your patron is Hera," Elliott rolled his eyes. "Hera is able to supersede any restrictions your planes of existence may hold. She is all-powerful."

"Damn," Jona whistled. "You're really up her ass, aren't you?"

"Shut up, Eleventh," snapped Elliott. "I couldn't breach your grounds yet, but I could manage this. But it's enough. Eva, get to the Covington House right now."

"I'm not really worried about the house right now." Eva glared at the newcomer with a hatred that was evident. "What I don't understand is why it's so damn important to you. Important enough to bring me a fucking message in the middle of the night."

"Because I'm ready to dance your damn grave," Elliott snapped "The sooner you go, the sooner I can do that."

"Look, if you set some sort of trap there, then I'm not going."

"Yes, you are. You're going to be a good little Sibyl, or my victims will never know peace."

Jonah nearly dropped his batons. This Elliott guy couldn't have the power. He was a Tenth.

Eva must have caught his expression, because she put all of her attention on him. "What does he mean, Jonah?"

Jonah couldn't speak for several seconds due to being dumbstruck.

"He—he's somehow got the powers of a Spirit Reaper,"

He responded in a hollow voice. "He is going to usurp spirits to make himself stronger."

Jonah saw horror, fear, and grief engulf Eva. Instantly, he was furious at this guy. Another damn bully.

"You're a big man when you're broadcasting from somewhere else," He snarled. "You're screwing with things you don't understand. Let those spirits go!"

"I warn you, Eleventh Percenter," said Elliott. "This isn't about you. It's about Eva. What do you care, anyway? You've known her one day, and from what I hear, your meet and greet wasn't pretty."

"Yeah, well, what a difference a day makes, huh?" retorted Jonah. "You won't hurt Eva. Not in my backyard."

"Don't befriend her," warned Elliott. "Do yourself that favor. Don't get close to that evil bitch. She'll betray you, just like she betrayed me."

Jonah sniffed. "Push someone around, and then paint yourself the victim. Classic. I only see one bitch here, and that's you."

Elliot's eyes hardened. "Okay, Eleventh—"

"Jonah Rowe's the name," interrupted Jonah with heat.

"Okay, Jonah," said Elliott. "I was going to leave you alone. This was simply a means to an end. But now, you're in the game, too. You'll die, just like the Sibyl."

Jonah gritted his teeth. "Death isn't real."

"Oh right," chuckled Elliott. "I almost forgot you people's cute little shtick. But death will be real. For you and your new buddy."

"Good luck with that." Eva lifted her chin as she glared at the image. "You haven't managed to kill me off yet."

Elliott pulled his eyes off of Jonah and slowly turned them to Eva.

"You know, even now, I still adore your green eyes. I

can't wait to see that fear in them again like I did back in Charleston."

Jonah snapped his attention to Eva. Her eyes were once again green. He looked back at Elliot's projection with loathing, but Elliott kept his focus on Eva.

"You will go to Covington House as soon as I am done here," He told her, "Or those fuckers I killed - including Martin and your whore of a mother - will never know peace."

Jonah tossed a baton at Elliott's projection. It shattered, but he knew that Elliot was on the Astral Plane somewhere, completely unharmed.

He went to Eva, who had fallen to her knees with her face buried in her hands. Jonah didn't know what to do other than fling an arm around her shoulder. Mere minutes ago, he'd have kept his distance, but the time for awkwardness was long gone now.

For a fleeting moment, Jonah's mind shifted. Eva didn't need Cyrus. She didn't need to be tied to an abusive, ancient keeper. He hadn't protected her from the Shades, and he sure as hell wasn't there when Elliot showed up. No. She didn't need Cyrus.

She needed him. The desire to hold her became so strong, he tightened the arm he had around her before he realized what he was doing.

What the actual hell was that about?

"It's alright, Eva," He murmured when he forced his thoughts back to the moment at hand. "He wasn't really here."

Eva looked scandalized, hurt, and broken. Then Jonah remembered those last words.

"Why did he say those things about your mom?" he asked her. "What victims?"

Eva raised her face from her hands and gave Jonah a

look that clearly said she was terrified to answer his question. She was spared the task though, because at that precise moment, the door banged open, and their friends burst inside.

"What in the hell are you doing?" Cyrus demanded. "Release her. Now."

"You better take that base out of your voice," Jonah snapped before he turned back to Eva. "What victims?"

"Elliot sacrificed twelve people to Hera last year. It was her payment for the power he possesses now."

"God dammit," Jonah growled a little in his throat. "I am tired of this shit! It can't be two a.m. and-"

They all looked at each other.

"Jonah," said Jonathan, "You and Eva have been in this room for a day and a half."

"What! But— "

Then Jonah remembered. Time on Earthplane and Astral Plane were different. Elliot's little Astral mind games made them lose time.

"We all lost a day and a half," said Reena. "We thought we were asleep for a few hours, but now it's Wednesday. Three p.m.."

"No," Eva jerked up, her eyes wide. "We missed the Covington House interview— "

"Never mind that, Eva." Cyrus began, but Jonah cut him off.

"Reschedule it," He commanded to no one in particular. "For today. Get whoever you need to speak to on the phone and tell them we'll be there in forty-five minutes."

"Why?" asked Reena.

"Elliot is holding spirits back from the Other Side," Jonah announced to them all. "He wants the Covington House thing done, or he'll usurp them like a Spirit Reaper."

# SIX

## EVA MCRAYNE

I KEPT DROPPING my brush as I got ready to go to the Covington house. The damn thing kept slipping out of my hand before I could stop it. I kept telling myself that there was no way Elliot could continue to hurt those spirits after they died.

Yeah. I also knew I was lying to myself.

I dropped the damn brush for the tenth time when Cyrus opened the door to the bathroom. He shut it behind him and I swallowed.

"Nothing happened between us, Cyrus."

"You were in that room with Jonah for more than a day and a half." He seethed. "I don't believe you for a second."

"Jonah can't stand me. I made sure of that."

"He can't stand you, but had no problem having his hands all over you?"

"He put his arm around my shoulder. I don't consider that-"

Cyrus punched my arm and I hissed between my teeth as I grabbed at it.

"That boy is not to touch you, understand?" He

snapped. "We'll take care of that new attitude you've developed since you got here."

"What new attitude?"

"Running off on your own, not listening to me, getting too damn close to strangers. This is for your own good, Eva. You have no idea what these people are capable of."

I knew what that meant. I felt my anxiety churn in my stomach.

"Ok."

"Ok?"

I nodded and held back the tears in my eyes at the thought of never seeing Jonah again. It was a stupid thought, anyway. Once we left North Carolina, he'd be just as glad to get rid of me as everyone else had been.

"Finish getting ready. You have five minutes."

Cyrus didn't slam the door, but I heard the force behind his motion as he closed it. I took a breath, closed my eyes, and forced myself to ignore the throbbing in my arm.

I couldn't help but think back to my conversation with Jonah last night. I could have told him the truth. I could have told him that I let Cyrus do whatever he wanted because of the power he held over me. He was the only one who could physically harm me. Kill me. That alone was enough to keep me in line.

I took another breath and headed over to the closet. I pulled off the short sleeve blouse I had on and replaced it with a long sleeve one. It was hot as hell today, but I didn't want my newest bruise to show up on camera. I just finished pulling my hair back into a high ponytail when I heard a knock on my room door.

My heart skipped a beat when I saw Jonah on the other side. He wasn't dressed all fancy; just jeans and a t-shirt, but that didn't matter. Jonah had a face that made everything look good.

"Ready to go?"

"Yeah. Just let me grab my bag."

I looped my messenger back over my neck and freed my hair from it. When I approached the door again, I gestured for him to go out into the hallway.

"Is Cyrus already down there?"

"Yeah," Jonah answered. "He's down there."

I glanced at Jonah and gave him a small smile. "He's just doing his job, Jonah."

"I get he has a job to do," Jonah grumbled. "But the way he goes about it isn't cool, Eva. It's not."

"It's fine."

"Is it?" Jonah reached out and caught my arm right where Cyrus had hit me. I made a low yelping noise and Jonah raised an eyebrow. "What's wrong?"

"Nothing. I smacked my arm on the door jam this morning. It's still sore."

I hated myself for lying. I hated myself even more for covering Cyrus' ass.

"Anyway, Cyrus has literally been like this forever. He learned how to be a commander back when it was ok to kill your own men if they disobeyed you. That hard ass approach just stuck."

"Big deal,"Jonah said, unmoved. "Just because something was commonplace doesn't mean it was right. He works for *you*, Eva. He should worship the ground you spit on."

"It..doesn't work that way with us."

"Why?" Jonah stopped in the hallway. I stopped, too, though I knew the clock was ticking. "Why won't you put him in his place?"

"It's not-"

"Why?"

"He can kill me, alright?" I let the words out before I

could stop them. I pinched the bridge of my nose for a second, leveled out my voice, and continued. "There is a clause in the whole Sibyl-Keeper relationship that says he can harm me or kill me. My immortality is mute if he strikes out against me. It's a protection amendment that allows the Sibyl to be taken down if ever possessed."

Jonah stared at me. "Eva, answer me honestly. Does he lord that over you? Does he remind you of that, and swing it over your head, like the sword of Damocles?"

"The what?"

"Never mind," Jonah waved an impatient hand. "Does he never let you forget that?"

"He's mentioned it a time or two." I rubbed my arm subconsciously. "Let's get going."

"Let me see your arm first. You could have reaggravated it."

"I'm-"

Jonah gave me a look that told me not to argue with him. I sighed.

"I can't roll my sleeves up and I'm not about to get topless on the stairwell. Can we just go?"

"Come here." Jonah opened a door we had just passed. "You can show me in here."

"It's just a bruise."

"Uh huh," He shut the door. "Go on. I won't look at anything other than your arm."

"I know that. I trust you."

I unbuttoned my shirt and slipped it off my shoulders.

"See? It's fine."

"Was that his grab from last night, or this morning?"

"Neither. I-"

"Eva, if anyone's never told you this before, you need to know that you are a terrible liar." Jonah ran the tip of his finger around the darkening red spot. "See this? Those are impact bruises. Fighters get them alot."

"You're not supposed to do that."

I whispered and Jonah looked up. If I moved forward just a bit, I could have kissed him. I didn't dare.

"Do what?"

"Care."

"Why not?" Jonah questioned. "Does Cyrus frown on that too?"

"Yes."

I pulled my shirt back on and was in the middle of buttoning it when I heard Cyrus coming back up the stairs. I forgot all about his five minute time limit.

*Shit, shit, shit.*

I slipped past Jonah when I heard Cyrus' footsteps pass the door. He gave me a look of confusion.

"What the hell-"

"I gotta get downstairs," I turned to him. "The second I hear Cyrus shut my room door, I gotta make a run for it."

I shouldn't have, but I moved away from the door and kissed Jonah quick on the cheek. It was nothing. Barely a caress, but I felt something stir in me that I couldn't place.

"Thank you for caring."

Jonah placed a hand to his cheek. He looked at me, surprised by the gesture, but he didn't wipe it away. That made me feel better.

Well, until he stepped around me to open the door. Jonah moved out into the hallway where Cyrus was standing.

"Come here, Jonah." Cyrus beckoned with two fingers. "We need to talk."

"No," Jonah said simply. "Get to your charge and do your job, pumpkin."

"Excuse me?"

Jonah headed down the stairs without another word. I heard the exchange out in the hallway then rubbed my forehead as I followed Jonah downstairs. Cyrus' eyes were like daggers on me. I knew that I was going to be in a shit ton of trouble, but I also knew he wouldn't do anything until we were alone.

He stormed after me and towards the rented SUV. Joey was already chilling in the backseat listening to music. My guess was *Broadway's Greatest Hits*. I was surprised to see Jonah heading to the other side.

"You are going to accompany us, Blue Aura?" Cyrus sounded cold. His tone was a hard one. "Why?"

"Jonathan said stay with Eva for the duration of this, remember?" Jonah got in the seat. "Like I told you before, if you're butthurt about it, go complain to him. Or maybe you can get in and we can reach Covington on time?"

Cyrus cut his eyes over at me and I turned away from him to get in the passenger seat. I buckled myself in and cleared my throat.

"How did we lose time?"

"Pardon?"

"How did we lose time?" I shifted to see Jonah snap his seatbelt on. "I don't understand how that's possible."

Jonah sighed. I could tell he really didn't want to answer this question. "When, uh, when there is a convergence of preternatural stuff and earthly things, sometimes normal things, Like time, get caught in the crossfire. Elliot meddled with ethereality and he isn't an Eleventh. It's like bad medicine, with loss of time as the side effect. This is something bullies don't understand, you know? Their actions have unexpected consequences and unexpected karma."

"Ok. Was it like that for everyone at the estate or just us?"

"All of us," Cyrus answered between clenched teeth. "One minute, I was talking to Jonathan and the next minute, it was daylight. He realized something was wrong and we all came upstairs to check on everyone."

Everyone? Or did he come to make sure I wasn't doing something I wasn't allowed to do?

I chided myself for the thought. It didn't matter. None of this mattered. In a few days, I would either be dead or on a plane back to California.

"Does that kind of stuff happen often at the estate?" I focused back on Jonah. "Or is this all because of Elliot?"

"Not often at all," Jonah answered. "Loss of time is a direct result of meddling. People have tried to manipulate time, but the consequences have always been disastrous. So no. It's not a common thing."

"Your girlfriend does that, does she not?" Cyrus chimed in as he looked into the rearview mirror. "Jonathan was speaking about her last night. The Time Item?"

I couldn't explain the sinking feeling I had in my gut. Of course, Jonah would have someone. Someone who wasn't necessarily at the estate. Someone that he hadn't mentioned because the only decent conversation we had was maybe twenty minutes long.

"What's her name again? Vera?" Cyrus cut his eyes over at me. "She is a proper actress. Perhaps Eva can help her get started on Broadway."

"First of all, Cyrus, Vera is not my girlfriend," Jonah sounded slightly brine. "She's actually out of town with another guy as we speak. As for proper actresses, what would you know about them? The scrolls Jonathan found described your wife as a woman who tried and failed every time she auditioned for the acting troupes. What was her name? Delphine? The first Sybil?"

"She was a wonderful actress," Cyrus responded with

pride in his voice. A pride I had never heard directed at me. "Delphine was ahead of her time in many ways. It is a pity she committed a Sibyl's suicide, but it was for an honorable reason."

"What reason?" I looked at him now. "You've never told me this."

"Because you don't need to know."

"I'd like to know."

"Fear not, Eva. One day, you will have your own reasons just as Delphine had hers." Cyrus went back to watching the road. "At any rate, I'm sure Vera will come around sooner or later, Jonah. Perhaps sooner, since Eva is going to put in a good word for her play. Right, Eva?"

"Yeah, sure," I cleared my throat from the knot that had formed there. "I'm not one with the Broadway crowd, but I can talk to some people."

"Ahead of her time," Jonah shook his head. "People said the same thing about Yoko Ono. And Eva, since Cyrus has decided to fashion himself the gatekeeper of information, I'll tell you. Jonathan told us that Delphine chose to exit her role after she outlived her two boys."

"Those two boys were my sons and I prefer to keep that information private."

Once again, Cyrus was speaking through gritted teeth. I wanted to feel sorry for him - the story was tragic - but I couldn't do it. I still said the words I was expected to.

"I'm sorry that you lost them, Cyrus."

"It's the true cycle of life. Everyone passes into spirit when their time comes."

Cyrus glanced back at Jonah and I knew what he was silently implying. I felt a sudden rush of fear so strong, I paused before I turned to look at Jonah once more.

"Are you sure you want to do this with me? I really

don't want to put you or anyone else in danger. And you saw Elliot. You see how damn determined he is."

"I'm not afraid." Jonah caught Cyrus ' look, and seemed thoroughly annoyed by it. "He may have abilities and knowledge, but he still eats and sleeps like any other animal. And just like all other animals, he can be put down. He might think he's safe behind supposed immortality, but that means a grand total of dick around here. He's determined? So am I."

I studied Jonah for a moment longer before I nodded.

"After the woods, I know you can handle yourself. I wasn't questioning your abilities. I just wanted to give you the option of bowing out. It's not fair for you to be dragged into my mess like this."

"What was the deal with you and Elliot anyway?"

"We were friends once, back in college. He offered me the spot on *Grave* and things went to hell after that."

"Why?"

"Jealousy? I failed to prove my loyalty to him?" I shrugged. "Who knows? Everyone has their motives. Elliot is no different."

"Elliot got pissed off because of me. Don't deny it, Eva." Cyrus flipped the blinker as we reached the downtown area of Rome. "He didn't like the fact your attention was divided. Now, I can understand why. You tend to get too focused on one thing when there are a thousand things going on in the background that are equally as important."

"Oh," Jonah said. He must have noticed the jab Cyrus had thrown at me. "So Eva sounds like a human being. Short-sightedness and tunnel vision aren't gifts, Cy. They're handicaps."

"That's precisely my point. Thank you for emphasizing that." Cyrus nodded. "Your tunnel vision is a weakness, Eva. They handicap you, just like Jonah said."

"Thank you for the reminder," I managed to keep my voice neutral. "I'll work on that."

"You should. In a fight, those handicaps could be deadly. Take the Shades for example. They were able to ambush you from behind since you were so focused on the ones in front of you. Had you been more observant of your surroundings, you wouldn't have needed our help."

"Or if I had just stayed on the porch, right?"

I went ahead and threw that in. I knew that was coming up next. There was no point in telling my keeper the truth. He wouldn't believe me if I did. Cyrus nodded.

"Exactly. We've been together for four years now and you still don't understand the importance of what I tell you."

"Just stabbing in the dark here," Jonah said, "But that might be because, from my perspective, it seems like it's all you telling things and not giving Eva the chance to get a word in edgewise. Relationships are all about one hundred percent from both parties. Sounds like the only ways here are the Way of Cyrus and Cyrus' Way."

"Ouch," Joey observed.

"Shut up, Lawson," Cyrus snapped, which prompted Jonah to throw up his hands.

"For God's sake!" He exclaimed. "You order him around too? Was there an update I didn't know about that made you the god, instead of Apollo?"

"I don't order Joseph around." Cyrus snapped. "I am not responsible for Joseph or his safety."

"I just don't get you, man," Jonah shook his head. "I don't. You know that you work for Eva, right? Not the other way around?"

"Eva has been exposed to our world for four years. She knows nothing about it. I do what I must to train her in it."

"Then train her!" Jonah spat. "And stop trying to be Big Bad Daddy! Because that shit is old!"

Cyrus sighed. "Jonah, have you ever been in the military? Have you ever had any formal training other than what your friends do at the estate? If you had, then you know my methods are not uncommon. You may not like them, but they are effective."

Jonah shook his head. "I figured you'd go that route. Well, speaking as someone who has volunteered with veterans of the military, I am well aware of your methods. I am also aware that attempting to spill behaviors and methods that worked in military life has very little success in the civilian world. You were a general, right? Cool. Respect. But you're not a general now, dude. That was ages ago. It's time to stop clinging to old glory and get with the times, dontcha think?"

"Why should I abandon methods that have worked for centuries?"

"Because most of those methods were outlawed here in the U.S. decades ago?"

"I am not a U.S. citizen." Cyrus shrugged. "My laws come from Olympus and I have broken none of them. Unlike you. Tell me, how often do you smoke weed, Jonah? I do believe that substance is illegal in North Carolina."

"Every time I'm sore from training," Jonah replied. "And last I checked, cannabis didn't leave bruises on women's arms."

I winced at Jonah's comment. I looked out the window instead of looking at Cyrus. It took a moment for him to speak.

"There are times when force is needed to emphasize a point. Do you not see this in your world as well, Jonah? Do you not fight ethereal beings - male and female - and leave bruises on them?"

"If I bruise Reena's arm, it's to pull her away from a Reaper or a Haunt or something," Jonah told the Keeper. "But last night, you bruised Eva *after* all the enemies were down. See the difference, pumpkin?"

"I was emphasizing my point. Nothing more. Nothing less. That is not abuse. That is being a commander. Someone who takes charge and action to correct the mistakes of his fellow fighters."

"Yeah," Jonah nodded. "And every abusive parent says they were just doing what they could. Excuse me if I'm not moved by your bullshit."

"I don't care if you are moved or not." Cyrus turned on the street that led us out of Rome. "You are free to question my methods while we are at the estate. But come Saturday, you won't think another thing about them. You'll go back to your actress and your weed and forget all about us."

"The actress ain't mine, I ain't telling you again. And I bet you'd just love to be away from Rome. Back to where you can try to assert control? Well you ain't getting rid of us that easily. Joey and Eva are friends now. That puts them in our zone. So your last desperate hope to be free of us? Fail."

"I've already explained to you that Eva doesn't have friends." Cyrus sighed. "It is far too dangerous and she is far too busy."

"I wouldn't mind being friends with the Elevenths," I spoke up since Cyrus was determined not to let me talk on my own behalf. "I'd like that very much, actually."

"Please stop embarrassing yourself, Eva. Joseph is the only one you haven't run off yet and the only reason he is still here is because of his contract." Cyrus snorted. "If you take Jonah up on this 'offer of friendship', it will just end badly for you and I don't want to deal with the aftermath."

"Now, you're a psychic." Jonah rolled his eyes. "My

God dude, ain't you just the Renaissance Man. Eva, Terrence, Reena and I would like very much to be friends. Since you don't hear it often, I'll tell you both: you don't need Cyrus' permission. If you're uncomfortable going over his head, I'll happily do so. Who do we need to speak to?"

"Now see here, you impertinent--"

"Look, pumpkin!" Jonah pointed. "There's the house. Eva, we'll talk later. Terrence is making meatballs tonight. We can all talk over dinner."

We pulled up to the front of the Covington Mansion not a moment too soon. I was sure it had been a sight back in its heyday. But after years of neglect, the old house just looked sad. The windows that hadn't been shattered were boarded up. The granite exterior was a mottled mix of gray, black, and mold. Three stories rose up, topped off by a rusted weather vane bent by the wind.

"What is it about this place?" I muttered to myself as I stepped out of the car. I needed to focus on something other than the argument I'd just heard in the car. "Why is Elliot so determined that I come here?"

"What?" Joey took off his headphones as he stood beside me. He whistled when he took in the same view I was seeing. "Classic, Evie. This episode is going to be classic."

"Right." I shook off the chill running down my spine. "Maybe we'll win you another award, Joey."

He grinned and wiggled his eyebrows at me before he rushed to get his equipment out of the back. Cyrus and Jonah came up to flank me on either side.

"This is the glitz and glamour of what I do, Jonah." I gestured towards the house. "Exotic places, beautiful faces—"

I let my voice trail off when I realized that Jonah had turned pale. He was still wearing his sunglasses, but I could tell by his expression that he was unnerved. Cyrus had picked up on it too.

"Scared, Rowe?"

Cyrus regarded him over my head. Given the events since we'd landed in Rome, I wasn't surprised that he had tensed up by my side. For his part, Jonah shook his head.

"Hardly. Where's the owner you were supposed to meet here?"

"I don't know." I shrugged. "We're only a day late. Maybe he got tired of waiting."

"Cute, Superstar."

I chuckled. "I thought so. Come on. I want to go check this place out."

I turned on my heel and marched up the steps. The place was encircled with a large front porch, but I had to be careful when I crossed it. The boards were green with rot. I started to warn the others when I heard a crack behind me.

"Dammit." Jonah grunted as he jerked his leg free from the hole he had made. "You couldn't investigate a place like the Hyatt, could you?"

"Nope." I turned back towards the ornate front door to see that it was standing open. "Wait, what?"

"What's wrong?" Joey had joined us, shifting his camera up to his shoulder. "Why are we all hanging out on the porch?"

"The door just opened." I frowned as I peered inside. "Maybe Frederickson is already here."

"Frederickson?" Jonah was dusting the dirt off of his pants leg. "The owner?"

I nodded. "Robert Frederickson. Bought the house at an auction back in 2012 as a tax haven. He contacted Theia Productions to do a show in the hopes that the exposure would help him dump it."

"Stay here." Cyrus stepped past me and over the threshold. "It could be a trap."

"Or just an empty old house full of spider webs and broken furniture." I offered up then shrugged as they all turned to stare at me. "It was worth a shot."

Cyrus ignored me as he disappeared inside. Joey sat his camera down then knelt beside it to fiddle with the buttons on it. Which left me and Jonah with nothing to do but wait.

"You don't have to defend me, Blueberry."

""Blueberry? Where the hell did you come up with that one?"

"It seems to fit you better than Country." I tested out the porch rail before leaning back against it. "And I'm serious. I know Cyrus can be a bit of a culture shock, but I'm used to him."

"I'm not." Jonah shook his head. "Superstar, I'm not even trying to be difficult. I'm not even trying to rock the boat. Please believe that. I know Cyrus has a job to do, and it's not an easy one. But the lack of respect he shows you just vexes me. He treats you like a pouty child who needs to be scolded. It's not cool. I don't do well with alpha males."

"I don't like it either, but-"

"I know you said he could hurt you, but the only way you would know that is if he has done it in the past."

I didn't know what to say to that. Jonah extended his hand.

"Let me see your phone."

"Why?"

"I'm going to program my number into it. If we're going to be friends, we need to stay in touch, right?"

"You were serious then, in the car," I pulled my phone out of my back pocket and passed it to him. "Are you sure? Cyrus was right when he said I tend to fuck things up with people. I don't want to do that with you."

"Eva, if anyone seems capable of fucking things up, it's Cyrus himself." Jonah took Eva's phone and stylus. "Dude is a pimple on the face of life, and he probably knows it."

I chuckled at that and Jonah gave me a small smile as he passed me my phone back.

"What's funny? He is."

"No, it's just I've never gotten a guy's phone number before." I laughed then repeated his hand gesture. "My turn."

Jonah passed his phone to her. "Never? Well, first time for everything, no?"

"Nope, never. Work people don't count. And I've never dated before, so there's that."

"Before Cyrus?"

I typed in my number and saved it before I passed his phone back.

"I don't think Cyrus counts. We don't go on dates. We spend time together when we train."

"Dear Lord, what does he train you to do?" Jonah asked. "How to scowl and judge everyone?"

I laughed again. I couldn't help it.

"No," I shook my head. "No. He's working with me on my fighting style. I'm too slow. Not powerful enough to knock an enemy out completely."

I twisted my face into Cyrus' trademark scowl as I mimicked his voice.

"You have to be faster, Eva. Do it again."

"It sounds as though too much focus is on fixing perceived flaws, as opposed to sharpening strengths," Jonah said. "Maybe you're not slow at all. Maybe that's all you've been trained to focus on."

"I can't tell you. I've never trained with anyone else."

"Really? Who taught you how to fight? Cyrus?"

"No. Athena. But that was...different."

"You'll have to tell me that story one day," Jonah said. "Maybe over Terrence's lasagna and homemade garlic knots."

"That sounds lovely." I smiled. "I take it Terrence is the cook? It's literally the first thing he said to us once we got to the estate."

"Yeah. Terrence cooks, Reena paints."

"What about you?"

"What about me?"

"What's your hobby?"

"Writer," Jonah said. "Not a great one at all. And the gym. I hated exercise before l met Terrence, Reena, and our friend, Bobby. But they made a gym junkie out of me."

"Will you share your work with me?"

"Sure. We can workout before supper."

"No, not your workout," I smiled a little. "Your writing. I bet you're better than you give yourself credit for."

"You don't want to workout with me, Superstar?"

"I can, but I'm not good at the gym. I haven't been to an actual workout space since I left Georgia."

"Interesting," Jonah observed. "You have a background in ballet and gymnastics, but you hate athletics?"

"How did you know that?" I asked. "That's not on my site."

"Fighting stance," Jonah told her. "I picked it up when you were fighting the Shades."

I flushed a little as my heart started pounding. People tended not to notice me. They were too enamoured by the character I had to be in Hollywood.

"You noticed that?"

"I did. I've been around all sorts of fighters. I'm able to pick up their backgrounds pretty quick."

"What's your fighting background?"

"You sure are curious about me."

"I told you I wanted us to be friends and I got your digits." I waved my phone at him. "So yeah, I'm curious."

"Blunt force," Jonah said. "I use batons, and I'm not fond of blades, so it's strength-based. Hits that'll rattle ancestors. So I do a *lot* of arm and back work to build strength. Since I'm not a hulking guy, I'm deceptive. Get to hide some attributes till they're needed."

"I can see that."

"That I'm not a hulking guy?" Jonah responded drily. "Thank you."

"No! That you use deception as a part of your fighting style. I do the same thing in a way."

"How's that?"

"Look at me, Jonah. Do I really look like I can kick someone's ass?" I shook my head. "My enemies think I'm an easy target. Even now. So they like to get me alone before they pounce."

Jonah shook his head. "So you're like Buffy."

"How?"

"You know, the blonde girl goes down the dark alley, but *she* is the dangerous one," Jonah said. "Nice to circumvent the trope, ain't it?"

"I'm a troupe?" Now, I was the one who responded drily. "Thank you."

"Well, you do fit the mold. Blonde, white, tiny."

"I'm no Sarah Michelle Gellar."

"But you *are* a slayer," Jonah said. "Terrence made me watch the first two seasons of *Grave*. So l have firsthand knowledge."

"Yeah? Terrence has good taste in television then." I grinned up at him. "What did you think about the show? Be honest. It's hard to hurt my feelings."

"I had no expectations, but found it very entertaining and informative," Jonah said. "All the research involved pulls me; research is another of my hobbies. So it's like...adventurous learning."

"That's my hobby."

"The show?"

"In a sense, but it's more about the research for me. I love the stories. The people. The history behind it all just fascinates me."

"Same," Jonah said. "It's why I know so much about mythology. I blazed through those books over and over."

"I'm glad one of us does."

"You don't know mythology?"

"I know some of it," I confessed. "But not everything. If I need to know it, Cyrus will tell me."

"So you know nothing," Jonah remarked. "Because Cyrus talks *at* you, not to you."

"Well, I know the gods I have met."

"But not their histories."

I shook my head. "No. I haven't had the time to actually read half the shit Cyrus put down in front of me. I can speak ancient Greek, though. I picked that up at the Academy."

"Really? Say something."

I tapped my finger against my chin then began to speak in the old tongue.

"I am very happy to have met you."

Jonah blinked. "I don't have one clue what you said, but it sounded cool as hell."

I chuckled. "I said 'I am very happy to have met you.'

"What other languages can you speak?"

"French and English. That's pretty much it."

"Cool," Jonah said. "I'm getting pretty good at Latin, because our friend Malcolm is teaching me."

"Latin?" I whistled. "I'm impressed."

"You speak ancient Greek."

"That doesn't make Latin any less impressive. I can't speak Latin at all."

"It just comes easily to me," Jonah said. "Like remembering dates and what have you."

"If the small talk is quite over," Cyrus said, his tone cold as he appeared beside us. "Our client has just parked."

I jumped when I heard Cyrus' voice. He trained those cold eyes onto me.

"The house is clear. It's full of cobwebs and broken furniture."

"It always is." I pushed away from the banister. "Let's go meet up with this man. But Jonah, you owe me something in Latin. I want to hear you say something, too."

Jonah leaned in and lowered his tone. "*Potes melior est, quam stulti.*"

I gave him a quizzical look. "What's that mean?"

"It means," Jonah looked over at Cyrus, who was still glaring at them as he went to help Joey, "You can do better than that fool."

I gave him a small smile then whispered in my ancient language. Jonah shook his head.

"Still cool. Still don't understand."

"I said "Thank you, but I don't know who would have me. I'm a train wreck."

"Eva! Are you coming?"

"Just a minute!" I turned back to Jonah. "Thank you all the same."

"You're very welcome, Superstar," Jonah replied. "Now, go do your thing."

Joey grinned as I approached him.

"Speak of the devil." He waved as an older man stepped out of the vehicle. "Time to get to work, Evie."

"Yay." I muttered. "Jonah, if you don't mind, stay by

Cyrus. I have no idea where Joey wants to film this thing. I'd hate for you to end up on the show."

"Me too." He took a step back. "Let's get this over and done with."

I bounded down the stairs to meet the man as he crossed the lawn. Robert Frederickson looked as if he had just left the Hamptons. Black hair distinguished with gray temples. White blazer and dark blue dress pants. He looked completely out of place here.

"Mr. Frederickson? Eva McRayne." I offered him my hand. "I apologize for missing our meeting earlier. We've had some—developments."

"Yes, well." He nodded to Joey. "My time is very precious, Ms. McRayne. I had every intention of being back in New York tonight."

"Theia Productions will cover the cost of this inconvenience." I smiled. "Have you ever done an interview before?"

"Not for television."

"This is Joey Lawson." I gestured. "Obviously, the cameraman. He will be focusing his attention on you when we get started. But first, he has to get you hooked up with a microphone."

"Got it right here in my pocket."

Joey passed it over to the man before passing a second one over to me. He showed our contact how to attach the device to his jacket to get the best sound. Then how to speak into it. When they got finished, I attached my own microphone to the collar of my shirt.

"Where can we get the best shot, Joey?"

"I was thinking on the porch. Mr. Frederickson, if you will."

Joey led us over to Cyrus and Jonah, both of whom

stepped as far away from us as possible. Mr. Frederickson straightened his jacket.

"Right to the point, then?" He nodded. "Good. The sooner this is over, the better."

"I couldn't agree more. But we still have to film inside. See if we capture anything."

"You will. I'm sure of it. My daughters swear by *Grave Messages*." The man shifted in place. "As you can see, I don't keep it locked. Nobody in their right mind would dare come here. You may come and go as you wish."

I bit back my response with a reminder to myself that this man was a client. So instead of snapping at him, I held up three fingers in Joey's direction, folding them down to give him the signal to start filming.

"Robert Frederickson is the owner of Covington Mansion, located fifteen minutes outside of Rome, North Carolina. Mr. Frederickson, what attracted you to Covington?"

"The history, my dear girl." He boomed with an exuberance so unexpected, I almost took a step back. "Rome has been the site of so much southern history. Covington is no different."

"What can you tell us about that history?" I tilted my head towards the man. "Murders? Suicides?"

"Oh, nothing like that." Frederickson chuckled. "But these walls serve as a monument to the Covington family."

"A monument." I focused on the camera. "It was believed that George S. Covington had his family buried here beneath the floors when the house was built."

"Yes, the old fool went insane with grief." Frederickson rocked back on his heels. "It happens, you know. When you lose a loved one. Or two."

I whipped my head around to see a faint spark of green

in the man's dark eyes. Could he—no. There was no way this man could be aligned with Hera.

My paranoia was simply at a fever pitch. It had to be.

I managed a thin smile and leaned back against my perch on the rail. "You purchased Covington in 2012, is that correct?"

"Yes. I was hoping to turn it into a getaway retreat for my own family."

"Wow, that's different." I raised an eyebrow at him. "You wanted to vacation with your family here? In the middle of nowhere? In an oversized tomb?"

The man coughed behind his hand as he narrowed his eyes at me. "Yes, well. As I said. Rome is a beautiful town. It is peaceful here. The fact that this manor is haunted was not a deterrent for me."

"Let's talk about that for a minute." I pressed against the rail. "What have people experienced here?"

"Everything. The stories rebound with objects moving on their own. Apparitions walk through the very walls!" He gestured to the heavens. "Screams resonate through the night and some reports state that previous occupants have been shoved down the stairs."

So far, so standard. I resisted the urge to roll my eyes at his theatrics. Why did people tend to act so crazy when there was a camera present?

"Alright. What about you? What have you personally experienced?"

"Me?" Robert Frederickson glanced nervously at the front door. "What do you mean?"

"Have you ever been shoved down the stairs?" I widened my eyes with mock innocence. "Have you heard these phantom screams?"

"No. I've—" The man huffed up, "I've never actually been inside."

I laughed. I couldn't help it. Under normal circumstances, I could contain my personal reactions to the people we deal with. But this?

This was too much.

"And—you just added another thirty minutes to my edits, Evie." Joey lowered the camera as I giggled. "What's wrong with you?"

"Seriously?" I ignored Joey as I focused on our contact. "You bought this house years ago. You call a television crew to come investigate it for paranormal activity. And you've never been inside?"

"I've never had a reason." Frederickson turned bright red. "Are we done here?"

I nodded. There was no way I could continue taking this man seriously. He waved his hand at me with anger before storming back to his car.

"Best. Interview. Ever." I grinned when I watched him drive away. When the others didn't respond, I turned to face them. "What?"

"Do you treat all of your clients that way?" Jonah frowned. "Why did you call him out like that?"

"Because he was an ass and a liar." I all but skipped through the door. "I can't stand people who turn all dramatic when they are in front of the camera. It screams fake to me."

"It should." Joey linked his arm into mine. "He bought this place as a tax haven?"

"Yeah. I figured that out after I checked the building permits. Frederickson never applied for one. I mean, why buy an abandoned house if you have no intention of fixing it up?"

I was still riding high as we stepped into the main hallway. Dust and grime covered everything. Pictures hung crooked on the walls. I was sure that if I held my breath, I would hear the rats scurrying about. We moved from room to room in silence which was all we encountered.

There were no screams. No one tried to push us down the stairs when we stood at the top. Nothing flew at my head.

Of course, I didn't have a mirror present. Cyrus must have taken them all down when he came in here earlier.

When we reached the bedroom upstairs, I stopped just short of the window as Jonah disappeared into a door I had mistaken as a closet. Cyrus stepped up behind me to clasp the back of my neck with his fingers.

"I overheard your little chat on the porch." He chuckled. "I found it quite entertaining."

"Why's that?"

"Because it became obvious to me that I was right. Rowe has no interest in you."

"I know he doesn't."

"Do you know how I know?"

"No."

"Because he had no interest in learning about you. Every question asked was directed at him. Perhaps, he is a narcissist."

"Or perhaps, he was simply answering my questions." I hissed when he applied pressure against my spine with his palm. "Ow."

"You have been warned, Eva. That is the last I will say on the matter. You have been warned."

# SEVEN

## JONAH ROWE

THE ROOM JONAH stepped into was no bigger than the bathroom in his old apartment. In other words, it was tiny and dark.

The walls were plastered with black. The small chair and table? Black. Even the mirror positioned across from the chair was dark.

"Ok." Jonah jostled against the door as it shut. "This isn't creepy. Not creepy at all."

He shifted around only to fall into the chair with a grunt. But just as he reached out to feel for the door knob, he heard a strange whispering fill his ears.

Jonah jerked his head towards the mirror as the black began to shift into faces. A blur of eyes and mouths until, at last, it stopped.

"Your soul is so hard to read, Jonah Rowe." The woman in the mirror pursed her lips together. "Oh, begging your pardon—spirit. What can I offer you?"

The image against the black shifted as she continued to speak. "Fame? Fortune?"

There were crowds of people screaming his name as

they waved books in the air. That image faded into a vision of himself, dressed to the nines as he sat down in a chair on the set of a talk show.

Those crowds—all holding his books and shouting his name—that talk-show spot. Jonah didn't even own a suit like that. It looked worthy of a designer collection. The type of clothing you wore when you didn't have any cares in the world.

And then a scene came into the mirror. One that made Jonah's eyes bulge. This one had Vera in positions he had only fantasized about. Hera didn't make this one a glimpse. It lingered. Jonah should have turned away. But for some reason, that was an impossibility.

*File it away, Jonah,* He ordered himself. *Scratch that. Forget it. You have more respect for Vera than just to regard her as a piece of meat.*

But it wasn't working. The woman had done it perfectly. The scene with Vera might as well have been a soft-porn short video.

The image faded, and the woman chuckled.

"You enjoy happy endings, Blue Aura? I do as well. Get the Sybil on the Astral Plane at the golden hour on Sunday. Do this for me, and the fame, the wealth, and the woman of your dreams is yours. Sunday at the golden hour. That's a sufficient amount of time to make up your mind. And, given your vision, time is something you long to enjoy. But there is more."

"More?"

"I will give you access to the one place your Jonathan can't get to. I will give you the key to the Other Side."

Jonah stared as if transfixed by the image. When he started to respond, the woman cut him off.

"Don't answer just yet, Blue Aura. There will be time

enough for that. Consider my words. Consider what could be. Then, when the time is right, I will return to you."

The woman's face disappeared as quickly as it emerged in the glass. He stood there, frozen in place.

Jonah didn't know what to think. Temptations with what he wanted? But it wasn't the Sirens.

This was one woman, with eyes as green as his friend Elizabeth Manville's. But Liz's eyes were full of happiness, warmth, and joy. This woman's eyes were venomous green, harsh, full of ambition and evil.

He'd read Greek mythology. Seen a bunch of pictures and depictions.

That woman looked like depictions he'd seen of Hera. But that couldn't be, Hera was the goddess of family, marriage—wholesome endeavors. But that woman he saw in the mirror was a thug. A thug and a bitch, with a trace of sociopath. He had no interest in doing anything that she said.

The memories of his experiences in this house resurfaced. He hadn't lied to Eva. He hadn't heard of the place. He'd never known its name. He'd just been there.

The Covington House was the site of his first great victory as an Eleventh Percenter.

The memories weren't pleasant. He'd nearly lost his physical life in an inferno in the basement. He'd gotten a deep muscle tear on his left shoulder, and that had been before the broken ribs. But he'd won that fight.

She'd also said that she could give him the key to the Other Side. Jonathan always said that that couldn't happen. It was inaccessible. The Protector Guides couldn't go there. The Spirit Guides couldn't go there.

But Hera said she could. She'd described it like it was a door that simply needed to be unlocked.

Seeing Nana again could be that easy.

A surge of fear shot through him like an electric current. *No*. What Hera promised wasn't natural. He couldn't think about Nana.

Hera wanted him to sell out Eva. Get her on the Astral Plane. Why?

"Jonah?" said Joey.

"What?" He said a little forcefully. "Sorry—I'm—"

He didn't even finish.

"Dude, you look like you've seen a…nevermind." Joey decided against it.

"Are you alright, Jonah?" Eva called out from her spot in the middle of the main room. "Find anything good in there?"

Jonah didn't know what to say. He wasn't up to telling her about his past with this house yet, and he certainly wasn't going to speak on Hera's visions. He thought the Sirens were bad, but Hera—he could never admit to the images she showed him.

"Old history," He muttered. "It doesn't matter."

"Why did Elliott send us here?" She asked with heat. "I was so sure there would be more to it than just the episode. If it weren't for Frederickson, this would have been a waste of time."

Her voice caught on the end of that sentence, but it looked as if she swallowed down the emotion.

Jonah was fuzzy on that part, too. Elliott couldn't have lured them here just for Hera to try to bribe him with fabulous prizes. She could've done that anywhere. So what other reason was there for them to bring Jonah and Eva to this place?

"We need to return to the estate and reconvene with Jonathan, Terrence, and Reena," said Cyrus. "Eva, Joey, go ahead. I want a quick conversation with Jonah."

Eva frowned. Jonah did, too. He wasn't up for private

conversation with the Muscle. Especially right now. He hadn't had time to reorganize his thoughts.

Cyrus jerked his head towards the door and the other two left. He then looked Jonah right in the eye.

"What did Hera show you?"

"I don't know what you're talking about."

"Yes, you do. What was your answer?"

"It's none of your damn business-"

"Did she ask you to betray Eva?"

"Why do you want to know?" Jonah sneered. "Afraid she gave me a better offer than she gave to you?"

Cyrus' eyes flashed. Jonah didn't give a shit. He stormed out of the room, still shaken by what he had seen.

It was Wednesday now. Hera gave him until the golden hour on Sunday.

He'd wanted this week to end as quickly as possible. Now he would have given anything to have more time.

# EIGHT

## EVA MCRAYNE

I TRAILED behind Joey as my thoughts whirled around in my head. First, there was the interview, then the house itself. Now Jonah and Cyrus were having guy time upstairs after all the tension between them in the car? After Cyrus said they needed to talk?

I didn't like this. Not one bit.

"Come on, Evie." Joey groaned as I lagged further behind. "You heard the man. We need to get back to Grannison. And time? She is a—wastin.'"

Waste of time. Isn't that what I said when we discovered Jonah in that dark room? I stopped at the bottom of the stairs, tilting my head in an attempt to listen.

I got nothing. Dammit.

"Hey, go on to the car. I'm going to wait for those two right here."

"Oh, no, you don't." Joey narrowed his eyes at me as he stormed back down the hallway. "You get into way too much trouble without supervision."

I rolled my eyes at him. "Fine. Stand here for all I care. I'm going to check that out."

"Check what out?"

"That." I pointed towards the end of the hallway. There was a door, barely visible in the fading afternoon sun. In fact, I'd missed it during our first walk through. "I want to know what's in there."

Joey caught my arm as I tried to go past him. He took one long look at the stairs before turning his attention back to me. I knew he was thinking about the hell I was going to catch for not doing what I had been told. Still, he whispered. "Camera?"

I nodded. "Where's it at?"

"On the porch. Stay right here." He looked down at me over his nose as he pointed a single finger at me. "Do not move a single inch."

"Then hurry up. They will be down here any second."

Joey jogged down the hall, out the door, and was back before I could cover the distance from the stairs to the mystery door. We slipped inside and closed it behind us.

I held onto the wall as we inched down another flight of stairs. I'll admit, I winced every time a board creaked. I was so sure that we would get caught for our exploration that I had to cover my mouth with my hand to hide my grin when we reached the bottom.

Joey tapped me three times on the shoulder, which meant he had night vision on and was rolling.

"We are in the basement of the Covington mansion." I took a look as my eyes adjusted to the darkness. "Dust, cobwebs, I'm not sure if we'll find anything here."

I was just being honest. As we explored the basement, it was nothing spectacular. Boxes and forgotten belongings covered in sheets. I started to tell Joey that we needed to go back upstairs when I turned and ran right into a large oval mirror.

I scrambled back without a sound as Joey kept filming.

I waited for the whispers to assault my ears. I waited for the faces to appear in the glass. Instead, a single figure appeared.

It was a man, his hair gray and neat. His clothing screamed the Victorian Era. He folded his hands together before his face as he studied me.

"There have been whispers in our realm, Sibyl, that you would come to this place of sorrow. I never dreamed I would have the opportunity to encounter you myself."

"Covington?" I frowned. "George S. Covington?"

"Yes, in the spirit." He chuckled to himself. "There are secrets here, child. A power I didn't understand but welcomed when I was in the flesh. The lines. They cross."

"What lines?" I kept my eyes glued to the mirror. "I don't understand."

"Of course not. You speak to the dead, but you do not listen." He shrugged. "At any rate, I have come with a message from your father."

"Apollo?"

"Yes, Sibyl." Covington grinned. "Your biological father. The Golden One. Apollo."

"Then get on with it. I have maybe two minutes to hear you out before I get caught down here."

Covington folded his arms. "Do you want the message or not?

I struggled against myself, and forced back my fear the longer this took. "Why would Apollo speak to you?"

"Well, that is the message!" The figure before me laughed. "He cannot assist you on the physical plane where the lines cross. He wishes you well, and has demanded that you listen to those who know better."

Huh. Well, that was about as helpful as nothing.

"Yeah? I'll try. But I'm not a very good listener." I snorted. "Is there anything else?"

"Only—" He paused as if to get his thoughts together. "Beware of false affiliations, child. They will lead you into nothingness."

"Ok. That was as clear as crystal. Nothing cryptic about that."

The figure didn't respond. He began to fade back into the darkness, so I grabbed the nearest sheet next to me to throw over the glass. My hand smacked against a hard pillar and I winced as I finished my task.

"Evie, I think we need to go back upstairs. I think I hear Cyrus looking for us."

"Cyrus won't hurt you, Joey." I turned towards the object I hit. "Can you shine your light over here?"

"Yeah, sure." He sounded resigned. "But only if you're quick about it."

Joey pressed a button and the spotlight on the bulk piece of his shoulder illuminated the object I had struck. It wasn't a pillar. It was a gravestone.

I brushed away the dust to read the inscription. *Edna Covington. B. 1792 D. 1827. In death, there is light.*

"It's the graves." I whispered before I stood up. "There should be two more. An uncle and mother."

I stopped as Joey swung the camera around to give me more light as I noticed the one thing I could never have noticed in the dark.

The walls were black. Strange symbols were scratched into the stone. I took out my phone as I heard Cyrus calling for me.

"Eva!"

"I'm down here!" I called back. "Joey, go grab them, will you? I don't want to face him yet."

"Nope. Filming." He responded. "You go."

"Fine." I pulled out my cell phone, pulled up the

camera, and snapped pictures of the symbols closest to me. "These are important."

"Eva!"

"Dammit." I sighed as I started back through the basement. "I'm down here! In the basement! We heard something and-"

I stepped on something hard enough to be felt through my boot, so I knelt down, brushed the dirt away, and used the light from my phone to expose the object. It was a trinket of some sort. Metal. Dented. Unrecognizable.

And strange. I pocketed it before I resumed my flight to the stairs. Cyrus was liable to beat my ass on camera if I didn't show up soon.

I burst through the door to see them heading towards the front. "Down here. You've got to see this."

"What are you doing?" Cyrus stormed over to me. "Once again, you defied a direct order."

I swallowed my fear as Jonah came up behind him. My new friend seemed seconds from smashing Cyrus across the back of the head.

"We heard voices in the basement." I lied as I headed back down the stairs. "Joey, I got them. Joey?"

I frowned as I went back to the gravesite. "He was here just a minute ago. He wanted to film the symbols we found on the wall."

"Symbols?" Cyrus had pulled out a small flashlight and held it in the direction I pointed. "I don't see anything."

"Look, I'm not making this up. And Joey—where's—"

My words trailed off as I considered what could have been the true reason why Elliot had been so insistent we show up today. He needed to get Joey off of the estate grounds. He wanted me to witness my friend disappearing.

I pulled my own flashlight out of my bag to check the entire basement, but the further we walked, the more my hands started to shake. Finally, Jonah caught my wrist to take the flashlight away from me.

"Eva, give me that. You're making my stomach turn."

"Joey!" I called out into the darkness. "Dammit, where are you?"

I heard a thud in the corner not far from where I was standing, but before I could rush over, I saw Joey poke his head up.

"Geez, Evie. Calm down, will you? You're ruining my moment of triumph."

"What moment?" I rushed over to him, trying to decide if I should hit him or hug him. "You scared me, Joey. I thought—"

"That the baddies had gotten me?" He grinned. "Your reaction is sweet, but I'm kinda hurt that you didn't think I would be able to fight them off by myself. Just because I don't have a ceremonial sword—"

"Shut up." I grinned as I threw my arms around him. "What did you find?"

"This." Joey held up a gold watch, still shining despite the dirt we were surrounded by. "Looks familiar, no?"

I took the watch as Jonah and Joey both shined their lights on it. My friend was right. It was familiar.

It was the same watch I'd given Elliot as a graduation gift a couple years before. It was cheap, but the only thing I could afford at the time. I flipped it over to trace the words I knew I'd find there.

*Shoot for the stars – Love, Eva*

---

I had work to do.

I waited until everyone else had gone to bed except me, Cyrus, and Jonathan. After assuring Cyrus I would not move from my post on the couch, he and Jonathan went into the next room for yet another secret discussion.

I spent the next few hours on my tablet, researching the symbols we had found at the house. Despite the intense briefing by Jonathan, Reena, and Terrence over dinner, I had kept my conversation with George S. Covington secret. So when I came up with nothing on the symbols, I turned my attention to the message he had given me from Apollo.

"Lines cross." I muttered as I typed the phrase into the search bar. "What in the world could that mean?"

"What could what mean?" Jonah batted at my legs to make room for himself on the couch. "You know, talking to yourself is a sign of madness, Superstar."

"So I've heard." I scrolled through results that ranged from song lyrics to church websites. "Just—trying to put the pieces together."

"Care to share? Or am I going to have to stare at the back of your toy while you play with it?"

"No. Not yet." I lowered the tablet. "Why aren't you upstairs? I thought it was past your bedtime."

"One, I'm supposed to be glued to you, remember? A job I failed at miserably this afternoon. And two? I can't sleep."

"So you came to talk? About what?"

"Nothing. Anything." Jonah shrugged as he leaned back. "I'm not picky."

"Then I'm going back to my research." I lifted the tablet up to start typing again when he interrupted me.

"Eva, can I ask you a question?"

"Ah, the ulterior motive." I sat the tablet aside and folded my legs beneath me. "What's up, Blueberry?"

"What's the power of immortality when life never ends?"

I blinked twice as I considered what he said. I knew

what the Elevenths believed. I knew that death wasn't a real occurrence. In a way, they were right. The spirits I had encountered all knew who they were for the most part. They were alive on their own playing field. I started to answer with a smart remark, but the sincerity in this man's face was so strong, I couldn't do it. So I sighed and tapped my tablet against my knees.

"Jonah, do you believe in the theory that energy can't be destroyed, only changed?"

"What does that have to do with anything?" Jonah frowned as he leaned forward to link his hands together. "What does that have to do with my question?"

"Everything, really." I sat the tablet on the nearby table and sat cross legged to face him. "Death is only a label we use to describe what happens when someone leaves the physical world. Some believe that's it. That's the end. Most can't fathom the idea that they will lose their existence. This is where we come in. Both of us, in a way. We commune with spirits because we put energy into the belief that they are real. That energy helps them manifest for us. But we are only using our energies to call forth other energies. Whether it be the gods, monsters—or spirits."

"So what's the point of immortality?"

"It keeps me on the physical plane." I paused long enough to get my words in order. "The way I understand it, when I became the Sibyl, Apollo granted me the ability not to pass into Spirit, as you say. My physical body has been frozen to remain as it was when I was transformed. I'll never grow old, never get sick. I'll just be. Here, on the physical plane."

I was expecting a snarky remark. Or for him to argue with me. Instead, he gestured to the watch I'd placed on the table next to my tablet.

"So what's the story with Elliot's watch? You up to telling me that one?"

I picked up the watch and rubbed my thumb over its face as if I could turn back time with it. I could still remember how embarrassed I was to give it to him, but how happy it had made him. He had worn it up until the day he found out about me and Cyrus. Then, it became discarded, just as I had been, when he decided our friendship was over.

"We weren't together, if that's what you mean. I told you that much already." I put the watch back down on the table. "Elliot and I met at UGA. We were friends. Inseparable. He's the reason I became the Sibyl in the first place."

"I thought you had your abilities before then."

"No." I raised an eyebrow at him. "Elliot sold the show to his dad's company just after we graduated. They needed a pretty blonde girl stupid enough to run into the fire. That girl was me."

"But things changed."

"Don't they always?" I shrugged. "We had gone to a conference where my predecessor tricked me into saying the Sibyl's oath. She died—I'm sorry—passed into Spirit within minutes."

"I don't understand." Jonah frowned. "If the Sibyl is immortal—"

"The current Sibyl is immortal. But Apollo blessed us with a way to free ourselves when we grew tired of the life we experience. The mirror must be passed down to another woman willing to say the oath. Once that is done, you either commit suicide or turn into dust."

"Like those bad vampire movies from the '50s?" He grinned as I leaned up to punch him lightly on the arm. "Hey!"

"When are you going to tell me about your connection

to the Covington house?" I fell back against the pillow. "Old history, I believe you called it."

"When I'm ready. Which will probably be never." Jonah cleared his throat, turning his head away from me and towards the door. "I wonder what they've been talking about for so long."

"Things that neither of us will ever understand." I reached for the remote on the coffee table when an alert went off on my tablet. I swiped across the screen, pulled up the alert, and groaned out loud. "Great. This is exactly what I need right now."

"What?" Jonah tried to see the screen, but ended up taking the tablet away from me. "Another threat?"

"No. Worse."

I leaned over his shoulder to tap on the article Google had let me know about. I pulled it up for Jonah to see in all its glory.

The website was connected to a cheesy celebrity tabloid. Whatever. But it was the headline that made Jonah sit up straight along with the picture of the two of us standing close to each other on the porch at Covington.

*Ghost Girl Spotted With Mystery Writer*

"What? How?" He looked at me and back at the article so quick, I was sure he would sprain his neck. "What is this?"

I scrolled down, sighing as I read how a source told them I was in Rome, North Carolina filming an episode for *Grave Messages* , and how I'd stumbled across a new writer. There was even a quote from Kenneth Quinn, some literary agent I'd never heard of. He swore a book contract to any man associated with Eva McRayne since he would have to be a man with connections.

"Yay." I collapsed back against the couch.

"Congratulations, Jonah. You're now officially part of my world."

"Will this—who will see this?" He couldn't tear his eyes away from the screen. "This can't be news."

"Oh, it is. To the right people." I shrugged. "You get used to seeing yourself under fake headlines after a while. Besides, by the time the week is out, the gossip hounds will be onto someone else. I'm sure this will be forgotten."

"Jonah? Can you come in here please?" Jonathan called from his study, so I snatched my tablet back with a snicker.

"Somebody's in trouble." I said in a sing-songy voice. "You better go before you make it worse."

I laughed again as Jonah threw one last glare in my direction. I could have sworn I heard him utter one word as he walked past me.

"Brat."

# NINE

## JONAH ROWE

JONAH WISHED Eva hadn't mentioned the end of the week. He also wished that his only concern was a stupid news story.

Had it been any other time, he might have enjoyed seeing himself online. But it meant less than nothing right now.

Eva had an interesting viewpoint of things. A far better one than he'd thought. They were on the same wavelength on many things, but what she called energy, he called essence. Elliot and Hera's plan, apparently, all hinged on getting Eva on the Astral Plane.

Jonah didn't tell her, but he couldn't see that Eva had any advantages in this. As was established, Eva was 'immortal." But life never ended. It merely changed form. Despite both of those points, Elliot and Hera were sure that if they got Eva on the Astral Plane, it'd be game over.

Jonah's entire thought process occurred between the family room and Jonathan's study. It was amazing how much work the mind could do in a short period of time.

Cyrus left after he gave Jonah another appraising look.

Jonah didn't really care. He needed to see what was so important to Jonathan.

Standing at a massive bookshelf, Jonathan asked Jonah to take a seat. Because of Eva's quip about him being in trouble, he had a fleeting feeling of being in the principal's office, but Jonathan didn't give off an accusatory vibe. If anything, he was his usual inscrutable self.

Even when an image appeared out of nowhere. Jonah blinked as sunlight appeared in the study. It was nearly midnight. What the fuck?

A man formed out of the light and Jonah got his first good look at him. He was blonde. Chiseled like a young Paul Walker. Jonah noticed the golden eyes and he realized this was no ordinary visitor.

"Jonathan, you asked for me, old friend?" The two embraced hands warmly and created even more questions in Jonah's mind. "How can I assist you after you have done so much for my Eva?"

"I wanted to discuss some concerns that have developed regarding Cyrus' treatment of Eva. But first, please meet my student, Jonah Rowe."

"This is the Blue Aura?" Apollo greeted Jonah with a nod. "Nice to meet you. Jonathan brags about you quite often."

"Does he, now?" Jonah shook hands with the god. The *god*. Wow, what a week this was already. "I have *so* many questions to ask you when you have the time. But the pleasure is mutual, sir."

"Please, have a seat, Apollo." Jonathan waited until Apollo was situated next to Jonah before he sat across from them. "As I said, we have concerns regarding Cyrus' treatment of your Sibyl."

"What sort of concerns?"

"I, myself, have noticed Eva's demeanor towards him. She acts as one who has been abused."

"That is no surprise."

"What?" Jonah turned his full attention onto the god. "What does that mean?"

"Eva suffered severe abuse from her mother throughout her childhood. Physically, mentally, emotionally. I am not surprised to learn that she responds to Cyrus in the same manner."

"Sir, first off, that's horrible, but with respect, it's more." Jonah shifted in his seat. "Cyrus treats Eva like she's his kid. He's like a domineering spouse. He cuts across her when she tries to speak. Like, *every* time. And that night with the Shades, he grabbed her roughly enough to bruise her."

"Was this during the battle?" Apollo asked.

"No, sir," Jonah said. "All the Shades had been put down. When confronted about it, he made no apologies and basically said that Eva needed to be toughened up."

Apollo raised an eyebrow as Jonah detailed the exchange. Then, Jonah remembered something else.

"Earlier, before we went to the Covington House, I noticed a large impact bruise on Eva's arm. It hadn't been there after the fight with the Shades."

"And her response when you asked her about it?"

"That she hit her arm on a door frame. I didn't press her on it, but I believe Cyrus punched her arm after the fight."

"Eva would have come to me if that was the case."

"Not necessarily." Jonah took another breath. "She told me about the clause where a keeper's actions can nullify her immortality. I think she is afraid he will kill her."

"Do you have any further proof?" Apollo leaned forward and clasped his hands together. "These are grave accusations against a slave who has been in my employ for over a millenia. I must know everything before I act."

"No concrete proof, sir," Jonah said. "Only that he seems to relish it and calls it strict discipline and old-school training."

"Then let's ask him."

"Are you serious?"

"Of course."

Apollo closed his eyes. A moment later, Cyrus appeared.

"Yes, m'lord."

"Sit down, Creten. I have something I wish to discuss with you."

Cyrus sat down. His eyes flickered over to Jonathan before he turned his focus back on Apollo.

"I am hearing disturbing accounts of the actions you have taken against my Sibyl. How do you respond?"

Jonah eyed Cyrus. His poker face was flawless, but something in his eyes flashed. "I'm afraid you have me at a disadvantage, my lord. Whatever do you mean?"

"Reports of disrespect and bruising my Sibyl in her private room."

"M'lord, the reports you are hearing are false. If Rowe is the one you have spoken to, then he has his own motivations."

"It was I who brought this up, Cyrus," Jonathan said. "Jonah was unaware of this meeting until I called it. So I must say that the fact that you were so quick to pounce on Jonah means you may be concealing something."

"I believe that Jonah may have spoken to you and you called this meeting."

"You have yet to answer for the accusations levied against you."

"They are false, m'lord. My task is to protect Eva. Not harm her."

"Why is it you have such caustic manners toward Jonah?" Jonathan asked. "You keep wanting to throw it back to him. Jonah told me nothing. It was I, in fact, that voiced concern about your behaviors. So if you desire is to be cold to someone, aim it at me. I should be the object of your irritation, unless of course, we're wrong."

"Rowe knows the source of my irritation." Cyrus snorted. "He has constantly insulted me and challenged my role as Eva's guard. Naturally, I would assume that he has made these accusations. I apologize to Rowe if I was wrong. As far as Eva is concerned, she has made no complaints to me regarding her treatment. This, I believe, is unnecessary interference."

"It is unnecessary interference because you've scared her into being silent about it." Jonah said.

Cyrus rose from his seat, but so did Jonathan and Apollo. When Cyrus saw that, he backed down. Jonah scoffed. Fucking bully.

"I have never gotten even the slightest inclination that Eva is afraid of me." Cyrus tucked his hands in his pockets. "I'm truly at a loss here."

"I believe it is time to speak with Eva on this matter. Cyrus, leave us."

Cyrus gave both Jonathan and Jonah a look of disgust before he vanished. Jonah headed to the door.

"She's in the living room. I'll go get her."

"Very well."

It didn't take long for Jonah to ask Eva to join them in the study. She was surprised, but she was even more surprised to find Apollo waiting.

"You're here? I thought-"

"The estate is neutral ground, my dear. Please. Have a seat."

"What's this about?" Eva asked as she sat down then crossed her legs at the ankle. "Is everything alright?"

"We are concerned for your wellbeing." Apollo spoke from his position beside her. "Answer my questions honestly, alright?"

"I'll try."

"Alright. Has Cyrus ever harmed you out of anger?"

The color completely drained out of Evas face as she stared at Apollo.

"I can't talk about that."

Apollo's golden eyes flashed. Jonah actually stepped back.

"So that's a yes," He said. "Has he threatened you if you said anything to anyone?"

"Look," Eva took a deep breath. "You know how forceful Cyrus can be-"

"Forceful in the ring is different than outside of it."

"He can kill me," She hissed. "You were the one who created that clause. If he knows I've said anything, there's no telling what could happen to me."

"When did this start?"

Eva covered her face with her hands then sat up after a moment.

"Does it even matter? Truly?"

"It matters to me." Apollo replied. "You matter, Eva."

"Sure, I do," Her tone became bitter. "You realize that no matter what you do to him, he's just going to turn around and put it right back on me, right?"

"Has he done that before?"

"Yes," The bitterness left her voice only to be replaced with resignation. "Yes, alright? Cyrus has hurt me before in anger. I can't tell you when it started because I don't remember all that much about it. I think it was after the Erinyes episode but I just...I just don't remember."

"Huh?" Jonah looked around the room. "Any particular reason she wouldn't recall?"

Apollo's jaw tightened before he spoke. "There are two reasons why Eva could be suffering from forgetfulness. The first is a head injury. The second is a method called Keeper's Restraint that allows keepers to wipe the minds of those they come in contact with."

Jonah's eyes narrowed. "Do you mean to say Cyrus could have been abusing Eva all this time and then wiping it away, like a damn Etch-A-Sketch?"

"It's possible." Apollo studied Eva. "But there are instances you remember?"

"Yes."

"What happened?"

"Why does it matter?"

"So I can confront him about his treatment towards you." Apollo was shockingly patient. "Jonah mentioned a bruise on your arm. He said you hit the door jam. May I see it?"

"Fine." Eva pushed up her sleeve to expose a large black and purple bruise. "Happy?"

"When did this happen?"

"This afternoon."

Apollo took her arm and examined it. "You should have been healed by now."

"I should be, but I am also being affected. My immortality is going in and out."

"The keeper did this?"

Eva sighed. "Look, don't make me say anything else. Please. It's just easier that way."

"Easier on who? Him?"

"No. Me."

"Why is that, Eva?" Jonathan asked. "Has Cyrus petrified you so absolutely that you're afraid to seek help at all? We are here for you, darling, if you need us. But you must help us help you."

Eva looked at Jonathan as Apollo put his hand over the center of the bruise. It faded instantly. When he released her arm, she pulled her sleeve back down.

"Thank you. And to answer your question, Jonathan, it's more than fear. It's nice to think someone out there can save you from...from things like this. But I have to be realistic about it. There is no help for people like me. No white knight. Once I accepted that, it became easier to keep my heart from being broken by disappointment when no one ever came."

Jonah winced. Eva couldn't have said a sadder thing if she tried. Apollo stood up. Calm, but frighteningly so.

"Eva, we will have further conversations about this when times are less dire," He said. "You all convene and handle the next steps. I will need to converse with my Keeper. He'll be back the morrow next."

"You think one conversation will put him in line?" Jonah couldn't help but ask.

Apollo turned to Jonah slowly. "One conversation with an all-powerful god of Olympus? Yes."

Eva said nothing as Apollo clasped her shoulder. He then shook hands with both Jonah and Jonathan.

"Thank you, old friend, for bringing this darkness into the light."

With that, Apollo vanished. Eva rubbed her hands over her face before she dropped them to her lap.

"May I be excused now? This has been a very difficult conversation and I wish to be alone."

"Of course."

Jonathan and Jonah watched her go before Jonathan turned to Jonah.

"You were right to be concerned, son. You should be proud of yourself."

"I am," Jonah said. "There is...more to this than I could believe, sir. I don't know what Cyrus is used to, but he ain't getting it here."

"Indeed." Jonathan went to the other side of his desk and sat down. "You met Hera as well today, did you not?"

"Cyrus tell you that?"

"He did."

"Yeah, of course he did," Jonah muttered. "Wasn't the most pleasant experience."

"One thing I have learned over the years is that there are gods you can trust and others who want to use you for their own personal gain. All I can counsel you is to be wary of any promises that are not sworn on the Styx."

"Noted, sir." Jonah nodded. "I'll bear that in mind."

“I also wanted to speak to you about going into the Covington House once again. That had to take a toll.”

What irony. A situation that Jonah didn’t want to discuss was a welcome distraction from the current subject. “Did you know about the graves in that underground room?”

Jonathan snorted. “Why do you think Creyton was attracted to the place?”

“Oh,” muttered Jonah, “But what I don’t understand is why Elliot and Hera wanted us there.”

“There is something that I’ve learned,” He said in a solemn tone as he sat back in his chair. “I learned it from George S. Covington, the patriarch of the Covington brood. It turns out that Rome, North Carolina is a place where the lines cross—”

Jonathan froze, and his eyes drifted to the left.

"Something is wrong," He said to Jonah. "Something foreign is on the grounds."

Just then, Reena burst in, with a yellow gleaming javelin in her hands.

"We have a problem." She looked furious. "More Shades are in the front yard. About twenty of them."

"What?" demanded Jonah. "But Cyrus and Jonathan shored up the defenses!"

"I know," said Reena. "But the Shades out there didn't get the memo."

---

Everyone else was already on the front porch of the estate. There were nearly two dozen Shades on the grounds, jeering, taunting, and inching nearer and nearer to them.

Despite her desire to be alone, Jonah spotted Eva with her sword at the ready. She caught sight of them and called out to Jonathan.

"Why aren't they up here tearing us apart?" She called out. "Not that I'm complaining, but I don't get it."

"I am a Protector Guide," Jonathan responded. "The home of my students is shielded. No foe will ever cross the threshold while I'm on these grounds."

Just then, a Shade proved the point by attempting to leap on the porch. It got knocked back and landed in a heap almost fifty feet away.

"Hell yeah!" shouted Terrence. "Knocked you on your ass!"

But it was only a brief comfort. The Shades were getting closer and closer to the porch. It seemed like they gained new ground with every step. Jonah didn't know how much longer they'd have safe ground. He remembered what Elliot said about breaching the estate "soon enough". How did he plan to manage that?

"What was that, Jonah?" Reena demandes out of nowhere.

"What was what?" asked Jonah.

"I read familiarity in your essence," said Reena. "What do you know?"

Jonah felt his mouth tighten. He'd known Reena for a while now, but it was still unnerving when she did that essence reading.

"When Elliot was doing that Astral projection, he said that soon enough, he'd be able to breach the estate itself," He told her. "I was wondering how he planned to do that. Did he have an in of some kind? A placeholder, token—?"

And then it hit him.

"The watch!" He shouted.

"What watch?" said Terrence.

Jonah rounded on Eva. "That watch you picked up at Covington House. Elliot must have planted it there. He must have done something to it, or Hera did, more likely. You brought it back here. It's got to be what's weakening our defenses!"

Eva tensed. "That's why he was so sure that he'd get in here soon. He did something dark to the one thing he knew I'd pick up."

"Where is it?"

"In the living room still. On the side table."

"Go get it!" said Joey. "Make a run for it. Why this house has to be so damn big—"

"No time!" said Reena. "Who knows how much headway the Shades will make while that thing sits in there, weakening our home! Terrence, take this!"

She tossed the javelin to him, which shifted from yellow

to burnt orange as it changed spiritually endowed hands. Reena stepped into thin air and vanished.

"What the hell?"

"It's the Astralimes!" shouted Jonah. "She'll be back—"

Reena stepped out of thin air as suddenly as she'd stepped into it, clutching the damned watch. She held it out in front of her and ran off of the porch using her ethereal speed.

A strange phenomena occurred. The more distance Reena put between that watch and the estate, the further the scope of the ground's defenses stretched, which repelled the Shades. She kept running—they kept getting pushed back farther and farther—.

She ran down the drive, and there was silence.

Eva looked here and there. "Where is she?"

"Be patient," said Jonathan. "We'll know soon enough."

Jonah stared at the dark drive like it was the only place on Earth.

*Come on, Reena.*

Then a blur raced up the drive and ceased at the steps. Reena's hair looked windswept—no surprise there—and her breathing was only a bit heavy.

"Jonathan, they're gone," She announced. "The ground's protection is restored. I pushed the Shades so far back that they were forced to retreat. Elliot won't be getting in here that way."

Eva actually pushed Jonah aside and placed a hand on Reena's shoulder. "I don't know you very well," She said, "but damn I'm glad you're on our team!"

# TEN

## EVA MCRAYNE

I STAYED OUTSIDE on the porch long after the others had returned inside. Not that I was alone. Jonah hung back, watching me. I was sure he believed I would break down after this latest attack by my enemy so soon after my confession to Apollo. But I wasn't about to panic. That would give Elliot power. It would allow him the opportunity to weaken me.

I'd be damned if I did that. Elliott had already infringed on my sanity one time too many.

"You gonna hang out here all night, Superstar?" Jonah gave up his post by the front door to come up behind me. "Cause there's really no point in searching for more fighters. They're gone."

"I'm not waiting on an army." I shook my head. "I'm waiting on the paparazzi."

It wasn't a total lie. The press hounds—independent or otherwise—had started showing up at our locations, hoping to get a glimpse at the great Eva McRayne. Daughter of Apollo. Messenger of the Dead. So many stories had been made up about me. So many lies had graced the covers of tabloids that I'd come to expect the sharks to start circling the moment I landed in a new town. And with the story I'd found online, it was only a matter of hours before they showed up.

I couldn't think about the Shades. I couldn't acknowledge the fact that Elliot had used such a sweet memory against me.

I closed my eyes as I thought about my interaction with Reena after the Shades had been pushed back. I'd been so ecstatic over her actions that I had thanked her. Told her I was glad she was on our side. Her response had been unexpected, but it shouldn't have surprised me.

I would have said the same thing in her position.

"I am not on your team, Sibyl." Reena had shaken me off. "I am protecting my home. Our home, to which your presence is posing a serious threat."

She took Terrence by the arm to go inside after Jonathan, but she turned to face me when she reached the door. "I may not question my mentor, but I do not have to like his decisions. You leave nothing but imbalance in your wake. I want nothing to do with you during the remainder of your time at the Grannison-Morris estate."

Her words were right, of course. I had become a symbol of hope to millions, but as a result, my presence had caused harm to so many who interacted with me. It could be so easy to release myself from this life. Get the mirror back from Apollo. Find another girl stupid enough to take my place. Run out in front of a car just as Katherine Carter, my predecessor, had done. Perhaps then, I could find peace.

And Elliot would win. That single thought alone was enough to pull me out of the self-pity I'd wallowed in.

"They can't follow you on these lands." Jonah leaned against the banister beside me. "And I told you how bad of a liar you are, right? Try again. What are you really thinking about?"

"Reena," I brushed a strand of gold from my eyes. "She's right, you know. I do bring imbalance in my wake. I do cause nothing but trouble. She's right not to want to have anything to do with me. You shouldn't want anything to do with me, either."

"You really are a defeatist, Superstar," Jonah observed. "I thought I was bad."

"Only the best for you, Blueberry," I nudged his arm with mine. "All or nothing. That's what I got to offer."

Jonah held up a joint. "Interested?"

"Gods, no," I shook my head. "Can't partake in that. Strictly speaking."

"Is that a Cyrus rule?"

"Yeah, but it's also a general rule."

"Suit yourself," Jonah put it in his mouth and lit it with a match. He took a drag then leaned back against the banister. "You ok, Eva? That meeting in the study-"

"Was a nightmare." I sighed. "I can't believe I ended up saying anything at all."

"Why is that?"

"Because it's not going to change anything. The most I can hope for is that things don't get worse."

"Seriously?" Jonah asked. "You think Apollo is that ineffective?"

"I think that Apollo means well. He always has. But he's not omnipresent."

"Yeah, but still. He can strike the fear of God - well, the gods - into Cyrus."

"If he was going to do that, he would have done that a long time ago, Blueberry. And I wouldn't be dealing with this shit now."

I saw the tip of his joint brightened as he inhaled. I gestured at it.

"How do you do that?"

"Weed? Pain management and stress relief. Never seen a stoner?"

"No," I laughed. "That's not what I meant. How do you smoke?"

"You never smoked before? Even cigarettes?"

"Once or twice in college, but our coach was exceedingly against it for obvious reasons. So I never got the hang of it."

"You really should partake," Jonah said. "If Bigfoot has an issue with it, get edibles or brownies."

"Let me try it."

"Seriously?"

"Well, yeah. Unless you don't want my mouth on it. Otherwise, give me the other one sticking out of your shirt pocket."

Jonah scoffed and passed his joint. "Follow the rules and regulations."

"Puff, puff, pass?"

Jonah grinned. "I see you are familiar with the rules and regulations."

I laughed. "I did go to college, you know. Those rules were taught during orientation."

I pulled on the joint and held it in for as long as I could. I released the smoke and closed my eyes as a very calm feeling came over me.

"That's nice," I passed it back to him. "I was expecting a coughing fit."

"You're more resilient than you thought, Superstar."

"That goes against the defeatist mindset, you know."

I watched him take his hit in the moonlight and wondered if he knew how good he looked. No wonder the

Sirens had wanted him. I took the joint back when he passed it to me.

"True, but I'm feeling good, so I don't want to focus on that mindset."

I blew out the smoke and passed it back.

"Tell me something good then."

"Like what?" Jonah knocked the ash off the banister. "What do you want to hear?"

"Something positive. I don't want to think about anything remotely negative right now."

"Well, this weed is absolutely amazing," Jonah murmured. "So there is that. Your turn."

"Let me see. I'm on an amazing estate," I took the joint and then my hit. "For the first time in a very long time, I'm completely relaxed and I'm getting to hang out with a pretty cool mystery writer. So there's that."

I passed the joint back to him.

"Are you ok? We haven't really talked about all the shit you've been exposed to over the past couple of days."

"Been used to weirdness, to be honest," Jonah replied. "Life ain't been normal for a while."

"I'm not even sure what normal means anymore."

"Eh, who needs normal? It's boring."

"You don't think you could go back to just....a normal life?"

"Not even," Jonah said. "I can't un-know everything I've learned. Normal would just drive me batshit at this point."

Jonah took the last hit off his joint and stubbed it out in an ashtray that sat on a table not far from where I was standing.

"Are you ready to go inside now?"

"Yeah, I suppose so. Thanks for sharing with me."

Jonah opened the front door and held it for me. I

walked past him then headed for the stairs. I stopped when he called out from behind me.

"Let me walk you up."

"Ok," I tilted my head as he crossed over to me. "You don't have to. I'm getting the hang of the layout and Cyrus isn't here. I think you deserve a night in your own bed, Blueberry."

"It would be nice to sleep on a mattress tonight."

"My point exactly." I started to walk up. "So take tonight off."

"No offense, but I think I will. It's been a hell of a couple of days."

I didn't say anything until I reached my room door. Jonah didn't, either. I started to open it before I leaned against it to speak.

"Good night, Blueberry. Thanks again. For everything."

Jonah gave me a nod. "Good night."

I watched him head down the hall before I went inside my room. I felt lighter from the joint, that was true. But I was also exhausted from the events of the day. Between losing time, the Covington House, and the conversation with Apollo, I just wanted to bury my head under my pillow and never wake up.

Despite my exhaustion, I took my time getting ready for bed. I didn't allow myself to worry about the aftermath of my conversation with Apollo. I knew there would be one. And I didn't allow myself to think about Reena's sharp words either. She was right. That's all there was to it.

"Rowe has made a deal with Hera. He has made plans to betray you."

I froze in the middle of braiding my hair when I caught sight of Cyrus' reflection behind me. His eyes colder than I had ever seen them.

"What are you doing here? Apollo said-"

"I haven't reported to Apollo yet. I am doing my duty to you before I go."

"Cyrus, I-"

"Rowe will betray you." He repeated. "Hera met with him at the Covington House. Do you want to know what she offered him?"

I felt sick from his words. A part of me knew that he was just doing this to hurt me. Another part of me wished he would just strike out instead. Physical wounds never lasted as long as emotional ones.

"Jonah isn't the type to betray someone."

"Oh, he very much is, Eva," Cyrus sneered at me. "Since you won't ask, I'll tell you. You will be the price for fame, the key to the Other Side, and the woman he is in love with."

The actress. I swallowed the knot forming in my throat. I should have known better than to hope for someone like Jonah. I was racked with a sense of disappointment so strong, I fell back against the sink.

There are no white knights. I knew this. The fact that I had dared to hope for one made me feel absolutely stupid.

"Poor Sibyl. What did you expect?" Cyrus closed the distance between us. "Did you expect love at first sight? Did you expect that Rowe would sweep you away from me? I will take my punishment from Apollo and be right back by your side the moment he allows it. You will never be rid of me. Never."

"Please leave." I whispered. "Please. I just want to go to bed. We'll...we'll talk later."

"Indeed we shall."

Cyrus grabbed me, covered my mouth with one hand, and slammed his fist into my side twice. I squeezed my eyes shut to keep my tears from falling as a flash of fire raced through my blood strong enough to erase my disappointment. I caught myself on the counter as he released me.

"Until next time, bitch."

He stepped back and was gone. I stayed in that spot, hunched over the sink as bile rose up in my throat. I felt sick from the pain, but once it passed, I cradled my side and moved over to the bed. I turned off the lamp and stretched out in the darkness as tears leaked out from my eyes.

I told myself not to cry. I told myself that everything was going as expected, so there was no point in tears. But that didn't stop them as I buried my face into my pillow and sobbed myself to sleep with only one thought in mind.

There would never be a white knight for me. Ever.

---

I wasn't at Grannison-Morris anymore. I took in the marble hall where I stood. I frowned and started walking. There were always answers to my questions. This would be no different.

I heard the sounds of laughter coming from a room not far from me, so I sped up until I reached the door. I started to knock until I realized it was cracked open. I leaned forward and pressed my face against the cold wood to see inside.

A woman was seated on a man's lap. I couldn't hear what she was saying, but I didn't need to hear what she said to know what was going on. I was witness to a very private moment. I started to back away until the man turned his face into the low light and I could see his profile.

Jonah. He grabbed the woman's hair to pull her into a kiss. I stared at the scene in shock. I shouldn't be watching this. I didn't need to be spying like this.

I couldn't pull away.

"Vera Halliday." Hera whispered into my ear as she appeared behind me. "The woman who has Jonah's heart. She will be his the moment he gets you on the Astral Plane."

"Why are you showing me this, Hera?" I didn't dare to turn away from the scene in front of me. "I've only known Jonah for two days-"

"Oh, but you have already fallen in love with him." The goddess waved a hand to open the door to give me a better view. "But your emotions are wasted. The scene you see before you is one of two people who are madly in love. An emotion you will never get to experience."

"I'm with Cyrus."

Hera's laughter rang in my ears. I crossed my arms over my chest as I stared at the wall above Jonah's head.

"Cyrus doesn't love you. He can't stand you. No one can stand you. Your own mother tried to kill you more than once."

I closed my eyes at her words. I knew they were true.

"So you see, little Sibyl, it doesn't matter how much wealth or power you steal from the Council. You will always be alone. No one - not Cyrus, not even the country bumpkin who barely has two pennies to rub together, will ever love you."

"What do you know about love, anyway? The mother of monsters—"

My voice trailed off as Hera smiled and shook her head.

"Oh, I am more than just the mother of monsters. I am the force of divinity behind a happy home. Marriage. Love. These are my realms, Sibyl. Yours is just departed spirits. Decay. Tragedies best left forgotten to time and the grave."

I did not respond to her as the scene progressed. Just moments ago, they were kissing. Now, they were naked. I tried to block the images. I didn't want to feel the hole in my chest that was forming. It shouldn't matter. Jonah and his actress shouldn't matter.

But they did.

"Take a look, girl. Look at what has been denied to you.Take a look at the dreams the Blue Aura is having at this very moment."

Hera then spoke with a whisper, but she may as well have shouted her next words. I heard them loud and clear.

"You are alone, little Sibyl. Your burgeoning affections? False. Your god? Helpless. You are mine to destroy whenever I choose to do so. You cannot remain in existence. You are too much of a threat to all I hold dear."

Her cold smile gave way to an expression of pure, undiluted hatred. But I barely noticed it. Her last words sounded eerily similar to what the Shade told me about being a 'threat to harmony.' What did they mean?

Hera disappeared, and the image of Jonah and that actress shifted into one of Hera and Elliot. It was the same scene I had witnessed firsthand in Montana.

Elliot declaring his hatred of me. He bowed his head before Hera as he swore his spirit to her service. How he had fought so hard against me in an attempt to strike me down.

"I will take anyone you have ever loved away from you. But alas, you can make this much easier on yourself."

Yet, as my memories faded from view, I still couldn't see her when her voice returned.

"You can relinquish your power. Allow those who are only tolerating you to know peace. Otherwise, I will finish what I have started. I will extinguish you and all who choose to align themselves with your service."

I woke up with a sharp pain in my side where Cyrus had hit me, but I ignored it. Hera's threat still echoed in my ears. I tried to tell myself it was just a dream.

I tried to explain it away as a product of too many months as her target. Yet, I knew better. She had already taken so much away from me.

Something was—different about Hera and the way she regarded me. It was as if her hate and anger seemed a bit sharper. A bit more focused. What was that about?

I kicked the covers aside as I wiped away the tears from the pain formed in the corners of my eyes. The scene of Jonah and Vera burned hot in my mind, but I shoved it aside. I needed to talk to him. I needed to know if what Cyrus and Hera had said were true. Had he made a deal with her? Was he really going to sell me out for the life of his dreams?

That was a stupid question. Who wouldn't sell out the girl they had only known for two days for the things they had always wanted?

I gritted my teeth as I headed out into the hallway. My side was throbbing now. So much so, I had to bite my tongue to keep from whimpering. My skin was slick with blood. Something was wrong, but I didn't want to consider it. The physical pain would pass. It always did. But the pain in my heart? The pain I felt when Cyrus told me that Jonah was dead set on betraying me?

I had to talk to Jonah. He would be straight with me. I knew it. And if it meant so much to him, then I would go willingly. Jonah deserved the life Hera promised him. He deserved to be happy.

Just as I deserved to be forgotten.

I leaned against the doorway as I considered what Cyrus had told me earlier. Jonah didn't seem like the type who would betray anyone. Granted, I hadn't known him long, but so far? He seemed trustworthy. Not to mention how he and I seemed to click once we dropped our guards.

A lie I had told myself. I'd never had an actual friend

before. Cyrus was right. The only reason Joey stuck around was because he had to. Hera was right, too. I really was alone.

I waited for the next round of throbbing in my side to disappear before I straightened my shoulders to head for Jonah's bedroom. If he was dreaming about Vera, then his dream would just have to wait a little longer.

I didn't get very far before Jonathan rounded the corner. He stopped and bowed his head to me.

"Is there anything I can help you find, Eva?" Jonathan gave me a small smile. "I heard from Jonah that this house is far too large."

"No," I hugged myself as a chill raced through my bones. "Actually, yes. There is. I need to speak with Jonah immediately."

"Of course." Jonathan took my arm. I tried not to lean on him too hard. I didn't want him to know that I was hurting like I was. "He is with the others in Reena's art studio. Shall I take you there?"

So he wasn't in the midst of some erotic dream. At least there was that.

I nodded. "Thank you. You are very kind to your students, Jonathan. An art studio?"

"Indeed." The man nodded as we walked. "I discovered decades ago that happiness breeds peace. All Eleventh Percenters are artistic. In Reena's case, her painting brings her happiness. It helps her focus."

"I could use some of that, you know." I sighed as we turned down yet another hallway. "Happiness."

Jonathan was quiet for a moment before he patted my hand. "Eva, please know, if there is anytime you need a retreat, then you and yours are welcome here at Grannison-Morris estate."

"I appreciate your offer, but I don't think your students

would be too happy about that." I gave him a sad smile as we stopped at the end of a hallway. "But one never knows. Thank you, Jonathan."

The Protector Guide bowed at me once more before retracing his steps. I could hear Terrence's voice coming from a few doors down, so I headed that way. Yet, I stopped just before the door when I heard a conversation already in progress. Yeah, I was eavesdropping, but I was too numb by what I was hearing to care.

# ELEVEN

## JONAH ROWE

"THAT WAS HARSH, Reena. She actually showed concern for your well-being!"

"I couldn't give less of a damn, Terrence. That woman is bad news. We didn't have this many attacks last fall, and at that time, we were dealing with vampires and sazers!"

Jonah let them go on like that forever. Terrence would make a passionate point, Reena would counter, Terrence would take a different route, Reena would counter that, and so on. They hadn't hung out in Reena's art studio for awhile, so it was a welcome refuge. If Jonah had to deal with Terrence and Reena's bickering, so be it. It took listening to their argument for him to build up the nerve to say the thing that would shut them up.

"Hera wants me to betray Eva."

It was guaranteed to work, and work it did. Terrence and Reena ceased as soon as he finished and looked at him in shock.

"Yep," He said once he felt eyes on him. "She appeared in a mirror at the Covington House and showed me fame. Showed me a reality where I was a prolific novelist. My books were the best of the best of the best . She showed me wearing suits that cost more than a car. She also showed me…other stuff."

Some of Reena's usual nature permeated her shock.

"Oh good grief, Jonah. We aren't in the third grade," She muttered. "Did Hera show you an image of you fucking someone? Namely, Vera?"

Jonah rubbed his eyes, ticked off and embarrassed. "Put the damn dampener back on."

"I'm wearing it, Jonah," Reena shot back. "I can't have it off around Eva and Cyrus. Their essences are so full of baggage that they could sink a cruise liner. It was simply written on your face that you saw some sort of carnal vision. Given how unnerved you are, it must have looked great to you."

"Can we please get back on task?" interrupted Jonah. "Can we do that, please? There is more. Hera also promised a way to the Other Side. She claimed it could be done."

Terrence's eyes narrowed somewhat. "So that's your dilemma? You think you might have a chance to see your grandmother again?"

Jonah closed his eyes. Nana. What he wouldn't give to see her again. But he didn't bring it up. It was old news. But Hera said it could be done.

The bitch was evil. She was calculating, and she made no secret of it. But she dangled the one carrot that gave Jonah the most pause.

It sickened him.

"The thing is, Cyrus knows that Hera showed me things," He said, ignoring Terrence's question. "Yeah, he's gone temporarily, but the second he gets back, you know he is going to turn her against us."

"What was Jonathan thinking when he approved this?" Reena demanded. "He brought this insanity into our home!

I admit that I was willing to give Eva a chance, but she's nothing but trouble. Plain and simple."

"She ain't the problem, Reena!" Terrence insisted. "It's Hera! And that Elliot guy! She is not a threat to us. How many times have people got the drop on us when we least expected it? Eva is a great woman. Let me tell you something about Eva. Do you know she grew up in a house on Sullivan's Island? A house that sold for millions? She refused to take a single penny from the sale and insisted the funds be donated to a victim's advocacy group in South Carolina. The Skinwalker episode? Won her a Primetime Emmy that she gave to a battered women's shelter. Eva did a special on it. Said these women were the true heroes who fight silent battles every day. Now tell me: would a fucking evil bitch do or say something like that?"

"Yes, actually," said Reena. "Celebrities know how to send the right message with the proper PR. You know how many corporate asswipes do charity work?"

Terrence roared in frustration. "Reena! This is serious!"

"You think I'm joking?" Reena snarled. "It's been serious, Terrence! It was serious when Jonah was attacked by the Sirens! It was serious when Elliot—a Tenth Percenter, might I remind you—was on the Astral Plane playing mind games! It was serious when Eva got attacked by Shades, and then brought back that stupid trinket that weakened our defenses! Who knows what would have happened if I hadn't gotten that watch in time? And now, Cyrus is going to twist her mind to see us as the bad guys?"

"You turned Eva against you, Reena," said Terrence. "She said that she was happy that you were on her team!"

"I, unlike you, am not so easily flattered, Terrence," said Reena. "Your stupid crush is blinding you. Eva doesn't give a damn about you. She doesn't give a damn about any of us.

She's made that clear from the moment she stepped off the plane!"

"Enough, guys," said Jonah wearily. "Terrence, you've made your point. Reena, you've made your point clear as a bright and sunny day. But this is on me. Hera tried to bribe me. Goddess of family, my ass. Maybe the goddess of those families on Steve Wilkos, or something. But Reena, think about when Jonathan rescued you from foster care after your uncle passed into Spirit. Think about when he welcomed Terrence into the fold. Think about when he rescued me after I learned that I was the Blue Aura. He could have ignored us all, but he didn't. He gave us the time of day, and now we're better people because of that. That said, I won't abandon Eva. No matter what lies Cyrus has put in her head about me. Jonathan did it for us, and now, we have the chance to do it for somebody else. This is our zone, and she is an outsider in danger. Elliott, probably because of Hera, is using a mixture of Greek magick and dark ethereality to fuck with us. There is also something about lines being crossed, but—"

"How would you know that?" a voice demanded.

Jonah whipped around. Eva was leaning against the door frame of Reena's art studio.

"How long have you been there?" He asked her.

"Long enough to know that you know information that was given exclusively to me at Covington House," answered Eva. "Jonathan said you'd be down here, so I came to talk to you. Hera showed me a vision, too."

"Are you alright? You're pale, Eva."

She didn't answer his question. "How do you know about lines crossing?"

"From Jonathan," Jonah muttered.

"What does he know about it?"

"I don't know," Jonah shrugged. "He didn't get past the phrase. That was when the Shades showed up."

Eva flashed an awkward look at Reena, and then returned her eyes to Jonah.

"Be straight with me, Rowe," She held her arms around her tighter. "Did you agree to hand me over to Hera?"

Through his alarm, irritation surfaced in Jonah. So he was back to Rowe now?

"What? No. She is trying to bribe me to do it."

"So you haven't said "yes"."

"Of course, I didn't."

Eva stared at him for several seconds then spoke again. "What does she want you to do?"

Jonah ran his tongue across his teeth. "She wants me to get you on the Astral Plane by the Golden Hour on Sunday."

At that, Eva looked hurt. She actually looked hurt.

"Hera was right. Cyrus was right."

"Now that ain't fair!" Jonah said, incensed. "That dude doesn't even know me! And the fact that I admitted what Hera wanted me to do speaks volumes!"

"And the fact that you didn't tell me right away speaks volumes, too," Eva countered. "You know, I thought we'd made progress, but you know what they say about first impressions."

"But I wasn't—"

"Hera wants me on the Astral Plane on Sunday?" Eva spoke over Jonah. "She promised you the life of your dreams? Fine. You tell me when we need to leave and I will go willingly. Maybe then I can finally be worth something."

"Now, wait a damn minute-" Jonah started before Terrence interrupted him.

"But what about the episode?"

Eva looked troubled, like that thought hadn't occurred

to her. Painstakingly, she put her defiant mask back on. "I'll think of something."

She turned to walk away, but then clutched at her side with a gasp and collapsed. If Reena hadn't used her ethereal speed to catch her, she'd have fallen face first onto the floor.

"What the hell!" Jonah joined Reena at her side with Terrence bringing up the rear. Reena must have suspended her dislike for Eva, because she fervently checked over her prone body.

Reena placed her fingers over Eva, and they gleamed the yellow of her aura. She then reached down to press her hand against Eva's dark shirt. When she raised her hand back up, her palm was covered in blood.

"Reena, what happened?" Jonah demanded. "Is it Cyrus? I thought he was gone!"

She raised her hand to her temple, focused very hard on something, and seconds later, Jonathan appeared from nowhere. Their mentor knelt down next to Eva without asking questions. His eyes widened within moments as he tugged at her shirt. A wicked gash lined her side. Her skin smeared with her blood.

"What, Jonathan?" asked Jonah.

"Her Sybil powers keep fading in and out," He told them. "That means the immortality fades in and out as well. Her previous wound from Athena's Blade has been reopened. We must give the girl time. There is nothing more we can do."

# TWELVE

## EVA MCRAYNE

I DON'T KNOW how to describe what happened next. One minute, I was on my way back to my room. The next?

I was standing over myself as the Elevenths circled around my body. I wanted to tell them I was fine. That if Reena would move out of the way, I'd wake myself up. But as Jonah studied me, I saw something I never thought possible.

He was concerned. Why? I meant next to nothing to Jonah. Between our bitchy first meeting to his talk with Hera, he had shown that time and time again. He only spent time with me because his mentor had forced him to.

Jonah lifted me up in his arms and turned to Jonathan. "I got her. Let's take her to the infirmary."

"Of course."

Jonathan gestured down the hall and they took off in that direction. I felt as if I should have followed. In fact, I started to head after them. But as I passed by a window, I froze into place.

I could see the grounds of Grannison-Morris estate glowing beneath me. I mean, literally glowing a strange pulsating light. I changed direction to approach the window and gasped as I pressed against the glass. From here, I could see the source of the white light was a perfect line slashed into the earth. It was strangely beautiful.

"Magnetic field lines."

I turned to see Apollo step out of the shadows to stand beside me. I frowned as he stuffed his hands into his suit.

We hadn't had a proper conversation since I discovered that he was my father. Not really. I didn't count the conversation about Cyrus.

I wondered how to approach the subject. How to feel. What to say. But before I could even try, he shook his head.

"Spare yourself, Evie. The details of our blood ties are a matter for another day. There are more pressing issues at this time."

He thought I could just compartmentalize it like that? As if it were a photo shoot for *Grave Messages*, or a guest spot on *The View*? Was that all I was to him? An event to pencil into his godly schedule?

Either he sensed my thoughts, or my emotions were written on my face. Either way, he gave me a look that was stern. Dare I say, it was paternal.

"I care for you deeply, my daughter. But this is not the time. For now, let it go."

I decided to roll with it, only because I realized that pushing the matter was useless at the moment. "I thought you would be busy with Cyrus."

"The matter has been handled."

"Ok. Then where are we?"

"As you can see, we are no longer on the physical plane," He looked pleased that I changed the subject, and turned his head to stare at me. "We are in-between."

I rubbed my hands over my face before I responded.

"What does that mean, exactly? Are you here to take me to the Underworld?"

Apollo burst into laughter. "Dear girl, no! Do you not understand what the word 'immortality' means?"

I raised an eyebrow to take him in. "What do you wish to tell me?"

He threw a look of disapproval in my direction. "Very well. For one, I won't allow you to destroy yourself so soon. You're my daughter, after all. You've done your duties to me well. For two? Come with me."

The room shifted in a flash. The window. The estate. It all disappeared.

I found myself in the basement of the Covington House, where the white light I'd seen outside Grannison-Morris estate was blinding. The symbols I had documented on the walls were glowing. I couldn't see well, but I could hear.

"Stand still." Elliot growled. He maneuvered someone into the center of the room. "You need to be in the very center for this to work."

"I need you to stand still." A man spoke. "How am I supposed to capture this if it's going to come out all blurry?"

"Stop talking."

Elliot raised his arms and began to chant. He began to shift into the wolf form Hera had granted him. I whimpered as I saw him turn on the man with a snarl.

"Joey," I whispered. "Not Joey."

Apollo flicked his wrist, and the scene disappeared. I looked at him in desperation.

"Please. Save him! Or let me go back. I have to help him!"

"No," said Apollo calmly. "You will have the opportunity to interrupt the Skinwalker's ritual when you wake. For now, I need you to listen."

Apollo turned to me and tapped his finger against my temple.

"It is true that you will return to Covington. Hera has requested that her dog conduct more sacrifices to draw you in. The first being your Joseph Lawson. But you must know how to protect yourself, Daughter. She has already begun to weaken your mental barriers."

"Yeah." I crossed my arms over my chest . "She is keeping me quite busy at the moment. I can't sit still long enough to think. Much less…"

"I am aware that she has been in contact with the Blue Aura." Apollo nodded. "And that your heart has been—stirring—since you met him."

"I don't want to talk about my heart." I narrowed my eyes at him . "Now, what can I do to save Joey?"

"The magnetic field lines." He gestured to the glow around us. "They run the whole of the Earthplane. Man does not believe they can cross, but at certain points, they do."

"Ok." I breathed out the word. "And that means—what, exactly?"

"That gods who mean you harm cannot reach you in Rome. Wretched name for a town, don't you think?" Apollo waved his hand. "At any rate, as long as you are on the physical plane, Hera can't attack you directly. Yet, if she can capture you and pull you to the Astral Plane, then she can steal your essence. Absorb it, if you will."

"Oh, for the love of—" I stamped my foot against the stone floor. "No offense, Apollo, but this is too confusing."

"She will lure you to the Astral Plane." He moved away from me to the very center of the room where Elliot had placed his victim in the vision. "This is the portal. You will be taken along with the Blue Aura. But what creates a barrier for mischievous gods can also be used against them."

At last, I realized what Apollo was trying to tell me. I grinned as I crossed the distance between us.

"Tell me everything I need to know."

---

I'm not sure how much time had passed, but when we returned to Grannison-Morris, the sun was fading off into the distance. Apollo walked with me until we reached a thick wooden door.

"Are you sure you understand what you need to do, Sibyl?" He turned with his hands stuffed into his pockets. "Once you are on the Astral Plane, I can no longer interfere."

"I do," I nodded as we passed through the door. I didn't try to rationalize our actions. There was no point, really. "Are you certain I can't say anything, though? They have a right to know."

"No, they don't. " Apollo made it sound final.

He whistled as he took in the sight before us. The room was empty save for my unconscious form, Jonah, and Jonathan. They seemed to be immersed in their thoughts.

Even Jonah—damnable, stubborn Jonah—was still concerned. He leaned against a counter which ran across the far wall with one arm crossed over his chest and one hand pressed against his mouth.

"Apollo, put me back." I took a step towards the bed. I couldn't stand to be the cause of all this worry. "Please."

"In a moment. I am not finished yet." Apollo moved to stand in front of Jonah to study him. He reached out, but stopped just short of Jonah's nose. For his part, Jonah jerked as if startled. "This man had no intentions of fulfilling Hera's request. He is quite intrigued by you."

"You mean I owe him an apology?" I groaned. "Apollo—"

"Yes." Apollo had that intractable look again. "He is exceedingly important to your fate. Heal the rift between you two."

"Fine." I sighed. I was ready for this to be over and done with. "I'll play nice."

"Please, do not mistake me. He considered following Hera's orders. Briefly." Apollo drew a circle in the air in front of Jonah's face. "But that is neither here nor there."

"What are you doing?" I frowned as I moved to stand beside him. "You aren't going to hurt him, are you?"

"No. Jonah Rowe is integral in ways that even his Protector Guide does not understand. Plus, the two of you will need each other in the future, as I've mentioned. More than you will ever know, child."

"What are you doing, then?" I asked him.

"I am merely granting him my protection since he will be your guard on the Astral Plane."

"I don't need a guard," I muttered for the fiftieth time since Apollo began his teachings at Covington. "I can handle it."

"I have no doubts, child. But it never hurts to have an extra set of hands." He smiled as the blue of Jonah's aura formed around his body. I watched as the blue shifted until it was flickering both blue and gold. "There."

"You didn't just bless him, did you? You did something else."

"I did." Apollo smirked, clearly proud of himself. "His aura will burn any who dare to fight against him."

"Ok. Look," I sighed. "As much as I hate for our little bonding time to end, I would really like to get back."

"If you insist. But remember all I have taught you, Eva. Your very existence depends on it."

I nodded as he moved to press the tip of his finger against the center of my forehead.

"Wait."

Apollo's finger paused inches from its mark. "Yes?"

I looked him square in his eyes. "Two last things. First, don't think you're off the hook. Someday, we will have the conversation that you wouldn't have tonight."

Apollo flashed another dazzling smile. "Fair enough."

"And the last thing." I softened my gaze somewhat. "Something is different about Hera now. She seems more vindictive—more determined to destroy me than ever. Do you know anything about that?"

Apollo regarded me for a few moments. "No. The bitch has merely elevated her vitriol, I suppose. Now, I must bid you farewell, Daughter."

He touched my forehead with his fingertip, and I sat up with a gasp, wrenching myself free from a wire that had been attached to my arm.

"Superstar?" Jonah said as he approached my bed. "Stay still. You don't want to aggravate that wound."

I buried my face into my hands as it all came rushing back. The argument with Jonah. The meeting with, and lessons from, Apollo. But the one thing that caused my heart to stop beating? The image of Elliot turning on the man at Covington.

"I've got to get to Covington." I lifted myself from the bed. "Now."

"Eva, stop." Jonathan spoke with such authority, any normal person would have backed down. "You've been unconscious for just over twelve hours. We need to assess you."

"Joey is at Covington with Elliot." I pushed my hair out

of my face. "He's doing a ritual, Jonathan. Please. Apollo—"

"Apollo?" Jonah frowned as he took the spot next to Jonathan. "What are you talking about?"

"I'll tell you on the way."

I jumped off the bed, but caught myself against it as the world started to spin. Jonah gave me a long look before he responded.

"Eva, you need to get back in the bed. Me and Terrence will go check Covington. You stay here."

"No, Jonah, you don't understand. Please. I have to go."

"Fine. But if you go, you stay in the car. Got it?" Jonah glanced over at Jonathan. "We'll be right back."

Jonah grumbled something else under his breath, but I didn't pay any attention to him. With him guiding me, we ran out of the house as soon as we could.

I could only pray that we would reach Joey in time.

---

The ride to Covington was uneventful. Of course, the entire heavens could have opened up and I wouldn't have noticed. I was in knots over what we would find when we reached the house. The bandages around my waist were so damn stiff I could barely move. Jonah had taken the wheel and as we approached the turnoff, I turned just enough to take a look at him.

He was sweating. Literally sweating. I could see the gleam of his skin in the low light.

"Jonah. I am sorry."

He jerked, but didn't look at me. So I tried again.

"I'm sorry for what I said. Look, it's not easy for me to admit when I am wrong. But I was wrong about you. I'm sorry."

Jonah muttered words I couldn't make out before he sighed.

"Apology accepted. Now, if you don't mind, will you tell me just what the hell we're doing?"

I didn't get the chance to answer. He brought the SUV to a stop and I was out before he put it into park.

"Eva!"

I barely heard Jonah yell my name. I dodged the hole Jonah had made on the porch when we were filming and disappeared inside.

I made my way to the underground room, ignoring the thick tension radiating around me. Joey was here. He was in trouble.

A scream filled my ears as I ran down the stairs, but it wasn't until I reached the bottom that I stopped.

The same white light I had seen with Apollo filled the room. I willed my sword into my hand as another wave of dizziness hit me.

Elliot was here. I could feel him.

I took careful steps towards the light as Jonah joined me. It wasn't until I reached the very center that I felt my blood run cold.

Joey's camera had been tossed aside. His body was crumpled into a heap as blood ran from his face.

"By the gods, no," I whimpered as I dropped down beside him. "Joey! Joey, wake up!"

I heard a snarl to my right, but when I focused on it, I saw a black blur lunge towards Jonah as Elliot attacked. Jonah fell back with a cry. I managed to stand just before Elliot snapped his jaws over Jonah's throat.

# THIRTEEN

## JONAH ROWE

WHEN THE WOLF DESCENDED, Jonah expected his physical life to flash before his eyes. The damn thing blindsided him, and he heard Eva yell.

But his physical life didn't flash before his eyes. Without thought, he gripped the wolf's upper and lower jaw before he got a proper clamp on his throat. Those teeth hurt like hell against his fingers, and he could see blood coming from the wounds that were now gouged into his hands, but he knew it would be a whole hell of a lot worse if the wolf succeeded in biting down on his throat.

Jonah's plan was to maneuver his feet so as to kick the wolf away, but before he could implement that plan, something very unexpected happened.

The wolf's maw began to steam and hiss, as though Jonah's fingers were scalding hot. It howled and distanced itself from him.

Jonah rose, puzzled. Why did that happen?

The wolf lunged before Jonah had the chance to retrieve his batons, so he threw up his hands by reflex.

Once again, its flesh hissed and burned when it came into contact with Jonah's bloody hands. It crumpled to the ground in a whimpering, disoriented heap. Jonah could see blisters on its skin where he'd touched it.

"Surprised?" He shouted at the beast. "Me too!"

He snatched up his batons from the ground, and had never been so thankful to see the blue gleam. But he didn't pay it too much attention. The wolf was down, but not quite out.

By this time, Eva was off to the side, cradling Joey's limp form. The wolf contemplated Jonah, clearly cognizant of its own wounds. With a snarl, it faded to black and dissipated amongst the shadows. Jonah narrowed his eyes. That wasn't the first time he'd seen figures vanish into the shadows, but it was never a thing he got used to.

He focused on Eva, who only had eyes for Joey.

"Joey, please wake up," She sobbed. "Please, just move!"

It made Jonah wonder. On a hunch, he closed his eyes, took a deep breath, and willed the curtain to rise and the actors to perform.

Sure enough, Joey Lawson's spirit was there. He stood over Eva, who still cradled his physical form. He then scanned the room in confusion, and locked eyes with Jonah.

Jonah wasn't unnerved by the event, of course, but he was glad that Eva couldn't see what he saw. She would probably have gone into hysterics.

"Joey." Jonah communicated with him mentally, as all Eleventh Percenters could with spirits. "It's up to you. I don't want you to pass into Spirit for Eva's sake, plus I like you a lot. But your life and your choices are your own."

Joey looked down at his damaged body, and then he focused on the sobbing Eva.

"I'm comfortable," He admitted. "At peace. But I don't think I'm ready to check out yet. I—I feel like I got more to do."

Jonah nodded. "I think so, too. Even without knowing you all that well, I think you've got more to do. So you're saying you want to stay?"

Joey's spirit nodded.

"Go on, then." Jonah tilted his head to Joey's prone physical form. " Make Eva's night."

Joey's spirit vanished. Seconds later, he coughed and opened his eyes. Jonah didn't think he'd ever seen such relief on Eva's face since he'd met her.

"Joey, are you alright?"

He coughed a few more times, but then gave her a slightly bloody smile.

"I've been better, Evie," He said, "but I'm thinkin' I might need a raise."

Despite everything, Jonah smiled. He'd communicated with many spirits and spiritesses in the past, but this was the first time he'd conversed with one who still had the chance to resume physical life. He was glad that Joey chose to stay.

"What were you doing with Elliot? You know better than to be alone with him. Don't you ever do that again!" snapped Eva, trying and failing to mask her relief. "Promise me."

"Tell you what," said Joey. "If you help me to my feet, I'll even pinkie swear."

They helped him to his feet. Joey cut his eyes at Jonah, who smiled and shook his head. Eva hadn't wanted to lose her friend. Jonah thought it was for the best if she never knew that, for a few minutes, she actually had.

"I'm glad you're alright, man," He said to Joey. "But I want to know what the hell was up with me! Burning Wolf

Boy like that? That was ethereality that I didn't know that I had!"

"You're just full of surprises, Blueberry." Eva brushed off her pants. "Who knows? It might come in handy again sooner rather than later."

For some reason, Eva sounded nervous when she said that, and she refused to look at him. So she knew something. There was more to it then.

Jonah filed it away. There was still Joey to think about. Apparently, Eva was on the same wavelength.

"Joey needs to get to Jonathan's infirmary," Jonah said. "But I'm not about to leave you to take him. Let me see if I can summon help. Never really done it before, but I think I can do it."

"Who are you calling?" asked Joey. "Jonathan?"

"Nope." Jonah concentrated. "I want the Protector Guide who put you guys on Jonathan's radar."

Eva scanned the room, like she expected more wolves to jump from the shadows. Jonah deactivated the Spectral Sight and continued to concentrate. Within seconds, he succeeded in his summons, and Akraia appeared. Jonathan was the only Protector Guide that Jonah had ever met, so he kind of assumed that they all dressed like him. Akraia proved that this was not the case.

She looked like she was in her late forties, but since she was a spiritess, age was a non-factor. She had bright-brown hair, a slightly angular face, and friendly, welcoming eyes. She wore a mauve business suit that included pants, not a skirt. For some reason, this gave her demeanor a bit of an edge, and Jonah figured that she probably commanded as much respect as Jonathan did.

"Jonah Rowe," She said. "It's a pleasure to put a face with a name. Why did you summon me?"

"There are some things that you need to know, ma'am,"

said Jonah. "But first, I would like to request that you transport an injured man to Jonathan."

"Certainly."

"Thank you, ma'am." Jonah cracked his neck muscles, which were a little sore after fighting the wolf. "I should probably introduce you to everyone. Eva, Joey, this is Akraia."

Eva's eyes widened. "Get away from her, Jonah! Akraia is one of the many names of—!"

"Silence!" Akraia flicked two fingers, and Eva flew into Joey, which sent both of them into an ancient table. "I'll not be exposed by the likes of you."

Akraia's form began to change. The bright brown hair became black, topped with a high, cylindrical crown. The features became stunningly beautiful, yet vengeful and malevolent at the same time. The mauve pantsuit became an immaculate white chiton dress. Lastly, the eyes changed to toxic green.

"Hera." Jonah was thunderstruck. "My God."

"Goddess, boy." Hera's eyes darkened. "I'm disappointed in you, Blue Aura. I would've given you everything you wanted if you'd had done as I had asked. But alas, now you shall share her fate."

Then Jonah felt what seemed like being pulled through fire, then ice. The next thing he knew, he was on the Astral Plane. He knew it well, after all. He and Eva were back to back, bound so snugly that he could barely move his arms. He felt movement from Eva, which must have been her turning her head this way and that.

"Jonah? You care to tell me what the hell just happened?"

"It's the Astral Plane," Jonah told her. "I don't know how Hera got us here without the Astralimes—"

"I don't need to quiver with such trivialities." Hera

tossed Jonah's batons one way, and Eva's sword another. "The fact that you didn't know that Akraia was one of my designations shows that you are ignorant of vital literature."

"I know my mythology just fine," snarled Jonah. "I just never heard that name."

"Well." Hera gave a minimal shrug. "Disregarding your teachings does have its consequences."

"Why did you bring us here?" demanded Eva. "You're a little early for the whole 'you will meet your doom at the Golden Hour' thing."

Hera laughed. "I know that you've been in contact with Apollo, Sybil. I am aware of what he shared with you. Let's see how you perform your tasks while bound to this stupid boy. And concerning Sunday? You've already experienced how Astral time and Earthplane time are different. It could be five minutes after I snatched you from Covington. It could be the next morning—or it could be Sunday, nine hours from the Golden Hour."

Jonah felt an icy chill. Eva posed the question.

"Alright, fine," She snapped. "Go ahead and tell us what happens then. I can tell you're just dying to rub it in."

Hera's smile faded, replaced by a hatred so pronounced that Jonah could barely look at her. "The Golden Hour is the time that the crossed lines will have contradicted each other's purposes and affects so completely that you will be rendered mortal once more, half-breed. At which time, you will be treated to your long overdue death. Think of it as a Grave Endowment."

"So, you wanna explain to me how you're managing to be here?" Eva was trying to work on the bindings behind her back, smarting Jonah with each movement. "How are you doing this? Apollo said that certain gods couldn't reach the Astral Plane!"

"But I am not a goddess, Sybil," said Hera, and she shape-shifted into her previous form. "I am the Protector Guide Akraia! See you very soon!"

She turned to mist and faded, leaving Jonah and Eva bound on the Astral Plane.

# FOURTEEN

## EVA MCRAYNE

THIS WAS GREAT. Just great. I struggled against the bindings for a minute before I realized that with each movement, they grew tighter. I finally gave up when Jonah hissed as the binds cut into our chests.

"Jesus, Superstar. Stop. That's not going to work."

"You know, as much as I enjoy being pressed against your back, Jonah. I would prefer it if we were freed." I relaxed as the fire I felt for him ignited with every brush I made against him. "I mean, I'm all for bonding, but this is too much."

Jonah was quiet for a second. After a moment, he broke the silence around us. "What do you know about my abilities?"

"What are you talking about?"

"How I burned Elliot. Spill it, Superstar."

"Fine. When I was out, Apollo stopped by for a visit."

"A visit?" His words were laced with sarcasm. "So you had a little father-daughter day while we were all worried sick over you?"

I knew Jonah knew nothing about it, but the pang went

through me at his words anyway. I did the only thing I could and matched his sarcasm."Oh yeah. It was great. He took me out for ice cream. Next week, he swears he'll take me to the movies and the park."

"Eva..."

"Look, he told me we were going to get snatched, alright? And he told me that you were going to be my guard in this place. But don't you dare get the wrong idea. I'm no damsel, Blueberry. And I sure as hell don't need you to protect me."

I turned my head as far as I could and he mirrored my movements. I could see the beginnings of a small smile on his face at the use of my nickname for him.

"You don't need a guard. You need a babysitter."

"I hate you so much right now."

I would have smacked him if I could, but the shadows around us started to shift as Elliot came into view. He had returned to his human appearance and even in the darkness of this place, I could see burns across his mouth. The vitriol in his expression was so pronounced that I shuddered despite myself.

"You are being transported." He snapped his fingers as a group of black masses appeared around him. "You will come with us."

"I don't think that's necessary," Jonah started, but he was cut off when Elliot came over to him and punched him hard enough to knock his head into mine. I winced as Jonah shook off the hit and spat blood out of his mouth.

"You're going to pay for that, Fido," He seethed.

Elliott didn't even dignify Jonah's words with a response. "I will undo the bounds and you will follow me."

He touched the binds with a single finger and they fell away. I lunged upwards the moment I was free, grabbing for Elliot as the Shades encircled us. He gave me a blistered grin as he caught me against him.

"About time you threw yourself at me, bitch." He leaned in as if to kiss me. "We have enough time before the Golden Hour. Maybe we should have some fun before it's all over for you."

"You're disgusting," I grumbled.

Elliott grunted. "Says the bitch that has the power to destabilize Olympus."

I narrowed my eyes at him. What did that mean? Seemed a little dramatic, even for Elliott. But I couldn't think much about it now. Despite being freed from each other, I had my orders from Apollo to follow, which sadly, did not include bashing Elliot's face in. So I let my enemy turn me around as we followed Jonah down a ragged path that faded into view as we walked on it.

"We have quite the show lined up for you two." Elliot broke the thick silence around us as we came upon a large door. As it was so dark, I couldn't see much else than the door itself. "I'm certain you will both learn a thing or two from it. I know I did."

Neither of us answered as we entered a room lined with two large jail cells. I watched as the Shades shoved Jonah into one of them then Elliot grabbed my arm to throw me into the other. I landed with a grunt against a frozen stone floor. Laboring my breathing as I hit my injured side.

"Enjoy your limited freedom, Eva." Elliot slammed the door behind me. "I am sure it will be the last you will ever know."

I waited until they were gone before I took in our surroundings. I didn't know much about the Astral Plane. Ok, scratch that. I knew nothing about the Astral Plane, but it seemed as if Hera could adapt it to her will. Could we do the same?

"You alright?" asked Jonah as he peered at me through the bars which separated us.

"Yeah," I nodded as I took in the dark mark across his right cheek. "You?"

"Apart from being pissed that I can't wring Wolf Man's neck, I'm wonderful." He winced as he slung his hands over the bars. "You said that Apollo told you about being captured. He didn't happen to mention how we were going to be freed, did he?"

"Yeah." I shrugged. "But I can't tell you. He made me promise."

"Ok." Jonah breathed out the word. "Then what did he do to me?"

"What do you mean?"

"Look, I know I don't understand all of my abilities yet. But fire? Not one of them. And if I can use it to get us out of here, then I need to know that."

"You can't. He blessed you with the ability of fire, Jonah. If you stopped jaw-jacking long enough to look at your aura, you can see how he changed it."

Jonah dropped his head to stare at his feet then whistled when he noticed the gold glistening against the blue.

"How long will it last?"

"I have no idea." I shrugged as I slid down the bars to rest my arms against my knees. "Apollo said you needed it. Turns out, he was right."

"Why?"

"Why did he give it to you? I have no idea."

"No." Jonah slumped down to his knees beside me to tap my arm with his finger. "Why you? I know you're not the first Sibyl. Has Hera gone after any of them before?"

I went silent as I tried to put my thoughts together then

shook my head. "No, she didn't have a reason to before. With me, she does."

"You gonna share what that is? Or am I going to have to play twenty questions with you to get it out?"

"I figured out something I wasn't supposed to." I shifted around to face him. "Did you know that a person can absorb the knowledge of a god?"

That gave him pause. He stared at me as if I'd grown a mustache until he started laughing."I think you hit your head a minute ago, Superstar. That's the most ridiculous—"

"You saw me fight, Jonah." I spoke in a whisper, afraid that our guards would return. "You think I learned all that from Cyrus? He's barely worked with me at all. It wasn't because of his training. It was because I absorbed Athena's knowledge."

"Athena." Jonah stopped laughing. I assumed he was trying to process what I was telling him. "The Athena. Goddess of War, Wisdom, and Battle Strategy."

I raised an eyebrow, which made Jonah scoff.

"Okay, so I read more mythology than just the bits I did on book reports. But that's who you mean, right?"

"Yes," I answered, "And Hera herself. Where do you think I got my charisma from? Why do you think people flock to me in droves? I mean, the Eva character is fantastic, I know. But with Hera's knowledge, I skyrocketed."

"And because you know this—"

"—I am a threat. I've become more than just the Sibyl, Blueberry. I've got attributes of two of the most powerful goddesses in existence."

"How?" Jonah demanded. "How is it even possible?"

I started to respond, truly I did. I wanted to tell him everything. But before I had the chance to open my mouth, I was slammed against the other side of my cell.

"Do not." Hera stepped forward. I shook my head with a groan as my vision began to clear. "You will not divulge my secrets to anyone, Sibyl. But I must admit, if stumbling across that secret was the worst threat you posed, I may very well have written you off as not worth my time."

My head cleared enough to focus my glare on her. "What are you talking about? I'm not here because of absorbing divine powers?"

"It is a piece of it, half-breed." Hera ran her index finger across her lip. "But it is only a piece. A small one at that. You pose a much larger threat to my way of life."

"Can you drop the riddles?" I demanded. They truly did wear on my patience. "I want a straight answer!"

Hera grinned. "Very well, half-breed."

She punched me across the face with the force of a man twice her size. It sent me to the back of the cell, where I slid down its wall. Jonah banged against the cell in rage.

"Leave her alone, Hera!" He snapped "I swear on my spirit, bitch—"

"Keep it to yourself, mortal." Hera waved her hand in his direction and he slammed against the cell wall himself. "Now, it is time for my fun to begin."

"Yay." I muttered as we both rose. "Jonah, promise me something."

"You sure are demanding a lot from me today, Superstar." He cracked his neck. "What now?"

"Promise that whatever she does, it won't break your spirit."

"I don't even know what that means."

"Trust me." I watched as Hera began to twirl her arms into the air. "You will. "

"Fine," he hissed. But Jonah wasn't her first target. It was me.

I saw the image Hera was creating out of thin air. I saw

myself as I thrashed about in my old college from a nightmare.

"Jonah!"

I heard Jonathan call out for Jonah as I looked away from the image in front of me. The door wrenched open to allow Jonathan entry. He took in our current predicament as Hera laughed.

"Wonderful! I couldn't have planned this any better. Please. Have a seat!"

She raised a single arm and he each hit the wall just as I had done moments before. This time, he wasn't bound. Jonathan seemed to be frozen into place. I hit my forearms against the bars with frustration until I heard Hera speak up.

"Pay attention, little girl."

I was forced to look at the screen as my image climbed out of bed, sobbing. I grew numb as I watched myself stumble into the bathroom. This was my darkest moment come to life. My weakness on full display. I had wanted it to be over. I had wanted everything to be over.

I dug out a blade from the razor on the sink. I collapsed with a sob as I began to slice away at my wrists.

*Soon,* I had promised myself as I ignored the blood pooling around me. *Soon.*

When my body slumped over, Hera froze the frame. I heard Jonah hissed out beside me.

"Jesus, Eva."

"I had my reasons."

"Your reasons, yes," Hera turned to me. "It is a pity that my Elliot found you. Perhaps, if he had been a few minutes late, the aggravation you have become would have been avoided."

I said nothing. She continued.

"You are worthless, Sibyl. As pitifully broken now as

you were then. You should have done the world a favor and passed on. Now, I am forced to do it for you."

"Leave her alone, Hera," Jonah snapped. "I am warning you."

"What does it matter to you, Blue Aura? This girl means nothing to you. She is not your friend, not your lover. Hell, she is barely even an acquaintance. You and I both know that once she is gone, she will be completely forgotten."

"Let Jonah go, Hera." I managed, though my voice was thick with my emotion. "He doesn't need to be tortured simply because he was nice to me."

"He should be tortured for that very reason alone. I swore to you, bitch, that I would strike you down. I would strike your allies down. But I have already tired of torturing you. As for you, Jonah Rowe. I am stunned by your idiocy. How could you deny yourself everything you've ever wanted?" The goddess sighed. "Yet, it is for naught. I have instructed Eros to give your prize to another."

The scene of my suicide attempt shifted into one of a woman with hazel eyes covered with dark brown strands. It was the same woman Hera had shown me the night before in my dreams. She glanced around as if waiting for someone. She must have spotted them because her face lit up like a Christmas tree.

The woman Jonah loved. I could see it in his expression when he stared at her face. My heart seemed to crack as I realized that he was truly in love with someone else. A crack that was followed by a spike of jealousy.

Who the hell was this woman? What the fuck made her so special? Why was she allowed to have all the things that had been denied to me my entire life?

"You came!" She squealed and threw herself into a man's arms. "Terrence, darling, you made it!"

"Your dearest friend." Hera smirked. "I thought it fitting. One betrayal for another, if you will."

"Jonah." I tried to get his name out as his expression became one of pain. I couldn't explain it, but seeing him like this increased my own heartache. I hated Hera for it. And I hated the woman in the vision for hurting him like this. "Remember what I said. Don't let her get to you. It will be your undoing."

# FIFTEEN

## JONAH ROWE

Jonah heard Eva's warnings. He even remembered when she warned him the first time. But being warned of danger and experiencing that danger was two different monsters. When he saw that vision of Vera and Terrence, as vivid as the one he'd seen in the mirror in the Covington House, it burned. Like being stabbed with an overheated knife.

"Jonah, stay with me!" shouted Eva. "It's not real. Remember the truth! Terrence is your best friend—"

"And when did you become anyone's voice of reason, Sybil?" said Hera with a laugh. "Elliot, what do you think of this abomination that has betrayed you time and time again? Do you regret saving her life when she was a mere mortal?"

"More than anything," He sneered. "I should have left her to bleed out. Would have made the world a better place."

With painstaking effort, Jonah yanked his eyes from the sight that ensnared his focus. He saw Elliot throw scrutinizing eyes over Eva.

"Janet was right." Elliot spoke calmly as Eva turned her head away from him. "You know that. That's why you tried to kill yourself before. It's why you destroy everything in your path now. Everything."

Jonah heard a pleasurable squeal, and refocused on the vision that involved Terrence. It tore him up all over again. It was almost like each time he saw it, the vision was accompanied by a fresh lash of emotion.

"Jonah," said Jonathan quietly, "Sometimes, the greatest internal victories occur when you assist others."

Jonah looked at the vision that plagued him. It made him sick to his stomach. But he'd also learned in the past few months that the things you fought only strengthened. That made him think about what Jonathan just said. If he kept focusing and refocusing on the vision that Hera sprung on him, he'd weaken himself because he'd keep trying to convince himself that it wasn't real. It was a battle that he'd lose from the start. But maybe his victory lay in assisting someone else.

"Come along, Elliot. Let us prepare for the Golden Hour."

The two of them vanished, leaving them to their torment. And like Elliott, Hera was simply another bully. That information cleared his mind somewhat.

He steeled himself, and regarded Eva, who was watching him with a fearful expression . He should have known that something wasn't right when the retorts and witty comebacks ceased. Eva had been through a great deal, with her powers. Now, she had to deal with the torment Hera had put her through. Reminders of a past that had driven her to take a blade to her wrist. Despite that, she still seemed more concerned for him than herself.

"Eva, you aren't worthless. You aren't the problem."

"Jonah-"

"No, Eva. I have to say this. When I first saw you, I thought you were a woman without a care in the world. You came across as a bitch, and I chalked that up to you just being another celebrity."

Jonah took a breath then continued.

"But it's all a front. A character you play so that people don't get too close. I never could have imagined that you were being beaten. Torn down. I never could have imagined that you would believe any of the shit Cyrus and Hera and Elliot threw at you. But if you've heard it all your life, what choice do you have?"

Eva closed her eyes. Jonah saw the tear slide down her cheek. He felt for her in that moment. He really did.

"Eva, I want you to hear me. Yes, I considered Hera's offer, but it had nothing to do with you. Hera claimed to have the key to the Other Side. I thought about a chance to see Nana again."

Eva looked at him. Jonah had her full attention now.

"I don't like to speak about my family much, but you'll get the nutshell," Jonah continued. "My dad was married, and he cheated on his wife with my mother, who was almost twenty years younger. I was the result. My dad went back to his family before I was born, and once my mom had me, she dumped me on my Nana and took off, too. I never knew them, and just discovered a couple weeks ago that my dad is in Spirit. I don't know anything about my mom. Nana was all I had. She was my best friend, and taught me everything she could about being a man. Then she passed into Spirit when I was eighteen. My life hasn't been quite right since. So yes, I considered Hera's offer if it meant I could see Nana again. Is she proud of the man I've become in the years since I last saw her? Would she approve of the choices I've made? Those are only two questions that I would ask her. But I decided that the chance to see Nana again, as much as I'd love to, was not worth violating the natural laws of life. I don't even know if Hera had a way to access the Other Side. But it doesn't matter. Nana is gone. I'd like to see her again, and I hope it happens one day, but she's in my past. I love her and miss her every day, but I had to move on. It is what it is."

He studied Eva until she met his eyes. "That's my point. You had a shitty childhood, yes. You have a shitty, abusive relationship now. But it's the past. Apollo said he could straighten Cyrus out. I hope he does. As of right now, what happened yesterday, two hours ago - hell, two minutes ago - is in the past. And living in the past ain't living."

Jonathan gave him the smile of a proud father. But it was Eva whom Jonah focused on. By ignoring the false image that Hera hoped to disarm him with, he had the strength to appeal to Eva.

But did he get through?

Eva bowed her head. Jonah could only imagine how difficult this must be for her. But he could say no more. It was out of his hands. So he waited.

Eva broke her silence at last. "You're right, Jonah. My past is...it's in the past, no matter what happens in the future."

With her words, the horrific image of her in that bathroom faded. The vision involving Terrence and Vera vanished as well. Jonah, Eva, and Jonathan were alone.

"Well done, Jonah," said Jonathan. "You truly are wise beyond your years."

"Well I wouldn't say all that—"

"I never knew those things about you, Jonah."

Jonah shrugged. "It doesn't make much difference," He replied. "My parents might have been sacks of shit, but Nana was awesome. Jonathan, I just thought about it. You're a spirit. Can't you walk through these bars?"

"Hera thought of that, and put checks against it," said Jonathan. "She thought of everything. Well, except one thing. Any second now."

Suddenly, the doors to the jail cells exploded. They literally blew clean off.

Jonah started. "What the hell?"

Jonathan regarded the empty holes with savage pleasure.

"The Astral Plane deals with freedom just as much as mystery," He explained. "If you are free in your mind, so, too, are you free on the Plane. Hera's feeble Astral cells couldn't hold us once you and Eva were free of the prisons of your minds."

"Great, Jonathan!" said Eva. "But-"

"The Golden Hour is approaching, Eva," said Jonathan. "Having said that, I would suggest we take our leave."

# SIXTEEN

## EVA MCRAYNE

As Jonathan and Jonah headed to the door, I resisted the urge to throw myself at Jonah and hug him. I knew that he said those things to pull me back. I knew that - somehow - we would become good friends.

That didn't mean he wanted me all over him. Especially now.

"Come on, Superstar," Jonah stopped at the exit. "We gotta get out of here."

He was right, of course. But what he didn't know was what Apollo had shown me. There was only one way out of the hell Hera had created.

And I was the key to it. Jonah, too.

"Get back here right this instant, Evangelina."

I turned around to see Hera standing next to my mother. Janet McRayne's face was twisted in a look of hatred that I recognized.

"No."

"How dare you?" She hissed. "How dare you defy me? You destroyed my life, had me murdered, and now you are refusing to help me ascend from the darkness?"

I stayed planted into place as Jonah and Jonathan flanked me. Jonah started to speak when I interrupted him.

"Jonathan, Jonah, please. Meet my mother. The late Janet McRayne. Except, this isn't my mother's spirit."

"How dare you? I am going -"

"Answer something for me." I closed my eyes until I found the strength to do as Apollo had demanded. Every fiber of my being was fighting against the fear of not doing what she wanted. "Mom, what's my middle name?"

"What?" The spirit before me faltered. "Evangelina, what a ridiculous question!"

"Just answer it." I closed the distance between me and the women standing across the room. "Surely you would remember."

"You are not worth remembering!" My mother turned to Hera then back to me. "But I will humor you. It's Claire."

I studied her with a look of pity. "No. I'm sorry, Nephele. You are incorrect."

The vision of my mother faded into a mirror image of Hera. Yet, this goddess was so very different. She wilted to her knees, burying her face into her hands as she began to weep.

"Who the hell is Nephele?" Jonah piped up behind me.

I knelt down before the goddess, but I didn't touch her.

"A tragic figure, really. She was created by Zeus in Hera's image when he got wind that a guest was going to rape his wife. She has suffered greatly since her creation." I glanced up at Hera. "The fact that you would use her in such a way is despicable. Elliot never had the spirits of his victims. It was a bluff to get me here in the first place."

Hera screamed. She actually screamed with frustration as she threw her hand out to strike me down. I grunted as she latched onto me when I fell flat on my back.

"You are too late, girl. Far, far too late. The Golden

Hour has begun and so too, has your death. I must complete my task. I must!"

The next few minutes happened so quickly, I couldn't grasp everything that happened. The room grew dark as the Shades surrounded us. I could hear Elliot's strangled growl as he reappeared before my protectors. I tore my eyes away from Hera's just long enough to see Jonah going crazy with his glow sticks and Jonathan ripped through Shades in an attempt to get to me.

But it didn't matter.

This was my fight. And I would be damned if I didn't win it.

I put my focus on Hera, who lifted up as she straddled me. I watched her hand shimmer until a golden dagger appeared. She began to slash it downwards in a manic attempt to stab me with the blade. I struggled to capture her arm as my free hand went into my pocket. I had seconds to do as Apollo instructed.

*Be with me* .

I felt my hand circle around the object I was trying so hard to find. When I pulled it free, Hera laughed as she leaned down to snarl in my face.

"Poor little Sibyl. Still alone. Still grasping for hope despite losing everything."

"Not everything." I fished out the metal I'd found at Covington House, and held it in Jonah's direction while I whispered an apology. One of his batons flew from his hands and into my grasp.

"Hey! What the hell?" demanded Jonah, but I took my focus off of him, returned it to Hera, and pressed both his baton and the slab of metal to her flesh.

"Tools of the Ethereal," I chanted, just like Apollo coached me, "Return us to Earthplane."

The white light that filled the room was blinding. When

it cleared, we were back in the basement of the Covington House. I shoved Hera off of me as I dropped the ethereal instruments and rolled away, willing my sword to appear all the while.

I'd never been more grateful to see it.

"Jonah!" I called out to him. "Use the fire! Make sure Elliot burns."

Jonah momentarily forgot his displaced baton. "With pleasure."

I heard his response, but I didn't dare turn to look at him. Hera circled me, snarling as she balanced the dagger in her hand.

"Stupid, stupid half-breed bitch. You do not know the wrath you have brought unto your own."

"Yeah, I get it. Darkness. Death. Destruction. Can't you come up with anything better than that?"

"Those things are the very threats you are!" roared Hera. "Now die! "

I dodged the blade and caught sight of a wolf surrounded by two men. Jonah had abandoned his other baton and lit his hands with Apollo's fire while Jonathan attempted to pull Elliot's attention away from Jonah. Elliot must have felt my eyes on him because he snapped at Jonah before he broke free from their barrier to head straight towards me.

He never got the chance to go any further than a few feet. As he passed him, Jonah grabbed Elliot's snout as his hands began to glow even brighter.

"Go to hell, White Fang!" He bellowed.

His blast knocked us all to our knees. The heat was so intense that it dried the sweat from my brow.

We were all disoriented for several moments, even Jonathan. For her part, Hera attempted to lift herself up, but collapsed back down as I held the tip of my blade to her throat.

"You can't do this," She spat. "I'll have your head within seconds."

"No, you won't." I pressed down. "Do you not realize where you are? Has your hatred blinded you so much that you have no idea that you are back on Earthplane? Back in Rome?"

"What—?" Hera's bright green eyes widened. "No."

"You have no power here. Especially now. I can take your head within seconds and end this for good."

I felt my companions approach us. Hera hissed as she tried to push herself back. But I wasn't finished. Not yet.

"See, you brought me here to use the ethereal world against me," I told her. "But what you didn't realize is that those same things can be used against you, too. For me, it was the magnetic lines that brought about vulnerability. For you, it's ethereal steel. All it took was a touch of one of Jonah's batons, combined with spare contraband I found here in Covington, and you are in a zone where you can do nothing against us."

Hera took a breath through her nostrils. "You bitch…"

"Yeah," I said, bored. "We've established that. Now, you like to make offers. Deals in exchange for getting what you want. I'm willing to do the same. Not that I'm giving you much of a choice. I'll keep my knowledge secret. I won't utter a single word about what I have learned. In exchange, you will leave me and mine alone. And I do include the Eleventh Percenters into that equation. No threats. No Shades. No wild dogs with a preference for psychological torture."

"Elliot," She breathed as she glanced around the room, "What did you do to him?"

"Put him out of his misery," I replied. "Jonah here did what I didn't have the strength to do in Great Falls."

Hera's eyes lingered on Elliot's body for a few seconds, so I tapped the blade against her jaw to pull her attention back to where it belonged.

"Eyes on me," I murmured. "You really have no choice in this, Hera. So if you'll agree, we can all go home."

"You dare threaten me," rasped Hera. "What makes you think you have the right? Apollo?"

I grinned. I couldn't help it. "Not this time. I've had contact with someone over his head. Somebody is really pissed off at you, sweet Hera."

For the first time since I'd known her, I saw concern on Hera's face. She struggled beneath me as the others surrounded us. Jonah with his batons of blue fire. Jonathan, whose hands glowed in the strangest fashion. But then, her game face was back on.

"You expect me to believe that you've had an audience with Zeus?" She rolled her eyes.

"Yep," I answered, "And you might want to pay attention, because I've got a message for you from him."

"I can speak to my husband myself, should I wish to," Hera spat on the ground. "I will speak to him about this once I return to Olympus—"

"See, that's the thing." I loved this, but I couldn't show it. Too much, anyway. "Zeus was not pleased when I told him about your activities out here in Rome. You were so ready to destroy me after the Council named me the Representative of Olympus. As Zeus is the head of the Council, your deeds were looked upon as transgressions against the throne. Your husband has seen fit to punish you."

Hera's expression turned to fear. She actually looked

afraid for the first time since I'd known her. "What are you saying?"

"I hope you like that mansion in Beverly Hills," I told her, "Because you're going to be Juno Helakos for a little while. Zeus has sentenced you to remain on Earthplane indefinitely, bound in this form you've taken. Your powers will be blunted, because there will be no one to attend to your shrines. You will pose no threat to me and mine. He told me to tell you these things because he was so angry, he couldn't bear the sight of you at the moment. Don't shoot the messenger. Anyway, you'd better leave all my friends alone, because if you so much as look sideways at any of us, I will personally see to it that Zeus finds out."

I lifted the sword, and Hera rose to her feet. She was so angry that she looked like she was about to explode. Zeus punished her in the worst way imaginable, binding her to human form with diminished powers and a short leash. She could hate me all she liked, but she wasn't willing to screw with her husband's orders.

"You've turned my husband against me, half-breed," Hera whispered. "Already, your cancerous influence eats away at my family. This only reaffirms the fact that you must be wiped away. I will follow my husband's orders. I will wait. But you are not long for this world, Sybil. I do not know how. I do not know when. But I will kill you, and prevent your decimation of Olympus."

The Queen of the Heavens disappeared into the shadows. I stayed still and waited, wondering what she meant. Decimation of Olympus? Like I was the one that was a threat to the realm of the gods.

It was just sour grapes. Had to be.

I turned to the men on either side of me. "Elliot?"

"Jonah finished him," Jonathan stepped up to me, his admiration evident. "And you have done well."

I tilted my head until I could see it for myself. Sure enough, Elliot was crumpled up where he had fallen. I went around them and knelt down next to the body as the memories of what we had shared flickered through my mind. Yet, the more I remembered, the more I thought of all the things I wanted to forget.

"We'll have to call the police. He's burned, but we can explain that away as an accident here on the property."

"Eva."

I didn't answer as Jonah called my name. I ignored Jonathan as he tried to approach me. Instead, I let my sword fade away when the exhaustion of this trip set in. I slumped down onto the dirty stone floor as Jonathan surveyed us all.

"Our time here is done, friends," He said. "Let's return home."

# SEVENTEEN

## JONAH ROWE

WHEN THE TRIO returned to the estate, they were met with the site of a huge bonfire that blazed right on the front lawn. Jonah roared and readied himself for an attack, but then Terrence and Reena appeared, completely unharmed.

"Well, don't y'all look like hell," commented Terrence. "No offense."

Jonathan ignored the quip. "Terrence, Reena," He said quietly, "Why—exactly—have you created a bonfire on the grounds?"

"And where the hell is Joey?" demanded Eva.

"Joey is fine," said Reena. "Apollo dropped him off. He is resting in the infirmary. And to answer your question, Jonathan— we didn't do this. You guys didn't have all the fun."

"We didn't?" Jonah lowered his batons. "Explain."

"About twenty minutes after Jonathan left to get you guys, we lost more time, which I'm sure you already know," Reena explained.

"When that happened, about two dozen Shades came on the grounds." Terrence interrupted. "They probably figured that since the bulk of our group was gone, we'd be easy meat. They were this close to attacking us—Reena and I were ready for what-the-hell-ever, but then this fire just—appeared out of nowhere, and the Shades hesitated. It was like they weren't so sure they wanted to attack us once they saw the fire."

"It didn't really matter in the end, though," said Reena, "Because while they bumbled around trying to make up their minds, the fire—well—spit out tendrils of flame from itself to the Shades. I've never seen anything like it."

"Barbecued them like brisket," said Terrence with relish. "Reena and I didn't have to lift a finger."

"Interesting," said Jonathan. "It functioned much like the Greek fire weaponry of the Byzantine Empire. Terrence, Reena, I'm sure you would have held your own, but that many Shades would have overtaken you eventually. Apollo saw to it that neither of you even had to take the risk. But it serves no purpose now. The threat has ended. Jonah, I think you will be of assistance here."

Jonah knew what Jonathan meant. He wasn't sure where the knowledge came from, though. It must have been a product of the mental clarity that usually came along with spiritual endowments. He concentrated, and his hands burst into blue flames.

"What the hell?" exclaimed Terrence, who took a step back.

"Long story," murmured Jonah.

He walked to the bonfire, where he cupped his hands like he held water in them. Lifting his cupped hands to his mouth, he blew the blue flames at the orange ones, while using his wind ethereality to guide it. The blue flames extinguished everything until there wasn't a single ember left. There wasn't even a trace that there had ever even been a fire on the premises.

"Now that was impressive, Blueberry," observed Eva.

Jonah snorted. "Yeah, I've heard that one before."

"So what happened with you guys tonight?" asked Reena. "I'd like very much to know the story behind those blue flames, Jonah."

"How about this?" said Terrence before anyone could reply. "Why don't we have the big talk over dinner? I'll whip up some breakfast food. Hope you don't mind breakfast for dinner. Eva, has big-city living made you averse to down home cooking?"

Eva made a face that almost made Jonah laugh out loud. "Not even L.A. can turn me off from home-cooked breakfast, Terrence."

Soon enough, everyone was gathered at the dinner table, while Jonathan, who had no need to eat, stood nearby. It was a much more light-hearted affair than it had been at their first meeting at this table. Terrence made bacon, sausage, scrambled eggs, biscuits, toast—one would have thought his aim was to feed a small army. He didn't leave out Reena, though, and placed toasted rice bread, fruit medley, cottage cheese, and grapefruit juice in front of her. No one else had an issue with the high calories. Even Joey was there, eating like he was at full strength. Jonah laughed at Terrence's look of shock when Eva revealed that she'd never had grits.

"What?" He cried. "That's impossible! You're...you're from Charleston!"

"It's...a long story."

"Well, we need to do something about that," said Terrence, who placed a steaming bowl of it in front of Eva, topped with a cube of butter. "Can't believe a southern girl ain't never had grits before!"

Once the grit debacle was rectified, Jonah, Eva, and Jonathan told their story to Terrence, Reena, and Joey.

Jonah hadn't even realized what a wild story it was until it was recounted. It had been a truly crazy week that was expedited by the fact that they had lost time twice. Jonah wasn't sure which part was the most insane. The fact that all the crap had actually happened, or the fact that they'd all survived it.

"Amazing," said Reena, whose eyes had a gleam that she usually only had during painting. "I underestimated you, Eva. You possess an edge that a lot of men don't even have."

Eva actually blushed. "I appreciate that, Reena, but I couldn't have done it without Jonah."

"Our Jonah doesn't yet realize his value to us," Jonathan smiled. "It is my hope that one day, he will see himself the way that the rest of us do."

Jonah didn't know what to say about the compliment he'd just received. Years of hearing that he was worthless had taken quite a toll, so hearing high praise like this made him feel a bit awkward. He acknowledged it with a smile and a nod, then switched gears.

"So Eva," He said, "I see that your eyes are green at the moment. When will you have your Sibyl powers back?"

"Oh," said Eva, surprisingly optimistic. "Apollo told me all about it. Without Hera and Elliott messing with me at every turn, my recovery will be a smooth one. My Sibyl abilities will be fully restored in about eight hours."

"Nice," said Jonah with a nod. "Got to admit, though, it was cool to see you handling business even with your powers out of whack."

Now it was Eva who looked awkward. "Thanks, Jonah," She murmured. "I appreciate it."

Jonah had no idea where her head was at the moment, but he decided not to pry. Instead, he rose from the table, sated and quite drowsy.

"I think that with all the crap passed," He said to the room at large, "We can all finally get a full night's sleep."

———

Everyone slept for nearly ten hours, and when everyone woke up, they discovered that two things had occurred. Eva's Sibyl powers had returned, and Jonah had not only released his spiritual endowment, but also - damn it all- Apollo's blessing.

"Eh, it's just as well," said Reena. "There is nothing like being yourself."

"Plus, we've got plenty of glitz and glam being ethereal humans, right?" said Terrence.

Jonah didn't respond, but he grinned. Terrence had a point, after all.

While Terrence regaled Joey with stories about his brother Lloyd and Reena showed Eva her art studio, Jonah walked the estate grounds. It was refreshing to have the serenity back, as well as to not see a single damn Shade anywhere. He sat at his usual spot in the gazebo, and lost himself in thought for—he didn't know how long. It was a lovely thing.

Then—

"Reena said I'd find you here."

He turned to see Eva. She seated herself near him in the gazebo, and took in the area.

"So this is where you come to de-stress?" She asked.

"More often than not." Jonah stretched. "So what's the plan? Do you intend to finish stuff up for your episode?"

"Yeah," said Eva, "But it won't take long. We'll pick up the cameras Joey set up throughout the house. I'll say something pithy about the house's history and Frederickson. We'll be done in plenty of time to catch our flight at eight tonight. Besides, after all you guys have done for us, I wanted to give you all some peace. I will say that I am glad we are parting on good terms. I don't think that would have been the case a couple days ago."

"Very true." Jonah gave Eva a sly smile. "I imagine that you're ready to get back to your own world."

Eva looked around the grounds.

"I like this world," She admitted. The wistfulness in her voice was not missed. "I need to confess something, Jonah. But you have to swear you won't repeat this. Ever."

She threw those gold eyes on him, and he snorted.

"Deal. What's up?"

Eva sighed. "I was thrown for a loop here. It is a strange thing for me to have people around me who give a damn about each other."

Jonah raised his eyebrows. "Really?"

"Really. In Hollywood, families have no problem throwing each other under the bus for a dollar. And given my history, I didn't know how to react when I realized that you cared enough to have an intervention for me. It's a lovely thing."

"Being cared about? Eva, the world loves you."

"The world loves the Eva they see on television. They love the badass blonde. They don't love me because they don't know the real me."

"Who is the real you?"

"I don't know. There are times when I feel as if I am the Eva people see on television. Other times? I'm the kid being starved to death in Charleston. But I can't focus on that little girl and I have you to thank for it."

"Me?" Jonah sat forward. "Why?"

"Remember that thing you said?" Eva asked. "'Living in the past ain't living?' That struck a chord with me. Really hit home. I don't know what the future holds, but I won't find out so long as I try to return to who I was in the past. When you said that, it made me realize just how heavy the past could be."

Jonah nodded, impressed by his own skills. "Well, you're welcome."

"You have a way with words, Jonah," Eva teased. "Have you ever considered writing books?"

Jonah laughed at her joke.

"I can get you in touch with some people in L.A. if you're interested," Eva clasped her hands in her lap. "Hera's not the only one with connections, you know. But after mixing our worlds like this, it'd probably be best to keep our distance from each other. Lines crossing—messed up powers—you guys having to deal with my fucked up emotional state—me having to deal with your smart mouth. It's just better that way."

Jonah regarded her. "That's a crock, Eva."

"Yeah, it is." Eva laughed. "It was fun. Dicey at times, but fun. I want to see you guys again someday. I've already invited Reena out to L.A. to get away from Rome—and even if I do come back, I won't have to worry about the lines anymore."

She held out her arm, and revealed a bracelet. It was a very interesting thing. The charm, clearly ethereal steel, was done in the design of a bundle of rods tied together in a cylinder, with a blade and axe among them.

"Jonathan gave me this," She explained. "He said it's a fasces. It's a Roman thing, so he thought it was fitting since we're in Rome and all. Apparently the Latin term fasces symbolizes—"

"—strength through unity," Jonah finished for her.

Eva grinned at him. "You really do know Latin. Anyway, it functions like a talisman, I guess. Jonathan said that I may be vulnerable to crossed lines in other places, too, but this nullifies any effect they might have on my powers."

"That's awesome," Jonah said. "I'm glad that you'll be safer in all those places you go for *Grave Messages*. May you continue to trash Landry in the ratings."

"I will do it with pleasure, but I'd best get going."

"Kick ass and take names, Superstar."

They rose, but both of them hesitated. After everything that had happened that week, a handshake just seemed tacky. They shook hands back at the airport when they didn't trust each other, but things were different now.

Jonah reached out to pull Eva into his arms. It was supposed to be a simple hug goodbye. The only right way to cement their friendship.

Except, it wasn't. The second Eva was in his arms, he knew something had changed. Jonah closed his eyes as he noticed how well they fit together. The lavender oil that seemed to permeate her entire body was intoxicating.

He had to get a grip. Now.

Jonah released her and resisted the urge to grab her again. His reaction, his thoughts had been automatic. Almost like breathing.

What the hell was wrong with him? He shouldn't be responding to Eva this way. Not when he had his heart set on someone else.

"Til next time, Blueberry." Eva leaned up to kiss his cheek. "Thanks again for everything."

She turned then threw a wave at him as she left the gazebo. Jonah couldn't keep his eyes off of her.

"Til next time, Superstar." Jonah cleared his throat as he watched her head back across the lawn. She didn't get five feet away from him before he called out. "Eva, wait!"

She stopped and turned towards him with a quizzical look on her face. "You alright?"

"Yeah," He jogged over to her. "I figured the least I could do was walk you to the car."

Eva grinned up at him. "Want to make sure I'm really out of your hair, huh?"

"Not exactly-"

He stopped when he saw Jonathan approaching them with Apollo. The god looked like he'd just stepped out of *GQ* magazine. Meticulous blonde hair, yacht club khakis and polo. Eva stopped walking and frowned.

"Apollo?"

"Forgive the intrusion, Eva." The god looked between them. "I must speak with you immediately."

"Ok. Go for it."

"Not here. Not outside, at least." The man turned to Jonah. "Jonah. You did well."

"Let us go into my study," Jonathan turned back towards the house. "It appears we have much to discuss."

Jonah and Eva shared a look as they followed the other two. This wasn't going to be good. It wasn't going to be good at all.

# EIGHTEEN

## EVA MCRAYNE

"THE HOIA-BACIU FOREST." Apollo began to pace when I took a seat on the sofa in Jonathan's study. "A forest just outside of Cluj-Napoca, Romania."

"A haunted forest?" I frowned. "That's hitting too close to home. I didn't have much luck last time I went to a forest."

"Romania is not Montana, dear girl." Apollo frowned. "The country was cursed with fables of vampires. But there is so much more to that land than you could ever imagine. To go to Hoia-Baciu could be a death sentence to a mortal."

"So if I'm going to a haunted forest, maybe I can turn that into a *Grave* episode. Tell me more about the ghosts." I ignored his words. I ignored the fear in my heart. "I want to hear all the gory details. Then we're going to call Connor and get the boys in Research to find out the rest."

For the first time since I'd known him, Apollo looked uneasy. His features were twisted in a grimace as he paced the rug in front of the sofa. I tapped my fingers against my knee as I waited for him to speak. When he didn't, I reached up to grab his arm.

"Come on. It can't be that bad."

No." He sighed. "The forest itself is horrifying, but there is a reason why the Council wishes you to go there. It's not because of ghosts, Eva."

I sat up a little straighter. I ignored my sudden pang of anxiety. I could do this. I could face anything the gods could throw at me.

Couldn't I? I'd just defeated Hera, after all. I cut my eyes over to Jonah, who had leaned back against the sofa next to me. He studied Apollo in silence. But we weren't in silence for long.

"Hoia-Baciu Forest is located in the Transylvania region of Romania. It has become famous with paranormal enthusiasts recently." My patron god ran his hand through his hair. "It is often seen as an easy location to snap photographs of orbs. Or catch the voices of spirits on film. There is also a clearing in the midst of the forest where the foliage will not grow."

"Ok." I shrugged. "So what's so damned bad about this place? Are you afraid I will get lost?"

Apollo's mouth became a tight straight line before he responded. "No, dear girl. The occurrences at Hoia-Baciu are not due to the paranormal as these enthusiasts claim. It is located on top of Tartarus."

"Tartarus?" I frowned. "The dungeon I keep getting threatened with?"

"The very same." This time, he pinched the bridge of his nose between two fingers. "On the outskirts of the clearing is the entrance to the infamous place. It has been sealed for centuries, but the barriers are being manipulated."

"Which means, what exactly?" Jonah asked. My new friend leaned forward to rest his elbows on his knees. "Manipulated ain't the same as broken."

"Not yet, Jonah," Apollo shook his head. "But if they

are weakened, then the greatest threat to the Council will be freed upon the world."

"Yeah." I snorted. "All the gods and people and creatures they cast down below could get their comeuppance. That doesn't sound so bad. That sounds like a long overdue dose of karma."

"Evie, no." Apollo gave me a look of pity. "You must understand as the Representative of Olympus, you would be targeted by these beings."

"Not to mention the Titans."

I whipped my head around to see Cyrus had appeared from the shadows. He seemed to have his focus planted on the two of us and his expression darkened for a second before he spoke. "What do you know of the Titans, Eva?"

"I've heard of them." I turned my attention back to Apollo. "That's the group that Zeus overthrew to gain his throne, right?"

"Right." Apollo agreed. "Shall I tell you the story since your Keeper was apparently lacking in your tutelage?"

Ouch. I knew that had to have stung Cyrus' pride, but I wasn't going to jump to his defense. The truth was, the majority of what I knew about the Olympian world came from the Academy led by Hecate, not my Keeper. I gave Apollo a small smile, but I couldn't ignore the knot forming in the pit of my stomach. I'd defeated the Erinyes out of my concern for Elliot. Hera? She had pissed me off. I had no idea what I was going to do against a group of gods if they were freed from their eternal prison. I folded my legs beneath me and settled in for what I was sure would be a long monologue.

Apollo didn't disappoint me. He perched on the sofa arm closest to me when he began to speak.

"Our world was created by two primary deities. Gaia, who is still celebrated today as Mother Earth and Uranus the father of the sky. During their marriage, they bore twelve children." Cyrus clasped his hands together in his lap. "A marriage that went well enough until Uranus cast two of their children into Tartarus. Gaia was so angry, she enlisted her youngest son to castrate her husband."

"So that's all true then." Jonah winced. "I know the old stories are violent but-"

"Wimp." I teased. "What happened next?"

"I'm afraid Cronos was successful. He waited in ambush with a sickle when his father met up with Gaia. I will only say that the result of his actions was the complete overthrow of Uranus." Apollo folded his hands over his knee. "The former King of the Titans cursed his son. He swore that Cronos would experience the same fate. His children would overthrow him to rule the heavens. The Titan became so paranoid of the curse that he swallowed each of his children as soon as he could."

"That can't be right." I twisted on the couch to face Apollo. "Zeus, remember?"

"Ah, but our history is full of trickery, dear girl." He gave me a soft smile. "Cronos had married Rhea, his sister. When it came time for the Titan to eat her youngest child, she hid the babe. She gave her husband a rock instead. The young Zeus was masqueraded in his mother's court. When he came of age, he gave his father a poison mixture that caused him to expel the children he had swallowed so many years before."

"I take it that this is how Zeus was able to lead the rebellion." Jonah shifted and his arm brushed against mine. I tried to ignore the warmth that spread through me. "Through venganance."

"It is." Apollo sighed. "Cronos had very powerful allies, but Zeus had the fire of revenge on his side. He enlisted his siblings. He freed the Cyclopes and the Hekatonkhieras. It was through the Cyclopes that the brothers were granted their infamous weapons. Zeus, his lightning bolts. Poseidon? His trident. Hades? His helmet. It was a brutal war. The Titanomachy decimated both the earth and the heavens over the ten years it was waged."

"But in the end, Zeus was victorious." I pointed out. "The Titans were imprisoned in Tartarus."

I let my last words die when I realized what Apollo was telling me. The Council's greatest threat was on the verge of being freed. The war which tore the world apart would be waged once more.

"There is more, Eva."

"More? What more could there be?"

"We do not know how to secure the barrier back to its original condition."

"Excuse me?" I felt the blood drain from my face. "What do you mean, you don't know?"

"We do not know. The Olympians didn't create Tartarus."

"Who did?"

"Chronos will be the only Titan who can provide us the answers you seek." Apollo rubbed his hands together. "Like many of the gods, he took refuge here on Earth."

"So where is he? Let's go talk to him."

"It is not so simple..."

"Don't start with me, Apollo. Not today." I crossed my arms over my chest. "If you don't know how to find him, tell me who does."

"Zeus." Apollo sighed. "He is the only one who knows how to contact the Ancient One."

"Then I need you to get me in touch with him, pronto. The sooner you do, the sooner I can create a game plan."

I went silent as I studied him. Although I had been told all my life that I looked like my mother, I could see myself in my father as well. We had the same wavy blonde hair. The same sharp nose. When I had first become the Sibyl, I assumed my beauty was a benefit thanks to my new role.

I was wrong. No matter how I tried to deny it, the man sitting in front of me was my father. I owed my very existence to a series of forbidden rituals conducted by Janet McRayne.

"Tell me what happened." I whispered. "Talk to me, Apollo."

He narrowed his eyes. Apollo knew that I was referring to my blood connection to him. I could tell by his tone when he responded. "I do not believe this is the right time, Sibyl."

I had so many questions. I needed answers desperately. But I was all too aware of the other three souls in the room. I bit my own tongue until the desire to scream at him passed.

"When do we leave? I have to go collect our gear from the Covington House then catch the flight back to L.A. to get this approved and-"

"Soon, Eva. The sooner the better."

"Not to overstep my bounds, but I'll go." Jonah looked me over. "It sounds like you could use the extra hands, Superstar."

I felt the blush rise in my cheeks. More time with Jonah? I wouldn't have to say goodbye to him?

Cyrus cleared his throat across the room and that snapped me out of my thoughts.

"Jonah, I would love to have your help. You are an amazing ally. But I can't jerk you away from your life and dump you in a haunted forest with me. It's not fair."

"Maybe I want to go," Jonah bumped his arm against mine. "I can ask Reena and Terrence, too. You'll be doing us a favor. Keeping us sharp."

"Jonah, perhaps you should reconsider," Cyrus

approached us to stand next to Apollo. "The forest is no place for mortals."

"All due respect, Cyrus, no one here is exclusively mortal, anyway. So that argument holds no water."," Jonah stood with a shake of his head. "Give me a few minutes to round up Reena and Terrence. You can hitch a ride with us to L.A., Superstar. Joey is dealing with the equipment, right?"

"Right."

"I'll be back in a minute then."

Jonathan followed Jonah outside and Cyrus glared at me from over Apollo's shoulder.

"Leave us, Alexius."

With those simple words, Cyrus vanished. Apollo folded his arms over his chest.

"Alright, Eva. Say your piece. I can tell you are aching to have -"

"Where were you?" I interrupted him. I knew I should have shut my mouth. Been respectful. Instead, the questions that had been forming in my mind since I'd learned the truth of my lineage tumbled out before I could stop them. "Why Janet McRayne? Why did they hide you from me?"

Apollo pressed his lips together before he turned away from me. I stared at him before I sighed.

"You're right. This isn't the right time." I stood and brushed my palms against my jeans. "Maybe it's better this way. After all, what right do I have to know anything?"

I moved to leave the room. I was almost to the door when his next words stopped me.

"I wanted what was owed to me. Is that what you want to hear?"

I froze in place. I was afraid that if I turned around,

Apollo would disappear from the room without telling me the story I was so desperate to hear.

"It had been so long since anyone had praised my name. Centuries of false promises and weakened power had worn me down. So when the girl entered the circle and promised herself to me, I accepted the invitation without a second thought."

I turned to see Apollo studying me as I had him a few moments before. He clasped his hands behind his back before he continued.

"Janet reminded me of Delphine. The conquest which had eluded me so many centuries before was now at my fingertips. This is where your resemblance to the original Sibyl comes from, you know. Your mother."

I bowed my head at his words. When I had first encountered Delphine, I had been shocked at how similar our appearances were. Now, I knew why.

Apollo had accepted my mother's invitation to finish what he had started when he created his first Sibyl. Here was a woman who praised him. Worshipped him as Delphine never had. Of course he was going to accept her. He would have been a fool not to.

"It was only three months after the rituals began that you were conceived." Apollo rocked back on his heels. "Janet was fearful. She had nowhere to go. No one to turn to other than the McRayne coven."

I narrowed my eyes at him. His story sounded too much like fantasy. A dream instead of the events which led to my existence. But how could I not believe him? I'd seen too much already to call him a liar.

"So why go to all this trouble?" I shrugged. "Making me your Sibyl? Why not ignore me, let me live a boring existence, and die of old age never the wiser?"

Apollo gave me a small smile. The Sun God reached out

to brush his knuckles against my cheek. "Because you are mine."

I didn't miss how his smile tightened when he spoke again. "Did you know the McRaynes were impoverished? Lillian McRayne dedicated her life to Hecate in an attempt to ease the pain her poverty caused her. It is true the witch gave the girl power, but it wasn't until I appeared to Lillian after your conception that they gained the wealth they desired."

"I don't understand." I frowned. "You paid them off to take care of Janet?"

"No." Apollo closed the distance between us to take hold of my arms. "I granted them wealth to take care of you. You must understand your status, Eva. The title of Sibyl? Being the Representative of the Olympian Council? Neither of these compare to the fact that you are my child. A princess of Olympus who is no less than the other heroes who came before you."

"I don't know what that means." I confessed. "I'm not stupid. I understand the biological part. But the whole demi-god thing is confusing. Not to mention how new this knowledge is. I thought that if I talked to you, I would understand. I would know how to handle things better. But the truth is, I'm just as lost now as I was before."

"Janet and Lillian decided it was best if you didn't know the truth of your lineage." His golden eyes softened. For a moment, the Golden One seemed sad. "You are my first child in centuries, Eva. I doted on you through them. I provided you a palace by the sea. A life without worry or difficulties."

"Except I had nothing but difficulties." I pointed out. "I've had nothing but difficulties since I was born. You know my history with Janet better than anyone."

"Ah, but by accepting your role, I was able to grant you

immortality." He smiled once more. "A gift that is your birthright. If I'd thought for a second we may lose you, I would never have allowed the Council to assign you to take care of the Titans. You must know that."

"I," I sighed. "I know. But Tartarus?"

"Yes," He clasped my shoulders. "Tartarus. I have every faith in you."

"Alright." I sighed. "We'll get it done."

Apollo gave me a squeeze before he faded into the dull rays that filtered in through the study window. I stared at the spot until I heard the study door open once more to see Jonah, Terrence, and Reena enter the room.

"We'll pick up supplies in L.A.," I spoke before they could. "But I'd pack a bag with jeans, long sleeve shirts, things like that."

"Not the first time we've been camping, Evie," Jonah grinned and my heart fluttered when he held up a duffle bag. "We're ready when you are."

I pulled my phone from my back pocket and texted Joey about our change of plans. I asked him to make sure everything got taken care of at Covington and told him I would send a driver to pick him up from the airport when he arrived. When I was done, I turned back to my new friends.

"Can we take the Astralimes to my condo in L.A.?"

"Sure. What's the address?"

I told Reena, who fiddled with her phone. When she passed it around, I raised an eyebrow. "What are you doing?"

"Memorizing the coordinates. We have to have them if we've never been to a place before."

Ok. That sounded just about as clear as mud. I blinked when Jonah approached me to offer me his hand.

"You have to hold onto one of us," He explained. "I

promised you the ride, so I volunteer."

I gave him a small smile as I took his hand. I don't know what I expected, but I wasn't expecting it to be so instantaneous. One second, we were in North Carolina. The next? We were in my living room.

"Oh, wow," Reena whistled as she sat her bag on the couch. "This is lovely."

"Thank you." I said, both for her compliment then to Jonah for the trip home. "How does that work exactly?"

"The Astralimes?"

"Yeah."

"Eva, a moment."

I turned to see Cyrus standing in the doorway of the kitchen. I released Jonah's hand with a reluctance I admonished myself for.

"Sure, Cyrus," I smiled at the others. "Ya'll go upstairs and get comfortable for the night. My room is the last on the right, Joey's is next to it. But there are four other bedrooms to choose from."

"Great!" Terrence slung his bag over his shoulder. "We'll see you in a bit, Evie."

"See you."

I watched them all go upstairs before Cyrus turned on his heel and marched into the kitchen. I had a brief flash of fear that he knew what had been going through my head about Jonah. But that was impossible. How could he know? Hell, how could anyone know?

"Cyrus?" I shut the door behind me. "What's wrong?"

"I am not going to accompany you to Hoia-Baciu."

"Really?" I pushed off the door. "Is this because Apollo-"

"It seems as if you have enough protectors already." Cyrus sneered at me. "Besides, I have been given my own task. I leave this evening."

"Ok," I breathed out as I tried to figure out what he

expected me to say. "Have dinner with us then before you go. I will miss you."

"No, you won't." Cyrus raised his eyebrows. "I sincerely doubt you will even notice my absence and I have nothing to say to those who betray me."

"Cyrus, I didn't betray you!"

"Yes, you did!" He took a step towards me. I took a step back. "You broke our confidence, Eva. You allowed the Blue Aura to spin lies about me. Now, you won't have to be concerned about me for a while yet."

"What lies?" I hissed as my temper flared higher than my fear. "I told Apollo nothing but the truth."

"You know what lies." He stopped within inches of me. "You are a fool, little girl. Rowe has barely given you the time of day, and you have followed after him like a simpering puppy. But he will reject you, no matter how desperate you seem for his attention. Just as I have in the past."

I stared at Cyrus in shock. He wasn't yelling at me. He didn't touch me. But I don't think a slap across the face would have hurt as bad as the reminder of how I had tried to seduce him once and he rejected me. My keeper took advantage of my silence to whisper in my ear.

"Nobody - not Rowe, not even a slave - wants you, Eva. Don't make a fool of yourself believing otherwise."

Cyrus pulled back and stepped into the shadows. When he was gone, I closed my eyes as a single tear threatened to fall. I waited for my eyes to stop burning before I opened them. Cyrus was right. He was always right.

I had to pull myself together and fast. I could hear Jonah, Terrence, and Reena coming down the stairs. Their laughter was an unfamiliar sound in these walls. I moved over to the sink, splashed my face, then turned when they joined me.

# NINETEEN

## JONAH ROWE

JONAH CAUGHT IT INSTANTLY. Eva may have had a million dollar grin on her face, but her energy had changed. And a stark change, at that. It made him instantly defensive. No one so beautiful, body and spirit, should have to wear masks all the time. No matter the reason.

But that was all in his head. Terrence was the one who voiced it.

"What's wrong, Goldie?" He wanted to know. "I'm not a genius, but I know a cheerleader smile when I see one. What's happened?"

"Old memories, Terrence," She moved over to the fridge and grabbed waters for them, wine for herself. Jonah took the water she offered them then sat down as she continued. "Nothing to concern yourself with. But Cyrus told me that he won't be with us in Hoia-Baciu. He has another assignment."

"Is that common?" Jonah asked as he opened his water. "Or is this because of Apollo?"

"I don't know. He didn't say." She shrugged and Jonah could tell she was desperate to change the subject. "But let's not talk about that now. Have ya'll ever been to L.A. before? What would you like to do tonight?"

"Never been off the Atlantic Coast before my adopted brother invited me to Hawaii," Terrence said. "So Cali is a first."

"Barring the whirlwind experience in LAX when we relocated from Hawaii to Virginia, nope," Reena answered as she chugged water.

"I've been to California, but not L.A.," Jonah told her. He wasn't buying the old memories line at all, but Eva deserved respect for her secrets. He'd only known her eight days, after all. "Just road tripping with my best friend from my old accounting job, Nelson. His folks are in Sacramento. Went there a time or two."

"We should go out then." Eva sipped on the wine and Jonah could have sworn he heard her purr a little. "We can do dinner downtown, go walk around Rodeo, or just go for a drive. I'll need to get the paperwork for the episode done, but I can do that once we get back. I don't want ya'll to be stuck inside all day."

"It's just after noon?"

"Yup. So you have plenty of time to see the city. Consider it my treat for ya'll putting up with my bitchiness this past week."

Reena grinned. "You realize that we saw through your bitch mask the whole time, right? But your hospitality is still much appreciated."

"I'm not surprised," Eva laughed. "I've always been a horrible actress. I'd suggest a spa day, but there's no point since we're about to go to the woods. There's the studio tours, Disneyland-"

"Disneyland?" Terrence perked up. "That's an idea. You know how long it's been since I've been on a roller coaster?"

"How old are you? Ten?" Reena teased him. "When do you have to get Joey at the airport?"

"I don't. I am having one of Theia's cars pick him up." Eva finished off the glass of wine she had poured for herself and put the bottle back in the fridge. "But if we're going to Disneyland, I need to put on shorts. It's hot as hell outside."

"Is that good with you, J.?" Reena studied him. "Want to go see the Mouse?"

Jonah chuckled. "I'm down for whatever."

"Disneyland it is, then." Eva slipped her glass into the dishwasher. "I'll be down in a few minutes if ya'll want to get ready to go."

Jonah watched her go and Terrence jabbed him in the ribs.

"You sure that psychic was wrong?

"Absolutely wrong. She's just a friend, brother." Jonah finished his water and tossed it in the trash. "Just a friend."

---

“Let’s get you in bed, Superstar.”

Eva groaned as Jonah shook her shoulders. He'd found her with her head down in her arms on her desk sound asleep. When he spoke, she jerked awake and gave him a look of confusion.

"Jonah?" She blinked back the sleep in her eyes. "What..."

"You've been holed up in here for the past three hours," Jonah took a step back. "Thought I would check on you since it's getting so late."

"What time is it?"

"Just after three a.m."

"Dammit."

"Whatcha working on? Romania?"

"No," She rubbed her hand over her eyes. "No, I have a luncheon at twelve I completely forgot about. It's for charity, so I have to go."

"What charity?"

"Autism research. I was working on the speech they asked me to do. Plus, I got word from Apollo that Zeus is supposed to show up anytime between now and when we leave."

"Zeus? The Zeus?"

"The Zeus." She hid a yawn behind her hand. "You won't be able to miss him. He's flamboyant."

"Come on. You can still get a few hours of sleep before we have to go."

"You want to go?" Eva sounded surprised. "I wasn't going to put that on you, too."

"I think it would do the three of us some good." He pulled her up to her feet. "We'll pick up outfits at the mall."

Eva giggled. "I'll take care of the clothes. No mall lines required."

The two of them walked through the quiet condo in silence. When they stopped in front of Eva's door, she turned to him.

"Is there anything I can do for you before I pass out again?"

Jonah struggled with himself because he knew Eva would have to be on the clock soon, but still. "Is there somewhere around here where we can smoke?"

"You can use my balcony."

The two of them entered her bedroom and Jonah whistled. The color scheme was blue and white, which contrasted nicely against the rich mahogany of her furniture. The far wall was nothing but glass, so he was surprised when she slid her hand over the glass and a door opened

"This is pretty damn cool."

"Yeah? Wait until you see the view."

She stepped outside and Jonah followed her to take in the sight of L.A. sprawled out beneath them. The lights were dazzling.

"I never thought to put chairs out here." She stepped aside before she shut the door behind him. "I'm not here often enough, to be honest."

Jonah sat down on the concrete and she sat next to him. He pulled his case out of his pocket and a lighter.

"You came prepared." Eva teased. "One day in the city, and you're already needing to take the edge off?"

"Nope. Nana always said that it's better to have and not need than to need and not have. So I'm always ready." He lit the joint, took a deep pull, and breathed out. "Here. Remember, the trick is to pull and hold it. Let it get in your lungs and do its thing. Then exhale."

"I remember."

Eva took the joint from him and pulled in a mouth full of smoke. She made a face as she held it in as long as she could before she exhaled into a coughing fit.

"That's the coughing fit I was expecting the first time," She croaked. "Do I need some sort of technique or something?"

"Nope," Jonah grinned. "The coughing signifies a great pull. Drink some water, and we'll do a few more. It'll calm you down, I promise."

Eva willed a bottled water in her hand and sipped on it while Jonah smoked. After a few more hits, she looked better. Less tense. She held the water bottle in her lap and rested her head on his shoulder.

Jonah froze at her movement. He could smell the lavender in her hair even more so than the earthy scent coming from the weed.

"Um, Eva?"

"What?" She jerked her head up. "Gods, sorry about that. I wasn't thinking."

"Eva-"

"Evie." She muttered before she sipped on the water.

"What?"

"Call me Evie. Or Superstar." Eva shifted away from him and closed her eyes. "People only call me Eva when they are strangers or when they are mad at me."

"Evie, it is," Jonah said. "But don't expect me to let you call me J.J."

"Why would I call you that?"

Jonah smiled. "You said you looked us up. So I'm sure you know that was my childhood nickname."

"I want to know everything about you." She covered a yawn with her hand. "The big things, the little things. I'm sure there's something that Google and Facebook haven't told me about you already."

"Like how I smoke weed on occasion?"

"Hmm, exactly like that."

Jonah chuckled as he finished off the joint. He stubbed it out on the concrete and they sat in silence for a while. Eva had almost dozed back off with her head against the outer wall when Jonah spoke again.

"So what's the deal with you and Cyrus now?"

"Don't know."

"Pardon?"

"I don't know." She lifted her shoulder in a shrug without opening her eyes. "I never really have. We're supposed to be together, but...it's never felt that way."

"Doesn't *look* that way either." Jonah knew he might be out of line, but he said it anyway. "Unless my observation skills are way off. "And don't try to cover for him. I know he's still pissed off because his ass got caught putting his hands on you. That's probably why he isn't going to Hoia-Baciu."

"Cyrus prefers it when I go at things alone. He always has. Says it makes me stronger." She opened her eyes to take in the city spread out beneath them as she ignored what he said about the abuse. "But me and you? We make a damn good team, Blueberry. I don't want you in those woods, but I'm so happy that you are here."

"You shouldn't be alone in there anyway," Jonah said, ignoring the brief giddiness of knowing Eva was happy he was there. "I don't think it'll be a digression of your strength if you had support."

"I like how that sounds."

"What?"

"Support. It's a nice word."

"Something you're not used to?"

"Something I don't dare expect," Eva shifted so that she could look at his face in the moonlight. "You have a group. A team. Friends and family you can depend on to always be there. That's a luxury not everyone has, Blueberry."

"You're Eva McRayne," Jonah said, bewildered. "You have a team *and* a staff, Superstar."

"But not people I can trust." She took a sip of her water. "If I tell the wrong person the right thing, they can go to any publication and make millions. If I fuck up in front of the wrong person, it'll be all over the internet within hours. I trusted Elliot once, and he shoved me out of a four-story window. I am only alive today because Hermes gave me the choice to pass into the ether or stay on the earthplane."

Jonah just listened to her, then pulled on the water. He couldn't believe Eva's circle was so small. Seemed as though it was only Joey. "What do you do to cope, Superstar? Since your circle is so small and you don't smoke weed."

"Work. Wine. That's pretty much it. I hate Hollywood parties. I don't do drugs," She gave him a small smile. "I'm the most boring celebrity in existence, I think. What do you do to cope?"

"Gym, Netflix, and camping," Jonah rattled off. "Nothing better for me, personally. When the holiday season hits, we do something called Butterball or Bust. Doug Chandler--another one of our friends--volunteers with this place called The Brown Bag Charity. They get all these donations of groceries, and we all box them up. We take them to the front doors of these needy and elderly families, ring the doorbell, and high-tail it away from there. It's fun as hell."

"That does sound like fun," Eva grinned at him. "Maybe next year, I can help out in some way. Gods know, I can donate cash if you need it."

She took a sip from the water and lowered it.

"Camping is gonna come in handy because I've never actually done that before. But Joey practically lived in the woods around his family's ranch in Wyoming. That's something you two have in common."

"Joey's woodsy? Huh." Jonah was intrigued. "How did he get into camera work?"

"He's an expert marksman, so he was really good at shooting things. He just traded his gun for a camera."

Jonah had rested back against the door frame. His legs stretched out before him and crossed at the ankles. Eva turned her neck so that she could watch him.

"So what's the deal with you and that woman?"

"What woman?"

"The one Hera used to torture you with. She showed you scenes of a woman with Terrence. That means she is pretty important." Eva fiddled with her earring. Jonah wondered if that was a nervous habit of hers when he spotted it. "Can I ask? Or is that too personal?"

Jonah sighed. He kind of wished he still had his joint.

"Vera. We are...Evie, it's kinda like grabbing the proverbial brass ring. You pull at it, think you've grabbed it, then--" He made a whooshing sound, "You're back at square one. It's kind of like that."

"What does that mean?" She looped her arms around her knees. "She makes herself unavailable?"

Jonah looked past Eva and to the lights. Eva stayed silent and he began to talk. He told her about the friendship that he had with Vera Haliday. He told her about the attraction between them and how he had tried to get her attention. Jonah told Eva about a date he had taken her on that ended with Vera giving him the silent treatment for months because he stopped to help a stranded woman on the side of the road. When he finished, Eva seemed pissed off. She had sat up and was staring at him.

"She ignored you?"

"Eva, it's not so simple-"

"Yes, it is." Eva frowned. "You helped a stranger who happened to be female and this Vera got all pissy about it. That pisses me off."

"Why?"

"Because you're...you're a good person. You're nice and you tried. You tried to do right by her and by the stranger, but you got burned because of it. That's fucked up, Blueberry. Vera doesn't realize what she is throwing away."

Jonah was taken aback, surprised by Eva's immediate defensive stance. Yet, he was also flattered. Odd. "I appreciate you, Superstar. Truly. It's just...one of the most confusing things I've ever experienced."

"Look, I know it's none of my business. And if I'm coming across too bitchy, tell me and I'll shut up. But of course, you're confused! Because she is making it confusing. And she's doing that shit on purpose to keep you dangling on a leash. It's not right. If she wants to be with you, then she'll be with you. There would be no confusion. No mind games."

Jonah shrugged. "That's what I thought. But Jonathan always says that people never fit perfectly in our boxes. So I was...I guess trying to accommodate her complexities."

"Complexities," Eva snorted. "Would you like an outsider's opinion?"

"Go for it, Superstar."

"Vera is not complex. Not in the way you think. You're a pretty big deal in the ethereal world, right? So she loves the fact that she has your attention. But it's more than that. She loves the fact that she can control you through snide comments, rudeness, and the silent treatment. She loves the attention because she knows that she doesn't deserve you, but you are a ready made audience to manipulate to her whims. And when you helped that stranger? She got pissed because her 'audience' was taken away. Because she was unable to control you in that moment. So she punished you." Eva's tone softened. "Just because someone doesn't fit in our boxes - as you say - doesn't give them the right to treat you like crap. The truth is, she doesn't fit in your boxes because she doesn't want to."

Jonah shook his head. A part of him knew Eva had a point. "I don't think I've ever heard it like that before."

Eva shrugged. "I'm a woman. Means I can see through other women's bullshit."

"Or you have experience with bullshit yourself."

"Plenty of experience." She tilted her head at him. "We just talked about my issues with Cyrus."

"How long have you two been 'together'?"

Jonah used air quotes for that last word and for some

reason, Eva must have found that funny because she laughed at him and he grinned in response.

"About four years now. You know about the things he has done, but the abuse isn't the reason I question things."

"What do you mean?"

Eva took her time before she responded.

"Well, there's no romance. Nothing physical at all. He has the role of mentor more than anything."

Jonah folded his arms. "No physical of any kind? Yet he wants you to check in on everything? Sounds like he's got a cushy arrangement where he begrudges you access to knowledge, but keeps himself distant enough to keep the perks."

Eva looked Jonah over. "You think so?"

"Where is he, Superstar?" Jonah asked. "I could talk about how he disrespects you all day. But the most glaring point is that he put his hands on you more than once. That's a non-starter."

Eva got quiet. So quiet that Jonah shifted against the concrete floor of the balcony.

"We can change the subject-"

"No, it's ok. I tore into how Vera treats you. If I can do that, then I can accept how you view Cyrus." She gave him a small smile. "Regardless, just know that I think Vera has no idea how lucky she is. You take the time to create special moments with her. She should be grateful. She sure as hell shouldn't be using you the way she is."

"And Cyrus shouldn't be acting all Alpha Male and smacking you around." Jonah said. "Just saying. "

"We're both in screwed up situations," She shook her head before she looked outwards. Jonah himself was surprised at how light the sky was getting. "I think I've kept you up all night again, Jonah."

"That means a sleep in," Jonah joked. "We have to head out closer to evening after all."

"Hmm, you can sleep in. I have that charity luncheon in a few hours." She smiled at his expression. "Seriously. Stay here. Sleep. It'll be a few hours, so by the time I'm done, you'll just be waking up."

"Okay," Jonah said, "I'm game. Answer me honestly. Did the smoke help?"

"It did actually," Eva made the move to stand then dusted her ass off. "But I think the conversation helped more. Thanks, Blueberry."

"You're very welcome, Superstar," Jonah grinned. "And don't forget. I'm always prepped."

She chuckled. "And you can always use the balcony if you need it."

They came back inside and Jonah hesitated before he left her room. He saw that it was just after five a.m. so he bade Eva a good couple of hours rest before he went to his guest room. He stepped down and crashed on the bed as he considered their conversation. Eva was right. They were both in screwed up situations.

Now, if he could just figure out how to fix it.

Jonah snagged his phone from the nightstand and swiped his thumb across the screen. He wasn't surprised to see there weren't any messages from Vera. Maybe he had hoped that if he had one, it was a sign that Eva was wrong.

There may not have been a message from Vera, but there was a text message from his friend, Asa. He frowned when he realized it had come in while the group was at Disneyland. He clicked on it and began to read.

*J, man! Call me! I got news!*

The next line had come in fifteen minutes later.

*Dammit, you must be at the library. I'm going to Hollywood, man! I got a call from an agent in L.A. today. They love my work! Gonna get me hooked up with one of the studios. Call me!*

Jonah was so stunned that he didn't even respond to the message. He threw on his pants and ran down the hall. He knocked on Eva's door. After a moment, she opened it.

"Jonah? What's wrong?"

He simply looked at Eva, still stunned.

"You made good on your promise to Asa. You actually helped him out."

"I told you I would," She raised an eyebrow at him. "I don't want him to know I was involved though. He should shine on his own merit."

"He's got a backpack full of projects," Jonah breathed. "You aligned him with people who'll hear him out? People who, forgive me, won't try to 'white' his stuff up?"

"Jonah, I hooked him up with the right people. There's no fear of his work being compromised." Eva leaned her head against the door jam. "They'll take good care of him. Hear him out and give him a good deal. Once he's signed, I asked them to send Asa to my personal lawyer to make sure everything works out exactly how he wants it. Your friend and his work will be just fine."

Jonah shook his head. "You're fucking awesome."

Eva snorted. "Because of my connections?"

"Because you're *you*." Jonah said. "Connections mean nothing. It comes down to the person who uses them. You're wonderful, Eva."

Eva shrugged a little. "Honestly, it's no big deal. I got a hold of Asa's manuscripts, sent a couple of text messages, and passed them around. The studio people loved them. Not because of me, but because the work is that good. Asa has the talent. He just needed someone to open the door."

"Thank you, Eva. So much." Jonah was still stunned.

"You might have just righted the trajectory of my friend's life. That IT job was crushing him."

Eva smiled as she crossed her arms over her chest.

"You're welcome, but I should be thanking you. Hollywood needs more diversity. You led me to someone who could very well make the biggest difference. Please, don't worry about Asa. Just celebrate with him."

She got quiet for a moment before she continued.

"I'm still working on those Broadway contacts. They are exceedingly difficult, but I was able to talk to a producer who will go to Vera's show. He's going to head to Seattle next week."

"She'll love that," Jonah said. "It'll be the highlight of her life, getting that play off the ground."

"I'll do what I can. I promise." She gave him another ghost of a smile. "I'd help you, too, if you let me."

"I'm good, Superstar ,"Jonah said. "There is no monumental favor l can ask for."

"Yeah? Well, if you think of anything-"

"Good night, Evie. I just...I just wanted to say thank you."

"Good night."

Eva closed her door and Jonah headed back to his room. He texted Asa back as he walked.

*Awesome! I can't wait to hear all about it, brother!*

# TWENTY

## EVA MCRAYNE

I COULD HEAR the crowds screaming my name as the door to the limo was opened by a very large, very serious security guard. He tapped his earpiece to announce my arrival as he helped me out. I brushed out the wrinkles in the sundress I wore while I turned to wave to those held back by a series of metal barricades.

"Eva! Over here!"

"Hey, Joey!" I called over the noise as I approached him. "Welcome home!"

"Eva!" I heard my name again from one of the reporters. "Come chat for a minute!"

I took Joey's arm as we made our way to the man who had called me over. Bryan Summers pressed a microphone in my face.

"We are thrilled to see you on the red carpet today, Eva." He flashed a bleached smile at us. "Your first one since the Spring, right? How are you holding up?"

"Autism research is an important cause." I managed to smile without clenching my teeth together. Not too hard, at least. "I wanted to come out and support the fine work these organizations do."

There. That sounded good enough. I sure as hell wasn't going to go into the murders of my parents or the rumors of my supposed suicide attempt. Smile. Gloss over the bad stuff. Romance the crowds.

That was my job right now.

"Where is Cyrus?" Bryan again. "I don't think I have ever seen you without him."

"What am I, chopped liver?"

Joey joked as he moved to stand in front of me. I gave him a relieved smile as I understood what he was doing. Joey was trying to shield me from the questions that I couldn't answer. I squeezed the back of his arm to give him my thanks. I took advantage of his distraction to focus on the line of photographers snapping away a million clicks a minute. I knew my picture would show up on their websites within hours. I would be in their magazines by the end of the week.

I was twirling around so that they could get the full effect of my outfit when I bumped into the man who appeared next to me. I expected it to be Joey, so I threw my arms around his neck to hug him.

The press loved it. Ate it up when Joey and I did our thing for them.

"That's a hell of a welcome." Zeus laughed as I jumped away from him. He gave the cameras a dazzling smile when he tightened his grip around my waist. "Apollo said you wished to speak with me."

"You have the worst timing ever." I hissed. "I can't talk to you about the barrier here."

"By the gods, girl!" He threw his head back with a laugh. "I wasn't going to miss a good party."

"Luncheon." I shifted away from him when we turned to continue down the line. "This is not a party."

"Will there be booze?"

"God, I hope so." I sighed. "Probably. This is Hollywood."

"Then it's a party, Evie."

Zeus gave a final wave when he held the door open for me. I rolled my eyes at him as I got my first good look at the white linen suit and loud pink shirt he wore. His white beard had been shaved back to stubble. He looked like a grandpa who tried too hard to understand his grandkids.

I stopped in my tracks at the thought. I snatched the first flute of champagne I could get my hands on when a waiter appeared. I tossed it back then grabbed another before I started laughing.

"What?" Zeus snatched a glass from the tray, too. He downed his as fast as I had mine. "What's so funny?"

"This is just too ridiculous." I giggled. "The great Zeus. Commander of the Heavens. My grandfather!"

He pressed his lips together for a second. "You finally made the connection, huh?"

"Yeah. And I am going to need more alcohol to handle that revelation." I pushed my way through the crowd until we reached the bar set up. "I need something stronger than champagne."

"Two scotch. Neat." Zeus held up two fingers as if the poor man couldn't speak English. When the bartender moved away from us, he twisted around to study me. "I don't understand what's so funny to you."

"Oh, nothing." I tapped my fingers against the wooden counter. "Other than the fact that I'm trying to figure out if I should call you Pappy Zeus or not."

"Zeus will work just fine." He growled. "About time Apollo told you the truth."

"Technically, he didn't." I pointed out. "Hecate broke the news when I was at the Academy."

"There you are!"

I looked up to see Joey catch up to us. He looked me over before turning to my companion. He freed one hand to extend it towards Zeus.

"Joey Lawson. Are you a reporter?"

I laughed. I couldn't help it. I snagged my scotch and took a gulp before I answered him.

"Joey, meet Pappy Zeus." I chuckled. "Pappy Zeus, my buddy Joey."

I guess Joey had been hanging around me too long. Too much exposure to the deities that circled around me. But even then, Joey's face went white. He didn't bother with an apology. He simply bowed his head instead.

"Please don't smite me." My friend muttered loud enough for us to hear. "Or if you do, do it in my sleep. I won't feel a thing."

Zeus snorted before he knocked back his own drink. He ordered us another. By the time they had arrived, I was more than ready to talk about Romania. But first things first. We had to sit through the luncheon. I had to repair the damage my time in Charleston had caused.

I had to convince my audience that there was nothing wrong. No monsters waiting in the wings. No threatening destruction.

"Come on. I need to sit down." I finished off my second glass. "We'll talk back at my place when this is over."

I didn't give either one of them the chance to answer. I lowered myself down at the first table I came to. I ended up sitting next to an actress known best for her baby daddy drama than her work. I pushed my chair farther away from her when the world began to spin.

"What the hell was in that scotch?" I muttered to Joey when he sat next to me. "I think I need to cut back today."

"Yeah, well," Joey frowned at the napkin he was trying to unfold. "You started drinking when the make-up crew arrived. I'm surprised you are still standing."

"True." I admitted. "In my defense, I didn't get much sleep last night."

"Water for my girl over here." Joey gestured to the waiter who approached us. "We're cutting her off."

"You, sir, are a royal buzzkill." Zeus spoke over my head. "Let the girl enjoy herself."

I watched as he glared at the actress on the other side of me until she excused herself from the table. He lowered himself down in the chair to push the plate in front of him aside. I tilted my head towards Zeus when I asked my next question.

"You said you gave me my sword because of the things I'd done for your family. I don't think that's true."

"Oh?" Zeus raised his eyebrows at me. "So you are calling me a liar."

"Evie…"

Joey hissed, but I ignored him as I continued.

"No, not quite. I'm sure that was part of it. But I think the truth is much simpler. I think you wanted me to like you. You have a history of bribery, after all. You knew I was going to learn about Apollo sooner rather than later. You wanted me to like you."

"Well, do you?" Zeus grinned. "Like me?"

"And the title. The Representative of Olympus. That was a present from you, too."

"Guilty." Zeus locked his fingers together when he rested his hands on the table. "The sword, the title. These are minor compared to the other blessings I have gifted to those in my bloodline."

"Did you throw them to the wolves too?" I widened my eyes in a mock innocence. "Or am I the only one to experience that particular honor?"

"It is time to get back to the task at hand, Sibyl." Zeus stiffened as he sat up straight. "The barriers."

"Fine." I mirrored his stance. It was obvious that I'd ticked him off. "I heard that you have no idea what I'm supposed to be doing. So I have to find Chronos."

"There was no need to know." The great King of the Heavens looked away from me towards a group of presenters heading towards the stage. "The barriers were supposed to be impregnable. Chronos insured it."

"So how do you know they are weakened?" I began to twist the stem of a champagne flute between my fingers. "How can you be so sure?"

"Because activity around Hoia-Baciu has increased ten-fold over the past two years. We overlooked it at first. We assumed that it would balance itself out over time."

"But it hasn't." I raised an eyebrow at him. "Ok. So our next step is Chronos. Where is he?"

"Ah, old Chronos." Zeus gave me a cold smile. "No. You won't be meeting him."

"Why not?" I frowned as a woman in green tapped on the podium to get everyone's attention. I lowered my voice a notch when she began to speak. "I need his help."

"Chronos is a permanent resident of the New Valley Retirement Home located in Anchorage, Alaska." He tossed back his drink before he pointed at me. "The old crow couldn't help you even if he tried. I had his memory erased."

I let my mouth drop open in surprise. I'd like to think I recovered nicely because somewhere in the back of my mind, I heard the speaker call my name seconds before the cameras turned towards me.

"Ms. McRayne and Mr. Joseph Lawson were our largest donors for this event. She has given *Autism Today* a record $250,000 to further our research into this condition. Eva," She gave me a smile. "Will the two of you come and say a few words?"

"Two hundred and fifty, what?" Joey leaned over to whisper in my ear. "You gave them our perfume ad money, didn't you?"

"Don't worry, Joey." I patted his hand. "It's only money. You'll get your share of the next endorsement we do. I promise."

As we rose up to approach the podium, my thoughts were flying at a million miles a second. Chronos was out. And Cyrus wasn't here to guide me. I didn't know how in the actual hell I was going to be able to pull this off.

I didn't have a choice. I had to think of something. Fast.

---

"You gonna tell me what I need to know or not?"

I kicked off my heels the second we walked through my front door. With Zeus and Joey following right behind me, I led them into the living room and curled up on the sofa.

The great god sighed before he looked at my friend. "Is she always so moody?"

"Only after she drinks scotch." Joey chuckled. "I'm going to get changed. See you in a few."

I waited until he was gone before I glared up at my guest. He grabbed the remote, flipped on the television then kicked his feet up on my coffee table. After a few minutes of watching him surf through commercials, I sat up and knocked his boots off my furniture.

"I'm waiting."

You're too extreme, Evie." He glowered at me. "Fine. Give me your tablet."

I rolled my eyes and reached into the side table to my left. I grabbed the device, switched it on, then passed it over. Zeus began typing something into it the second it loaded up.

"You need to speak with Prometheus."

"Who?" I frowned. "Wait. Is that the fire guy?"

"Sort of."

I twisted my head and smiled when I saw Jonah come down the stairs. He gave me a sleepy smile in return as he sat in the armchair next to the couch.

"Who are you?" Zeus narrowed his eyes. "I didn't see you at the luncheon."

"Pappy Zeus, Jonah Rowe. Jonah, the one and only Zeus."

Zeus beamed at my introduction as he shook Jonah's hand. "Any friend of my Evie's is a friend of mine."

"Uh huh. Go back to this fire guy."

"Prometheus?" Zeus looked up at me before he pulled up a Google map image. "Oh, right. He is a Titan. Smart enough to choose the winning side of the Titanomachy. He was spared Tartarus for that very reason."

"Ok." I leaned over to look at the screen. "How can he help me?"

"For one, he's a Titan. Two, he is an expert in Titan history." Zeus glanced over at me with his ice grey eyes. "And three, he is known for his trickery. If anyone knows how to strengthen those barriers, it will be him."

"So where is he? What are you showing me?"

"San Francisco." Zeus smirked. "He lives there now. Goes by the name Paul Martin."

"Paul Martin?" Jonah felt like an intruder on the

conversation, but the name was one he was familiar with. "The famous grifter?"

"That's the one," Zeus said. "He was ways adept at craftiness."

"How Do you know of him?" I asked, curious.

"Paul Martin was on *Masterminds*," Jonah explained. "He was an amazing grifter and con man. Only got caught when one of his jobs needed extra hands and someone slipped up. But I can't believe that the master criminal was a damn Titan. One would think he'd be untouchable. Zeus, Paul Martin...*Prometheus*...did five years. How could they contain and incarcerate a Titan?"

"Prometheus remained incarcerated simply because he wanted to be." Zeus passed the tablet back to me. "He may be a trickster and a con man, but he is one that you will need, so play nice. Here is his address in San Francisco. Fancies himself to be a hipster these days."

"How do you know what a hipster is?" I frowned at him. "You know what? I don't want to know."

Zeus patted me on the knee before he stood. I watched him stuff his hands in his pockets and I knew he was about to leave. I didn't know if I should be relieved or worried since he hadn't told me that much.

"I want you to be careful in the Forest of the Forgotten." Zeus shifted his focus down to me. "Monsters from every corner of the globe were trekked in to keep curious onlookers away from what lies beneath it. So brush up on all legends. Not just our own."

"Forest of the Forgotten?" I frowned. "Why is Hoia-Baciu called that?"

"Because the creatures who roam through the trees were discarded by their cultures long ago." He gave me a sad smile. "Be on guard. Flip through the cards whenever necessary. And trust in your instincts."

“What in the hell does that mean? Flip through what cards?” I swung my feet off the couch as he disappeared. “Dammit.”

I dropped down on the couch and rested my forehead against my armrest. Finally, I spoke.

"Mornin', Blueberry. Sorry you walked in on that."

"All good," Jonah promised. "Any idea what creatures they were talking about?"

"No," I muttered against the armrest. "None. I need to find and meet with Prometheus. He's the only one who can tell me what we need to do to shut the barrier down."

"What happened with Chronos?"

"Zeus wiped his mind. Stuck him in an old folk's home." I lifted my head. "So it's onto San Francisco before the flight to Romania."

"Flight?"

"Yeah. We have to get all the cameras flown in. And I don't want to abandon Joey on a long flight like that. You don't have to fly if you don't want to. I'd hate to put you through that since you, Reena, and Terrence are helping me with this."

"Eva, how many times do I have to tell you that we are helping you no matter what?" Jonah said. "We're in. Even if it's a flight."

I smiled at him. I couldn't help it. I wondered if Jonah knew how gallant he seemed to me right now.

"You're a hard one to shake, Blueberry. Thank you for not listening to me."

I sat up as Joey came tromping back down the stairs. He looked at me then to Jonah before he looked back at me again.

“Hey, you ok?” Joey took the seat that Zeus had abandoned. “You look like you’re about to throw the remote through the television. Don’t do that.”

"Hardy har," I shook my head at him. "I need you to go to the office. Get the equipment ready to go. I have to go to San Francisco to get information."

"I thought we were leaving tonight."

"We are. This won't take long. The drive to San Francisco is what? A few hours?"

"A few seconds," Jonah snagged the tablet and studied the map Zeus had left behind. "You can catch a ride with me."

I sat up. "Really? Because the sooner we go, the sooner we can get to Romania."

"Yeah," Jonah stood to take in the cocktail dress I had on. "You might want to change though. You never know if there will be a fight or not."

"I never do, Jonah," I squeezed his hand before I realized what I was doing. "I never do."

---

What could I possibly say about San Francisco to do it justice? The town was beautiful. A shining example of the wealth that California had to offer its people. As we walked through the Haight-Ashbury neighborhood, I couldn't help but stare at the brightly colored houses that lined the road.

"Painted ladies." Jonah explained. "That's what these houses are called."

"Really?" I gave him a small smile. "Jonah, the more I see of you, the more I think that you are Wikipedia personified."

He chuckled as he stuck his hands in his pockets. I knew from Google Images that we were looking for a blue house with green embellishments. And I vaguely recalled how Zeus had called Prometheus a hipster. But other than that, I had no idea what to expect. I was searching for the house when I heard Joey whistle out from behind me.

"Now this is where we need to be investigating."

I shook my head as Reena announced we had found the house we were looking for. It was ornate. Flamboyant. And utterly magnificent.

I took the gray stairs two at a time until I was standing in front of the door, but when I raised my fist to knock, it flew open. A man squinted at me until he noticed the others coming up from behind me. I was just as surprised by his appearance as he seemed to be at my presence. His hair fell in dark waves over his shoulders. His beard was the stuff of legends. He wore thick black glasses better left in 1965. Glasses he was now glaring through as he struggled to see me thanks to the late afternoon glare of the sun.

"Sorry. No solicitations."

He started to shut the door back, but I was quick. I smacked my palm against the wood with a smile.

"Mr. Martin, my name is Eva McRayne. May we speak to you for a minute?"

"Eva who?" He scoffed. "Look, girl, I told you. I'm busy. I don't care what you're selling."

"Titanomachy. Does that word ring a bell with you?"

I dropped my hand when he released the door. He leaned out, glanced up and down both sides of the street, then stepped aside. The god didn't say another word as he turned to go down the hallway.

"You Titans sure know how to welcome a girl." I called after him. When he didn't respond, I sighed. "Let's go before he changes his mind."

I followed him through the thin hallway until we reached a room that was covered with more trash than furniture. I stepped through piles of newspapers and wrinkled my nose at the smell which filled the air.

"What is that?"

"Pot." Prometheus responded. "I'd give you a hit, but I don't share with strangers."

"Personally, I don't want your weed," Jonah said. "All due respect, you may very well have laced it with something. I have my own. So, Eva, what do you need from this guy?"

I couldn't explain it, but having Jonah standing next to me made me more confident. More assertive. Or maybe, I was. I knew that with my friend beside me, I could handle anything. Even a drugged out Titan. I gave him a quick look of appreciation before I focused back on Prometheus.

"Listen, I need your help."

"Can't. I won't be no help. Not anymore."

"Sir," I closed my eyes and tried not to breathe as he picked up a thin cigarette. "The barriers of Tartarus have been weakened. The Council is sending me out to Hoia-Baciu to secure them. But I haven't the first clue as to what to do."

"Ah, a hero then." He smirked at me before he took a drag off of his nasty cigarette. "That is how you recognized me."

"Sort of." I frowned. "Can you not do that, please? I need you to have a clear head."

"Never been clearer." He blew out a cloud of smoke towards the ceiling. "There's nothing I can tell you. Sorry. You've wasted your time."

"Aren't you an expert?" I didn't bother to hide my actions when I covered my nose with my hand. Jonah's weed hadn't bothered me. So why did the smoke around us stink so bad? "Zeus said..."

"Zeus says a lot of things. All of which are lies." The man sat up to point the joint at me. "Sorry to disappoint you."

I glanced over to Jonah, who was glaring at the Titan with the frustration I felt. I was sure the god was lying to me. In fact, I was convinced he knew everything there was to know about Tartarus and the barrier. He was just making this needlessly difficult.

Well, there was more than one way to get the information I needed.

"My apologies as well." I sighed. "You know, I thought for a second that you were the god I was looking for. Although for a Titan, I'd imagined you would be taller. Stronger."

The air in the room shifted in a second. The god threw his little brown cigarette into an ashtray. He stood and stormed back down the hallway to the front door. For the second time in less than five minutes, he held the door open for us. This time though, he was throwing us out.

Just before I crossed the threshold, I turned on my heel and stuck out my hand. I was more than a little surprised when he accepted it.

"Thank you in advance, Prometheus."

I gritted my teeth as his power flowed through my body the second I said his name.  Cyrus had claimed my ability to steal the knowledge of the gods was based solely on my status as a demi-god. I couldn't dispute him since I knew next to nothing about the benefits of my bloodline. But as I struggled to stay upright when the Titan's knowledge slammed into my brain, I knew more than I had ever wanted to know.

The thrill of stealing from the gods. The pain of having my body ripped open again and again by a bird's sharp beak. The drugs Prometheus used to mask the memories he couldn't forget.

"Let go of me!"

I heard him snap before I realized I was still holding his

hand. I dropped it in an instant as Jonah grabbed my shoulders.

"Eva? What the hell?"

I turned to search his face as the world shifted in colors and sounds I had never experienced. I stumbled into him as I tried to form words.

"Stole...memories. I know everything."

Those were the last words I would say before I collapsed against my friend in a fit of laughter.

# TWENTY-ONE

## JONAH ROWE

JONAH LOOKED at Eva in alarm and confusion. All she did was touch the guy's hand, and now she was laughing like a full-on stoner who'd been toking for hours.

"Dude, what the hell?" He demanded of Prometheus. "What did you just do?"

The Titan shrugged. "I *did* tell you to get out of here."

"Look, Cheech the Titan," Jonah got in his personal space. "What the hell *was* that? What's happening?"

"Jonah," Eva cackled, "Have I ever told you that your accent pulls me in *every* single time? You could be reading the directions on *Minute Rice* and it could be like Shakespeare."

Jonah felt his face heat up, and Reena took Eva by the shoulders. "Holy hell. Does Eva have a bipolar diagnosis? Is she manic?"

"Oh, for God's sake," Terrence said. "Speaking as the only one here who actually watches *Grave Messages,* Eva has the ability to absorb traits from other beings. Don't ask how; they never touched on it in any of the episodes. My guess is that she absorbed Hippie Dude's um...highness."

"Right you are, Terrence." Eva airily lifted her hand for a fist bump. "Right you are."

Joey knelt down next to Eva then looked up at Jonah, Reena, and Terrence.

"Let's get her out of here before the press shows up. This don't look good at all."

"What were you on?" Jonah turned to the Titan. "Asshole-"

"A speedball," He gave them a vicious grin before he stepped back. "Have fun with the goddamn thief!"

Jonah started forward but Reena grabbed his arm. Terrence and Joey were lifting Eva to her feet but she slumped between them.

"Funny. Feels funny." She frowned. "Why are there so many birds?"

"Birds?" Reena frowned. "Eva, I haven't seen a bird all day."

"Let me have her," Jonah reached over and lifted Eva off her feet. "We need to get her back to the condo. She can't go anywhere like this."

"Sweet," Eva muttered against him. "So sweet. Why are you so good to me, Blueberry? You don't even know me."

"To the alley, J.?"

"Yeah," Jonah ignored Eva as they headed into the alley between Prometheus' house and his neighbor. "We can leave from here."

"I want to get to know you," Eva muttered as she buried her face into the side of his neck. "You smell good. And you're nice. You're too good for me though."

"What?" Jonah turned the corner, but he was momentarily distracted. "What did you say, Eva?"

"You're mad at me. Can tell. Called me Eva. It's ok," Her eyelids fluttered. "It's ok. Nobody wants me. Just leave me here."

"Eva, you're making no sense." Jonah was very alarmed by her words. But it was no shock. Not if she was feeling the effects of a damn speedball. Opioid mixed with a stimulant...no wonder she collasped. Prometheus grinned from the side of the porch with no mirth as he watched them.

"Looks like you all will be in for a long day. That'll show you about trespassing."

"Hey, Chong, look!"

Terrence held up his phone, and a video of an incoming crow popped up. Prometheus yelped and staggered back, falling in a heap over his own feet.

"Yeah." Terrence snorted. "That's what I thought."

Joey glanced over Terrence's way.

"That was a cool thing you did," He remarked.

Terrence pocketed his phone. "That was one story I actually remembered. Bitch."

Jonah led them to the farthest part of the alley then initiated the Astralimes. When the group appeared in the living room, Jonah lowered Eva down on the couch and Joey went about the process of slipping off her shoes.

"What are you doing?"

"Making sure she don't get the couch dirty. She'll hate that when she wakes up."

"And you know that from experience?"

"Yeah," Joey stood with Eva's shoes in his hand. "Let's just say this isn't the first time Evie has passed out due to intoxication."

Reena, Terrence, and Jonah all looked at each other before Joey returned from the foyer.

"What did you mean by that, Joey?"

"About what?"

"The intoxication comment. Eva doesn't seem like a druggie to me."

"Or me." Reena crossed her arms. "And I would know."

Joey sighed as he lowered into an armchair and rubbed his hands over his face. Finally, he spoke.

"Evie has never met a wine bottle or liquor she didn't like."

Jonah looked over at Eva. That was a huge surprise. "Do you mean to say Eva's an alcoholic?"

Joey nodded. "Functioning. You should see her room and office, man. Bottles, mini samples from the air lines...there is this intern who threw away a gift of three dozen bottles of rum before Eva saw them. She has it under control. Usually."

"When did that start?" Reena sat across from Joey. "The alcohol use?"

"I can't tell you." He shrugged. "She and Elliot used to go out when they went to Georgia together. It got worse after things blew up between them."

"What does that mean?"

"Guys, I really shouldn't be saying all this."

"Joey, if you want to help Eva? You have to help Eva." Reena again. "So talk. What happened between her and Elliot?"

Joey looked between them. He seemed to be trying to gauge how much he should say.

"Elliot kinda...stalked Eva. Long before she became the Sibyl. He would just appear where she was. They built a friendship off of that, somehow. Maybe she never believed he would actually stalk her. Anyway, they had a fight during the premiere of *Grave* and Elliot never forgave her for questioning him. He would put her in shit situations to prove her loyalty. Even used her as bait to catch a rapist in San Diego - she was fine, by the way. Wasn't hurt in the least. But she started drinking more after that. Dinner drinks moved up to lunch. Lunch moved up to breakfast. It was the only thing that calmed her nerves as she continued to work on the show."

Jonah just stared at Joey. "Has anyone tried to call her on it?"

Joey scoffed. "Eva is the centerpiece of Theia. No one in their right mind would make her mad."

"Uh-uh." Reena shook her head. "I call bullshit on that. Eva is not a primadonna or a bitch like that."

Joey shrugged. "All due respect, Reena, You've known her ten days."

"All it took was knowing her for ten minutes, Joey," Reena countered. "She isn't that kind of person."

Joey regarded Reena, then shrugged again. "Maybe it's the alcohol that makes her like that, then."

"What does Cyrus say about all this?" Terrence rocked back on his heels. "It can't be good to have his Sibyl drunk all the time."

"I know that he tends to indulge her." Joey spoke slowly. "Says it's common for someone with Eva's history to need to take the edge off."

"You're not talking about Elliot anymore, are you?"

"No." Joey's expression twisted into one of guilt. "I've said too much."

"What are ya'll doing?"

The group turned to see Eva sitting up on the couch, holding her head with one hand. She frowned at Joey, who was still standing next to the open cabinet door.

"Joey? What the hell is going on?"

"Joey claims you're an alcoholic," Jonah answered. "Is that true?

"Can we just back up for a second?" Reena stepped forward. "First off, how are you feeling?"

"Better," Eva admitted. "I don't feel like I'm an extra in a movie about Jim Morrison anymore if that's what you mean."

"Alright," Reena sat on the couch next to her. "We need to talk."

"About?"

Eva looked confused as hell. Her eyes were narrowed and Jonah wondered if she was still feeling the effects of the speedball. Yeah, she said she felt better, but Eva was a lightweight. He'd learned that from their smoke sessions.

"Joey says you drink. A lot." Reena studied her. "You need to stop that."

"A lot?"

"Yeah. It's not good for your mind or your body-no matter how fast you heal."

"Um, ok." Eva looked even more confused. "But I have to drink at social events."

"How much do you drink in a day, Superstar?" Jonah sat on the coffee table and faced her. "Be honest."

"Why would I not be honest?" She shrugged. "It depends on the day. On average, one, maybe two bottles of red? That sounds right."

Jonah took a venture. "Eva, how many drinks would you say you have a week? Sixty?"

"Gods, no!" Eva exclaimed. "Not even close! Maybe... thirty? Between the social functions and what I drink at home."

Jonah felt his mouth tighten. It wasn't missed by Eva, whose eyes narrowed.

"Jonah, did you just trick me?"

"Afraid so." Jonah decided to be honest. "That's a trick to check frequency of alcohol intake. Go outlandishly high, which makes the true answer seem small in comparison."

"Ok," She breathed out. "I'm sorry for the confusion, I just don't understand where all this is coming from."

"Joey mentioned that you were a functioning alcoholic." Reena studied her. "Because we care about you, we want to help you stop."

"Joey! What the hell?"

"Look, the conversation just snowballed, baby girl. I wasn't trying to throw you under the bus."

"Right." She narrowed her eyes at him. "In any case, sure. I drink a lot. But never on locations. And never when I have to be behind the wheel. I see wine like you guys see weed. It's just a way to unwind."

"Yeah," Jonah said, not really buying that. "May I challenge you?"

"Sure, why not."

"Go one full day--twenty-four hours--without one drink," He said. "If you can do that, we'll back off."

"Ok." She hid her yawn behind her hand. "I can do that."

"I have another question." Terrence eyed her. "Did you absorb Prometheus' mind?"

"Unfortunately," Eva wrinkled her nose. "He wouldn't help and we needed to know what he knew. I wasn't expecting to take on his high, too."

"How many times have you done that, Evie?"

"Three, now." She ticked off the names on her fingers. "Athena, Hera, and now, the jackass."

"Explains your line about birds," Reena muttered. "But did you find out anything that would benefit you?"

"I don't know yet." Eva answered. "Honestly, I don't know. I won't know until we reach Romania."

"Why is that?" Jonah shook his head. "If you have his knowledge-"

"Because I don't know what is real or what was created in his memory bank by the drugs."

She had a point, but Jonah was still annoyed because of

the revelation that Eva was an alcoholic. Plus, she had taken a risk absorbing that bastard's mind. A risk that could amount to nothing. She folded her hands in her lap and frowned at him.

"You can't be mad at me, Jonah."

"Why not?" He raised an eyebrow at her. Eva had mentioned something when she was high about him being mad. Maybe she was convinced that he was.

"Because I may have useful information. And my head hurts." She gave him a small, playful smile. "And I'm just too pretty for you to be mad at."

Jonah smirked. "Bringing up your looks to talk your way out of this? Afraid that's not going to work. Gonna take a bacon double cheeseburger and some milkshakes."

Eva chuckled. "That sounds reasonable. And ya'll should have a decent meal before we leave."

Terrence perked up. "Burgers and shakes? I'm game!"

Reena shook her head. "Evie, where's your kitchen? I'll make a salad."

"You can order a salad, Re. You're in the vegan capital of the world, after all."

She perked up and everyone shifted off the couch. Eva was the last to move but she led them to the kitchen. She pulled open a drawer that was filled near to the brim with menus.

"Take your pick," She joked as she stood back. "Every place in L.A. that delivers."

"You don't cook?" Terrence looked scandalized. "In this kitchen?"

"Ew, no." Eva wrinkled her nose. "Cooking was never my talent."

"Seriously?" Reena asked. "It's just been take out all this time?"

"Um, well, I think there's some waffles in the freezer.

Joey likes those." Eva leaned back against the counter as she flipped through the menus. She passed one to Reena then one to Jonah. "VegaHana for Reena. Texas Roadhouse for the guys."

Jonah just laughed to himself. He was going to have to work with Eva. First, he'd have to teach her to boil water. "Bacon Double cheeseburger. Onion rings."

Eva winked at him as she took down their orders then made the calls. Once everything was set in place, she stretched.

"Ya'll know where the living room is. Go chill out. Enjoy modern living for a bit longer. Joey, what do you know about our flight?"

"It's not ready."

"What do you mean, it's not ready?"

"The plane's not ready, baby girl." He looked over at her. "Don't give me that look. I talked to the guys at the hanger before we left for San Francisco. They were having to change a fuel line or something."

"Great." Eva drew out the word. "So what does that mean, exactly?"

"That we'll leave out in the morning instead of tonight. Besides, that'll give our people more time to get things set up in Romania."

"We could always use the Astralimes," Reena suggested. "No harm in that."

"We can't." Joey shook his head. "Not with all the equipment we have."

"You don't know much about ethereal beings, Joey," Reena said. "We can get it done. It'll just be more than one trip. Even with multiple trips, we'll still slash the flight time. It's not an issue at all."

"We can't, Reena," Joey's expression was one of apology. "I appreciate the offer, but all that equipment? It's already been loaded. And Theia made the arrangements for us to check in tomorrow night. Which reminds me, we're going to be bunking up on rooms. Two per. Connor wouldn't go for more than that."

"It's for one goddamn night." Eva frowned. "Seriously?"

"You know ol' Scrooge as good as I do." Joey shrugged. "One of us will get a solitary room. The rest of us will share. So how do we want to do this? Draw straws?"

Jonah shrugged. "Whatever. I'm game either way."

"How much are the rooms?" Eva narrowed her eyes at him. "Because I'll pay for the ones that Connor won't."

"Evie, it's fine." Reena shook her head. "We got three rooms, right?"

"Right."

Reena tore off a paper from the notepad on the fridge. She grabbed the pen and wrote out the numbers 1-3 twice. She folded them then put them in her hands and shook.

"Pick one."

Eva picked up a paper, then everyone else followed after her. When everyone had their pieces, she opened hers first.

"I got number two."

"So did I," Reena murmured. "Looks like it's going to be ladies' night for us."

"I got three," Jonah said. "So who's bunking with me?"

"I got one," Joey glanced over at Terrence. "What'd you get, T.?"

"I got one. Looks like Jonah is getting the big bed."

The doorbell resounded through the condo and Eva excused herself to go answer the door. She came back with the bags and trays then began handing them out. When she was done and everyone was settled at the table, she went to make coffee.

"Whatcha eating, Superstar?" Jonah popped open the

lid to his Styrofoam box. "They didn't forget yours, did they?"

"Nope." She made herself a cup of coffee. "I never eat before we film. It's unlucky."

"Unlucky?"

"Yeah." She joined them at the table then sat down. "Been doing that since I was a kid and old habits break hard, ya know?"

"Huh." Jonah looked her over. "So you're gonna drink some calories? Afraid to eat due to nerves?"

"Not alcohol, if that's what you mean. Joey always packs *Ensure* drinks for me."

"Strawberry." He grabbed a handful of fries. "She usually downs those things faster than I can supply them."

"Is it nerves?" Reena dug into her salad. "I'd think you'd be past that."

"No," Eva sipped on her coffee. "I, um. I was a classical pianist when I was little. My mom believed it was bad luck for me to eat before a performance. So I just...can't now. It's been ingrained too long."

Jonah nodded. "I get it. Coffee or smoothies will also work. They can function as good meal replacements too. And because it's liquid form, it'll go right into your organs."

Eva raised her coffee cup. "Damn straight, Blueberry. There's enough sugar and creamer in here to kill a horse."

"We should probably sleep after this." Joey gestured with his burger. "And make sure you all have enough entertainment for that flight. It's going to be brutal. Sixteen hours. Maybe more."

Jonah pointed to his phone. "I have Audibles. Got two books, maybe three."

"I have work to do." Eva pointed out. "But if you don't steal my tablet again, Reena and Terrence can use it."

Jonah laughed. "I'm sure your work will be a lot more engaging and exciting than my damn books."

"Somehow I doubt it," Eva grinned. "I stalked your facebook, remember? I know what you like."

"Yeah?"

"Uh huh. But if you want to help, you can." Eva shifted in her seat. "Or we could just play Scrabble the entire time. I'm not picky."

"Scrabble." Terrence looked at Eva with surprise. "You want to play Scrabble with an author? Love a challenge, eh?"

"I could use it as a learning experience," Eva smirked. "Besides, I might not lose."

"Really, Evie?" Reena shook her head. "Jonah is the undisputed champion of Scrabble."

"Either way, it'll be fun as hell." Eva finished her coffee and stood. She put the mug in the dishwasher then headed back to the table. "I'm crashing. It's been a hell of a day between Zeus and birdman."

"Rest well, Superstar," Jonah said. "Hope the coffee didn't ruin it."

"Never does."

She squeezed his shoulder before she headed upstairs. When she was gone, Reena turned towards Joey.

"What's up with you?"

"What?"

"You said Eva is an alcoholic. She hasn't even mentioned wine once."

Joey stared, then shrugged. "I'm just concerned. Eva has a mountain of stress on her and doesn't always cope well. I was leery. That's all."

"How well do you know Eva?"

"What do you mean?"

"Just curious," Reena finished her salad then sat back. "You two ever date? Work buddies? Or just roommates?"

"Date?" Joey damn near choked. "Are you kidding me?"

"It's a fair question," Reena watched him. "After all, we're just getting to know each other."

"No. We're just friends. Roommates. Cyrus snatched her up pretty quick." He finished his burger then wiped his hands. "Evie is like a sister to me. I'm a bit protective. I care about her even when she doesn't care about herself. That's all."

"I get that," Jonah said, eyeing the cameraman, "But you were just so quick to throw her under the bus. It was just a little jarring."

"I wasn't throwing her under the bus. You asked me a question, I answered it." Joey shrugged. "Besides, if we are going to hang out together, it's better that you learn the truth now, right? Before you get too deep."

"Okay, Joey, fair enough." Reena sipped some water. "Since we're all learning truths about one another, how long have you been clean from narcotics?"

Joey stared at her. "What?"

"It's obvious," Reena told him. "You have to keep your hands and mouth busy at all times. You use spearmint toothpaste, which is the best at hiding cigarette breath. Most addicts latch on to cigarettes or exercise after they get clean. You also have tribal sleeves up both arms, yet you're a white man from Wyoming, so...no tribe. At first, I thought they were capers from your younger days, but now I'm going to say that you got your arms tatted up to hide tracks. So...heroin, right?"

"Yeah." Joey sighed. "Heroin. Started back in film school to keep myself awake during long shoots. It's...been a struggle but I'm clean."

"The fact that you have tats means you had good veins,"

Reena said. "You're lucky that Theia didn't see them and assume you were a gang member or something."

"It's Hollywood," Joey chuckled. "Everybody here has tattoos. Theia just thinks it was a move I made in college."

"Uh-huh," Jonah said. "Good for you. Also explains why you went there concerning Eva. You've been there yourself."

"The worst critic of an addict is a recovering one." Joey shrugged. "But...Eva's stubborn. She's been like that for as long as I've known her. But you guys aren't as squeaky clean as you seem either, are you? Everybody has to have something."

"Hey, dude, I never said I was a saint," Jonah muttered. "I'm not just gonna jump to the worst conclusion is all."

"Not saying that," Joey shook his head. "Just....trying to get to know you guys, too."

"What do you want to know?" Terrence asked. "I'm an open book, bro."

Joey thought for a second before he chuckled. "I honestly don't know. It doesn't seem as fun to throw out questions and just get an answer to everything."

He collected his trash and tossed it in the trash can. "Let's go play Madden or something. I don't think I'm going to be able to sleep for awhile."

Terrence shrugged. "I'll never turn down Madden. Competition clears the mind."

They left. Reena stared after them, and Jonah tapped her wrist.

"Joey was really quick to flee, wasn't he?" Jonah asked.

"Uh-huh," Reena said. "You picked up on it too."

"You think he's full of shit?" Jonah questioned.

"That's an unfair judgment," Reena said. "We all have secrets. But he's definitely worth a lookup."

She took her last bite of food then closed the container.

"Jonah, I have to ask you something."

"Yeah, Re, what's up?"

"Why are we here? In L.A.? Getting ready to chase a television show into the woods?" She studied him. "Don't get me wrong, I would have bought your 'already bored' speech if we hadn't just faced off against Hera. But there's more here, isn't there?"

Jonah nodded. No point in lying to Reena. "I have the strongest feeling that something isn't right. That Eva was meant to be screwed over here. Like she'd be easy meat for...something. Just felt like someone intended to do her legit harm with this one. But having help is the game changer. Make sense?

"It makes perfect sense." Reena tapped her fingers against the table top. "And while that was well said and completely gallant, I'm not sure that's your only motive."

"What are you talking about?"

"Only that you jumped to help before you knew what help was needed. Do you feel obligated or something? I know how you are once you give your word."

Jonah thought about her words before he answered. "No. No obligation. I wanted to. Just felt right."

"I heard from Vera earlier." Reena grabbed her container then Jonah's. "She and the gang are living it up in Vegas. She wants to Skype before we leave for parts unknown."

"Okay, cool," Jonah said. "But...were you done talking?"

"No," Reena studied him. "I'm a bit worried about you."

"Doesn't have anything to do with a fucked up demon forest, would it?"

"Maybe a little. But I know you, J. I want you to be careful around these Hollywood people."

"Damn, Reena," Jonah said. "You're agreeing with Joey, after all?"

"Not at all." She sighed. "Not in the least. But Jonah, if you get too attached to Eva, how are you going to handle that when she's gone all the time? We can't follow her on the road from now unto eternity."

Jonah looked at Reena and laughed. "You think I'll latch onto her like a puppy. No, Reena. Don't even worry about that."

"Ok," Reena nodded. "As long as you recognize that's a bad idea."

"To make new friends is a bad idea?" Jonah wanted to know.

"This isn't about being friends we can just hang out with. These are people who run for their lives on a weekly basis. On - and off - television, J. And when our shit hits the fan in the ethereal world, we don't want to pull them in it. What would happen to Joey if he met Jessica? How do you think Eva would fare against Creyton?"

"So...you're saying leave Eva to her own devices, consequences be damned?" Jonah leaned back in his chair. "Reena, what would Jonathan think of a stance like that?"

"I'm not saying that in this instance. I'm not." Reena shook her head. "J., I just think that those two could very easily get mixed up in our mess and they won't survive it."

"You make it sound like they are about to move into the estate."

"No," Reena frowned. "Nothing like that. It's just-"

"What, Re? You're talking in circles and I'm not following."

"I don't know. I don't. I just want us to be careful. That's all. Do I think Evie is on the up and up? Yeah. But I'm not sure about everyone else around her."

"Oh definitely," Jonah said. "I get that completely. She's

probably got snakes all around her. That Connor guy sounds like that the worst."

"Maybe." Reena sighed. "Want to go ahead and Skype with V.? I don't think I am long for bed myself."

"Sure, Re," Jonah pulled out his phone. "Let's give her a call."

# TWENTY-TWO

## EVA MCRAYNE

I COULDN'T SHUT my mind off. That was typical when I was trying to sleep. So too was my decision to work in the hopes that I could calm my thoughts down.

But my laptop was in the study. And I wanted to grab water from the fridge. Oh, who was I kidding? I wanted to see if Jonah was still up. The truth was, I was infatuated.

I padded downstairs and froze at the kitchen door. Reena and Jonah were still sitting at the table with a phone propped up. There was a dark-haired woman on the screen who seemed to be talking more to Reena than Jonah.

A familiar dark-haired woman. I'd seen her in Hera's twisted visions. This had to be Vera Halliday. Fabulous.

I caught the look of frustration on Jonah's face just before Reena called the woman 'V'. I was right. This was Vera.This was the woman who dared to dangle my friend from a chain.

Maybe it was time to break it.

I should have just pranced my ass right back upstairs. I was dressed for bed in a t-shirt and short shorts. But I couldn't stop myself as I entered the room, flung my arms around Jonah's neck, and kissed him right on the cheek.

"Who's your friend, Blueberry?"

The woman drew up. Even through the screen, I could see the ice in her eyes as she examined me.

"My name is Vera-"

"Oh! Verna! Nice to meet you!" I tugged at Jonah's chair until I could plop down right across his lap. "Right, right."

Jonah seemed as surprised as Reena by my actions, but I kept going. I was hoping to show that bitch that Jonah couldn't be controlled or manipulated by her. That she wasn't the only option.

"And who are you, exactly?"

"Just a friend," I grinned down at her image sweetly. "What are ya'll going on about?"

"Not that it's any concern of yours, but I was talking about Mariah Carey's performance at Caesar's Palace," Vera answered rather haughtily. "She has a residency here, and we got to see her."

"No kidding?" I grinned. "I haven't seen Mimi in months! Nice to know where she's been hiding."

Jonah frowned at me. "Mimi?"

"Oh yeah," I patted his hand. "Mariah let's her close friends call her Mimi. Next time you're in Vegas and you want to see her, Blueberry? Just let me know. One call, and l can get all in."

"There's no way you actually know Mariah Carey." Vera frowned at me. "She's much too famous."

"Nobody is 'much too famous'," I rolled my eyes. "People are people, after all. She just happens to sing."

"And what do you just happen to do?"

I was pleased by her icy expression. Maybe now, she'll realize what a gift she is wasting with Jonah.

"Me? I happen to play in dusty old houses and look good doing it. What do you do again?"

"I am an actress and a playwright."

"Oh. Well, good luck with that."

"Why would I need luck?"

"Because you must not be very good. I've never heard of you before."

That was the moment her icy expression shifted into one of fire. Apparently, she didn't like to be reminded of her status as someone that nobody knew.

"Maybe there's more to life than fame." She snapped.

"There is," I agreed. "Unless you are in the entertainment industry. Then you're just wasting your time."

Jonah nearly choked and I patted him on the back. Reena snickered, but straightened her expression. Vera sneered as she looked at her phone.

"Eva, was it? Why don't you use your so-called fame to do some good in the world? Seems like all you do is promo tours and photo shoots. Personal opinion? You need a steak sandwich or two. When men are hungry, they go for the fruit, not the twig it hangs from. Just a thought."

"When you actually get known for more than selling tickets at the county fair, then I'll be more than happy to take your advice, Verna."

Reena laughed aloud. Vera gave her a look of pure scorn.

"Reena!"

"What? It's amusing." Reena didn't look awkward at all. "Vera, we're all grown here. You saying you can't take banter?"

"That's not banter-"

"Oh, sure it is," I shifted against Jonah's lap. "You can't

tell me I've hurt your feelings. Why would the apple care about what the twig thought?"

Now, her eyes narrowed. "Are you calling me fat?"

"Not calling you anything," I hid a yawn behind my hand. "If you think that, then maybe it's you who are insecure about your weight."

"Can I talk to my friends without you hanging all over Jonah's neck?" She replied with gritted teeth.

"Jonah does have a fine neck." I kept my arm around it. I wiggled a little to emphasize that I was on his lap. "He's fine, period, don't you think, Verna?"

Vera looked Jonah in the eye. "You have anything to say, Jonah?"

Jonah looked right back at her. "Nothing more than you failed to answer Eva's question. You think I'm fine or no?"

"I can't believe you would put me on the spot like this." Vera sipped from her wine glass and I wrinkled my nose. "What? Are you too good for wine?"

"I'm too good for box wine, yes. I can tell by the color how watered down it is. And you shouldn't feel on the spot at all. Look at this face! This body! I'd get Jonah in magazines if I thought he'd go for it."

"Jonah," She decided to ignore me completely. "Do you really want me to answer that question?"

"Actually, yeah, I do."

"I think you look quite nice then."

"Quite nice," Jonah said. He stiffened and I could tell that response had rankled him. "Well thank you. You look alright too."

Vera actually drew up and I squeezed Jonah's neck to show that I was proud of him. He had made it clear that Vera had a negative effect on him. If I could save him from that, then I would.

"Anyway-"

"I think she's blind, Blueberry. Or maybe she can't see you that good through Skype." I tilted my head towards him. "Any girl who was on your arm would make sure to keep you as the center of her attention."

"I just remembered that there is a party in the hotel bar." Vera backed away from the screen. "Hope you have fun in The Forest of Hell."

"We will, Verna Pie," I grinned. "Hope you have fun trying to breathe in your party dress tonight."

"*What*!"

I ended the Skype call and looked at Jonah and Reena.

"What? It's true. I bet that poor dress will burst at the seams."

"Eva, did you just hang up on Vera?"

"Damn straight I did." I pouted at Jonah. "She deserves worse than that. The entire time, all she wanted to talk about was herself. She didn't ask either of you how you were, what you were doing. It was all 'me, me" me.' That's not right."

Jonah shook his head. "She *is* an acquired taste. Didn't think she'd go all prickly bitch like that."

"I did." I should have gotten off his lap. That would have been the polite thing to do. Instead, I stayed right where I was. "Women like Vera don't like it when another woman encroaches on her territory. I'll admit it. I was acting out. But I had my reasons."

"Shit was funny," Reena said. " I thought Vera would see it for the foolishness it was."

"She's too blind to her own bullshit," I shrugged. "I regret nothing. The only reason l fat-shamed her was because she brought weight up first."

I finally made myself get up and grab the water I had come down for in the first place. "If I stepped out of bounds, I'm only sorry to you guys."

"No apology necessary," Jonah said, though he still looked aggravated. "If anyone should apologize, it's Vera."

Reena raised an eyebrow at him. "You ok, J.?"

"Just irritated," Jonah replied. "We're all being foolish, and she goes from zero to bitch. It was uncalled for."

"You know why." I dropped down in the chair next to him. "She's jealous."

"She's in Vegas," Jonah argued. "She needs a catcher's mitt for all the men she could be catching."

"Maybe, but catching men and controlling one are two very different things." I pointed out. "And she is pissed because she realizes that her hold on you is breaking. You'll see her sooner rather than later when you guys get back to the estate."

Jonah sat back. "You know what? Let her shake her ass at that bar while we play Scrabble."

Reena snorted. "Jonah, as bright as you are, you are still such a man. Vera's not at the bar. She's seething in her room, probably with wine."

"Damn straight she is." I nodded. "She's sulking in her box wine. I hope you don't mind that I was all over you. Vera needed to see that you had other options. She would have brushed you off otherwise."

Jonah's cheeks flushed a little. What the hell was that about? Had I embarrassed him? "Don't mention it. How about the Scrabble? We could also do MadLibs."

"I'd love to, but I have to go dig through accounts from Romania." I shook my head. "I'm still trying to get a grasp on what we will be facing."

"Okay, cool." Jonah rose. "Gonna hit the shower them. Maybe that'll cool down my mind."

"Your mind or something else?" Reena asked shrewdly.

I noticed the look between them, confused.

"I feel like I'm missing something here."

"You're missing Reena's attempts at dry humor," Jonah said through gritted teeth. "The banter ended with the Skype call, Reena dear."

"Just making an observation."

She laughed. I wondered if it was an inside joke then decided to play it off.

"Alright, well, I'll be in my room if ya'll need anything."

I got up, snagged my water, and left the room. I was pleased with Vera's reaction. Good. She should be aggravated. Maybe then, she'll realize that Jonah was someone she couldn't take advantage of.

# TWENTY-THREE

## JONAH ROWE

Jonah could feel Reena watching him as Eva left. She waited until they heard Eva head upstairs before she spoke.

"J., if you stared at that girl any harder, your eyes would pop out of your head."

"Reena, if you stared at everything around you any harder, *your* eyes would pop." Jonah countered.

"I'm not making fun of you. Not in the least. But Evie? She's innocent. She has no idea the effect she had on you. That's probably why she sat in your lap like she did."

"Exactly," Jonah said. "Eva is innocent, in a world of snakes. I'm surprised *Vera* didn't pick up on it."

"Vera was too busy seeing green to notice anything." Reena grinned. "You gotta give it to Eva. She's got moxie. Thank god that wasn't in person."

"Damn straight," Jonah said, shuddering at the thought. "I don't know what would've been worse; Eva stabbing Vera or Vera abusing ethereality in a cat fight."

"Hmm."

"What's that sound for?"

"I think I was wrong about which one of you was going

to be the puppy dog." Reena tapped the table. "Pretty sure it's gonna be Eva."

Jonah laughed. "Reena, go to bed. Your ponytail is cutting off the blood flow to your brain. "

"I don't think so. Eva is infatuated with you. The only reason she even came in here was because she saw Vera. You must have told her."

"I thought she was too high to pay attention."

"Well, she knew enough about Vera somehow that she knew exactly how to get under her skin. And those two don't run in the same circles."

Jonah sipped the remainder of his water. "And they say men are the petty ones."

"Well, if the roles were reversed, how would you react? If a guy was jerking Eva around like that?"

"He'd be icing his nuts," Jonah said. "Because I'd have punted them. "

"See? It's not petty. She thought she was defending her friend." Reena stressed the word 'friend'. "So I got a great bit of amusement from it."

"I did, too." Jonah laughed just thinking about it. "I thought V. was going to break that wine glass."

"I think it told you a lot, too." Reena said carefully. "In her responses about you."

"Perhaps," Jonah said, as careful as Reena. "But like you said, Eva is an innocent in these regards. She could be infatuated by a guy who is kind to her. Especially after the shit we learned about Cyrus."

"Normally, I would agree with you. But men are kind to her every day." Reena pointed out. "And...I haven't read her essence or yours, mind you. But there's something there. It's like...a magnet. Jonah, if you'd talked to Vera before meeting Eva over Skype, how would you have felt? Still irritated?"

"Face facts, Re," Jonah persisted. "Vera was being testy anyway. She was freezing me out of the conversation once she found out that I spent the night in Eva's bedroom, despite knowing that it was Jonathan's decision. So I was kinda irritated already."

"True, but you're avoiding my question." Reena snagged his wrist to pull him back into the chair. "J., you can be honest with me and I'll be honest with you. That's how we work. So here's my theory. You have feelings for Vera. Did all this shit for her and time after time, she either strung you along or shut you down. You still clung to those feelings and the possibility that she could have the same ones. Here comes five foot six inches of blonde badass and you've been knocked on *your* ass. Hard enough to finally start seeing the truth. Tell me I'm wrong."

Jonah looked at Reena and sighed. "Reena, I wouldn't actually say knocked on my ass. My God, Cupid hasn't jabbed me with a bow. But yeah, there is...something concerning Eva. She's cool people, very down to Earth. But I'm going to be cautious. My track record isn't amazing. You know about Priscilla. The women who decided they didn't need me after a couple great fucks. And of course, Vera. So, you ain't wrong. But caution will be my friend here."

"Caution is your friend, J. And while you have a history, I wouldn't count out a future, either. Even if that's not with Eva? Maybe you'll finally see the truth about your relationship with Vera. You don't need another Priscella - someone who makes you think they are doing you a favor by being with you - and Vera is doing exactly that. You deserve better and you know it. Eva is opening your eyes up to that."

Reena's phone rang against the table and she snorted. "It's Vera."

"Looks like the party got put on hold then."

"Don't say a word. Let's see what she has to say." Reena grinned as she answered the call. "V.? You ok? What happened to the party?"

"Fuck the party. Who the hell was that bitch hanging all over Jonah?"

Reena sighed in exasperation. "She's not a bitch, V. That's our new friend, Eva McRayne. Star of *Grave Messages*."

"Don't give me that 'new friends' line." Vera sniffed. "Friends don't hang all over each other like that. What's the deal with them?"

"Why does it matter?"

"Re! You're killing me! Is Jonah screwing her or not?"

"Um, V.?" Reena frowned. "Aren't you poly now? Don't you have that woman in Seattle and that guy in Colorado? Why would you be worried about Jonah?"

Jonah was curious about that, too. Vera got quiet for a minute. He wondered what she could possibly say. Finally, he got his answer.

"You know that Jonah is one of my friends, Re. I care about my friends. And I don't want him to get tangled up with some blonde bimbo who is going to drop him the second she finds a better lay."

Reena looked at Jonah and rolled her eyes. When Vera initially left to "find her way," Reena was supportive, and told Jonah that he needed to take steps to move on. But when Vera's relocation seemingly transformed into an excuse to flash herself all over the western United States, her support soured rather quickly.

"Your friend is fine, V. You forget about Terrence and Liz and me? Spader and everyone else? We've got Jonah's back were that to happen. But it's not going to. One, Eva is a wonderful woman and not at all the persona everyone has built, and two, she and Jonah aren't even like that. Now get to your party."

"Wait, I still have questions."

"Ok. Like what?"

"How did they meet exactly? At the estate? I saw this article online that was about the two of them at the Covington House."

"Yeah, we helped with the episode."

"Re, what if Jonah gets wrapped up in the whole Hollywood scene? How could that be good for him?" Vera sighed. "Maybe I should come home. I can make sure little Miss Touchy Feely keeps her hands to herself."

Jonah nearly responded in annoyance, but Reena waved a hand. "Vera, as long as you've known Jonah, has he ever been one to stray like that? And after all the fuss you made about finding your way, why the hell would you come back here? Surely you realize that makes absolutely no sense."

"Yeah, but-"

"But what?" Reena snorted. "What is this really about, V.? Are you jealous?"

"Of what? That twig? Hell, no." There was the sound of shuffling on the line. "Where are you? Maybe if I talked to Jonah in person, that could help."

"We're at Eva's condo in L.A."

"Wait. That kitchen I saw. That's *hers*? Who'd she sleep with for a place like that?"

"Bye, V."

"No, wait. Look. Yes, I'm trying to find my way, but as soon as I'm done, I want to come back home. Maybe me and Jonah can start over or something. If he gets too close to that bitch, that could ruin things for me."

"Are you serious right now?" Jonah saw that Reena almost laughed. "Ruin things for you, with Jonah? You're in two relationships right now. What about ruining things with them?"

"Oh, come on. I'm just having my fun right now." Vera huffed. "You know I like variety. But it's different with Jonah."

"How so?"

"Jonah needs a challenge. He doesn't need a quick fuck on the side. I give him that."

"Challenge, as in ignoring him for six months?"

"He came back to me. There's obviously something there. And sometimes, you have to draw out your boundaries. Him flirting with another woman is a boundary."

"Jonah didn't come back to you, he came to support your play," Reena said. "And might I remind you that was where it was revealed that you'd moved on after only two months? Where were the boundaries then, Vera? And why, exactly, did none of us hear a damn thing about your desire to return here and be there for Jonah until after you saw him just talking with another woman?"

"Reena!"

"What? It's a serious question."

"Because he was going to wait on me, alright?" Vera snapped. "Or at least, he was supposed to. I'll call him tomorrow. We can talk about everything then. Hash things out."

"Feel free," Reena shrugged though Vera wouldn't see it. "But between now and that call, check your motives, Vera. And properly determine if any of them actually involve a legitimate commitment with Jonah, or the fact that you're afraid someone might beat you to it. Just a thought."

"There is no way that...that...blonde is going to beat me to anything." Vera scoffed. "First off, there's absolutely nothing there. She's a damn stick. Second, she's probably got the conversation skills of a wall. They have nothing in common."

"You still sound pretty jealous, V."

"I'm not jealous. I know that Jonah is in love with me. That's why I know he'll wait for me to get myself settled."

"You seem pretty damned set that Jonah has to make all the sacrifices, V."

"Why not? He's always doing stuff for me. And waiting is a hell of a lot cheaper than those tickets he bought me when we went on our date."

Jonah didn't know what was more infuriating. The fact that Vera believed that or the fact that she viewed him like some sort of lapdog. Reena's eyes flashed, but she shook her head.

"If you say so, V."

"Is he still up? I'll call him now."

"Yeah, he just left the kitchen." Reena glanced over at Jonah as he pulled his phone out. "Go for it."

"Bye!"

"Later, V."

Reena hung up and whistled. "That was interesting."

Before Jonah could respond, his phone started vibrating against the table.

"That was real damn fast." He let it ring twice more before he answered. "V.? What's up?"

"Hey, J!" Vera's voice sounded like honey as she greeted him. "Listen, I know you're in L.A. I was wondering if you wanted to meet up somewhere since we're on the same coast again."

Jonah rolled his eyes but kept his voice level. "That won't work, V. I've got a full plate while I'm out here. And you do, too. You still send us your itineraries, remember?"

"We can always make time for each other, right? Surely you can spare an hour. We'll meet for lunch somewhere. Or you can come to Seattle. We can talk about things."

"What things?"

"Me and you. Where we stand. I know I'm playing around right now, but it won't last forever. And when I come back home, maybe we can work something out."

Jonah shook his head. "Vera, this is so silly of me, but doesn't that sound just a little entitled?"

"Pardon?"

"You get to play around, leaving me to wait. Then when you're ready, I'll be at your beck and call? Do you hear how that sounds? What if that was my expectation of you?"

"Jonah, you know that's not fair-"

"Well? What if that was my expectation?"

"You know I have to get things out of my system. I can't commit to just one person right now. But when I'm ready, I think we could come up with an arrangement."

"What sort of arrangement?"

"Something to where we could both have our fun."

"Vera, why do I have the feeling we wouldn't be having this conversation if you hadn't seen Eva over Skype?"

"I'm not jealous, J, if that's what you mean. There's no way in hell you would choose some vapid television hack over me."

"Vapid hack? Or a woman so maladjusted and arrogant that she expects a man to twiddle his thumbs while she paints the world red?" Jonah scoffed. "Not a judgement, Vera, but merely an observation. Who knows? Maybe I need to get shit out of *my* system or something."

"Why? Jonah, you've had your fun." Vera scoffed. "You've had your fair share of lovers. Now, it's my turn. But that won't last forever."

"Yeah, I've had lovers," Jonah responded. "But I wasn't stringing anyone along while I had them. So your expectation is for me to wait while you do God knows what, then welcome you back with open arms once you're done? Vera, honestly now, would you do that for me?"

"I...I would try."

"Try?"

"Yes. I can't help it that I get jealous when someone tries to latch their claws into you, Jonah. I can't. I am very possessive about those I care about."

"Admirable, Vera," Jonah said. "But I couldn't help but notice that you said you would try. As in, you'd put your best foot forward, but you'd still be fucking around."

"Well, it's hard to make a commitment right now. You know that I'm exploring all possible avenues. That's why it's better if we wait before we try to settle down. Isn't that what you would want if you were in my position?"

"Actually, Vera? I'm not sure that I really want anything with you."

Silence. Jonah raised his eyebrow, confused.

"Hello?"

"Excuse me?" Vera whispered.

"You heard," Jonah said. "You want to explore all avenues and see if something sticks? Great. I wish you the best with it, truly. I desire to do the same. I did want to have a future with you at one time, but growth and perspective have shown me that that season has passed. I wish to pursue other avenues myself."

"Jonah, you can't be serious! Come to Seattle. We'll spend the night together. You'll see. All I am asking for from you is time. Let me get my feet on the ground."

"Your feet have been on the ground, the bed, the hot tub, the cruise ships, and everywhere else for almost a year, Vera," Jonah told her. "You forget that you post *everything* you do on social media. I'm not coming to Seattle. That's a pass. But thanks for the offer."

"Is this because of the blonde bitch?" Vera seethed. "Jonah, fine. If you have to, fuck her a few times and get it out of your system. Just don't tell me about it and we'll be fine. I can forgive you for that."

"It's *not* about Eva, I'm gonna need that to be the last time you call my friend a bitch," Jonah said, sensing Vera's heat and contemplating matching it. "I don't need to fuck someone out of my system, I just realize that I deserve more than just to wait for someone to get their mind right when I'm already taking the necessary steps to fix mine. I don't need your approval or your forgiveness, Vera. I've just moved on. Same as you."

"Jonah, you can't say that! You can't say that you moved on! After the night we had? Be reasonable. Do what you have to do. I will, too. Maybe in a few months, you'll give up in this ridiculous stance of yours "

"No, Vera." Jonah wasn't even angry anymore. This wasn't infuriating. It was just sad. "Yeah, the night we had was magnificent, but when we had the chance to transform that night into bigger things, you balked and needed to go off somewhere. I didn't appreciate it, I was bummed out by it, but I made my peace with it. Now, I've moved on. We're on an even keel in regards to exploring new options. So the only ridiculous stance is your own, no offense."

"I'll remember this conversation next time we talk, J. Talk about us, that is. Have fun with the bimbo."

"Have fun with the CEO and the lacrosse player, V.," Jonah said. "Bye."

She hung up the phone and Reena didn't laugh. She studied him in silence.

"You ok?"

"I'm great." Jonah said, and he meant it. "Feels like an iron bar is off my shoulders."

"I'm proud of you." Reena patted his hand. "You didn't back down from what your stance was."

"I'm not the same guy who pined for Vera," Jonah said. "I'm worth more than that. Wish I'd figured it out sooner."

"You're also not the same guy who showed up at the estate. Or the same guy you were yesterday. Or five years ago. Give yourself some slack, J."

"Indeed you're right," Jonah said. "And I don't need Vera's manipulative ass."

"No. You're don't. You do deserve better." Reena tapped the back of his hand. "And it's a good thing you recognize that now instead of later."

"It had been coming along for a while," Jonah admitted. "But Vera made it so *damn* easy, too."

"It's easier when you see what someone really thinks of you." She leaned back in her chair. "I can't believe she admitted to jerking you around."

"She isn't the first entitled and arrogant person we've ever met, and she won't be the last."

"True." Reena frowned as Jonah stood up. "You heading to bed?"

"Yeah. Night, Re."

"Night."

Jonah headed upstairs and stopped by Eva's door. There was light coming from beneath it, which meant she was still up. He took a chance and knocked. He heard rustling and a few minutes later, Eva opened the door.

"Hey," She smiled. "Want to use the balcony?"

"Not exactly," Jonah rubbed his hand through his hair. "Listen, I didn't want to be alone. Can I come stay with you? I'll even sleep on the floor."

Eva looked surprised then shook her head as she opened the door to let him in.

"My bed is huge, Blueberry. Have at it." She closed the

door behind him. "I'm still reading about the forest though. Is the lamp going to bother you?"

"No," Jonah slipped past her into the room then turned to face Eva when she shut the door. "Vera called Reena right after you left. Then she called me. I told her to go screw herself."

"What?"

"Vera." Jonah sat on her bed and stared at her. "I told her I didn't want to be her fool anymore."

"Oh, Jonah."

Eva sat down next to him. She seemed hesitant but she clasped his hand. "What happened?"

"Well, she pretty much told me that she expected me to wait for her to sew all her wild oats, for as long as she needed, and then she'd come back to me to discuss a future. I'm being totally serious here."

Eva's mouth parted before she shut it. Jonah gave her a quizzical look.

"What?"

"No. I don't trust myself to speak right now. I'm pissed off and I might say something you don't like."

"Wait, why are you pissed?"

"Because she is so damn selfish! Jonah, what about your emotions? What about your time?" Eva stopped, took a breath, and started over. "It pisses me off that she hurt you. You're a wonderful person, Jonah. You don't deserve any of the shit she has put you through."

"You're right," Jonah said. "*Fuck* me for not realizing that sooner. All this time, I thought Vera was the way she was because she'd been made that way by hardship. That she had complexities and dark spots to work on. And *all* the while, she was just a manipulative, solipsistic-"

"Twat."

"What?"

"Huh? Oh, nothing," Eva said. "Just thinking out loud."

"No, I heard," He gave her a small smile. "But I realized something."

"What's that?"

"You can go through hell and still treat people with respect and kindness. She used her past as a way to manipulate people."

"Hmm."

"Hmm?"

"Yeah. See," Eva shifted so that she faced him. "Having a hard background can have one or two effects on people. One, they get selfish. They embrace their victimhood and wear it like a shroud. Or two, they do their damnedest to protect people from the hurt and disappointment they felt."

"You're right," Jonah agreed. "And Vera? In retrospect, I can see clearly that if manipulation was an Olympic sport, she'd bring home the damn gold."

"Lay down, Blueberry." She patted the bed then giggled when he raised his eyebrow. "Trust me. You're safe. I won't bite. You can sleep here tonight."

Jonah moved to the other side of the bed and crawled under the covers. Eva settled in with her back pressed against the headboard. She began to run her fingers through his hair.

"I'm just trying to help you relax. You've earned it."

"I appreciate you," Jonah told her. "You know? There has been a time when I'd have thought that how Vera treated me was a pretty okay deal. The whole 'beggars can't be choosy' thing. But...nah. It was bullshit, and I deserve better."

"You really do," She agreed. "You deserve someone who will give you their entire attention. You deserve someone who wants to be with you, not keep you as a backup. If Vera wants to keep exploring avenues? Then that means she's always looking for something she'll never find. Including in a committed relationship."

"Committed? That's a laugh." Jonah scratched his beard. "Since she's moved to Seattle, she's began to identify as genderfluid and polyamorous. She's got her girlfriend, and some guy in another state. Plenty of other partners too. Because her girlfriend and boyfriend have a 'don't ask, don't tell' arrangement when she's out of town, touring with the play."

"That's kinda sad, don't you think?"

"What do you mean?"

"It's sad because she's obviously missing something that she is trying to get through sex, but she will never be satisfied. It doesn't matter what or who she does, she doesn't seem like she will ever be truly happy."

"It truly does." Jonah sighed. "The shit doesn't even piss me off. If anything, I pity her. Fucked up way to live. Trying to fill a void and nothing will ever be enough."

"I'm proud of you. That wasn't easy, I know. But Vera isn't the only woman out there. You'll stumble across the right one. I just know it."

"Lord knows I've had my share of the wrong ones," Jonah muttered. "But I won't bore you with that."

"You're never a bore, Blueberry," Eva continued stroking his head. "I told you I wanted to know everything about you. The good and the bad."

"Why?"

"You fascinate me. The way you think. How you respond to situations. It's different than anything I have ever known."

Jonah chortled. "Okay, fire away. I'm an open book."

"Well, tell me about your Nana. She seemed to be exceedingly important to you."

"Yeah, and then some." Jonah let his mind roll back.

"Nana was my best friend. My father, Luther, took off, never met him. But I found out that I have four brothers and sisters. Eh. Anyway, my mother, Sylvia? She was about as maladjusted and screwed up as Vera. Nana didn't even really like her. When she left, Nana actually said she did me a favor. Nana always looked after me, she always made sure that I never went hungry, and that I always had shoes that fit. And she took care of my ass when I was bad."

Eva grinned down at him. "That happened a lot, huh? You being bad?"

Jonah laughed. "Not as much as you'd think. I would say I was a pretty good kid for the most part. I was no more mischievous than anyone else. I have great memories of Nana. She was into every game show, western, and soap opera, so I was, too."

"Her favorite?" Eva asked.

"*The Young and the Restless*," Jonah said. "Bar none. She got me into wrestling and *Walker, Texas Ranger*. I still remember the first wrestling match I ever watched. I swear I was only a few years old, sitting on Nana's knee. Dusty Rhodes was fighting Lex Luger in a steel cage."

"I know next to nothing about wrestling."

"Really?"

"Really," She laughed. "No television, remember? I was in college the first time I watched a television."

"Wrestling and books were my coping mechanism throughout my whole childhood," Jonah said. "When I was bullied, I'd just imagine I was in the ring, taking out frustrations on other wrestlers. I know a ton, and still watch to this day. You may not know a lot about wrestling, but I'm sure you know a few classic wrestlers. Like Hulk Hogan."

"I know him," Eva nodded. "I also know Randy Savage and the Macho Man."

Jonah snickered. "Eva, Randy Savage *is* the Macho Man."

"Oh damn." Eva laughed. "Well, I just proved my point, huh?"

Jonah snorted again. "Nowadays, I'm sure you'd know a couple. Dwayne Johnson? John Cena?"

"I know John Cena because I met him when he was doing some of his Make-A-Wish visits," Eva said. "Stand up guy. And Dwayne Johnson...Jonah, I'm a female."

Jonah rolled his eyes. "Uh huh."

"It's not my fault he's pretty to look at."

"Uh huh."

"I'm serious!" Eva laughed. "But even if he offered, I'd turn him down."

"Yeah? Why's that?"

"One, he's a family man and I'm no homewrecker. Two? I just like to look at him. I'm not sexually attracted to him."

Jonah cracked open one eye to see the curve of her waist by his head. Oh. That explained a lot.

"So you're a lesbian?"

"No. I'm not sexually attracted to girls, either." She gave a small shrug. "I think I'm wired differently. Sex has never been on my radar. I'm sure it's nice and all, but I'm just too busy for all that."

"Hmm." Jonah thought about it. "Well, it's not like it's a crime to be more focused on your career. But maybe, just maybe, the right guy will come along. But you gotta let it happen naturally. Nana always said forcing it would just leave you wanting, because what you *need* will come to you all its own. So don't worry. If it's meant to be, it'll happen."

"Maybe." She sounded a little sad. "The truth is, I don't think there is much hope for me."

"You don't know that, Eva."

"You told me the other night that you were always told

you were worthless, and a part of you still believes that, right?"

"Right."

"Well, it's the same with me except change the word worthless with love. I have been told I am unlovable for as long as I can remember. So I don't hold much stock in things ever happening for me. I just...live. Do the best I can to make people happy. Not worry about love or sex or all the drama that comes with it."

"You're more invaluable than you know, Eva," Jonah insisted. "Just because you didn't hear on the daily doesn't mean it's true. It just means you've been around stupid assholes for too long in your life. Same as me."

"Sounds like something we both need to work on."

"Loving ourselves?"

"Yes. And realizing that we've let other people fuck us over for too long." She smiled down at him. "Like you did with Vera tonight. You stood up for yourself because you realized how much worth you actually have."

The two of them fell into a comfortable silence. Eva stretched out her legs and put her laptop on her lap. She lightly scratched his head with one hand as she typed with the other. After a while, Jonah muttered.

"Aren't you going to sleep tonight?"

"Eventually," She replied as she continued. "I don't need much sleep. Never have. And I can't sit still and do nothing. So I am using my insomnia wisely."

"By doing what, exactly?"

"Working. I'm reading some accounts from Hoia-Baciu right now. The locals say that the trees scream at all hours. The scientists who have gone in can find no evidence as to why."

"Science," Jonah scoffed. "The number of things that

have been disputed and torn down because of lack of scientific evidence. Mind-boggling."

"We certainly don't fit in that mold, do we?" Eva gave him a half smile. "Ethereal beings, demigods. I think we'd make their heads explode."

"Eh,"Jonah shrugged, pessimistic. "They'd probably figure out a way to explain us. Swamp gas from a weather balloon was trapped in a thermal pocket and refracted light from Saturn, which resulted in Elevenths and demigods. Some shit like that."

Eva burst out laughing and Jonah grinned against his arm.

"No offense to the scientists, but if someone told me I was the product of space swamp gas, I'd cut them."

Jonah laughed. "Come on, Eva. You got to be a slave to logic!"

"I'm logical," She grinned wider. "I know I exist, thus, that is my reality. Just as you exist and that is your reality. It's not my fault those fuckers don't know what they are doing."

"Agreed," Jonah said. "Then you have people like Vera, who is the ambassador of Planet Entitlement."

"Which - if she changed her attitude - could have a fantastic life." She shook her head. "I just don't get entitled people. What the fuck makes them so special that they think they should be handed whatever they want only to throw it away?"

"Right?" Jonah shook his head. "Might be why I like Rome. You don't need to be a fake blow up doll in those parts. Just a nice demeanor and the ability to mind your own business."

"Rome was nice. I can see how peaceful the estate can be without the Shades and pesky television people around."

"Right? But travel is cool too. Astralimes allow us to

save money, but sometimes you can't beat a good old road trip."

"I spend six months out of the year on the road, Blueberry. Road trips are pretty much my speciality."

"Those aren't road trips, Superstar," Jonah told her. "That's an obligation. "

"Technically, yes."

"Technically?"

"Well, it is an obligation," She grinned. "But I'm well versed on how to pack, how to have the most appropriate playlists, and my superpower is the ability to read an old fashioned paper map."

Jonah grinned. "Take the victories where they are, eh?"

"Uh huh," She nodded. "So if we ever go on an actual road trip together, I can navigate."

"So can I," Jonah said. "I never use my phone's GPS. Honestly, I rarely even use maps."

"Seriously?"

"Yeah," Jonah said. "If I've been there once, I never forget it. Like historical facts."

"You must have a photogenic memory then. I have to admit, I'm not jealous of you for that."

"It's got it's benefits and drawbacks," Jonah admitted. "But I have appreciation for my memory. Always been like that."

"So your memory is your superpower? Or something else?"

"Doubt it," Jonah said, trying to stave off the fear in his face. Eva wasn't a sexual being; she didn't know what that sounded like. "Just always been that way. My power is balance. Ironic, because I have anger management issues. And also controlling fog. And this."

He extended his hand. Electric sparks flew.

"I can control electricity, whether I'm spiritually endowed or not."

"Oh."

She breathed out and sat her laptop aside. She shifted so that she could better see the sparks.

"That's like magic." Eva studied his hand then his face. "It's so pretty, too. Can you use it in a fight or when you're in trouble?"

"Uh huh," Jonah said. "Like a taser. But I usually harness it through the batons. Sometimes I help folks out."

"How?"

"My friend Doug Chandler helps at the Brown Bag charity," Jonah said. "Food bank and clothes and whatnot. He told me Duke Power was screwing this one family because their light bill was short by like...ten dollars. Cut the power off anyway. They got the measly ten dollars, but still claimed they had to wait a day and a half for reconnect. They'd just gotten groceries, so their stuff was gonna spoil while they waited. So I camped out in their neighborhood and kept their lights on with my ethereality all night so their food didn't rot. They've in the same neighborhood as where Brown Bag is located, so I just told people I was volunteering all night. The family called it the grace of God. Maybe it was divine timing, I don't know. I try not to boggle down too much mentally with the cosmic stuff. It was just me helping someone who was getting screwed."

Eva's face softened. "You must have been exhausted after that."

"Yeah, well, it was necessary."

"You are a good soul, Jonah. A very good soul." She shifted against the mattress and sat back. "I hope you realize that."

"You ok?"

"I'm great," She tilted her head to the side. "Why?"

"Your energy just changed. I could feel it?"

"Oh, I'm just...touched, that's all. I admire acts of kindness and the people who do them." She reached out then stopped short of his hand. "Can I touch the sparks? Or will that shock me?"

Jonah found her request odd, but wasn't awkward about it. He was lying on her bed, after all. "You might feel a buzz, but it won't be debilitating or anything."

"I'm only being nosy," She took his hand and laughed. "It's not even a buzz. It tickles."

"Good then," Jonah grinned. "It's kind of a pleasant feeling, like that mild buzz you have on your skin while you get a tattoo."

"You have tattoos?"

"Of course. Don't you?"

"No," She shook her head. "I have my mark of the gods, but no tattoos. It just appeared on my side after I passed a test at the Academy."

"Interesting," Jonah said. "But yeah, I have four. All on my upper arms, chest and back. Have to keep them hidden for the most part because the good Christian people I have worked for in the past don't believe in marking yourself up. But if I ever reach the point where l don't have to work for prudish blowhards, I'll get them all up my arms and everything."

"You should do that anyway." Eva adjusted her shirt back into place. "Can I see them?"

"You want to?"

"If you're willing to share them."

Jonah pulled off his shirt. "Just so you know, I'm not ripped, or burly like Terrence. No abs to be seen here, but I have dropped some gut fat. Having a big belly ain't possible when you live with Reena Katoa. But feast your eyes. My left arm here is Archangel Michael. So I'm always protected. Left shoulder is my zodiac sign in Celtic. I'll be damned if I'm putting that 69-looking thing on my arm. Left pec is Egyptian ankh. My back is Nana's name and birthdate."

"Alexa, turn on the overhead lights."

The room was filled with light and Jonah blinked. He wasn't used to that.

"You got the Amazon thing?"

"Yes, now hush and let me look."

Eva shifted onto her knees as she took his arm. She turned it so she could see the Archangel tattoo. She gazed her fingers over it before she did the same thing to his back tattoo. Eva traced the lines on his skin with each tattoo she came across. When she came back into view, she did the same with his ankh.

"These are beautiful. The art is extraordinary." She traced the downward stroke of the ankh. "You should definitely get more."

"That's the plan," Jonah said, "Once I don't have old fogeys who control my paycheck telling me it's in the Bible. Which it's *not,* by the way. The Bible forbade body mutilation, not body art."

"If you're ever interested, I could always find a way for you to work on *Grave.*" She lowered her hand. "Research, writing monologues. Or, if you wanted to be on camera, we could work something out. There's no tattoo judgment in Hollywood, after all."

"Seriously?" Jonah asked. "They don't forbid tattoos?"

"Have you seen Joey's arms?" She teased. "No, they don't forbid tattoos. And if you did something behind the scenes - like writing or research - nobody could give two damns about your body art. Theia pays well, too. Very well. Yeah, there would be meetings in L.A., but there'd be no reason why you couldn't work from the estate."

"Shit, I just might take you up on that one," Jonah told Eva. "I could even treat myself to a tattoo with my first check. But how about you? Think tattoos on a woman are cool?"

"Let me know what you want to do, Jonah. I'll make it happen. As far as tattoos on women? I don't know. I never really thought about it, but I can't see how a large number of tattoos on women are attractive. Maybe a few small ones?"

Jonah stifled a yawn. Eva shook her head.

"I'll keep yapping at you until sunrise if you let me, Jonah. Let's turn in. We have to be on that flight in a few hours, and it's going to be more exhausting than you can imagine. Feel free to stay in my bed if you want. Gods know, it's big enough."

"Yeah, I think I will," Jonah said. "I've gotten comfortable and everything."

Eva flipped off the light with another voice command and she got buried beneath the comforter. She lifted up only once more.

"Good night, Blueberry. Thanks again, for being here."

"Good night, Superstar," Jonah responded. "Thanks for having me in the first place."

# TWENTY-FOUR

## EVA MCRAYNE

"JESUS, Evie. How long have you been up?"

I glanced up to see Joey pad into my room. He threw himself down on my bed to bury his head in the pillow by my side. I chuckled as I glanced at the clock. It was just after eight. I patted Joey on the shoulder and went back to my tablet.

He was so quiet, I assumed he had gone back to sleep. But after a few minutes, my roommate mumbled something I couldn't hear.

"I'm sorry?" I raised an eyebrow at him. "What did you say?"

"What are you doing?" Joey opened one dark eye to look at me. "That better not be work. It's too damn early. I thought you'd be hungover or something."

"I didn't drink at all yesterday, despite the fact that you told Jonah and the gang that I'm a drunk." I glared down at him. Not that he bothered to open his eyes to gage my reaction to his little revelation. "And yes, it's work. I have to keep myself busy, Joey. If I don't, then I start to think."

"Why does this pillow smell like Jonah?"

"Does it?"

"Evie-" He growled a little in his throat. "What's going on?"

"Not a damn thing. He came and crashed in here last night. Left about fifteen minutes ago."

"Evie, I want you to be careful with Jonah."

"I don't know what you mean."

Joey grumbled again against the pillow before he bunched it up under his head.

"For one, this separation with Cyrus is only temporary. You know what he would do if he found out you let Jonah crash in your bed?"

"I'm not worried about Cyrus. Apollo handled that."

"You should be." Joey snorted. "You really think Apollo is going to do that much good? No. You can't beat a man's personality out of him."

I didn't say anything. I certainly didn't want to tell Joey that you could, in fact, beat a man's personality out of him.

"And anyway, it's not like he's interested in you."

"Joey, why are we having this discussion?"

"Because I don't want to see you hurt anymore than you already have been." Joey sighed. "It's only the truth. And I'm a man, Evie. If Jonah was interested, he'd act differently around you."

"Like how?"

"He'd actually want to learn more about you, for one." Joey snorted. "Every conversation you two have is you asking questions about Jonah and he responds, but never asks about *you*. What little he does know about you, you've had to volunteer in the context of the conversation about him.

"Why would Jonah be interested in me, Joey? Seriously? Do you not realize how much of a trainwreck I am? Between work and Olympus and Cyrus, I'm surprised he agreed to help me at all."

"I'm not. He's bored out of his mind. *Grave* gives him and his friends something to do."

"They are our friends, too."

"I hope so. But you keep acting all giddy around Jonah and he's gonna run off and take his friends with him. Mark my words."

"I offered him the research position on Grave."

"What?" Joey opened one eye to stare at me. "Dammit, Evie. Why? Are you crushing on him that hard?"

" Jonah is just a friend, Joey."

"Is he? You're already going out of your way for him."

"Can we just get back to talking about work?"

"O.k. What about it?"

"The Council. Hoia-Baciu." I shrugged as I went back to tapping my fingers against the screen. I ignored the pang of hurt in my chest over what he had said about Jonah. I knew the truth already. That didn't make it hurt any less. "How much I need to be prepared."

"By doing what? Research?"

"No. By contacting a friend of Prometheus. He is stationed in Prague, but for an insane amount of money, he has agreed to meet us in Transylvania to take us to the outskirts of the forest."

"When you say 'friend'," Joey snorted as he shifted his arms under the pillow. "Do you really mean 'drug dealer'?"

"I don't think so." I frowned. "Though it's a possibility. His name is Arc. Said he will give us a map to the circle."

"Right." Joey closed his eyes. "I'll believe that when I see it."

"Are you going to be productive today or just keep my bed warm?" I smacked his arm this time. "I thought you were going to go buy the equipment we will need to survive the wilderness."

"I ordered the equipment online and had it shipped to the hotel last night, Miss. Taskmaster." He frowned at me. "While you were hanging out with Jonah, I called Theia. Connor's assistant got our rooms confirmed."

"Well, at least now I don't have to worry about that." I sighed. "Thanks, Joey, for taking care of everything."

"Did you look at the gun laws?" He finally decided to sit up. "Cause I want to take my pistol in case we need it."

"Why would we need a gun?" I scowled at him. "I'll have my sword. And Jonah, Reena, and Terrence will be armed, too."

"Oh, I don't know." Joey rolled his eyes. "We're only going into a freakin' forest, Evie. One filled with wild animals that eat small American girls like you for a snack."

"Oh. I didn't think about that."

"So I'll take that as a 'no' then." Joey stood up and ruffled my hair. "Fine. I'll do it."

"Ok." I shrugged. "I know you wanted me to take the day off, but I have to run over to the office. Get my hair done and pick up the massive kit that the make-up witches prepared. Then over to wardrobe before I start writing the monologue."

"Keep it light." He wagged his finger at me. "Remember, Evie. We're going camping. You gotta carry all this stuff."

"But that's what I've got you for." I teased. "Didn't you just get a raise for carrying stuff for me?"

"Camera." He stressed the word. "I carry a camera for you. Not beauty crap."

"Meanie-head."

"And…now you're four."

I laughed as he winked at me. When Joey was gone, I went back to reading the article I'd found on the hauntings reported in Romania. Surprisingly, nothing I'd read had said anything about vampires. Instead, they talked about a biologist named Alexandru Sift who'd been deemed crazy by the locals for wanting to step foot in Hoia-Baciu in the first place. His reports from the 1950's detailed instances such as shadows moving. The feeling of being watched. Even the trees seemed to change.

Another hour of reading passed before I yawned. I didn't have to be at work until eleven. Plenty of time to take a quick nap.

I started to close out the internet browser when a small mail icon began to flash in the corner of my screen. I tapped on it to see a new message from Prometheus' buddy, Arc.

*Darling Sibyl –*

*I have been in contact with Prometheus. He told me what occurred in San Francisco. Lucky for you, I never turn down the opportunity to meet someone almost as beautiful as me.*

*I will meet you in the lobby of the Opera Hotel at 5 a.m. on Friday. Have the money wired to me by tomorrow evening.*

*Arc*

I typed up a quick response and decided against adding a smart comment about his desire to meet someone who looked as good as he did. So the dude was vain. It didn't matter as long as he told me what I needed to know.

Like where the hell I needed to go. I threw the tablet in my purse before I jumped in the shower. I used my time under the water to sift through Prometheus' memories. It was true that I knew what I had to do. The problem was, Prometheus had spent all of his free time trying to erase the knowledge I needed now. I squeezed out a glob of conditioner into my palm as I tried to make sense of the flashes that flickered through my mind.

Tall, shadowing trees. Carvings. The clearing.

I focused on the image of the clearing. Although I'd

never been to Romania before, I knew that Prometheus had been there. I knew what it would look like. And I would know where to go.

Maybe. I finished washing the soap out of my hair as I considered how much had changed since I'd become Apollo's Sibyl. When I first started, I thought my only responsibilities would be to talk to the dead through mirrors. Chasing monsters and strengthening the barriers of Tartarus had never once crossed my mind.

I finished up, dried off, and threw on a robe before wrapping my hair in a towel. I was irritated that we weren't setting out until that afternoon, but at least I could buy more time to get everything ready.

I was in my closet trying to decide what to wear when I heard a knock on my door and Jonah's voice fill my room.

"Evie? You in here?"

"Yeah," I stepped out of my closet and tugged the towel off my head as he stepped inside then closed the door. "Trying to figure out what to wear. What's up?"

Jonah took in my robe and I swore his cheeks flushed. He shook his head.

"I can come back-"

"No, it's fine. I'm covered." I sat at my vanity and began to detangle my wet hair with a brush. "You alright?"

"I wanted to see what the agenda for today was." He sat on the edge of my bed. "Any news on the flight?"

"Yeah. We're stuck leaving at three, so I have to go to the office and get prepped for the episode, pick up my wardrobe, stuff like that. Joey is making sure that all the gear we need is going to arrive at the hotel."

"So we need to be at LAX at three?"

"Yeah." I grabbed a bottle of hair smoothing cream and pumped some out on my palm. "Jonah, I gotta ask you. What do you make of all this? The barriers, the forest, the

Olympians. Compared to the Elevenths, I feel like we are a mess."

"I think that with the Council and the dissenters, it's a lot of cooks in the kitchen. It also seems that a great deal of Olympians, not all of them, but a bunch, are resistant to change. Fresh air might *help* them."

"I think that fresh air is a good thing," I agreed as I combed the product through my hair. "But I have to be honest, Jonah. I'd never heard of ethereality until we had that meeting in the living room of the estate. Are Eleven Percenters hiding their abilities? Or are you guys like, an open secret?"

Jonah snorted. "There are more Elevenths than the Curaie even know. Some live in communes with other Elevenths, and there are homesteads, like the estate. But many just live in Tenth society, content with being as 'normal' as they can hope to be. So *those* Elevenths definitely hide their abilities. Or do as little ethereality as possible."

"So we're ok to feature you guys on the show." I finished with my hair then reached for the lavender oil. I dabbed it on my wrists as I continued. "I was going to do that anyway, but I wanted to clear it with you first. Especially now that you are going to be in not one but two episodes back to back."

"None of us are worried about that. Hollywood is ridiculously fickle. We'll be completely Flavor of the Month."

"I wouldn't be so sure, Blueberry," I dabbed the oil behind my ears, my neck. I bent over to put some behind my knees too. "You are ridiculously attractive. Reena, too. Terrence doesn't show up on the footage as much, but he'll have his share of fangirls start forums and write fanfiction about him. I see you three getting all sorts of attention. I want to make sure you're ready for that."

"Thank you, Superstar." Jonah sounded touched by my concern over them. "But I'm sure we'll be fine. It'd be a bitch if we lived in a celebrity hotbed or something. But out here in the sticks? Piece of cake."

"I loved Rome," I sat up and fluffed out my hair. "Don't laugh! I did. I enjoyed the peace and the quiet. I enjoyed the fact that I could be outside without a bunch of photographers trying to take pictures of me for the tabloids. If it didn't seem like I was stalking you guys, I'd buy a house there. I'd have to stay in L.A. when I'm doing a season because the logistics of getting back and forth between L.A. and Rome everyday is impossible for me."

"Would it really be all that impossible?" Jonah asked and I wondered why. Me being across the country was a great excuse for him not to have to deal with me. "With shadow and ethereal travel and everything? Or is it just like location purposes?"

"It really would. I'm not ethereal, so I couldn't use the Astralimes. And Cyrus told me once that I am banned from using shadow travel because Sibyls have tried to escape before or something?" I frowned as I tried to remember. "And anyway, it's not like I could show up at the estate everyday with my briefcase and say 'Hi, Blueberry! Can I get a ride to L.A.?"

Jonah frowned. "Go over Cyrus' head and ask Apollo. Or even Zeus. That shit makes no sense. Besides, if the estate was too crowded, you could always lease a cabin or something. "

"Why lease a cabin if I can just buy it? Or a house for that matter. Aren't there gated communities in Rome?"

"You'd consider moving there? Seriously?"

"I'd consider it, yes," I smiled at him as I rubbed lotion

on my arms. "I'm afraid you'd get sick of me if I stayed at the estate for too long. And Jonathan might try to get us to share a room again. I couldn't possibly make you sleep on the floor so I'd get in all sorts of trouble."

Jonah laughed "You know you're always welcome. Spader would love you."

"Whose Spader again?" I capped the lotion and moved over to sit next to him on the bed. "In fact, who all lives at the estate? Why didn't I meet them before?"

"Because everyone was off on vacations or with family," Jonah explained. "Me and Reena are each other's family, and Terrence didn't care for the family trip the Decessios went on. The estate is a revolving door of people, but the people who actually live there are me, Terrence, Reena, Malcolm, and Trip. Everyone else just loves it there. Spader lives there as well most of the time. He's this Goth guy who always wears flannel and likes disabling locks. He looks like trouble, but he's scary smart. He could be in the Ivy League if he desired to be. Instead, he's content ripping off casinos and pining after Liz. He started watching *Grave* with Terrence and vouched for you. Now, he adores Liz *and* you."

"That poor man loves *Grave* and adores me?" I raised an eyebrow. "He must have horrible tastes."

Jonah chuckled and I grinned as he continued.

"You haven't seen a single episode of *Grave*, have you?"

"Of course not," Eva scoffed. "I never look at my work; I experienced it, after all. I haven't even seen Covington."

Jonah snickered. I raised a single eyebrow at his reaction.

"What?"

"No offense, Eva, but that's kinda odd. I mean, if you won't watch yourself, why do you expect the fans to?"

"There's a huge difference between them and me." I

explained. "Because most of those locations left me either injured or nearly traumatized. People watch *Grave* because they like the stories. The action. You said you've seen some episodes of *Grave*. You know how it is."

"Yeah, I'm pretty deep in it now," Jonah said. "When Jonathan said you'd be coming, I wanted to get some background information on you. Was only wise. So instead of just reading the websites and just going at face value, l watched the show. l even watched your *Ted Talk*."

"Ew, why?" I made a face. "The *Ted Talk*? It was awful. But now, I get to put you on the spot. Do you have a favorite episode?"

"Oh definitely," Jonah said. "Tied between that one where you helped that family who'd been driven nearly insane by Mania in the Bayou, and the one where you discovered that those Titanic explorers were being haunted because of the brooch they found. Never dawned on them that it might be cursed."

I considered his answers before I responded. "So you like the ones that are a fair distance away from Olympian things."

"I love Greek mythology," Jonah nodded. "That'll never change, especially now. That said, it's only one cog, and the paranormal world is *huge*. So the elements that encompass other matters are a breath of fresh air sometimes, you know?"

"I totally get it." I smiled a little. "Olympus can get...overwhelming at times. And to be honest, the focus used to not be on Olympian affairs. I try to stay away from them most of the time. I should have known that Covington would end up with a tie to Hera since Elliot was so determined to go there."

"What about you? Do you have a favorite?"

I thought about it. After a moment, I nodded.

"I think my favorite was all the way back in Season One. Elliot invited Amy from *Rise and Shine* to go with us to a haunted amusement park. She wanted to trip me up and so did he. But the spirit there was a woman who had passed in an accident back in the sixties. The park paid off her family to keep her death out of the papers and she had been buried under the gift shop. Finding her remains was the best feeling in the world because I helped her move on."

"Why was Amy trying to trip you up?" Jonah shifted to face me. "Seems like a dick move to me."

"I was new and the media may build you up, but it's much more lucrative to tear you down," I explained. "She was looking for the big story. Eva McRayne is a fraud. A charleton! And Elliot was pissed at me because I embarrassed him on national television."

"How's that?"

"I said in very polite, family friendly language that he had a small dick and then threw flour in his face," I grinned. "The resulting food fight was live then it got over three million views on Youtube."

"Wait a second, Terrence loved that!" Jonah exclaimed. "Didn't that have a positive turn?"

"Sure did," I grinned. "The resulting goodwill brought twenty new sponsors to *Grave*. They said it made me look human and therefore, relatable."

Jonah chuckled. "I'm sure it did."

"I have to be at the office by eleven." I studied him. "Do you want to hang out in here with me for a few more minutes?"

"Evie, it's not even ten yet."

"L.A. traffic and I suck at driving. So I have to get a head start."

"How bad do you suck at driving?"

"Um, sometimes I forget how to actually start the

Rover?" I bit my lip. "And reverse and drive are pretty confusing too. Plus, I forget about that whole emergency brake thing. So there's that. And don't even get me started on parking."

"Um, Eva? Legit question here. Who taught you to drive?"

"Nobody. I took the ferry and walked everywhere in Charleston. I didn't need a car at UGA, but I had to have an ID for Theia, so they got me one. I taught myself."

"Clearly, not well."

I gave Jonah a look but he didn't back down.

"Hey, you appreciate me being real with you," He shrugged. "You need someone to actually teach you. I'll happily do so, unless you want Reena."

"Wait," I raised an eyebrow at him. "You're willing to risk life and limb to teach me how to drive? Seriously?"

"Everybody starts somewhere," Jonah said. "The thing about driving is that the only way to learn is to drive. It's that simple."

"Ok. If you're sure." I eyed him. "But I'll owe you one, you know. This is a pretty big deal."

"You won't owe me anything, Superstar," Jonah shook his head. "All I ask is that you be patient and not give in to frustration."

"And why would I do that?"

Jonah snorted again. "Because driving is the one thing you can't pick up through absorption. If it were, you'd have done it already."

"I don't absorb knowledge often," I stood up and stretched. "Only when I need to. It's awful. Like, a freight train slamming into your brain. I get everything - the good, the bad - all of it."

I decided to change the subject. I didn't like talking about stealing the minds of the gods.

"When would you like to do this?" I headed back over to my closet. "I need to get some clothes on, but we can go play around in a parking lot or something."

"Sure," Jonah stood and I saw a flicker of relief cross his face. "We can roll when you're ready."

I disappeared into the closet and considered the relief I had seen on Jonah's face. I must have made him uncomfortable in the robe. I sighed. I should have known better. I should have realized he wouldn't want to see me like that.

My conversation with Joey replayed in my mind. Jonah wasn't interested in me, huh? Well, let me see how he responded to something that showed a little more skin.

I grabbed a sports bra and yoga pants then threw them on. I stepped out of the closet while tightening my ponytail.

"Ready." I brushed the loose strands of hair from my face. "You?"

"I thought you were going to the office after this. You're going to wear that to the office?"

"No, I'm going to take my robe too. I have to get my hair touched up and do all kinds of beauty crap before I can be seen on camera."

I saw Jonah wince a little and realized in that moment that - no matter how comfortable I was with him - he may not be that comfortable with me. Joey had been right. Cyrus was right. I should have known better.

"Oh, gods, I'm sorry, Jonah. I didn't mean to make you uncomfortable. Hold on."

I disappeared back into the closet and pulled out a tshirt. I slipped it on and snagged my sneakers. When I came back out, Jonah was still there, thank the gods. I hadn't run him off.

"Sorry. I really wasn't thinking." I smoothed out my ponytail as I stepped into my shoes. "Let's go."

Jonah gave me a look of surprise. I focused on tying my shoes instead.

"Eva, what exactly would make you think that you made me uncomfortable? I'm *totally* at ease with you. I'm more comfortable with you than I've been with just about anyone. Keep the sports bra. You look beautiful in it. More beautiful in fact than half those women half-naked out there right now. Put the sports bra back on. Let's put those vain bitches to shame."

I studied Jonah in shock. I couldn't help it. Was he being serious? Or just being nice?

He looked serious, and I believed him. But he was right. I was going to the office after this. Even if he was comfortable with me, I didn't need to be going into the office like that.

"Thank you," I reached out and squeezed his hand. "Your words mean more than I can say. I'll keep the shirt. I'm going into the office, after all. I need to keep some level of professionalism."

I willed the keys to the Rover in my hand. I was truly touched by Jonah's words, and I couldn't let him see just how much.

"Want me to drive now? Or wait until we find an abandoned parking lot?" I gave him a small smile. "It's up to you."

"Let's find a nice remote place," Jonah said. "When you have the fundamentals down, then we'll move to traffic."

"Sounds good to me."

I passed him the keys and we headed downstairs. Joey looked up from his spot on the couch as we approached the living room.

"Going out?"

"Uh huh, Jonah is gonna teach me how to drive."

"You brave, brave soul," Joey teased and I stuck my tongue out at him. "Best of luck."

"Figure out those gun laws. I'll see you at LAX at 2:15."

"Yes, m'am."

Joey gave us a salute and we headed out into the garage. My Land Rover was one of the few treasures I loved. Mainly, because it was my first big purchase with my *Grave* money. My condo was the second. Jonah hit the key fob with a whistle.

"Fancy."

"She's my baby." I responded as I slid into the passenger seat. "What kind of car do you have?"

"I have the same Silver Ford Taurus that I had at nineteen," Jonah responded as he started the car. "That and my old Eastpak backpack are the two oldest possessions."

"They must be sentimental items."

"Why do you say that?" Jonah backed out of the space and got out on the road. "Maybe I'm that broke."

"You could be, but you're not," I turned down Slipknot as we talked. I ignored Jonah's look of surprise at my choice in music. "I don't know about your finances, and it's none of my business. But you've had both of those items since college. That means you have attached meaning to them. You said your grandmother was the most important woman to you last night. Did she give them to you?"

Jonah was quiet for a moment while he drove. "Nana didn't give the car to me, per se, but she was helping put money towards it before she passed into Spirit. I was able to afford it five months after...you know. But the Eastpak?"

Jonah laughed before he continued.

"That thing was no gift. I got it from Wal-Mart after a summer job when I was fifteen, and never got rid of it. High school, college, grad school...that's been my bag."

"Don't you think it's time for an upgrade?" I wondered aloud.

"No need," Jonah said. "That bag's a trooper. Broken in and everything."

"I'm surprised it lasted that long." I teased him. "Are you sure you're not confusing 'broken in' with 'beat all to hell'? I mean, you are a writer. And you work at a library. You need a proper bag to carry all those books around."

"My Eastpak is durable and weathered, just like me," Jonah insisted. "I'll show it to you next time you're at the estate. You'll see it's better than new."

"You may be durable, but you're not weathered in the least," I grinned. "I don't see a single wrinkle on your face."

Jonah furrowed his brow to make lines appear across his forehead and I giggled.

"That doesn't count. And if your bookbag is beat all to hell, I'm buying you a Patagonia. I'll even get you a blue one. I bet your Eastpak is grey. And is coming apart at the seams."

"You will do no such thing," Jonah told her. "Use that money on coffee or dessert or something."

"We'll see," I smirked at him. "I do want to see this monstrosity of a bookbag though. Maybe we can have a party and burn it."

I burst out laughing at the look of horror that crossed over Jonah's face. His expression broke out into a grin as he looked over at me.

"Not to get you off my ass about my perfectly fine bookbag, but why is Joey looking up gun laws?"

"Oh. He's an expert marksman, remember? A sharpshooter? I think that's the term he used. He wants to bring his gun to Romania in case we run into any wild animals that want to eat us."

"Will he have a gun on the plane?" Jonah said. "Is that possible?"

"On a private jet? Absolutely. He usually carries one on location just in case. We don't go to the safest areas, after all. And while I could kick a robber's ass, we don't want to risk being in a gunfight without a gun."

"I don't think I've ever seen Joey shoot one thing on the show," Jonah remarked

"He's never had to. I've always been able to take down any threat we face. But it's good to have insurance. Especially if I get knocked out and Joey is on his own."

"This looks like a place as good as any." Jonah pulled over into an abandoned strip mall parking lot. "Show me what you know."

"You sure? I was having fun just riding with you."

Jonah winked at me as he shut the Rover off and passed me the keys. We switched places and I fiddled with the keys for a second before I found the right one. I stuck it in the ignition and started it up.

Jonah didn't say anything as I started to put the car in reverse. The warning light for the emergency brake came on and I grumbled.

"I always forget that part."

I pushed down the brake and pressed on the gas. We went backwards and I hit the brakes before I burst out laughing.

"See? I told you. This is hopeless."

"The pilot episode of *Grave,*" Jonah tightened his grip on the handle over the door. "You said you'd be the most hopeless Sybil ever. You proved that to be a lie. This will be no different."

"We'll see." I sat back in the seat. "Ok. Let me try this again."

Jonah spent the better part of the next hour working

with me. I got better with steering, a little better with braking, and he explained things to me like what the dials all meant and the gears. By the time I had to head to Theia, I wasn't great. I wasn't even safe to actually get on the road, but I was better.

I cut off the car then passed the keys over to him. "Thanks, Blueberry. I learned a whole bunch. I suck, but less."

"You never sucked," Jonah said, his voice firm. "All you ever needed was to learn."

I gave him a small smile then kissed him on the cheek. "Thank you. You're very sweet, Blueberry."

We switched seats and Jonah pulled us into traffic. He glanced over at me and I tilted my head at him.

"What?"

"You're an enigma, Superstar."

"How so?"

"You're one of the most famous people on the planet, but you don't act like one. You don't brag, you don't throw money around, and most of the women I've seen here always run around half-naked. You, however, ran to throw on a t-shirt because you thought I would be uncomfortable. I can't figure out why."

I thought about his words for a moment. I wasn't about to get into my past with my mother. Or Cyrus' influence. So I took the easy way out.

"Jonah, we've only known each other for a few weeks, but you've become very important to me. I don't want to do anything to fuck up the friendship we're building."

"And you thought just wearing a sports bra would fuck everything up?" Jonah frowned. "That was never gonna happen."

"Well," I thought of the best way to put this. "Let me start this by saying one, I'm not throwing a pity party for myself or two, I'm not fishing for compliments. I'm just stating facts, ok?"

"Ok."

"I know that I don't have the body women would envy. I'm too thin. Too boney. There's nothing I can do about it since my immortality froze me like this. So I try not to run around exposing people to how I look. Whenever I do photoshoots, they are so photoshopped by the time they hit the magazines, you can barely tell it's me. Not to mention the make up. All that helps."

I kept my tone level. I wasn't emotional or anything. I was just being honest.

"Anyway, when I came out of the closet, I saw you wince and I realized that you didn't want to see me like that. You were probably relieved when I went to get dressed in the first place. So I was afraid that I'd run you off."

Jonah just stared at me. I tried to keep his gaze, but in the end, I just sighed and studied the city around us.

"Eva, you're fucking gorgeous," He began. "You're the dream girl. I don't know how you came to believe you weren't beautiful, but the opposite is true. You're too bony...you're more athletic build than skinny. You're not 'exposing' people to how you look. You're being yourself, letting your light shine brightly. If people don't like it, fuck them. That's on them, not you. So anyone who'd supposedly run off? They're dealing with their own inadequacies and projecting them onto you. That's all that is. If you want to change some things up, consult Apollo. He's a god after all...perhaps he can do something about the frozen piece if you desire to make changes. But only if you desire to, because you're beautiful. Of that, there can be no question."

I didn't know what to say to Jonah. I didn't. That was

the second time today that he had said I was beautiful, and I didn't know how to respond to that. If he'd told me I was a mess? I could have handled it. I was used to that.

I took a leveling breath before I gave him a soft smile. "Thank you again, Jonah."

"For?"

"For being you. For being so undeniably sweet. Your words mean a lot."

"You don't believe me." Jonah reached over to clasp my hand. "Eva, I'm being honest with you. If you looked in the mirror-"

"No," I shook my head. "There's no need for that."

"Why though? Why would you say such things about yourself?"

"Jonah," I squeezed his hand. "I am not going to burden you with the shit from my past. Let's just say that I have heard those words from a lot of different people over the course of my life. And it's easier to believe and accept them than it is to get heartbroken about it. Does that make sense?"

Jonah regarded me before he responded. "Eva, what if I told you I spent my teen years being called a bum and a fat piece of shit? That it should have been criminal for me to be as ugly as I was? What would you say?"

"I would ask for their names and addresses so that I could gauge their eyes out. Obviously, they don't need them. They aren't using them."

Jonah raised an eyebrow. I shrugged.

"I'd say that they were fools and liars. I'd say that you are an amazing human being who is handsome as all hell and if they hurt you, I'd be forced to act on it."

"Well, Eva, that happened."

"What?" I stared at him this time. "Are you serious?"

"Dead serious," Jonah nodded. "From Kindergarten till

damn near senior year of high school. I was told I was fat, ugly, poor, stupid...this fucker named Billy Silverstone was the absolute worst to me. He even started a rumor that I was homosexual. No, I'm not throwing shade on homosexuality, it's just in my case, things got even worse for me because it opened the door to an additional dimension of bullying. His little fuck buddy and leader of the the girl cliques, Regina, helped. She even spread the gay rumor to another damn school."

"No one even bothered to *ask* if you were gay?" Eva demanded.

"You serious, Eva?" Jonah laughed with no mirth. "It was school. People attack you first and figure you out later. My childhood best friend, P.J., was literally my only friend. And even he came under fire just for being my friend. Outside of Nana and him, I wasn't told anything positive. My first serious girlfriend, Priscilla? Even she didn't ever call me handsome. She said I was 'fuckable.' So I've been thrown that shit, too. It's one of the reasons I have anger issues. So you're not alone. You can put it behind you. Slowly but surely. I am working on it as we speak. I'm choosing *not* to live in that dark mental place. You can work on it too."

"Jonah, pull over."

"What?"

"Pull over."

When he pulled over into a restaurant parking lot and shut off the car, I threw my arms around his neck and held him. I couldn't help it. It broke my heart to think that this hero of a man had been treated so unkindly. I didn't care how long ago it had been.

Jonah stayed stock still as I held onto him.

"You are absolutely nothing like how they described you." I said against his shoulder. "Absolutely nothing. You are handsome and I wasn't kidding when I said I'd get you in magazines if I thought you would go for it. Those people can go fucking rot. I really should go after them for hurting you like that. I really should. It's not right."

Jonah seemed too stunned to react to my show of affection. He kept his hands glued to the steering wheel as he spoke.

"Thank you, Eva. So much. Now I want you to begin the process of believing me when I say that everything bad you've heard about yourself is trash. The people who made you believe that shit- they are-fuck them. May they fall off the Empire State Building and catch their eyelid on a nail."

I held on a little longer. I wanted to tell Jonah everything. I wanted to tell him all my horrible experiences. Somehow, I was convinced he would make them all go away.

But I couldn't do that. This wasn't my pity party and Jonah wasn't a white knight come to save the day. There were no white knights, after all. No matter how much I needed there to be one.

Finally, I pulled back with a laugh.

"A nail, huh?"

"A rusty one. Sharp as hell."

"Jonah, what year did you graduate high school?"

"Um, why?"

"I'm just curious. I mean, I could do the math myself, but it's easier if you tell me."

"2005."

"Ok." I smiled sweetly as I put my seatbelt back into place. "That helps. A lot."

"I don't understand." Jonah frowned. "What does my graduation have to do with - wait."

"What?"

"Evie, you can't go harassing people who were assholes to me."

"Sure, I can." I flipped my ponytail over my shoulder. "They need to learn a little humility."

"So what do you have to do before the flight, Superstar?"

"Hair and pick up the clothes they want me to wear. It's a pain in the ass, but I have to play by the rules."

I shifted in my seat to study Jonah. I took in the lines of his face as if to commit them to memory. Unfortunately, he noticed me staring.

"Yes?"

"Nothing. Just trying to figure out why you are so easy to talk to. I thought at first it was because you have such an inviting face. But I think it's just you and the aura you project."

"Hey, I wouldn't know myself," Jonah said. "People just always found it easy to speak with me."

I smiled at him then began to direct him to the office. Once we got there, Jonah's first visit to Theia Productions was an absolute bore. I know it was, though he didn't say as much. He hung out and chatted with my stylist as I got my hair done. I introduced him to the people in wardrobe and make-up. Then I showed him the studio, the area that was currently accounting but would become Theia Music Group within the next year. Finally, I took him up to my office.

I opened the door to see Joey sitting cross legged on the floor with a list. He was digging through black equipment cases and checking each item off.

"Hey, Joey," I held the door open so that Jonah could follow me in. "Everything look alright?"

"Perfect, as always." He grinned up at us. "I got the call

that we got some new equipment in so I wanted to check it out. How was the lesson?"

"Fine. I was just giving Jonah a tour of Theia."

I watched Jonah take in my office, which was more of my home than the condo. He walked around with his hands in his pockets, stopping by the wall to wall bookcase filled with books about the occult and the paranormal. He looked at everything - from my white and glass furniture to the framed promotional posters of Grave that hung on the wall. Finally, he stopped at the large floor to ceiling window that was more of a wall than a window.

"So what's in the bag, Joey?"

"Which one?"

"That funny looking one."

"My bow and a hell of a bunch of arrows."

"Your bow?"

"Yeah. Turns out, Romania has some of the strictest gun laws in the world. So I had to improvise."

"Huh. I didn't realize you knew how to shoot a bow."

"I'm from Wyoming, baby girl. We can shoot anything."

“I don't think you'll use that thing once.” I fell back onto my butt beside him. “And if I remember correctly, weren’t you the one who said we should pack light?”

“You’ll thank me when you’re running from a bear.” Joey smirked at me. “Besides, it’s not like you took my advice at all. How many bags are you bringing?”

“Four. But I can narrow it down to one when we get there.” I glanced over at Jonah. “What are you bringing, Jonah?"

"Just my batons, Superstar," Jonah replied without looking away from the view. "All I've ever needed."

"See?" Joey stuck his tongue out at me. "Jonah knows how to pack."

"Oh, be quiet." I stood up when the phone on my desk rang. "Just a second."

I glanced down at the caller id and started not to answer it. But my producer had to know I was in here to be calling. I plastered on a fake smile as I answered it.

"Hi, Connor! Listen, we're super busy-"

"Cut the crap, McRayne." Connor huffed into the phone. "You leave for Romania in a few hours?"

"Yeah," I sat down in my chair. "Why?"

"Because you just got a promotion. We're giving you Elliot's old title of Creative Director for *Grave*. You need to sign the paperwork."

Whoa. Really? That meant that *Grave* - everything about my show - was up to me. The stories we featured, how we promoted it, everything.

"Thanks, Connor. Send the contract to my lawyers. If it sounds good, I'll sign before we leave."

"Why don't you sign it now?"

"Because I'm not convinced you won't screw me over."

"Fine."

He hung up the phone and I beamed at Jonah and Joey.

"You're never happy after you talk to Connor." Joey gave me a look of pure suspicion. "What's wrong?"

"He just gave me Elliot's old title of Creative Director." I grinned wider. "*Grave* finally belongs to us! We can do what we want as long as we don't go crazy with the budget!"

"Wow." Jonah was impressed. "Congrats, Superstar. I heard you say you'll have a lawyer look at it first. Reena would be *so* pleased at that."

"Always, Blueberry," I beamed now thanks to his praise. "Connor can be a snake, but he's a snake I'm familiar with."

"It's almost one, Evie," Joey glanced up at the clock over my head. "Let's go to lunch to celebrate."

"Ok." I stood. "Jonah, why don't you call Reena and Terrence? They can meet us at the sushi place across the street then we can go to LAX from there."

"Oh, Reena will love that," Jonah said. "I'll shoot a text now."

We helped Joey pack up the equipment he had been playing with and got everything set to be sent to LAX. We headed across the street and I went ahead as Jonah, Reena, Joey, and Terrence all greeted each other at the entrance.

"Hey, Ayiko," I kissed her on each cheek. "Do you have a private room available?"

"Of course!" She grinned. "Will you be joining Cyrus?"

Wait. What?

"Cyrus is here?" I tilted my head at her. "Which room is he in?"

"The Magnolia room." She checked her book. "It's a smaller dining room."

"Is he alone?"

"No. He brought a business associate with him. A Dominique Breaux."

Interesting.

"I tell you what," I gave her a bright smile. "We won't disturb them. But will you show my party to another dining room? And can we start with the sampler platter? I want to say hello to Cyrus first."

"Of course." She bowed her slender neck when the others approached us from the street. "Follow me, everyone."

"I'll be there in a moment, guys."

I left it at that as I slipped past the hostess station then headed down the server's hall. Normally, I couldn't be so bold, but I owned this restaurant. Aiko's had been an investment of mine for over a year now.

A fact that gave me freedom to roam. I stopped next to

the bamboo door and slid the viewing window cover back just enough to see a woman of color on Cyrus' lap. I may not have known anything about sex, but I knew enough to realize what I was seeing.

I should have been angry. I should have charged in there and demanded an explanation. But I didn't. I felt nothing. I was numb to what I was witnessing.

I closed the window covering back then stood there a moment longer. I had suspected Cyrus had his lovers. After all, how many times had he told me our relationship was in name only?

I looked up at the ceiling as I recalled the day I had tried to seduce him. The humiliation that followed had been enough to turn me off of sex forever. It was the first time he'd ever directly said that he didn't want me. That I wasn't desirable. It was the first day he had begun to parrot the words my mother used to say.

It didn't matter. Let him have his fun. He was a man, after all.

I took a breath, plastered a smile on my face, then went into the kitchen to personally chat with the staff. By the time I approached our dining room, I felt better. Calmer.

"Hey, people," I slipped in and held the door for Ayiko as she left us. "How is everything?"

"I was just telling everyone how this is your place, Evie."

Joey snagged a sushi roll from the large plate that had been placed in the center. I was pleased to see that the four of them had attacked the large amount of food.

"I'm only an investor-"

"Your name is on the stationary." Joey scoffed. "Let me tell you all the story. Evie and I would always come here for lunch - she'll get the miso soup, she always does - and she overheard Ayiko crying in the women's room. She found out that Ayiko was about to lose her restaurant, so Evie took her savings and invested in this place. That wasn't long after *Grave's* first season wrapped. Now, Aiko is thriving and making Evie richer by the day."

"Gods, how you exaggerate, Joey." I accepted the green tea the waitress had brought to me then sat back as she put a bowl of soup in front of me. "You make it seem like I did it out of the kindness of my heart. It was for purely financial gain, I promise."

I winked at him and he grinned at me.

"Anyway, ya'll order what you want. We won't get this kind of food in Romania."

"This spread is amazing," Reena said. "It's with food like that you'll see me binge out."

"This," Terrence muttered, "Along with my chicken salad with homemade mayo. Don't play squeaky clean, Re."

I giggled at their banter as Jonah shook his head. After the group ordered another round of food, Jonah tapped me on the wrist.

"You alright?"

"I'm fine," I looked at him, startled from my thoughts. "Why?"

"One, you're quiet. And two, your knuckles are white on that spoon. I think you've bent it."

Oh, well, damn.

"I'm ok," I loosened my grip and gave him a soft smile. "I've gone without alcohol for almost forty-eight hours, Blueberry. I think I'm starting to feel the withdrawals. That's all."

"Want to do cardio with me?" Reena suggested. "Fires up the same receptors that alcohol does."

"I don't think we have time," I checked my wristwatch. "It's almost two and we have to be on the plane by three.

Did you guys need to run back to the condo to pick up anything?"

"Nah, we're all squared away," Jonah snagged another roll from the platter. "When do we board?"

"Two forty-five, so if we're done here, we might want to head that way."

"I saw the Rover in the parking deck," Joey extended his hands for my keys. "Give 'em up."

"I didn't drive. Jonah did."

"You let Jonah drive the Rover?" He whistled. "Damn. You barely let Cy drive that thing."

I started to come back with a smart ass remark when Ayiko poked her head in.

"Sorry to disturb you, but I told Cyrus you were here."

She stepped aside and pushed the door open. Cyrus was there in his usual black suit with the woman next to him with the same militaristic aura he did.

"Eva, everyone," He bowed his head at the group. "I knew you were leaving out today. I wish you well."

"Thanks-"

I started before he cut me off.

"Allow me to introduce you all to Dominique Breaux. She is a keeper who is assisting me on matters for the Council."

"Nice to meet you."

Joey waved. The others gave her smiles. She returned them, but cut her eyes over at me.

"You are the Representative, yes?"

"Last time I checked." I wiped my hands on the cloth napkin. "They haven't fired me yet."

I caught the look she shared with Cyrus. I should have ignored it, but I was aggravated now. He didn't know I had seen them together, but I felt he was flaunting her just the same.

"Is there a problem?"

"No, no problem." She gave me a hateful grin as she bent at the waist to get a better look at my face. "You just seem...more fragile...than I would have imagined."

"More fragile?" I smiled. "I suppose so."

I lashed out faster than anyone could have imagined and grabbed onto the back of her hair. I slammed her face into my half eaten bowl of soup so hard, the porcelain cracked. I stood as she fell to the floor, now cupping her broken face. I turned to Cyrus, who actually looked surprised.

"Next time you bring your whores to my restaurant? Try not to fuck them in the dining room. It goes against the California Health Code."

"Whoa!" Jonah jumped from the table. "What the hell is going on?"

"Bitch-"

The woman seethed as she struggled to stand. I met her nose to nose.

"Strike out against me and I will have you tried for treason, Keeper. I'm already going to Tartarus. I will be more than happy to drop you off."

"Eva!" Cyrus barked at me. "Have you lost your mind?"

"Not in the least. You want to take a hit at me, too? Or did Apollo finally get through to you?"

The disgraced keeper looked away from me and I nodded.

"Just as I thought. Come on, guys. I'll explain later."

"Um, how about you explain now?" Terrence looked between us. "Because that was not a normal way to say hello."

"Fine. Ayiko told me Cyrus was here with this woman. I went to say hello and saw them fucking in their dining room. I was going to let it go, but then, she had to call me fragile. So, I showed her how fragile I really am."

"I should kill you." She snapped as she grabbed a napkin to wipe her face. "You should be punished-"

"Oh, fuck off. You're obviously good at it."

"Eva." Cyrus snapped. "Get outside. I want a word with you."

Now, my heart dropped. There was no way in hell I was going to be alone with him after I showed out like that.

"Sorry, Cy, I don't have time. You can yell at me later."

Cyrus looked unpleasantly surprised. "Eva, I said to step outside--"

"And she said she did not have time."

Everyone turned. Apollo stood there, looking stern. Maybe a little pissed.

"Lord Apollo." Cyrus was stunned to see him. Everybody was, in fact. "To what do I owe this very unexpected pleasure?"

"Oh, it was brought to my attention that you had predilections that may be detrimental to your tasks," the god replied.

"I'm afraid I don't follow--"

"Of course you don't," Apollo said, "Which is why I'm here. So whatever you needed Eva to go outside with you to say, you may now come outside and say to me. Eva, friends, continue onto your flight. Cyrus will interrupt you no further."

I felt so much relief, my shoulders dropped. We filed out of our private room and I stopped only to tell Ayiko to charge our bill and the tip to my credit card. We didn't say anything until we all piled into the Rover.

"Guys, I'm sorry," I twisted around in the front passenger seat. "I shouldn't have showed out like that. I owe you all a huge apology."

"If Cyrus was fucking someone in plain sight, you need

not apologize to anyone," Jonah spat. "I wonder who contacted Apollo anyway?"

"I have no idea."

"Ok. Can I ask a very personal question?" Reena eyed me from the back seat. "Feel free not to answer this. But you caught Cyrus cheating on you and you said you were just going to let it go?"

"Um," I fiddled with rings as I tried to think of an answer. Finally, I decided on transparency. "Yes. I was. I didn't see a reason to make a scene about it. And the truth is, when I saw them? I just didn't care. I still don't."

The silence in the car was deafening. I sighed and continued.

"Besides, sex has never been on my radar. I'm not a sexual person, I suppose. So if he goes to someone else? Great."

Reena stared. "Eva, in no world is that great. Not if he's supposed to be with you. Now if you're asexual, fine. But that still doesn't give Cyrus a carte blanche."

I shrugged. "Can we change the subject -"

"I can't believe you broke the bowl with that bitch's face," Joey laughed from the driver's seat. "I love it when you do shit like that. She wasn't expecting you to do anything at all and you broke a bowl. With her face!"

"Yeah, well, I have my moments." I smiled at him. "That was fun though. A lot of fun."

"Good thing she was caught unawares," Joey added. "If she is a Keeper, she's probably dangerous herself."

"*Eva* is dangerous, Joey," Jonah said. "You've never needed your gun, have you?"

"Aw, thanks, Blueberry," I grinned at him. "I love that."

Jonah smiled back, but it didn't reach his eyes. I continued.

"But I'm not worried about the keeper. Or Cyrus. I am worried about us making this flight on time, slow poke."

"I'm going as fast as I can, Evie." Joey rolled his eyes at me. "Besides, they won't leave until we get there. No worries."

"Good," Jonah said. "Maybe we can rest on the plane. How smooth is the flight usually, Eva?"

"It's great, actually. There's a double bed, too, so we can take turns. We should arrive at seven a.m. their time."

"Layovers?"

"One in Shanghai, for fuel. Then it's back in the air."

"Good," Jonah said. "Several hours noiseless, dramaless, Cyrus-less. Can't think of anything better."

I didn't say anything else. There was nothing more I could say, really. So I focused on the road. I focused on us making it into the hanger ten minutes before takeoff. I focused on giving everyone a tour of their new home for the next seventeen or so hours.

Once we were settled and in the air, we started a game of scrabble. I was losing badly to Jonah and Reena. Terrence, too. So when Jonah leaned over to look at my letters, I just turned them towards him and said.

"Help please. I need an adult. Who can spell."

"You can spell perfectly," Jonah said. "Look, you've got at least three words there."

"For three points, two points, and...three points."

"No, goofball, look." Jonah took my *A* and put it next to Reena's *X*. "With the triple word score, that's 27 points."

"Oh," I breathed out. "Oh, you are good at this game."

"Nope," Jonah grinned. "Just good with words."

I laughed at his expression as Terrence gave us a look.

"If we playing doubles, we playing doubles." Terrence joked. "Re, come help me."

That started an all out scrabble war between the four of

us. I couldn't remember the last time I had laughed that hard. By the time the steward brought our dinner trays around, we had tied each other in wins two each.

"I better go get Joey up." I stood and stretched. "He'll be pissed if he misses dinner. Thanks, guys. That was the most fun I've had in awhile."

"Happy to provide," Terrence said. "Next time we'll be on the ground and I can cook for you."

"I'd like that." I slipped past Jonah's seat. "When we're home though. I don't know what kind of food they have in Romania."

I moved over to the bedroom door and knocked. It took a few minutes, but Joey came shuffling to the door.

"Dinner time, Sleeping Beauty."

"Thanks, Evie."

He yawned as he grabbed his shirt then followed me back out to the main cabin. He tugged his shirt over his head as we gathered around the table that had once held our scrabble board.

"What'd I miss?"

"A kick ass Scrabble tournament." I grinned at him. "Me and Jonah won!"

"Twice." Reena looked at me with amusement. "You won twice out of four games. We're even."

"So a tiebreaker is in order at some point," Jonah grinned. "I'm game."

"How about after ya'll eat?" I took my smoothie from the steward as the others uncovered their trays of chicken, rice, and something green. "I think we can take them down, Blueberry."

"Blue and gold, huh?"

"Blue and gold."

He tapped his water bottle against my glass. Reena and Terrence did not look amused.

"I am kinda sad I missed whatever you are talking about." Joey laughed. "Sounds like an asskicking."

"Nah," I grinned. "Just some good ol' fashioned fun, Joey. There'll be plenty of asskickings later."

---

Let me start by saying that it took a very long flight to get to Romania. By the time we landed in Cluj-Napoca, I was ready to pay any price imaginable to get off that damned airplane. We had a good time thanks to Jonah, Reena, and Terrence, but even they were ready to put their feet on the ground by the time we landed.

The car ride that followed was nothing but pure torture since it meant sitting for another thirty minutes while our driver maneuvered through the narrow streets. Even Joey was ill by the time we reached the Opera Place, our hotel for the night. He didn't say a word as we pulled up to the massive yellow building that seemed to dominate the grey winter sky above us.

I got out of the car and stood there for what felt like forever, studying the clouds overhead. I couldn't help but remember how I'd felt when Elliot had sent me to Montana to do the Kentauros episode. I'd hated it since I didn't like farms. Or horses. Or the outdoors. Yet here I was. In Romania. Ready to trek into the most haunted forest in the world on the orders of the Olympian Council.

"You comin', Evie?"

I nodded before I jogged over to Joey. He and the others had headed towards the front door the second they got out of the car. I reached out and squeezed his hand before I slipped by him. I didn't want to let on how scared I was.

So I chalked it up to myself as being exhausted from the

flight. After we'd gotten set up in our rooms, we wouldn't say another word to each other. We didn't need to. The two of us had worked together – and lived together – for so long now, all it took was a look to understand exactly what the other was thinking. Thankfully, Jonah, Reena, and Terrence understood our unspoken language and they seemed to agree.

Food. Bed. The rest could be dealt with later.

Too bad the Fates had other plans. When I grabbed my key from the hotel clerk, I heard a man call out to me from across the lobby. He wasn't a large man. Quite the opposite. But his smile was so big, I shrugged and headed in his direction.

"Yes?"

"Miss. McRayne," He took my hand as if I were made of glass between his own. "I am Andrei Savu. I am the proprietor of Opera Place."

"Nice to meet you." I gave him a tight smile. "Thank you for having us."

"No. No trouble." The poor man's grin got even bigger. "All of Romania is here to greet the princess of *Grave Messages*. Please, won't you take a moment to speak with our press?"

Their press? I blinked as I looked into the room he was standing next to. Inside, a podium had been set up. A crowd of men and women had gathered in front of it. Some with cameras. All with microphones. I let my mouth drop open in shock for a moment as I tried to decide how to handle this newest nightmare.

"Please. Only a few words."

"I," I turned back to him with my eyes wide. "I look horrible. Mr. Savu, you must understand, our flight was over sixteen hours…"

"Beautiful." He threw up his hands when he interrupted

my protests. "A true creation of God. Now come along. Romania loves you."

I felt myself being ushered into the room. I heard the reporters as they began to cheer for me. I searched the door when I reached the podium, but my people didn't join me. Instead, they stayed planted by the door. Jonah was rubbing his eyes with his hands, Reena looked irritated. Joey just gave me a massive grin. I mouthed a single, solitary word in his direction as the press began to shout questions at me.

"Traitor."

I don't know how I did it, but I switched from the travel-worn girl I was to the celebrity I had become. I smiled. I laughed. I answered every question I could without mentioning the real reason we were there. I focused on the history of Hoia-Baciu as they knew it. I promised them that I would use my abilities as the Sibyl to learn all I could about the cursed lands. And I used the time I had to beg for space. I emphasized how curious onlookers could taint any evidence we may find. I pointed out the dangers of being in any forest alone, but especially one known to cause people to disappear.

When it was finally over, I let Mr. Savu take over my spotlight. I made my way over to Jonah and all but collapsed against him. I looped my arm through his, gave the reporters one final smile and wave, then whispered to him.

"Run. Now."

"You don't have to tell me twice." Jonah muttered he led me through the lobby. When we reached the elevator, he waited until the doors shut behind us before he spoke. "How do you do it, Evie? You can be dead on your feet and still charm the hell out of everyday folk."

"Hera." I pressed myself against the wall of the elevator

to keep myself upright. "I absorbed her charisma, remember? I pull it out whenever I need to."

"Like you do with Athena's knowledge when you get into a fight?"

"Yeah." I sighed as my best friend joined the conversation. "Joey, can we drop this for now? I'll tell ya'll anything you want to know later. Right now? I need a shower. A change of clothes. And if I make it through all that, sleep."

"You know; you are usually the one talking my ear off when I have jetlag." My friend teased. "It's kinda nice to be on the other side of the coin right now."

"Please stop talking." I tilted my head back to look up at him. "You know I love you. But I love silence more at the moment."

"Burned." He sighed when the doors opened. "Come on, Sleeping Beauty. Let's get you to bed. We have a very long day ahead of us tomorrow."

I didn't argue. I didn't protest. I let the group lead me into my room where my luggage was already waiting. But with it, there were piles of boxes. The equipment Joey had ordered before we left Los Angeles. Reena and I were sharing a room, so we said our goodbyes at the door with plans to meet up for supper later that evening.

I dropped down on the closest bed then grabbed the pillow behind me. I worked it into place then released a happy sigh despite the fact that I was still fully clothed. I couldn't explain it, but I felt safe here. Secure. I tried to pull myself up to start unpacking, but I couldn't make myself do it. Instead, I buried my head deeper into the pillow and closed my eyes.

I was asleep within seconds.

# TWENTY-FIVE

## EVA MCRAYNE

"You've got to be kidding me."

I stared at the backpack Joey was trying to convince me held all the essentials I would need when we were in the woods. I went from staring at the backpack to him.

"I can't carry that. It's bigger than I am."

"It's not so bad." He shook his head at me. "Now turn around. I have to adjust the straps for you."

I glared at him for a good five seconds before I did what he asked. I could see Reena trying her best not to laugh as he hefted the heavy thing onto my back. I frowned when he came back into view.

"Joey, what the hell is in this thing? Concrete?" I lifted my shoulders as he reached out to adjust the right strap. "Stones? The entire Theia Productions shoe collection?"

"Survival kit." He kept his eyes down as he tugged at the nylon. "Your bag has your tent, your food, your clothes. No makeup though. You're going to have to do without that."

I rolled my eyes as he began to work on the left side. "I think I'll live without my eyeliner for a few days."

"Good. Cause it wouldn't fit." He took a step back. "There. The weight is balanced. How does it feel now?"

"Like I'm carrying a house." I grabbed the straps. "But better. Thanks, darlin'."

"Don't mention it." He helped me take the damn thing off. "I got something else for you too."

"What?"

"Body camera." He reached into the small black bag by his feet. "I'll attach it once we get to the forest. We might lose each other, Evie. This will help me figure out just where in the hell you are."

"Ok. So that's helpful."

There was a knock on the door, so I made moves to open it without falling over thanks to the weight on my back. I opened the door to see Jonah and Terrence on the other side.

"Ya'll are just in time to get fitted with your own house."

"What?"

"Our camping gear." I stepped aside so they could join us. "And body cameras."

"No sweat," Jonah glanced at the bag. "You, Terrence?"

"Already on it." He grabbed a bag and passed it to Jonah. "You good with the straps, bro?"

"Yeah, I got it." Jonah put his on and started tugging at the clasps. He glanced over at Reena. "You already got yours?"

"Yup. Evie made me go first." She laughed. "I think she was avoiding it."

"I maintain that this is silly. Why carry a bag when I can just will stuff to me?"

"Oh, I don't know," Joey responded dryly. "Maybe because - with our luck - that little trick won't be available in Hoia-Baciu? I'd rather not risk it."

"Yeah, yeah," I snorted. "Get me out of this thing, will you?"

"You said something about body cameras?" Terrence was working on his own bag. "How does that work?"

"Easy. We attach it to your clothes and it will capture anything you see." Joey unhooked me and pulled the bag off as he talked. I shook out my shoulders. "It'll also track your location in case any of us gets lost."

Joey patted me on the arm before he continued. "I've got everything I need. What time are we meeting with your contact again?"

"At five a.m." I took the opportunity to shake out my arms. "Arc said he'd meet us in the lobby."

"Who's Arc?" Jonah asked as he slipped out of his bag. He placed it next to mine. "A guide?"

"Of sorts." I nodded. "He is a friend of Prometheus. He is going to give us a map of the forest in exchange for a ton of money."

"Sounds classy."

"That's better than what I said," Joey grinned. "I said he sounded like a drug dealer."

I cut Joey a look as I crossed the room, grabbed the phone, and hit the '0' on the keypad. Two rings later, a woman's chipper voice greeted me.

"Hey, good morning." I cleared my throat. "Can you send someone up for our bags? We need to have them packed in the car and ready to go."

"Of course, Miss. McRayne. They will be up in a few moments."

"Great. Thanks." I hung up the phone to see Reena raise an eyebrow in my direction. "What?"

"We could have taken them down ourselves, you know."

"I mean, we could," I pulled at my ponytail to tighten it. "But I prefer that we save our strength for the hike, right?"

I began to check through our bags one last time to make sure we weren't forgetting anything. I was sure we were going to be away from civilization for at least a week. And I was pretty damn sure that no one was going to be willing to deliver anything if we needed it. So by the time the hotel porter showed up, I was convinced there was nothing I would possibly miss. Even if I was stuck in the middle of nowhere.

We entered the lobby a few minutes before five to see the place abandoned except for a lone woman standing behind the impressive wooden counter. I frowned at the massive clock that hung on the far wall before I saw movement just off to my right. A tall man was standing by a large window holding a stick up and moving his head around. I stuck my hands in my pockets as I approached him. It wasn't until I was by his side that I realized what was in his hand.

A selfie stick with a cellphone attached to the end. The man gave his image on the screen a brooding look before I saw the flash go off.

"Excuse me." I cleared my throat. "You wouldn't happen to be Arc, would you?"

"I am." He was so focused on catching himself in the right light that he didn't look at me. "You must be Eva."

"I am."

I almost ducked when he reached out to grab my arm. He pulled me next to him and gave his camera a massive grin. "Smile, girl. You're about to be famous."

"I am already famous." I glared at him. "Who are you?"

"Arc. You know that."

"Yeah, ok." It was my turn to reach out. I snagged the stupid stick and pulled it out of his hand. "How do you know Prometheus?"

"How do you?" He pouted. "Give me my camera back."

"Answer my question first."

"Fine. He and I became close when we were in Tartarus."

"So you're Greek."

"Of course I am." Arc widened his bright green eyes. "What else could I be and still look so stunning?"

I started laughing when the pieces fell into place. The selfies. The vanity. Tartarus. Arc was none other than Narcissus. The god who loved himself so much, he became a flower because he stared at his reflection so long.

"What?" He snatched the stick from my hand. "I didn't say that to be funny."

"Joey, guys," I managed to contain my laughter long enough to speak in clear sentences. "Meet Narcissus."

"Wait, the Narcissus?" Joey looked between me and our new acquaintance. "I thought he was turned into a flower."

"Things change. Sadly." The strange man sighed. "Alas, Zeus saw better use for me in this new, improved world. I help him with his fashion sense. He lets me remain free to roam the top soil. Or rather, grace it with my presence.

"He is going to get real annoying. Real fast."

Jonah whispered in my ear. I clamped my hand over my mouth as I tried to hide my giggling behind a cough. I will admit, Narcissus was quite the sight. He was chiseled. Lean. Every strand of his thick blonde hair seemed to behave. Even his beard had been trimmed to perfection.

I knew from the stories Cyrus had forced me to read that he knew how good he looked. And that vanity had been his curse. But there was more to him than a pretty face. Narcissus had been a hunter once. He would be very familiar with the woods. I wondered if I could get him to come along with us, but decided against it. This little mission was going to be dangerous enough as is.

"Ok. So let's have it. Hoia-Baciu." I looped my arm through his to pull him to the closest sofa. "Where do we need to go?"

The demi-god was too busy staring at himself in the reflection of the wooden table to answer me. I ended up nudging him with my elbow before he reached into his pocket to pull out a sheet of paper.

"Here. I drew it out for you."

"Um, thanks?"

I took the flimsy piece of paper and unfolded it. It was the crude drawing of a circle. But around that circle were little lines that I recognized. Directions written in ancient Greek. I smoothed out the paper and held up my phone to snap a picture of it. When I was done, I tucked my phone into my jacket pocket.

"Any tips you can give us? I know about your past, Narcissus, as a hunter."

"Don't call me that. It's too 3rd century." He finally tore his eyes off of his reflection to look at me. "I go by Arc now."

"Fine. Arc. What do we need to watch out for?"

"The forgotten ones." The man shuddered. "Wretched, forgotten beasts who will not hesitate to rip you to shreds."

"Any idea how the barrier was weakened in the first place?" Joey perched himself on the other side of me. "I mean, sure, Eva can do her thing to strengthen it. But how can we prevent this from happening again?"

"No idea." Narcissus shrugged. "I'm no historian nor am I a Titan. I am just here for the money."

"Of course, you are." I stood up and stretched. "Alright, Arc. Let's head out. You can tell Joey here where we need to park the car."

"Already? The sun has just risen…" His voice trailed off before he broke into a smile that brightened the entire room. "The light is best in the golden hour. Let's go. I need some new outdoor shots anyway."

As Narcissus led us outside, I shook my head. The Olympians never ceased to amaze me. So when he climbed into the car, I joined him with a single question in mind.

"Have you considered a career in Hollywood, Arc? I think you would fit in nicely."

"Nah." He waved his hand in the air to dismiss my question. "Too much work. Too little time for my beauty routine. I could never devote myself to the silver screen."

"What is your line of work, exactly?" Reena, this time. "Aside from your beauty routine, that is."

We shared an amused look. Narcissus didn't catch it.

"Photographer." Narcissus twisted around to see me. "I model on the side, though. Good pay. Beautiful clothes. What's not to like?"

"Everything." I shuddered. "Sorry, Arc. I'm not a fan of modeling. Too much responsibility for clothes I don't even like."

"I don't have that problem." He shrugged. "I just do what I'm told. Admire the results. If something happens, it happens."

We fell silent when Joey started up the car. He drove through the narrow streets until the town fell away. Though I don't know how Joey could see anything. The farther away we got from civilization, the thicker the fog became until we were crawling down the road. Which gave Arc plenty of time to talk about his favorite subject.

Himself. I learned that he had become a vegan during the 19$^{th}$ century. That he spent the majority of his time taking Pilates and photographs of himself. Our new tour guide boasted to have collected over two thousand selfies in the past two years alone.

By the time he told Joey to pull over, we were all ready

to throw Narcissus out of the car just to get some peace and quiet. Me, in particular. I wanted to think. I wanted to go over our game plan. I wanted to enjoy the warmth of Jonah's body as he was crammed next to me in the backseat. Instead, I had been forced to listen to a god whose biggest fear was that MAC would stop making his favorite contouring kit.

"Thank God." Joey muttered when he joined me at the trunk. "I was tempted to run us off the road just to give Arc something else to talk about."

I awarded him with a small smile before I shook my head. "It wouldn't have worked, Joey. The sky could have fallen in around his ears and he'd still talk about how good he looks in coral and beige."

"Yeah, yeah." Joey lifted the lid. "What'd ya say, Evie? Ready to do this thing?"

"As ready as I will ever be." I turned to our friends who looked just as relieved as we were to be out of that car. "Guys, we're going to do the set up. Come on over to get your mics on."

Joey and I went through the same routine we did at every location. A brief talk about what we were going to shoot first. Made sure I knew what I was going to say for the introduction. Equipped our mics. This time, Joey had new toys to play with. He grinned like a kid at Christmas as he attached the body cameras on to himself, Jonah, Reena, and Terrence. Finally, he put mine in place. My friend snapped the last wire in place just below my left shoulder before he told me how to use the damn thing.

"It will stay on the entire time." He took a step back to admire his work. "So we'll capture footage from your angle, Evie. But if we get separated, I want you to press this button here."

"What button?" I tried to look down. "All I see are wires."

"Here." Joey lifted up a tiny black box he had hooked onto my side. "Press this and your location will show up on my phone. And stay put. I might not be able to keep up with you if you take off."

"Fine." I glanced over to where Arc was waiting. "Anything else?"

"Your bag, madam." He grinned. "Turn around. I'll help you put it on."

"I hate this thing. So much."

Joey chuckled as I did what I was told. Soon enough, he had me strapped into the bag that held everything I would need to survive for the next week. As we joined the others, I tried to think of something smart to say. Something sarcastic about investigating a beach next. But my words died in my throat as I noticed our surroundings.

Despite the dense fog, I could still make out thick black trees. Memories of what I had been through in Montana played at the forefront of my mind, but I shoved them back. Now was not the time to remember. This was different. And there was so much more at stake than a simple haunting.

Granted, I couldn't classify Montana as a simple haunting either. The monsters there turned out to be the work of Hera. It was my first true interaction with her. But it didn't matter. Not now. I wasn't at some ritzy horse farm. I was in Romania. At Tartarus.

I had a job to do. Be the hero. Be everything everyone expected me to be.

It was time to get to work.

It wasn't until we were halfway across the field that led up to Hoia-Baciu that I noticed the mob waiting for us. Men and women - some with cameras, some with microphones -

started cheering when they saw us. I closed my eyes, took a breath, and let my face fall into the mask I wore around the press. It was easier to hide my fear that way.

"Who invited them to the party?" Terrence frowned as he came up beside me. "I thought you asked them yesterday to leave us alone."

"In the woods, yes." I nodded. "I didn't say anything about them greeting us at the proverbial door, though."

"Well, I can't say that I blame them. I am pretty spectacular." Joey grinned. "I am just surprised, that's all. I'd expect this in the U.S. Not here."

"Bună dimineaţa!" Arc pushed past Terrence to grab my arm. He waved to the press with a laugh as he pulled me towards them. He fired off another round of a language I couldn't speak before he finally decided not to be rude. My newest companion switched to English. "Oh, good. They speak your language, Sibyl."

"Great." I gave him a tight smile. "Not surprising though. I thought everyone spoke English here."

Arc scoffed as he introduced himself to the press as my guide. I didn't bother to hide the disbelief on my face as he talked about his fear for us as we went into Hoia-Baciu. But this group had no interest in the great Narcissus. A woman pushed her microphone at me as she asked me about my time in Romania so far.

I did the best I could. I tried to be patient. Answer all of their questions. But time was running out. When Joey cleared his throat, I found my way out.

"It's time for us to film the introduction to the episode." I took a step away from them. "Joey, let's include our new friends this time."

"Whatever you say, Evie." He narrowed his eyes at me and lifted his camera off the ground. He put it on his shoulder as I turned back to the group.

"Just stay still. Cheer or shout when necessary, ok? Jonah, Re, Terrence? I want you guys flanking me."

"Sounds good to us, Superstar."

I gave Jonah a grateful smile as he moved up beside me. I squeezed his arm then chided myself. I found it all too easy to be touchy-feely with him. I needed to control myself with that.

Once everyone was in place, I nodded to Joey. He dropped his hand to tell me we were rolling, so I grinned hard enough to make my cheeks hurt.

"Welcome back to *Grave Messages*! Today we're greeting you from a field outside of Cluj-Napoca, Romania. For those of you familiar with the paranormal world, you know exactly where I am. But for those of you who aren't? Well. See those trees behind me? That's the infamous Hoia-Baciu Forest. The most haunted forest in the world."

I opened my arms to gesture to the press behind me. "And check out the welcoming wagon! Romania sure knows how to make a girl feel welcome around these parts."

The crowd behind me cheered and I caught sight of Arc rolling his eyes. Not that his opinion mattered. So I smiled brighter. Wider. And kept talking.

"It's true that we are here to document the paranormal in these woods. But our purpose in Romania is much darker. Much more deadly. You see, buried beneath these lands is none other than Tartarus itself. Never heard of it? Good. That'll keep you away from here. Let's just say it's a very bad place for very bad souls. Thanks to the Olympian Council – yeah, those same gods you learned about in middle school – we've been assigned to keep those bad souls from escaping. Now, Joey and I are here with the Eleventh Percenters from Rome, North Carolina. Jonah, Reena, and Terrence. Say hello to the viewers at home, guys."

I didn't bother to hide my pride when each of them gave

small introductions about themselves. When Joey turned his camera back to me, I was still beaming.

"Anyway, we've got a grocery list of activities planned for the week ahead. Document the paranormal on these lands as Alexandru Sift attempted to do back in the 1950s. Shut down a weakening barrier. Find a way for me to survive the week without Wi-Fi. Good times. So let's get started, shall we?"

I winked at the camera and saw the little red light shut off. I turned back to the press behind me to thank them for their participation, but as I waved goodbye to them, I noticed Arc was glaring at me.

"Why didn't you have me up there with you?" Arc bounded over with a scowl on his perfect features. "I should have been on camera!"

"I left it open." I shrugged. "You should have joined the crowd. Besides, didn't anyone tell you that your face can get stuck that way? Don't do that."

A look of pure horror flashed in his eyes before he realized I was teasing him. But instead of taking the joke as I had intended, he huffed.

"I'm leaving. You got your map. I brought you to the forest of the forgotten. I've fulfilled my part of the bargain."

"That you did." I stuck out my hand. "Thanks, Arc."

I wasn't surprised when he ignored my gesture. I watched him turn on his heel to stomp after the press before I whispered.

"Good riddance."

"You can say that again." Jonah snorted. "I could never understand Apollo's love for him in the stories."

"Perhaps he loves him as we all love beautiful things." I shrugged. "Too bad the beauty is only skin deep though. He could have been quite helpful to us."

"Yeah. Like the kid's drawing he gave you as a map?"

Reena fell in step with us as we crossed through the trees. "Or how he abandoned us before we actually entered the forest?"

"Well, we're here now. No use complaining about it."

I fell silent as we continued through the thick trees. I couldn't shake the feeling that we were being watched. Maybe it was a rogue reporter who decided not to listen. Maybe the biologist Sift had been right when he said he felt eyes on him at all times. Either way, I hoped that whatever was watching us was as miserable as I was. Despite the early morning sun, the fog around us had yet to lift. It was dark. Dank. Cold and lonely.

"Ok." Joey held out his arm to stop me. "Let me see that map, Evie. We need to see where we are and which direction we need to be heading in."

"How'd you learn so much about the woods, Joey?" I handed him the map while he pulled out his phone. "I mean; I know you used to shoot guns with your dad growing up. But this whole Grizzly Adams part of you is new to me."

"I grew up in Wyoming, Evie." He gave me a grin. "I learned real quick how important it is to know where you are when you're in the woods."

"That was before GPS, right?" I gave him a look of mock seriousness when he stuck his tongue out at me. "What?"

"You're only a few years younger than me, missy." Joey shifted until I could see his phone. He'd pulled up an aerial shot of Hoia-Baciu. "Ok. We're here."

My friend pointed at the very bottom of his screen. I watched his finger trail over the trees before he stabbed it down in the center of a barren circle. "This is where we need to be. Should be a two-day hike if we don't run into any trouble."

"And if we do?"

"Then we deal with it." He tucked his phone into his pocket before snapping the camera he'd used to film the intro to his bag. "We'll use the body cameras for now. Anything big and I'll pull Betsy back out."

"Betsy?" I snorted. "You named your camera 'Betsy'?"

"Yep." He nodded. "Good, solid name for an old standby. She's never let me down."

Joey was interrupted by the short, sharp scream. The six of us froze into place as it faded away.

"What the hell was that?" Joey whipped around to look at me. "It sounded like a girl."

Another scream resounded through the trees as Prometheus' memories began to surface. I held onto the straps of my bag as I looked upward. We hadn't gone a mile into the forest yet, but the horror of this place was already making an appearance.

"That wasn't a girl, Joey. It was the forest. The very trees themselves are screaming."

"Ok." He drew out the word. "Next time the gods need you, I vote for somewhere less creepy-forest and more sunshine-resort."

"I second that motion." I moved around him to keep walking. "But it is what it is. Let's keep going. The sooner we reach the clearing, the better."

We all fell silent as we continued onward. The deeper we went into the forest, the more it seemed to change. The trees began to curl around each other. The vegetation grew thicker. The air was heavier. By the time we reached a small creek, I was so anxious, I was shaking. Joey, despite his history of playing in the woods, seemed to be having a hard time breathing. The rest of our party seemed to be just fine. I thought about Reena's suggestion for cardio when we had lunch in L.A. I kinda wished I had taken her up on the offer now.

"I call for a break." I glanced down at my watch. "It's after ten, which means we've been on this little nature trail for a good three and a half hours."

Joey unsnapped his bag and dropped it before he bent over. He grabbed his knees before he began to gasp for air.

"Joey?" I frowned. "Are you alright?"

He shook his head. "Can't...breathe. Burning."

"Burning?" I dropped my own bag before I went over to him. "Where?"

My friend released the grip he had on his knees to tug at the collar of his shirt. I smacked his hand away, lowered him down to the ground, and pulled the cloth away from his skin.

"Oh, my god." I glanced up to Jonah. "He's burned."

"Burned? By what?"

He bent over me to see the wound. Joey's pale skin was the darkest shade of red I'd ever seen. He was so badly burned that blisters had started forming up the back of his neck. I shook my head in response to the question I didn't have an answer to.

"Grab my canteen, will you? Joey, take your shirt off."

"Evie, I never thought I'd say this to you, but there is no way in hell...."

"Just do it." I resisted the urge to smack him across the back of his head. "I'm going to grab the first aid kit."

Joey grumbled as he began to do what I asked. By the time I'd dug through my supplies to find the small white box, he seemed to be breathing better. The color was back in his face. Reena had set to work, pouring water over the burn. When she saw me stand, she moved to let me take over.

"That's no ordinary sunburn." She glanced between us. "It looks like radiation."

"It may be." I agreed as I applied burn spray to Joey's

neck. “There were reports online about people coming out of here with strange markings. Burns. Believers chalk it up to UFOs. But if Tartarus is here…”

“Then it could be residual from the fires of hell below us.” Jonah finished for me. “In the stories I used to read, any human would have been affected by them.”

“Then why aren't we affected?” I tossed the can back in the bag and grabbed a white square bandage. “We're human, too.”

“No, we're enhanced.” Jonah looked puzzled. “Our ethereality is enough to protect us. Maybe your Sibyl abilities are enough to protect you."

"Maybe."

“Guys, really,” Joey hissed when I taped the bandage in place. "I’m fine now. I feel fine.”

“Good.” I handed him his shirt. “In that case, I’m going to refill my water bottle. We’ve still got a whole afternoon of hiking to get through. I’m not going to make it without it.”

I snagged my bottle from Reena's hand. "Can ya'll stay here with Joey? I don't know if he'll be able to shoot his bow with those burns."

"You really shouldn't go alone, Superstar." Jonah frowned down at me. "I'll go with you."

"Jonah, if some big baddie comes out of the woods, I don't want to leave anything to chance." I gave him a soft smile. "Reena and Terrence - as bad ass as they are - would be torn between a fight and watching Joey. If there are three of you here, then two could fight and one could guard."

"You've already thought this out."

"I tried," I admitted. "Besides, the creek is just beyond those trees. If anything comes for me, I'll make such a fuss, you'll know it."

I resisted the urge to grab his hand before I turned

towards the creek. I wasn't stupid. I knew I shouldn't go too far. No matter how fancy Joey swore our new technology was, I wasn't convinced that they'd be able to meet up with me in this mess of trees. So I pushed through the brush that lined the edge of the water and bent down. I said a quick thanks to Apollo that I lived in the age of portable water filters when I dunked the bottle in the creek.

I was just about to pull my hand out of the water when I heard a snarl to my left. I froze at the familiar sound. After all, I'd heard it every time Elliot had transformed himself into a wolf. A huff of breath followed the snarl and I rose to my feet to face the animal.

I was wrong. It wasn't a single wolf. There were seven of them. Each staring at me with cold yellow eyes. My first thought wasn't of Elliot. It wasn't about my weapon. It was about the injured man who was stupid enough to put himself in my care. I stole a glance back towards the brush where my party was waiting. Then, I did the only thing I could think to do.

I ran

# TWENTY-SIX

## EVA MCRAYNE

AT FIRST, I could hear their paws pounding against the forest floor. I heard the leaves being crushed beneath our weight. I could feel the branches as they scratched at my face. But soon enough, the beating of my heart began to fill my ears. My body went numb from fear. All I could do was push forward. Further the distance between the animals and my friends.

"Evie? Evie, where the hell are you?"

Jonah's voice filtered through my tiny earpiece. I took a second to look behind me to see the wolves less than three feet away from me. I didn't respond. There wasn't time. I ran straight for a fallen tree and prayed it was low enough for me to vault over.

It was. I landed in a crouch on the other side before I pushed off once more. I heard one of the animals' whelp behind me. Then another. But I didn't stop to see what had happened to them. The trees had become a blur. The world sped past me as I moved as fast as I could though this cursed place. I only slowed down when the foliage became too thick for me to run through. I worked my way through them, shoving my way through two trees before the ground disappeared beneath my feet.

I released a short scream as I tumbled down the hill. I threw my arm up over my face and let my body go limp as I rolled. When I finally came to a stop, I looked up to see a wolf had leapt into the ravine after me. I shoved myself up, ignoring the sharp pain that ricocheted through my ribcage. I had two seconds to move. Two seconds to shove myself out of the way.

I forced my body to the side to watch the animal as he jerked in mid-air. He landed in a heap right beside me. I forced my head up to see Joey and Jonah standing at the top of the hole I'd fallen into. Reena and Terrence joined soon after. My dearest, darling cameraman was lowering the bow to his side. Joey must have noticed that I was staring at him in shock because he tilted his chin towards me with the smuggest look possible before he called down to me.

"Who got you, Baby Girl?"

Despite my attempts to catch my breath and the pain in my side, I started laughing. I fell back in the leaves as they scrambled down the hill to meet me. When they reached me, Joey extended his hand towards me with a grin.

"And you said I wouldn't need my bow."

I took his hand with a chuckle. "That was awesome, Joey. Too bad we didn't get that on camera."

"Ah, but we did." He tapped at the wire still attached to my chest. "From your angle and mine."

"Eva, what the hell happened?" Jonah slid to a stop beside me. "Why didn't you call out for help?"

Because I didn't want to put you in any more danger? Because I couldn't stand the thought of you getting hurt? Because I would gladly give my own life for yours?

I didn't say any of this outloud. Instead, I dusted off my arms to keep from meeting his eyes.

"I didn't want to yell because I didn't want to startle them any further. I ran in the hopes of finding a larger clearing to fight them in."

Jonah sighed before he wrapped his arm around my waist to help me out of the ravine. When we reached the top, Joey wrapped me up in a bear hug.

"Eva McRayne, don't you ever run off like that! You scared the shit out of me when we couldn't find you."

"Joey," I gasped against the sharp pain that raced through me. "Please...stop. You're killing me."

"What?" He released me. "Are you alright?"

"Yeah." I took a deep breath, which turned out to be a very bad idea. "Just...ow."

"What's wrong?" Reena frowned at me. "Did you hit a stick or something?"

"I'm fine. I'll be fine."

"Evie..." Joey tried this time but his words faded when he caught sight of me. "Alright. Look. Let's go get our stuff. We'll take it slow for the rest of the day. Give you time to heal."

"Thank you." I turned towards the hill. "So who knows the way back to camp?"

"I do." Joey pulled out his phone with his free hand. "Tracking app. I didn't realize it would be this handy to have."

"Lead the way, Grizzly." I waved him in front of me. "My bed in L.A. is calling out to me. The sooner this is done the sooner I can get back to it."

———

By the time we got back to our gear, I was sweating from the exertion of trying to breathe. My side was on fire. My lungs hurt. And worst of all?

Jonah and Reena kept giving me looks of concern before they would glance at each other. For the most part, I ignored them until Jonah tried to strap my bag back around my chest. I couldn't hold back my whimper as he pressed the plastic clasp together.

"Ok. That's it." He undid the clasp and tugged the bag free from my back. "Off with the coat, Superstar."

"Jonah-"

"Don't you 'Jonah' me." He crossed his arms over his chest. "You may heal, but we need to assume that you won't."

"I will. I promise."

"Off." He narrowed his hazel eyes at me. "And start talking. What hurts?"

"My side." I winced as I unbuttoned my coat. "I feel like I have needles pricking my skin."

"Another burn?" Reena, this time. She took my coat when I handed it to her. "Or maybe you sprained something when you fell down the ravine."

"Guys, can you give us a minute?" Jonah looked at the group. "This won't take long."

I watched as the others moved away from us. I wondered why Jonah had taken this task upon himself. After all, Reena had been the one to tend to my wounds back at the estate. But I didn't want to question him. He was helping me after all.

"It hurts along your side?"

I didn't answer as Jonah lifted up my t-shirt. I heard him whistle before he pressed his fingers over the spot that hurt so bad. I bit my lip to keep from sobbing as the throbbing returned. He seemed to be focused on prodding my ribs, but I couldn't help but notice how his fingers seemed to linger over the white phoenix tattoo on my side. My mark of the gods. Finally, he lifted up.

"You've cracked a couple of ribs, Evie. You're going to have to take it easy until your Sibyl powers kick in."

"Jonah, I can't."

I started to tug my shirt back down, but he stopped me. He shook his head and gestured to Reena to bring him the first aid kit I'd abandoned earlier. She passed it over before they exchanged another silent conversation before she rejoined the others.

"As I was saying before you interrupted me," Jonah took the kit and pulled out a roll of bandages. "Since I know there is no way you would agree to my sensible suggestion I'm going to wrap you up. Can you lift your arms?"

It was a struggle, but I did it. Jonah pulled my shirt over my head then made quick work out of wrapping me up tight in those thick bandages. I felt my face flush each time his fingers grazed my bare skin. When he pressed a silver clasp into place, he stepped back to admire his work.

"How does that feel?"

"Better."

I admitted as I reached for my shirt. He passed it over to me and I slid it back on before I grabbed my coat next. I really was grateful, but I was embarrassed because he had to help me. And because my heart was pounding a mile a minute from a few strokes on my skin.

I had to get a hold of myself. I gave Jonah a small smile as he batted my hands away to button up my coat.

"Thank you, Blueberry." I managed. "You really are the best, you know?"

He cut those hazel eyes up at me and I couldn't breath. Maybe the bandages were too tight, after all.

"Don't mention it." He helped me put my bag back on then loosened the straps to fit around my bandages. "If it gets to be too much, you let me know. Promise?"

"I promise."

Jonah clasped me on the shoulder before we rejoined the others. He passed Reena back the first aid kit and she attached it to her backpack.

"What's next?"

"Let's get across the creek. We won't go as far today as we had planned. Especially since I've never put up a tent before. I'm going to need some time to figure out how to do that."

"You've never put up a tent before?"

"No. I don't go outside unless absolutely necessary. Much less sleep outside."

"Well, I grew up on a cattle ranch." Joey checked his camera before we all started walking. "I practically lived in the woods during the summer. And if it wasn't too cold, I stayed there in the winter too."

"So why be a cameraman? Why not stay on the ranch?" Reena wrinkled her nose as she stepped into the creek. "I don't understand."

"Because I was bored." Joey raised his voice over the sound of the water as we waded through it. "Life doesn't change in Wyoming, Re. Same horses. Same snow. Same woods day after day. I wanted to travel and I was damn good at shooting things. I just replaced my gun with a camera."

"You got your wish then." Terrence shook out the water from his boots when we reached the other side. "But why *Grave*?"

"Because filming couples fighting with each other on reality television gave me the same feeling that Wyoming did." Joey shrugged when he fell in step with me. "I was bored out of my mind. It was always the same. They argued over money. Sex. Stupid shit that didn't mean anything."

"Did you just cuss?" I grinned. "I didn't think anybody cussed in Wyoming."

"Blame California." He matched my smile. "So yeah. When Connor approached me to do Elliot's project, I jumped at the chance. Did I think it would take off? No. I thought we'd last for a few episodes then fade away when Joseph's influence wore off."

"So what changed your mind?" Jonah came up on the other side of me. "About the show?"

"Evie." He shrugged when I grinned at him. "It's true. I'd never met anyone as fierce as you, Eva. As determined. When you say something is going to happen, it does. When we filmed the first episode in Kansas and I saw how you reacted to the ghost there, I knew I'd struck gold."

"The show has turned out to be pretty spectacular." I admitted. "I didn't want to do it at first. But Elliot talked me into it."

"The money?"

I nodded. "Yeah. It's crazy, though. Despite everything we've been through and everything I've learned, I feel like I'm right where I need to be."

"Because you like kicking butt so much." Joey chuckled when I stuck my tongue out at him. "Seriously? I think Connor should have given you the producer spot from the get-go. This is going to be the start of a whole new *Grave Messages*. We'll make it better. Darker."

"More dangerous?" I chuckled before I went back to being serious. "I don't think we can make it any more dangerous than it already is."

We fell into a comfortable silence after that. For my part, I was trying to see the beauty of the woods. I was trying to find one redeeming quality about this horrible place. Its horrible history. But I couldn't. It was too dark. Too wild. And I wasn't kidding about it being dangerous. I can't tell you how many times I almost twisted an ankle as I stepped over the roots that attempted to trip us up. In fact, I was in the process of avoiding one when Terrence broke the silence around us.

"Um, Evie. We've got company."

I jerked my head up to see a young girl standing on the path in front of us. She was filthy. Dressed in white rags covered with a mixture of blood and dirt. I stopped when I got close enough to see that she was Asian. The lower half of her face was covered with a surgical mask.

"Glad to see I'm not the only one who looks completely out of place here." I quipped. "Who are you?"

The girl stared at us for a good minute before she tilted her head to the side. When she finally spoke, I was surprised. I could understand her, although she didn't speak in English. It was Japanese.

"Do you think I'm pretty?"

"What?" I glanced over at Reena, whose mouth was in a hard line. "I don't understand…"

"Do you think I'm pretty?" The girl's eyes flashed as she took a step forward. A long thin blade appeared in her hand before she stopped. "Do you?"

"Um, at the risk of being run through, yes?"

Joey piped up. I whipped my head around to stare at him, but my mind was racing. I was attempting to use Prometheus' knowledge to recognize the threat in front of us. At long last, I found the information I was looking for.

"Joey," I hissed. "Whatever you do, do not answer her questions."

"Why?" He looked down at me before he turned back to our new addition. "Oh, god!"

The girl had removed her surgical mask to reveal a

ghastly wound where her mouth should have been. I swallowed down my nausea at the sight when she spoke again. "Do you still think I am pretty?"

"What about me?" I unhooked my backpack and dropped it on the path. "Do you think I'm pretty?"

I kept my eyes on her as Jonah did the same. He pulled out his weapons as Reena and Terrence followed suit. Fabulous.

The girl looked confused for a minute. She bounced her knife against her leg then asked her stupid question again. This time, Joey started to speak, but I cut him off as I willed my sword in my hand.

"She's called Kuchiake-onna. A spirit from Japanese folklore." I explained. "You can't answer her questions, Joey. If you say 'yes' twice, then she will give you the same deformity that she has. If you say 'no', then she'll slice you in half. But she is powerless if you answer her questions with another question."

My friend clamped his mouth shut. So I turned towards the spirit who blocked our path.

"What happened to you?"

"Do you still think I'm pretty?" She hissed. I watched as her eyes gleamed white. "Answer me."

"Do you know who I am?" I smirked. "Do you not know that I don't answer anything I don't want to?"

The girl screamed in frustration at my questions. She launched herself forward to slam her shoulder against my chest. I grunted as the throbbing in my ribs returned, but I ignored the pain. I brought the hilt of my sword down onto the top of her matted hair and shoved her off of me.

Jonah struck out to crack his baton against the top of her head. The spirit released an unholy scream as she turned her attention away from me to Jonah. He struck out again as Reena swept her feet out from under her. Terrence grabbed her as I scrambled to my feet. Despite my injury, I didn't give her the chance to attack me for a second time. I whirled the blade in a circle by my side before I brought it down across the back of her neck. The girl released one last scream before she disappeared into a mist of white.

"You guys are the best." I looked at the Elevenths. "Seriously. That was awesome."

After a moment, Joey returned to my side. He clasped me on the shoulder before he took a deep breath.

"Ok. So I'm sure there's an explanation for that."

"The forest of the forgotten." I let my sword disappear before I took up my gear. "Remember what Zeus said? Monsters and spirits from all over the world were brought in to keep humans from wandering in these woods."

"How did you know what she was?" Reena caught up with me as I resumed our hike. "No offense, Evie, but I didn't take you to be an expert in Japanese mythology."

"History. Japanese history." I corrected her, but my smile faltered when I realized I'd just said the most Cyrus-like phrase possible. I'd put him and his little escapade at Aiko's out of my mind. I needed to do that again. I shook my head to chase the thoughts away. "And I'm not. But Prometheus is an expert on Hoia-Baciu. He knows every monster, every being, every path here. So by extension, so do I."

"So why do we need Arc's ridiculous napkin map?"

"Because I don't want to pull into Prometheus' memories any more than I have to." I shuddered. "They are too much, Re. Even for me."

I tilted my head to look up at Joey. "I have a question for you, though. How did you know what she was saying? I didn't realize you could speak Japanese."

"There's a lot about me that you don't know. Yet." He

gave me a lecherous grin until I punched his arm. "Ow! I'm kidding. I'm kidding. Anime."

"What?"

"I used to watch anime when I was a kid." He chuckled. "I picked up a few words over the years."

"Why am I not surprised?" I rolled my eyes at him. "Half-naked girls being saved from the big-bad ogres. It's right up your alley."

"Hey, that's not fair." Joey grabbed the straps of his backpack. "I watched it for the stories. Some of them were damn good, Evie. I can recommend some good ones if you want to see what I am talking about."

"Yeah, we'll see." I looped my arm through his. "We might even make a night out of it if you promise to show me the ones where the girls kick ass."

"Now who's cussin'?" He grinned down at me. "Deal. But you're buying me dinner. It's the least you can do for my expertise."

"I always buy you dinner." I rolled my eyes before I looked around. "Is it just me, or is it darker than before?"

"It's getting darker." Jonah glanced at his watch. "My watch says it's just after four. Let's find a good spot to put everything down for the night."

"Sounds like a plan to me." I shrugged. "My side is still sore. And I'm surprised Joey hasn't eaten half the forest by now."

"Can I do that?" Joey's face brightened. "I thought the Romanians would frown on it, but..."

"Just go." I gave him a little shove. "Find us a spot, Grizzly. I'm ready to call it a day."

---

By the time the group had eaten dinner and I'd had my meal shake, I was more than ready to call it a night. I hugged Joey, thanked him for the twentieth time for putting my tent together for me, and crawled inside with a happy sigh. It was true that we didn't get as far as we had hoped on the first day. But we were here. We were in the forest.

We were alive.

I considered that progress. I sat on my sleeping bag for a moment as I recounted the events of the day. Narcissus. The press. Hoia-Bacu. The wolves and the spirit girl. But in the end, I shook my head. There was no point in trying to go back over the things that had happened. There were no lessons to be learned there. Nothing I would have done differently. I worked off my boots and unzipped my bag as my thoughts of the past shifted into my concerns for the next day. Apollo willing, we would reach the clearing. I'd use Prometheus' knowledge to strengthen the barriers. Film another award-winning episode.

I laid down with a sigh as I tried to get some sleep. The guys had left the fire burning in an attempt to keep the local wildlife at bay. But I wasn't afraid of the wildlife. I was more concerned with the monsters meant to keep people like us out of Hoia-Baciu. I willed my sword into existence and placed it on the ground next to me. After all, I'd already used it once on this little journey. Who knew if I was going to need it again by the time the night was over?

I jerked when I felt a hand grip at my shoulder. I sat up and nearly bumped heads with Cyrus. He looked wicked in the shadows.

"Jesus, Cy. You about gave me a heart attack."

"We need to talk, Eva."

"No, we don't." I shook him off. "You've made it very

clear where we stand. Seeing you with that woman just confirmed it."

Cyrus gritted his teeth. I could tell how his jawline tightened.

"I am not supposed to be here. I am taking time away from a very important mission-"

"Then go. Don't be here." I hissed back. "You have your hands full and I'm fine."

"You have forgotten your place, Eva," He growled. "Chasing after Rowe to no avail. Showing your ass against a woman who did you no harm. You insulted my honor-"

"Your honor!" I lowered my voice before anyone else heard me. "You showed everyone how honorable you truly-"

I gasped when Cyrus delivered a sharp punch to my broken ribs. I doubled over and tried not to throw up as he glared down at me.

"You deserve worse for the humiliation you have bestowed upon me," He grabbed my chin and forced me to look up at him. "Your punishment can wait, but do not force me to leave my post again "

Cyrus vanished as I began to cough. I wrapped my arm around my torso and reached around in the darkness for my water.

Gods but damn that hurt. I finally found the bottle and sipped on it. I didn't know what was worse. The pain in my side or the reminder that Cyrus had no problems knocking the shit out of me.

I felt tears spring up in my eyes but I wiped them away. It was nothing. He was caught up in his anger. He had been trying to get my attention, that was all.

I knew I should have stayed right where I was, but I didn't want to be alone. I unzipped the tent and saw that Jonah had a lantern on in his. I took a painful breath and moved across our makeshift campground. I had no right to be bothering him. I knew this.

But if Cyrus had taught me anything, it was that I was a selfish creature. I bent down with some effort and whispered at the zipped door.

"Jonah? Are you awake?"

A few moments later, Jonah unzipped it and gave me a look of surprise.

"Superstar? What's wrong?"

What could I possibly say? That my boyfriend had shown up out of nowhere and punched me in my broken ribs? That I needed to be around him and his light now more than ever?

In the end, I released a shuddered breath.

"My ribs are killing me. Would you mind looking at them for me? If not, it's ok."

"Come on in," Jonah shifted back. "I'll check you out."

I breathed another shaky sigh of relief as I crawled into his tent. Jonah sat back on his knees as he studied me.

"I can't see that much in this light, but I can see how they are coming along."

I nodded as I pulled my shirt over my head. I closed my eyes as Jonah leaned in closer to me.

"Are you sure I'm not bothering you? I won't keep you awake, I swear. I know you're exhausted."

"You're never a bother, Eva," Jonah scoffed."I don't know what you're used to, but you're welcome here."

I nodded as Jonah took my shirt away from me. He gestured for me to lift my arms and he went to work unraveling the bandages. When they were off, he snagged the lantern then brought it closer to my skin.

"The bruising has gotten worse," He frowned as he ran his fingers along the edges. "Like you've had another impact here. Did you hit something on the hike today?"

I shook my head, unable to speak. His fingers felt amazing against my skin.

"You're going to have to take it easy since you aren't healing, Superstar."

"I don't know how that's possible."

"Here, let me wrap you back up."

"There is no need for that." Cyrus' voice filled the tent and I closed my eyes with a small groan. "Eva. A word."

Gods dammit. I thought he was gone.

I met Cyrus' blazing gaze when he pulled back from the opening of the tent and I knew I had to follow.

"What in the hell is he doing here?"

"Cyrus is upset with me." I tugged my shirt all the way down. "I'm sorry I disturbed you."

Jonah rocked back with a sigh as I crawled out of the tent to see Cyrus storming to the tree line. I took a breath and followed him. When we were out of earshot from the camp, he rounded on me.

"I leave you and you run straight to fucking Rowe?"

"You punched me!" I frowned at him. "I went to have Jonah look over my ribs since you got me right where they were broken!"

"Just to check your injuries?" Cyrus laughed, but the sound wasn't a nice one. "I'll bet."

"Are you jealous?" I narrowed my eyes at him. "Why? You said it yourself that nobody wanted me. That you are burdened with my existence. So if Jonah doesn't want me, then why are you all fire and brimstone right now?"

Cyrus looked at me, stunned. "I'm not jealous. I'm not intimidated by Rowe at all. I'm more concerned with you making a gods damn fool of yourself with the protege of a Protector Guide that I respect wholeheartedly."

Ok. So that one stung. I must have winced because Cyrus nodded before he closed the distance between us.

"You are my burden. My shackles. I won't have you ruining the network and the relationships I have built because you've decided to act like a damn lovesick schoolgirl." Cyrus examined me. "Have you no shame? Are you truly as a big a whore as your mother?"

If the first comment stung, that one sliced right through me. I wanted to be the exact opposite of my mother in every aspect of the word. I wrapped my arms around myself and studied the dirt beneath my feet.

"But you aren't a whore, are you?" Cyrus clicked his tongue against the top of his mouth. "Because there is no one willing to take you in their bed. One look at you and they are repulsed. It's only after the photoshop and the make-up that you are even slightly attractive."

"Cyrus, stop-"

"No. You are not listening to me. You are not listening to reason. So I am forced to be harsh with you. I am forced to show you the reality of your situation. Once you get these crazy ideas out of your head, then you can move forward."

"What crazy ideas?"

"Love. You, Little One," He sneered at me. "Your mother didn't love you. Elliott, Joey - none of them loved you. I don't either. But I will put on the mask I am forced to wear to save you public embarrassment."

I was numb by the time he finished. I should have lashed out with the woman I had found him with. But what did it matter? Cyrus was doing me a favor. He was making it seem as if I were lovable. As if I were happy. I should have been thanking him instead of running my mouth like I was.

I cleared my throat as I willed the burning in my heart to subside. His words had burned like acid and ate at me.

"You are not to go in Jonah's tent again. I won't allow it."

I said nothing. What could I say to that? Cyrus knew the reason for my silence and he nodded.

"You understand, Eva?"

"Yeah," I cleared my throat as I looked up. "Yeah. I understand."

"Dude!" An unexpected voice came from nowhere. Terrence. "How can you say those things to Eva? Did Apollo not just rip into you for doing that exact same shit?"

Cyrus actually looked surprised to have been overheard. "This doesn't concern you, Terrence-"

"It concerns me when I see a guy tearing a woman down like she's his damn daughter!" Terrence was standing next to a tree. I looked away from him as he stormed over to us. "How would you feel if that were turned back on you?"

"You can say whatever you like, Terrence." Cyrus wasn't upset. If anything, he appeared amused. "In fact, I am glad that you are here. Tell me. Would you sleep with Eva if given the chance?"

"No, dude-"

"You have just proved my point. Thank you, Terrence." Cyrus turned back to me. I heard him clear his throat so I looked up at him. "As I was saying, do not let me catch you in Rowe's tent again. And by the gods, keep your shirt on."

He vanished into the shadows and I stared at the spot until I was sure he was gone. Terrence broke the heavy silence.

"Eva, I'm so-"

"It's fine." I released a breath and gave Terrence a shaky smile. It was the best I could manage at that moment. "You're fine. I promise."

I didn't know how much he heard, and I didn't want to know. I felt humiliated and weak. Most of all? Cyrus' words hurt. And even though I wasn't attracted to Terrence in the least, his response had only proved Cyrus' point.

"I'm ok." I tightened my arms around myself. "I promise. But...I'd like to be alone. For a little while."

"Are you sure?"

"Yeah. The camp is just beyond the trees. I'll be back in an hour."

"If you're sure-"

"I am. Thank you, Terrence, for your assistance. I mean that."

He nodded then headed back to the camp. I waited for five, then ten minutes before I sat down on the ground, buried my face into my hands, and willed my heart to stop breaking.

# TWENTY-SEVEN

## JONAH ROWE

JONAH WONDERED when Eva would return. She had come to him for help. She must have been in a lot of pain to actually ask for assistance. He was going to do just that before Cyrus had damn near broken into his tent.

What the hell was Cyrus doing here? Jonah was sure they wouldn't see that asshole again until after this mess was over. Wasn't he on some assignment? One that didn't involve the woman he supposedly loved?

Jonah started when he heard Terrence yell out. He left the tent just in time to see Terrence storm back into the camp utterly furious.

"What the hell happened out here?" He demanded.

Terrence told him. Jonah felt the purest rage imaginable within seconds. Small dick energy was one thing. But dismantling like that was another.

"He had the audacity to twist your words to prove his point?" Jonah growled. "I'm going after her."

"Dude, she said she wanted to be alone."

"I'm not letting a woman who's had suicidal thoughts be alone, Terrence."

"But she's immortal," Terrence said.

"And in the not-even month we've known her, how valuable has that been?" Jonah shot back. "I'm going."

"Jonah, wait. Wait just a minute." Terrence caught him by the shoulders. "I need you to think. Just for a minute."

"About what?"

"About Eva. J., she's been humiliated. Not just with Cyrus twisting my words around, but the fact that I witnessed him tear her down like that."

"Terrence, she doesn't need to be alone."

"Give her time, J. If you go in with guns blazing, she is going to be even more humiliated because she'll know that I told you."

"But-"

"But now, we know that whatever Apollo did to Cyrus, it wasn't enough. If Eva isn't back in an hour, then go. You can say you were concerned because she was gone for so long. Deal?"

Jonah thought about it, and sighed. "Deal. He'd better be glad Reena didn't hear that."

"She wouldn't have," Terrence muttered. "She brought those damn noise-cancelling headphones."

"They drown out yelling?"

"Jonah, those goddamn things would drown out an aerial bombing."

Jonah went back to his tent and shut off his phone. He sat in the low lamplight with his eyes locked on his watch. Eva had one hour to get back to camp. As he waited, he thought about their previous interactions. How Eva was all fire until she came out in her sports bra that day. In that instant, he saw something he didn't think was possible. Something that was confirmed when she told him how she saw herself.

Eva's strength and her ability to fight was a front for a

very broken, very damaged woman. After what Terrence had shared with him, he had a better understanding as to why. And what had she said? That it was easier to believe the bad so that it didn't hurt so bad when she heard it?

Damn. Just damn.

Exactly one hour later, Jonah caught sight of movement in the campfire. He climbed out just as Eva sat down next to the fire. It sparked as she stared into it.

"Hey," Jonah lowered onto the patch of grass beside her. "How are you feeling?"

"I'm fine. I thought you all would be asleep by now."

Jonah locked eyes with Terrence as he joined them and decided not to force the issue. He simply glanced back at Eva. "Weed?"

"Sure."

Jonah sat down next to her and passed her a water. He pulled out his case then snagged a joint from it. He lit it, took a puff, then passed it over to Eva.

"Thanks." She took it and inhaled. When she released the smoke, she sighed. "That hit the spot, Blueberry. Thank you."

"You're very welcome," Jonah said, measuring his tone. "We've got your back. Whether it's with a weapon or weed."

"Except for Reena," Terrence joked. "She's passed out. She'll have your back tomorrow."

Eva passed the weed over to Terrence while giving him side eye. "You told Jonah, didn't you?"

"Yeah," Terrence shrugged as he took his hit. He blew out smoke before he finished. "I wasn't snitching on you or anything."

"It's fine." She rubbed her forehead with her fingers. "Really. And I'm fine. It's just words."

"Nah, it's not." Because of the weed, Jonah wasn't as

forceful as he could've been. Still, he was adamant. "Those were some horrible things to say to someone you supposedly care about. It's almost like he wants depression all around him so he can thrive. Fucking asshole."

Eva didn't say anything for a while as they passed the joint between them. Finally, she responded.

"There's nothing I can say that won't sound like I am defending him."

"Can I ask how often he talks to you like that?"

"Depends." Eva shrugged. "It depends on his mood or if he has a bad day or if he feels I need to be put back in line."

"Can I ask what started all this tonight?"

"Um," Eva pulled her knees up to her chest then hugged them against her. "He is convinced that I am embarrassing him and that I'll screw up his connections to the ethereal world."

Jonah frowned. "Eva, if there is anything that might damage his connection to us, it's him. No hero is abusive like he is. Saying you are screwing things up for him teeters on gaslighting. That shit won't be tolerated."

"I'm surprised he came here where he could risk being overhead." Terrence passed Jonah the last bit of the joint. "He was pissed because you were with Jonah, wasn't he? Why do you let him talk to you like that?"

Eva took a long breath then stared into the fire. Jonah knew the answer to this question already. Terrence did not.

"He's the only thing in existence that can outright kill me, you know? It's a failsafe in the Sibyl arrangement in case I get possessed. So I tend to tread lightly."

"Eva, let me tell you this now. If you need to walk on eggshells with someone because you're afraid they might hurt you, that's a person you just might need out of your life." Jonah responded when Terrence didn't.. "That's a bedrock of worry, not trust. And it ain't healthy."

Eva rested her forehead against her knees after that. She made it clear that she was done with this conversation.

"You shouldn't be alone tonight." Jonah studied her. "Come stay with me in my-"

"No," Eva jerked up and looked at him with wide eyes. "Jonah, I can't. He said outright that he wouldn't allow that and I am not going to put you in the middle of my mess."

"Eva, listen." Jonah was undeterred. "One, we're all here to look out for one another. Two, it's not like I'm putting moves on you; I just want to keep you company because you are clearly not in a great headspace. Three, nobody here gives a single damn what Cyrus will allow."

"I appreciate your words, Jonah. I appreciate you all and your concern. But I just...I can't."

Jonah nodded slowly. "Alright then. The stipulations were that you couldn't be in the tent with me?"

"Yes."

"Then we'll just sleep outside. Let me grab the sleeping bags."

"Jonah, there is no way you are going to get a full night's sleep like this. The idea is so sweet, but I can't ask you to do that."

"You didn't ask me," Jonah said. "I volunteered."

"I mean-"

"Eva? Stop. Just stop worrying. It'll be fine."

Jonah moved over to the tent and pulled out both sleeping bags. He set them out as close to the fire as he dared. When he was done, he patted on the one for Eva as Terrence bade them good night.

"Let's just sleep. We have a long day tomorrow."

"Alright." Eva shook her head. "But if it starts raining, you should go back to the tent. Promise?"

"Deal," Jonah said. "Now, go on and get some sleep.

Rest assured that you do not need anyone's permission to do so."

Eva stretched out and turned over on her side. Jonah watched her from his own sleeping bag for any sign of duress, but there was none. She hadn't seemed upset when she returned to them either.

How long had Cyrus been saying that shit to her? Probably years.

"Stop thinking, Blueberry." She spoke over her shoulder. "I can hear your wheels turning from here."

Jonah felt his face warm, but luckily, it was dark. "No such wheels are turning, Superstar. Your boy is way too stoned."

She laughed a little at that then flipped over on her back to look up at him.

"I didn't think you could get stoned. You don't seem high at all."

"I'm pretty stoned," Jonah said. "I'm just good at maintaining it. One day, you will be, too."

"I don't feel any different. Just relaxed. Is that what it's like for you?"

"Yeah," Jonah answered. "All the bullshit in life just gently fades away. I can balance my emotions should I wish to, but I'd rather not go that route. It's tedious as fuck, plus I have no right to sidestep my emotions just because I have the power to do so. But the weed allows relaxation that not even gaming or writing can provide."

He examined her face in the campfire. Most people looked wicked in the shadows cast by flames, but not Eva. If anything, the light softened her features. As if not even the darkness could hide her beauty.

Fucking gorgeous. That was a much better description of the woman stretched out next to him.

"You should sleep, Jonah," She finally said. "High or no, we're heading out at first light."

"Alright. Good night, Superstar."

"Good night."

Jonah stayed on his side to watch her as her breathing evened out. He knew that she was still hurting. He could see it with each breath she took. But there was nothing he could do to help her. Not with Cyrus, not with her injuries. It pissed him off, but it wasn't his place to step in where he wasn't invited. Finally, as the fire burned down to embers and his thoughts became blurred with his exhaustion, he fell asleep.

# TWENTY-EIGHT

## EVA MCRAYNE

I WAS NOT in the best mood as we continued to trek through the forest. Even though Jonah had slept right next to me, I hadn't slept well. And although the camping coffee maker was a sweet gesture on Joey's part, the resulting drink was no Starbucks. It was so bad, I dumped out my third cup after the first sip. An action I would have never done back home. So when Joey started whistling our theme song, I had to close my eyes to beg patience with him. I knew he wasn't the source for my aggravation.

I decided then to strike up a conversation. I focused on Reena, who was just ahead of me.

"What's your origin story? The dynamic trio?"

"What?" Reena glanced over her shoulder at me. "What do you mean?"

"Your story," I dodged a branch before I ran smack into it. "How did the three of you meet?"

Reena allowed herself a smile. "Jonathan brought Jonah to the estate. It was Labor Day weekend. Terrence gave Jonah a high calorie breakfast before he got down to my veggie juice. I introduced myself, Trip, well...he was

Trip. Jonah said his aura was blue, And I dropped my damn knife in the sink."

"I had to give him an incentive to stay," Terrence teased. "Otherwise, he would have ran for the hills and never come back."

"Was that really an option?" I glanced over at Jonah. "I just can't imagine you anywhere else."

"Well, that day was shit," Jonah recalled. "A girl I'd had a few dates with said I wasn't her type, my boss made the work day an hour longer, and the world turned blue. So if there were individuals who could help distract me from all the crazy, I was game."

"And look at how well that turned out for you," Reena laughed when he stepped into a mud puddle. "You've fought ethereal baddies, Greek gods, Creyton. Now, you're in the most haunted forests in the world."

"What's a Creyton?" I asked. "Is that like an ethereal creature? Like the Shades?"

Jonah and his friends looked at each other. Jonah finally broke the silence. "Creyton is the most dangerous Spirit Reaper who's ever existed. He made whole towns insane by perverting essence to keep himself young for decades."

"That and he's a stone-cold killer," Reena added

Now, it was Joey and I who looked at each other. Despite the horrors we had survived, I couldn't think of anything that matched the sound of this Creyton.

"So a Spirit Reaper, what is that exactly?" I asked. "Are they common? Are there any traits to look out for?"

"They're Eleventh Percenters who've embraced the Dark Side of ethereality," Jonah answered. "Guess they are about as common as anyone else. There are bad Elevenths like there are bad regular people."

"They've embraced the Dark side, so their ethereality

glows kinda darker," Terrence said. "Some are jokes, some are Creyton. Their danger levels cover a wide-ass range."

"So it's not like they are born that way." Joey nodded. "It's a choice."

"But what would be the benefits to going to the Dark Side?" I frowned. "I don't get it."

"I suppose people like bullying and power," Terrence answered. "They'll say something like there is more power to be had."

"I can see that." I nodded. "That's something I've seen in Olympian circles. Some have a willingness to do anything to grab for power. I suppose it's the same in your world, too."

"Serious question," Joey fell in step beside Terrence. "Now that we know about ethereal beings, how big of a threat are they to people like us?"

"About the same level of threat they were beforehand, brother," Jonah replied. "Ethereal humans are still human, therefore still vulnerable. You know?"

"I'm certain the pantheon has had experiences with Elevenths in the past," Reena said. "Ask Apollo. We can't be new to Mount Olympus."

"I'm sure Elevenths aren't new." I looked up at the canopy of leaves overhead as it began to rain. "Did you see how chummy Jonathan and Apollo were when he came to the estate?"

"Yeah," Jonah said. "I wonder how far they go back to be honest. "

"Apollo never mentioned the Elevenths to you?" Terrence spoke up behind me. "Really?"

"I am just starting to interact with Apollo," I tugged at the hood of my poncho to pull it over my hair. "Cyrus has been an intermissionary for us until I graduated from the Academy. Then he started contacting me directly."

"Good," muttered Jonah, salty about Cyrus. "I'm glad you get to establish your own path without Cyrus ' input."

"Well, to a certain degree," I shifted my backpack on my shoulders. "His role isn't to guard me any more so much as it is to guide me. So I'm kinda stuck with him."

"Sensational guidance he's providing." Terrence observed.

I shrugged. "What can I do, Terrence? I can't physically chain him to me. And to be honest, I wouldn't want to. I kinda like being on my own."

"Can the bind be dissolved?" Jonah asked. "Can...I don't know...Atalanta be your Keeper? Wait, Is Atalanta actually real?'

I giggled at the face he made as he asked that question.

"Yes, she is real. She was an Amazon warrior originally and then the Keepers recruited her."

"An Amazon?"

"Yeah. Olympus is quite diverse. We have people and beings of all races and nationalities. Most of Zeus' children aren't caucasion."

"Okay great," Jonah said. "Can Atalanta be your Keeper? I'm all for girl power."

"I don't know," I wrinkled my nose at the rain that dripped from it. "I never thought to ask if I could get a new keeper."

"In Evie's defense, Cyrus was great until her parents were murdered."

"Joey!"

"What? It's true."

"So what happened, Evie?" Reena narrowed her eyes at me. "Be honest. I can tell when you are lying."

"Why would I lie?"

"Why are you stalling?"

Dammit. I took a minute to climb over a rock before I spoke.

"Ok. Fine. You all know I met Cyrus when I became the Sibyl. We started our personal relationship not long after I filmed the Bachelor's Grove episode. He was never one for personal affection. And I understood. He was a soldier, after all. That just seemed to go with the territory. But..."

I swallowed. This next part wasn't easy to talk about. I'd never told anyone. Even Joey.

"But," I continued. "The day before the McRayne funeral, I needed a distraction. I tried to seduce him and he told me in no uncertain terms that I had misunderstood our arrangement. I won't go into the details. Lets just say I made a move and everything has been fucked up ever since."

Jonah regarded her. "Sounds like he was the one who made things awkward. Why would he be so testy?"

"I didn't get close enough to find out." I took a breath. "But that's when he got weird, Joey. And why he got weird."

"It's also when he started disappearing a lot." Joey noted unnecessarily. "When you were in the hospital after Elliot shoved you out the window, he was rarely there. Then he dropped you off at the Academy and split."

"Thanks, Joey."

"I'm only stating facts," He cut his eyes over at me. "And now, we find out how rough he's been with you?"

"Since when did *you* become the one with the uncomfortable truths, dude?" Terrence quizzed. "A week and a half ago, you were the fun guy. Now you're dredging up Eva's bad memories?:

"I'm not trying to start anything, Terrence. I'm not." Joey grabbed the straps of his bag with both hands. "But it's only fair that we're all on common ground, right?"

"How is Cyrus common ground?" Reena wanted to know. "What does he have to do with this assignment?"

"Well, he showed up last night, didn't he?" Joey shrugged when I glared at him. "What? I heard him talking to you in your tent. He sounded pissed."

"Give him a Man of the Year award if you want to," Jonah said, unwilling to have Eva relive those soul-crushing words. "Point is, he ain't no hero. Joey, I got nothing but love and respect for you, but we're just calling it like we see it. If you have any more glowing endorsements of Cyrus, keep them to yourself, no offense."

"None taken." His face lit up in a bright grin. "But if what you're saying is true, that means I'm a hero, too."

"Didn't you shoot down a wolf in mid-air?" I punched his arm lightly as I teased him. "That's definitely not something a hero would do. Not ever."

I was relieved at the chance to lighten the mood. I hooked my hand into the crook of Jonah's elbow as we came across a path of trampled grass wide enough for us to walk side by side.

"Tell us more stories of the ethereal world." I looked at the others. "What is it like to fight a Spirit Reaper?"

Jonah thought about it. "It's like the craziest adrenaline rush. Say what you want about Mike Tyson, but he was right. Everybody's got a plan until they get hit. You can have the biggest and best strategy, but in the end, it's your gut, nerve, and sharpness of wit."

"And that primal need to survive," Reena added. "We know that if we go down, that's it. There's no safety net."

"Not to mention that most of them are backstabbing bitches." Terrence grinned down at me as he took my other arm. Between him and Jonah, I felt a bit like Dorothy in the *Wizard of Oz*. You need to tangle with one at least once, Evie. You'll see how easy they fold."

"I don't think that's such a good idea," I spoke my thoughts out loud. "I mean, I would if I had to. But how does one fight ethereality without being ethereal themselves?"

"Do the skills matter?" Reena said. "Everyone brings their expertise to the table. Whoever is standing at the end is the winner. No matter their background."

"Hmm, that's an excellent-"

I stopped so quick, I nearly pulled Jonah and Terrence back with me.

"What the hell, Superstar?"

"Shush." I tilted my head in the direction I heard the sound. "I thought I heard something."

I caught a glimpse of a figure standing in the trees. Or at least, I thought I did. When I removed my bag, the trees shifted so that my view was obscured.

"Joey, stay here."

"Oh, no. I don't think so." He shrugged his equipment off to drop it next to mine. I heard the thuds of three other bags as they hit the ground. "What did you see?"

"Shadows." I pinched the bridge of my nose between two fingers. "Maybe I've been in the forest too long. I'm starting to see ghosts where none exist."

"Maybe. Or maybe..."

Jonah's words changed over to a yell when a vine wrapped around his ankle to yank him off his feet. He started clawing at his leg as I brought my sword forth to cut him free.

"Jonah! Are you-"

I was cut off when I heard Reena release a short scream. I watched in horror as a series of arrows came out of the trees. Terrence went down next, then Joey.

"Shit!" I turned to Jonah. "We gotta get them in the foliage! It'll cover them!"

I grabbed Joey's arm and shoved him to the side seconds before another arrow slammed through his shoulder.

"God." He hissed as he grabbed at the arrow. "Damn. That hurts."

"Come on."

I ducked as a second arrow followed the first. This time, our attacker missed. I managed to get Joey on his feet, threw his good arm around my shoulders, and forced him to move as fast as possible. Jonah already had Reena and Terrence. I dropped him against a tree in the underbrush as I got my first good look at the hunter after us.

'Hunter' was not the right word. 'Crazy creature from a fairy tale' was a much better description. The being that stepped out on the path was tall. Much taller than anything I'd ever seen before. His features seemed to be carved out of wood. His beard? A twisted mixture of vines and grass. I blinked twice to make sure I was really seeing the hooves that served as his feet and the horns that grew out of his head.

Jonah slammed into me seconds before he grunted. I caught him against me and tried not to scream as he collapsed against me. I saw the arrow sticking out of his back and it became much harder to hold that scream back.

I lowered Jonah to the bed of pine needles and whispered to Joey.

"Joey, whatever happens, don't make a single sound. Got it?" I pressed my lips against his ear to whisper as low as possible. "Stay put."

Joey was pale. Gasping before his eyes rolled back in his head. My friend had passed out from either the pain of his injury or shock. I gritted my teeth together as I stood. I walked through the brush and bounced my sword in my hand as I took in the beast.

"Leshy." I called out its name. "Some lord of the forest you are. Picking on those who wish to save your lands."

The creature turned his vibrant green eyes upon me with a laugh. His bow transformed into a wooden club that looked bigger than I was. I tried to find out more information about this thing through Prometheus' knowledge. Sadly, all I got was its name. So I waited. I circled it. I wanted to see it attack to know what my best course of action would be.

I didn't have to wait for long. The thing swung its club up and over. I jumped back as I watched it crash down in the exact spot where I had been standing.

"Oh, hell no." I snapped. "You put that down before you hurt somebody!"

The thing swung at me twice more. Each time, I used its speed against him. When he missed for a third time, the thing threw its head back and screamed. I froze as I recognized the voice it used.

Joey.

My hesitation cost me. The creature threw out one massive arm and landed a backhand across my face. I collapsed in a heap as it began to laugh. I laid as still as I could when it wrapped its hand around my waist. I kept my eyes closed when the man lifted me up to get a better look at me. I could hear him giggling as he loosened his grip enough for me to move.

I cried out as I brought my sword up. I slammed it to the hilt between its eyes. The monster stared at me for what felt like forever before he began to fall backward. I went with him, shifting my body around until I had one foot on his chest and the other on the ground. I pulled my sword free, whispering my apologies to the beautiful weapon as I wiped the remaining brown muck off of it.

"Guys," I breathed as I turned back to the foliage where my friends were injured. "I'm coming."

I took off like a shot towards the woods where I had left them. But when I reached the spot I had left them, they were gone.

"Joey!" I screamed out. "Jonah! Terrence! Reena! Get your asses back here!"

I checked the surrounding trees. There was no sign of my fallen comrades anywhere. Yet, I forced my panic to subside. I couldn't find them, couldn't save them, if I lost it. When I made it back to the path we had been taking, I felt the tears burning in my eyes at the sight of his bag. No. I refused to believe they were gone.

I started to lift up my bag, but my hand was still covered with the muck I had wiped off my sword. I dropped the damn thing and kicked it in frustration as I told myself the same thing over and over again.

They would be fine. They would all be fine.

But they weren't. Each member of my party had been shot. They were all hurt. They needed me.

I was proud of myself. The tears I wanted to shed so badly never fell. I unhooked Joey's precious camera. The stupid bow I had teased him about. A flashlight. The first aid kit and canteen they would need when I found them. I went back to my backpack, threw out every item Joey had packed for me and tossed in the few items I had picked off the bags that remained. When I lifted it, the weight was more balanced. Lighter.

Granted, the stupid thing was almost empty, but still.

I squared my shoulders, tightened my grip on my sword, and set off. I would find my friends. I would find the circle. And I would strengthen this damn barrier if it were the last thing I would ever do.

---

I was forced to stop just before nightfall. Not because I couldn't see, mind you. But because my legs were shaking so badly, I kept stumbling over the damned roots that lined my path. I lowered myself down beside a small lake to splash water on my face. There was no hope to get the grime off, but I had to try.

"Lovely evening, eh, Representative?"

I jerked my head up, my hand on the hilt of my sword when an old woman appeared beside me. She sat a pile of bloody clothes in the water and began to hum to herself as she went to work washing them.

"Who...what...are you?"

"Bean Nighe." She gave me a grin that exposed one huge tooth hanging from her gums. "A witch. An omen. I am a fairy of the Scots. Meant to bridge this world and the next."

"Ok." I shifted away from her. "So what do you want with me? Cause if you tell me you have an apple for me to eat, I'm not going to fall for that."

"Why, to give you a message, of course. What use would I have for apples?" She cackled. "You have the memories of another. Many others. Yet, you do not use them. Why?"

"Because I'm not nosy?" I snorted. "That wasn't a message. That was a question."

"Indeed it was." She nodded. "Tis only right I be able to make inquiries at my age. I've earned the privilege."

"Fine. I don't like to remember the horrors Prometheus went through. Or the wars that Athena went through. Or the heartbreak Hera experienced. Does that answer your question?"

"Yes. And no." The old woman resumed her washing until the water turned red. "From one messenger of the dead to another, my words are only this. Blood is the tie which binds the doors of Tartarus."

"I'm sorry, what?" I wrinkled my nose up at her. "I don't understand."

"You will, dearie." She gave me a long, drawn out sigh. "Ignorance is such bliss for the young."

"Right. Cause that made absolute perfect sense." I rolled my eyes as I stood up. "Are you done with me? I need to get going."

"The circle is that way." She extended a long jagged finger towards my right. "Pull the memories forth before you get there, child. Do not be caught unaware."

"Yeah. We'll see about that." I picked up my sword and stood. "Thanks, though. I appreciate the warning."

I crossed the river the only way possible. By sliding around on rocks worn down by the current I was scared to death I was going to fall into. It was one thing to be immortal. But to be an immortal and caught beneath a river current? To almost die only to come back was a vicious cycle I did not want to get caught up in.

"Congratulations, Evie. You just gave yourself a whole new nightmare to wake up screaming over."

I muttered to myself as I jumped off the last rock and onto the bank. I landed on my side, but instead of getting up out of the mud, I laid there. Don't get me wrong. I wasn't mourning the loss of my friends because I refused to believe they were gone. I wasn't wallowing in self-pity over being alone in these wretched woods. Or even depressed that the father I just found out I had was one of the twelve gods responsible for putting me here in the first place.

The truth was much simpler than you could ever imagine. I was exhausted. Every bone in my body hurt. My head and jaw ached from the hit I had received from the Leshy. My ribs were still tender from my tumble into a ravine and Cyrus' punch that may have broken them further. At that very moment, I would have given my very soul for a shower and my own bed.

"A wish, dear girl. You must make a wish."

I froze when I heard the man behind me. I knew I needed to sit up. I needed to grab my weapon. But I couldn't move. Instead, I stared straight ahead as a pair of men's boots appeared in front of me. He began to stroke my hair as he spoke.

"Your soul demands release. I can sense it."

"Ok. You're creeping me out." I managed as I got my first good look at him. The man was pale. His skin tone seemed to glow in the moonlight overhead. His eyes were the same shade of pink as a rabbit. "I don't have a wish to make."

"Everyone has a wish." He smiled just enough to expose the fangs on either side of his mouth. "Allow this Strigoi to grant it to you, child. What will it be? Beauty? Fame? The illusion known as love?"

Strigoi. I searched my mind for information on the man who was knelt down before me. Romania. Considered the grandfather of vampires. Has the ability to incapacitate their victims by stealing their ability to move. Made them easy prey.

God, I was sounding more and more like a video game guide by the second. I released a short breath before I responded.

"Despite my current appearance, I've been told I am attractive." I worked out the words that Jonah had told me back in L.A. "I'm already famous. And love? I don't need that. Now go away."

The man pushed my hair back from my throat. His face twisted into an expression of pure euphoria as he stroked my skin there. I fought against the enchantment he had cast over me, but I wasn't kidding when I said I couldn't move. The only thing I could do was talk and even then, that was difficult.

I cried out when his teeth sank through my neck. It felt as if my throat had closed in on itself. I tried to move. I tried to claw at the creature latched onto me. Turns out, I didn't have to. The horrible man jerked himself free and began to pant.

"Who…what…are you?"

His face had darkened from the blood he had taken from me. His pink eyes had shifted to red. But as he began to wipe my blood away from his mouth, I saw the blisters forming across his mouth. He scrambled to his feet as he doubled over with a shriek of pain.

I felt the enchantment he had over me shatter as smoke began to billow out of his nostrils. His mouth. The monster gave one last scream as he fell in a heap. I watched his hand fall limp with confusion.

"Yeah, well. That's what you get for taking what isn't yours." I pressed my hand against the side of my neck and snagged my sword as I stood up. "Damn vampire."

I kept my eyes on the corpse until I was back on the path the old woman had pointed out to me. I couldn't help but wonder if my exposure to the Stigoi was going to turn me into a vampire. But I shook off the thought. Vampires were the least of my worries at the moment. Me turning into one? Even lower on my list.

I focused instead on finding my way through the trees. On keeping the flashlight steady. On not jumping at the sound of every noise that greeted me through the trees. If I could face down the greatest monsters this forest had to offer, I could survive the final trek to the circle.

I'd be damned if I didn't.

# TWENTY-NINE

## EVA MCRAYNE

I KNEW I was close to the clearing when I was rocked by the sickest feeling I'd ever experienced. It was so strong, I stopped to lean against a tree until the nausea passed. Thanks to Prometheus, I knew what was happening. Those susceptible to the tortures Tartarus had to offer grew ill when they were close to it. That's why the forests were filled with monsters from other cultures. Those of the Greek persuasion would have been too sick to do any good against nosy tourists or curious bystanders.

I shut my eyes as I swallowed back another round of nausea. I had to get through this. I was too close to let this stop me. So I shoved myself away from the tree and stumbled through the thorn bushes until I could see the circle I'd been after since we'd entered Hoia-Baciu. It was completely free of vegetation. No trees grew in the center. No stones dotted it. It was nothing but a smooth patch of grass.

I leaned forward as I caught sight of movement just to my left. On the outskirts of the circle, four forms appeared to be tied to the trees. When the clouds overhead shifted and the moonlight was exposed, I caught sight of Jonah and Reena. I was sure the other two were Joey and Terrence.

I worked my way back through the thorn bushes. I couldn't explain my sudden need to be stealthy, but something was telling me not to expose myself just yet. When I reached the back of the tree that held my companions, I realized just who I needed to hide from.

Narcissus stepped out from the wood line across from us. I watched as he ran his palm over a strange carving in the bark. He began to sing as he turned in a slow circle with his arms above his head.

"Soon, my darlings. Soon. You will be free to knock the Olympians from their throne. You will return my beloved to his spot in the heavens."

Beloved? I rolled my eyes towards the sky. Nice. The demi-god wasn't just vain. He was a romantic, too.

I waited until he fell to his knees in the center of the circle before I shrugged off my bag. I knew what was about to happen. And I didn't need the extra weight slowing me down. I pressed my body against the tree until I leaned in to whisper against Reena's ear.

"Re, it's me. Don't move. Just listen."

Reena jerked against her binds. She kept her head down in the position I'd first seen it in and she did what I asked.

She stayed silent.

"Ya'll are beat all to hell. But I need you. I'm going to cut you free. Then you are going to grab Joey, free Jonah, and Terrence. Use the Astralimes and get everyone the hell out of here. Understood?"

She clenched her fist over my wrist to show me she understood. I kept my eyes on Narcissus as I slipped my blade beneath the rope and pulled. The damn binding snapped. I saw Reena catch herself before she caught Joey in her arms. I didn't get the chance to look my friend over. The keeper wrapped her arms around him and the two of them disappeared into nothingness.

I moved over to Jonah next. He was out cold. The arrow was still protruding from his back. I whispered my apology in his ear as I jerked it out. He didn't move until I pressed my hand against the wound. I focused my ability to heal onto it and prayed to Apollo to save him.

Reena tapped me on the arm the second she returned. Once we had Jonah and Terrence free, I waited in the shadows as Reena took them both home until I was once again alone.

Good. That would make this much, much easier.

"Narcissus!" I called out when I stepped out of the brush. "What a pleasant surprise! You should have traveled with us. It's been one hell of a ride."

The demi-god's head snapped up to watch me as I strolled into the clearing. He scrambled to his feet and even from here, I could see the fury in his expression.

"Don't call me that! I told you, my name is Arc!"

"Yeah, I don't think it fits you though." I stabbed my sword into the ground to lean against it. "Ass hat? Yes. Arc? Not quite."

"How…"

"Did I make it?" I shrugged. "No clue. I have to admit though. The Strigoi thing was a nice touch. Made me feel right at home here in vampire country. But that doesn't matter. What I want to know is just how long you and Prometheus have been planning this little scheme of yours."

"No." He snapped. "You can't stop us. You're too late."

"Oh, we've got time to clear a few things up." I tilted my head to the side. "If I'm remembering Prometheus correctly, you two started your little fling at Tartarus, right? Bosom buddies to the end. What did he promise you to come here? Power? No. That doesn't feel right."

I tapped my finger against my chin. "Ah. There it is. Revenge against the Council. You wished for Zeus and the others to suffer as you were made to do. That's just sad, Narcissus. I would expect a better reason from you. Something more creative."

"You have no idea what I went through." He screamed. "The tortures that lasted day after day. The damned gods will suffer as they have made me suffer! Every ounce of their blood will spill, Sibyl. As will yours."

"Yeah. I've heard it before. Try again. Go for more 'your soul will be ripped from your body' instead of 'I will see you dead'. Makes for better television."

The demi-god roared as he turned towards the tree with the carving. I watched as he grabbed a knife from his belt and slammed it in the very center of the symbol. I jerked my sword free as the ground around me began to rumble. It would have been an amazing sight if I hadn't been standing in the very center of it.

And I didn't know what he had done. I fell back as the ground began to rip open beneath me. I rolled to my feet to see a series of creatures clawing their way to the surface. Some had been human once. Others were obvious creations of a twisted mind. I would have stopped to stare at them if a woman hadn't charged me at that exact moment.

"Time to play."

I launched myself into the mob. The first few fell easy enough. But it wasn't long before I was vastly outnumbered. I cursed as I swung. I forced myself to focus on Prometheus' memories as I slammed the hilt of my sword into one monster after the other. I had to get to Narcissus. I had to get to that carving.

I had to catch the world on fire.

I worked my way back to the edge of the clearing and ducked as a bull-looking thing swung its horns at me. I fumbled for Joey's bow and the single arrow he had left. I cried out as the creatures began to overwhelm me. Ripping at my skin with their claws. Their teeth. I managed to work the bow onto my shoulder as I grabbed my sword once more. I slashed the blade upward and forced myself to kick out to make room to move. It didn't take long. The beings so determined to destroy me were weak. Worn down from their exposure to Tartarus.

I shoved my way through the crowd until I had the carving in sight. I heard my sword drop to the ground as I took up the bow.

*Blood is the tie which binds the doors to Tartarus.*

The old woman's words came to the forefront of my mind as I flipped through Prometheus' memories. I felt my blood begin to boil when I slashed my hand open with the razor sharp tip of the arrow and covered it with the thick red liquid. It didn't take long for the abilities I had stolen from the Titan rose to the surface. I snapped my fingers over the arrow and gritted my teeth as the flames erupted.

The beings clawed at me and each other seemed a million miles away as I shouldered the bow. I stared down the arrow and pulled the string back as I took the advice Zeus had given me over a week before.

*Flip the cards.*

Athena's knowledge flowed through me. It kept my arm steady despite the fight going on around me. I released the bow with a quick prayer to the goddess. She must have heard me. The flaming arrow slammed into the knife Narcissus had stabbed into the wood.

I stared at it with my mouth open before the world began to rumble once more. The creatures began to scream as the ground opened up to suck them back down below.

But I wasn't afraid of falling into Tartarus. I threw down Joey's bow and took off like a shot as the trees around me erupted. Their branches lined with flames. The wood crackling as it burned. I was so focused on getting to the other side of the clearing, I forgot the one person I should have kept my eyes on the entire time.

I slammed to the ground when an arrow pierced my leg. I rolled onto my back just in time to see Narcissus launch himself on top of me. He slammed his weapon across my throat as he screamed.

"No! You…you've ruined everything! Dammit!"

I fought for breath as I brought my sword up to block his next blow. I wrapped my leg around his waist and forced him over. When I got him down, I slammed the palm of my hand into his nose. I brought my hilt down to finish the job. I heard his jaw snap despite the fire raging around us.

The demi-god attempted to work himself free. He dug his fingers into my thighs. He tried to grab for my throat. But I was too pissed off to notice the pain he had caused me. I lifted up enough to twirl my sword around twice as the fire around us arched overhead.

"The sad thing is, you aren't all that attractive." I sighed. "Goodbye, Narcissus."

I sliced my sword across his throat with ease. His expression was one of pure shock before he vanished.

I fell to my knees as the ground stopped shaking. I started laughing as the forest burned around me. I had done it. I'd restored the barrier. I'd saved my friends from the horrors of Hoia-Baciu. I tumbled over to lay on my side as the need for sleep threatened me. I'd meet back up with them soon. I'd make it out of this damned forest.

I was sure of it.

"Eva, goddammit!"

I felt Jonah lift me up from the grass. I rolled over and opened my eyes just enough to see the fear in his eyes.

"What's the matter, Blueberry?" I slurred. "There are no monsters here. Turns out they were just trees."

"I've got you, Superstar. I got you."

He was shaking as he pressed me against his chest. I could hear him making promises to get me home as my body gave way to exhaustion and the fire raging around us faded into nothingness.

# THIRTY

## JONAH ROWE

EVA WAS STILL ASLEEP three days after Jonah got her to the infirmary at the estate. Despite Reena and Jonathan lording over him to check out his own wounds, he was fine. If it hadn't been for the soreness in the middle of his back, he never would have believed that he had been shot with an arrow.

Well, that and the footage from the body cameras. Joey had borrowed Terrence's laptop and plugged the footage in. Jonah had watched himself get snatched away from the foliage after he had been shot. He watched as he had been tied to a tree by the fucking Olympian prima donna.

That was enough to piss him off. Then, they watched Eva's footage. Her encounters with a Scot spirit and the vampire dude were harrowing, but it was the final fight that made Jonah grit his teeth in frustration.

She shouldn't have been alone, but she was. She shouldn't have had to be so damn strong, but she was. Strong enough to save them when they couldn't.

"Jonah?"

He turned to see Jonathan and Apollo standing in the doorway of his room. He would have been down at the infirmary, but he didn't want things to be assumed as Reena had back when they were in L.A.

*Use caution,* she had told him. *Keep your distance.*

So he had, though he stopped by Eva's room every now and again to check on her.

"Yeah?" Jonah crossed the room. "Is Eva-"

"No. She isn't awake yet," Apollo stressed the last word. "But soon. I came to tell you that we discovered the poison used against you by the Lechy."

"What's that?"

"A combination of belladonna and nightshade. There were only trace amounts, but enough to knock out an elephant. It is a wonder you were awake before you returned to retrieve Eva."

Jonah didn't have an answer for that. He recalled how he woke up at the estate as Reena was trying to get him in the infirmary. He recalled immediately using the Astralimes to Eva's exact location. How he knew where to find her, he didn't know. But he wasn't going to question it.

Apollo nodded in response to his silence. "Regardless, I owe you a great deal of gratitude. Eva is quite precious to us."

"Jonathan, Apollo," Reena appeared in the doorway. "Eva's awake."

Jonah followed after them then slipped into the room as Eva sat up. She rubbed her eyes with the back of her hand before she blinked them into focus. When she saw them, her face broke out into a huge smile.

"Thank Olympus," She breathed out in relief. "Ya'll are alright."

"Never mind us," Jonah said, grinned to mask the

majority of his relief. "The good thing is that you are alright."

Eva looked around, still half bewildered from sleep. "I half expected to see Cyrus here."

"No," Apollo said. "He is of no use to you at the moment. He will return to you when he has learned his place."

"What are you doing with him?" Jonah asked with no shame. "Enquiring minds would love to know."

"Never you mind son." Apollo gave Jonah a sly, slightly creepy smile. "Never you mind."

A part of Jonah wondered if Cyrus was back in the forest. The bigger part of him didn't care.

"So what's the damage?" Eva studied the group. "How's your back, Jonah?"

"Fine." And he meant it. "How are you feeling?"

"Like I could sleep for a week." Eva admitted before she looked to Apollo. "So it's over? Truly?"

"Indeed. The barrier has been restored. Narcissus has been returned to the chains he belongs in."

"I think the most torture you can do to that man is to take his make-up collection away."

Jonah's comment earned a few laughs. Eva wrapped her arms around her knees as Apollo spoke once more.

"Eva, I have made arrangements for you to remain at the estate for the next few days. That should give you the time you need to recover."

"And also, Cyrus is not welcome on my grounds till he learns manners," Jonathan said. "I won't stand for such treatment. You'll have no Keepers. Apollo knows you're in good hands."

"Are you sure, Jonathan?" Eva looked between Apollo and the protector guide. "I'll earn my keep, I swear. I can't cook, but I can clean. Sorta."

"No," Jonathan smiled. "You may train when you are able. But consider this a vacation. There is no need for you to do anything."

"Thank you." She grinned. "Does that mean I get my old room back?"

"It does," Jonathan laughed. "Indeed, it does."

---

Jonah had been itching to get home all afternoon from his shift at the library. He loved the job, loved the people, but it was Eva's second day at the estate. Since Reena and Terrence had plans, and Joey had been forced to take the Romania footage to California, he knew that she had spent the day alone.

He walked into the mud room off the kitchen then froze when he heard music coming from the formal living room that they only used at Christmas. Music that didn't come from a radio, but from the baby grand piano that had been there nearly as long as the house itself.

Jonah moved silently through the rooms until he reached the doorway. Eva's back was to him as she played.

Jonah stepped on a creaky point of the floor, and Eva and looked around. She shook her head at his expression.

"Yes," She said. "I can still play."

"Who knows?" Jonah asked, still mystified.

"No one, nowadays," Eva replied. "That's the first time I've played in almost eight years."

She scooted over on the bench and patted the spot next to her. When Jonah sat down, she continued.

"Do you have any requests?" She asked teasingly. "This is a once in a lifetime performance, after all."

Jonah thought about it as he listened to the music. "Can you play Route 66?"

"Nat King Cole?" Eva smiled. "Not a problem, Blueberry."

Jonah's request came to life in the formal room of the estate. Jonah closed his eyes to listen to the music. When it was over, Eva cracked her fingers and began again. Another melody. Chopin, maybe?

"I mentioned before that I was a classically trained pianist." She spoke as she ran her fingers expertly over the keys. "It's not something I like to talk about and I won't talk about it now. But I tuned this old girl in case someone else wants to play her. I was just...testing it out."

"Eight years, you said?" Jonah was unabashedly impressed. "But you do it like it's nothing. Can you at least tell me when you started?"

"I took my first piano lesson on my third birthday." Eva turned her eyes back to the keys, but Jonah had a feeling she wasn't really seeing them. "I played daily from that moment until I was fifteen."

"Did you ever play in recitals?"

Eva didn't answer at first. Finally, she nodded as the music switched to a more somber tune. It seemed heavier.

"Of course. I was labeled as a child prodigy back then. I played in concert halls, private homes, anywhere my mother wanted me to, really. If I made the papers? Great."

"You were in the news?"

"More often than not, but you won't find me under Eva in those archives. I shortened my name when I got to Georgia."

"What's your legal name?"

Eva's lips tightened, but then she smiled. "You don't get that one today, Blueberry. I will happily take another request, though."

"Why don't you choose?"

"Alright."

Eva stopped for a minute before she began again. This time, the music started slow but became faster. Deeper. Jonah took in the crescendos, the valleys. After a few minutes, he cleared his throat.

"What's that piece called?"

"What do you want to call it?" She gave him a soft smile. "Because it doesn't have a title. I'm just coming up with it as I go."

"No kidding?" Jonah raised his eyebrows. "How about um...Symphony of Gold? Like that?"

Eva grinned. "I like it. How about this one as Symphony of Blue?"

She increased the speed of the same piece. It wasn't as dramatic, a bit more serious, but Jonah laughed as she brought it to an end.

"Not bad, eh?"

She chuckled as she reached for the key cover. Jonah gave her a look of surprise.

"You're stopping?"

"I don't have to." She stopped then turned to him. "But surely you have other plans for the day, Blueberry. Listening to me reminisce about the past isn't on that to do list."

Jonah shrugged. "I usually binge on Netflix after work. You'd be bored out of your mind huh?"

"Not even a little," She pulled the cover down and secured it. "I told you, I don't really watch television."

"That's so strange to me because you're on television. I'd think you'd be an expert."

"Yeah, well," She grinned. "I'm already part of the best T.V. show. What more is there?"

Eva laughed at his expression before she continued.

"I tell you what," She moved over beside him. "You pick the show and you will have my utmost attention."

"You won't be bored?"

"Not as long as I'm with you, Blueberry."

Jonah watched her while they headed towards the family room. When Eva got settled on the couch, he grabbed the remote and sat next to her.

"Speaking of television shows, have you given my offer any more thought?"

"I have," Jonah grinned as he looked at her, "And I'd love to."

"Really?" Eva twisted to face him. "You would?"

"Researcher from my own home for *Grave Messages*?" Jonah laughed. "Too perfect an opportunity to pass up. Yeah, I'm in."

Eva grinned so big, her entire face lit up. "I'll get your contract together and you can start as soon as it's signed. We'll work out the details then."

"What sort of details?" Jonah studied her. "I'm curious."

"Well, you won't be under Connor like I am, so you have to meet your boss. David Thompson. He's ex-CIA, so he has contacts to help if you need it. And other things, like your assignments and your pay."

"What is the starting pay for this?"

"One hundred and twenty thousand a year. Plus bonuses if your work is the basis for one of our award winners."

Jonah gaped at her. "Seriously? I didn't even get half of that with my accounting job, and I had a damn Master's Degree!"

"Yeah. I told you it pays well," She shrugged. "And you'll be great."

"How did this position come open?" Jonah eyed her. "You aren't just creating one for me, are you?"

"No," She laughed. "Not even I have that sort of power. One of the researchers is leaving Theia. He is going to chase his acting dreams in New York. So the position is open and you would be perfect for it."

"I'm more qualified than the list you have in place?" Jonah narrowed his eyes. "I know you guys have one."

"Yes." Eva shrugged again when he narrowed his eyes at her. "Ok, it helps that I'm endorsing you. But I told David about your background. He thinks that you will fit in great."

That was all Jonah needed to hear. "Awesome. I'm game. So when exactly does the transition begin? When does the current guy cycle out?"

"He's already gone, so you can get set up today if you want." She grinned. "Why don't I go ahead and call David?"

"Right now?"

"Why not? It's only two on the west coast."

Eva willed her phone in her hand and scrolled through her contacts. She hit the icon to connect the call. Two rings later, a gruff man's voice came over her speaker.

"Evie, baby, we're working on it. Europe is a pain in my ass."

"Europe is always a pain in the ass," She laughed. "I was actually calling to give you some good news."

"Yeah? Your boy decide if he want to play with us or not?"

"Yes and he does, so don't go pulling out that ol' government goon schiek on him. He's right here. Jonah, David. David, Jonah."

"Hi, David," Jonah said cordially. "It's an honor to meet you, sir."

"Eva. He's polite."

"Yeah? So?"

"So I don't know how to respond to someone being polite. I work in L.A."

Eva laughed and Jonah raised an eyebrow.

"How about you start drafting his contract?" She responded. "The sooner the better."

"Evie give you the details already?"

"She did," Jonah replied as he grabbed a pad from the side table and pen. "What expectations do I need from you, sir?"

"I'll send you a list of the locations we're looking at. You pick the ones you want to do." David pauses for a moment. "Then you'll find every legend, every story about the place. The research comes in because you'll be trying to find factual accounts to either back up - or disapprove the story. For example, the house had a triple murder. You'd look for newspaper accounts, police reports. You get it? Great. You don't? Document that. Eva needs house plans, too."

"House plans?"

"Yeah. She goes to these places in the dark. Helps to know where the stairs are."

Jonah nodded as he wrote down details. It sounded like he'd get along well with this guy. He always did function better in situations where the expectations were clear cut and then he was left to his devices. "Research is my thing, man. I think I got this, no problem."

"Great. I'll send the contract to you today. Evie, I'll send it to you."

"Why don't you send it to Charles? Jonah and I can be at his office in thirty minutes."

"You and your lawyers."

"Not gonna let Theia screw over my friend, D. Send it over. Well take care of the rest."

"Later. I'll send the locations list with it, Jonah. Nice to have you."

Eva hung up the phone with a motion of glee. "We gotta go get ready!"

Jonah mockingly rose up. "Dammit Eva. Making me shower and shave."

"I like your beard, so keep that." She grinned. "But you could stand a change of clothes."

"You know where we're going?"

"Yeah. My lawyer, Charles Stephens. He'll drop everything to take a look at the contract for you."

"Seriously?"

"Yeah." She squealed again as if she were getting this job offer instead of him. "I'm so excited for you!"

"I'm excited too!" Jonah exclaimed. "Never have things come together so quickly!"

"Welcome to my world." Eva laughed. "Now, hurry up so we can get you to work!"

---

Two hours later, Jonah and Eva were tucked into a private room at one of L.A.'s most exclusive restaurants. It was so exclusive, there was no sign. No advertising. And you had to be instantly recognizable the second you walked up to the security detail at the door.

"Jesus, Evie," Jonah leaned across the table as she sat down. "How did you know about this place?"

"The Haunt?" She shrugged as she accepted her water from the waiter. "It's one of my investment properties."

Jonah stared at her. "You...how do you advertise this place?"

"Word of mouth," She grinned. "Everybody who is somebody wants to be invited in. Those who are invited brag about being able to get in the doors. It's a place to be seen but to also have privacy without the tourists clamoring all over you. I figured that since we are celebrating your new job, we'd do it right."

"Nice," Jonah breathed. "We'll need to bring the Rome crew here."

"Yeah, I'm sure we will someday," Eva gestured to the attendant standing by the door. "Can you bring a chicken salad for me and the steak dinner for my guest?"

The man nodded once and slipped from the room. Eva turned back to Jonah when the door was shut.

"So you're happy about the contract? One twenty plus bonuses? You've already signed so we can't change it now. But it's good for a year. We can always negotiate more next year."

"I'm *great* with the contract," Jonah said as he unwrapped the cloth napkin from the silverware. "It's more money than I've ever made in my life. And as frugal as I am, it'll go a *long* way."

"Well, and you won't have to worry about me being in your hair all the time. I go to the research meetings every once in a while, but not often. So I won't be lording over you or anything."

"Getting paid to research." Jonah shook his head. "Nana would laugh her head off at this because she wouldn't be surprised."

"She's gotta be proud as hell of you," Eva gave him a small smile. She raised her glass. "To you and your new career, Jonah. I hope it serves you well."

"I'm so thankful and excited," Jonah said. "You're the best in the world, Superstar."

"Eh, I'm alright," She lowered her glass when he didn't raise his own. "Either way, this is a whole new beginning for you. Congratulations."

"And I have you to thank for it," Jonah tapped his glass against the side of hers. "To you, Superstar."

"To us." Eva gave him a small smile at his gesture. "May we have many more adventures together."

## END OF BOOK 1

Dear reader,

We hope you enjoyed reading *Gods & Ghosts*. Please take a moment to leave a review, even if it's a short one. Your opinion is important to us.

Discover more books by Cynthia D. Witherspoon at https://www.nextchapter.pub/authors/cynthia-d-witherspoon

Want to know when one of our books is free or discounted? Join the newsletter at http://eepurl.com/bqqB3H

Best regards,

Cynthia D Witherspoon, T.H. Morris and the Next Chapter Team

You might also like:

The Daughter of Olympus by Cynthia D. Witherspoon

To read the first chapter for free, please head to:
https://www.nextchapter.pub/books/the-daughter-of-olympus

# ABOUT THE AUTHORS

T.H. Morris has been writing in some way, shape, or form ever since he was strong enough to hold a pen or pencil, and was born and raised in Colerain, North Carolina. He has been living in Greensboro, North Carolina for the past twelve years. He is an avid reader, primarily in the genres of science fiction and fantasy because he enjoys immersing himself in the worlds that have been created. He began writing The 11th Percent in 2011. He resides in Colorado with his wife, Candace.

Cynthia D. Witherspoon is an award winning writer of Southern Gothic, Paranormal Romance, and Urban Fantasy. She currently resides in South Carolina, but spent three years in Fayetteville, Arkansas. Always an avid reader, she began writing short stories in college. She graduated with a Bachelor's Degree in History from Converse College, and earned a Masters in Forensic Science at Oklahoma State University Center for Health Sciences.

Lightning Source UK Ltd.
Milton Keynes UK
UKHW021222161220
375273UK00008B/486

9 781034 034346